11/13

D1402265

continued . . .

Emerald

"A passionate tale that brings late seventeenth-century England vividly alive . . . fast-paced and filled with action from the very first page to the climax."
                                        —*Midwest Book Review*

"With strong characters and an action-filled plot, *Emerald* is a royal flush."   —*Affaure de Coeur*

"An entertaining read. When the two [protagonists] come together, they make for a fun-loving, sensual couple."   —*The Romance Reader*

"Warm and wonderful. . . . The story is one that will enthrall. Exhilarating."   —Heart Rate Reviews

"Brimming with action, adventure [and] love. Ms. Royal brings Restoration England to life right before the reader's eyes. I highly recommend *Emerald*."
                                        —Romance Reviews Today

Amethyst

"An accomplished debut."   —Patricia Gaffney

"All of these characters are so well drawn and developed. . . . A promising debut."
                                        —*The Romance Reader*

LOST IN TEMPTATION

Lauren Royal

A SIGNET ECLIPSE BOOK

SIGNET ECLIPSE
Published by New American Library, a division of
Penguin Group (USA) Inc., 375 Hudson Street,
New York, New York 10014, USA
Penguin Group (Canada), 90 Eglinton Avenue East, Suite 700, Toronto,
Ontario M4P 2Y3, Canada (a division of Pearson Penguin Canada Inc.)
Penguin Books Ltd., 80 Strand, London WC2R 0RL, England
Penguin Ireland, 25 St. Stephen's Green, Dublin 2,
Ireland (a division of Penguin Books Ltd.)
Penguin Group (Australia), 250 Camberwell Road, Camberwell, Victoria 3124,
Australia (a division of Pearson Australia Group Pty. Ltd.)
Penguin Books India Pvt. Ltd., 11 Community Centre, Panchsheel Park,
New Delhi - 110 017, India
Penguin Group (NZ), cnr Airborne and Rosedale Roads, Albany,
Auckland 1310, New Zealand (a division of Pearson New Zealand Ltd.)
Penguin Books (South Africa) (Pty.) Ltd., 24 Sturdee Avenue,
Rosebank, Johannesburg 2196, South Africa

Penguin Books Ltd., Registered Offices:
80 Strand, London WC2R 0RL, England

First published by Signet Eclipse, an imprint of New American Library,
a division of Penguin Group (USA) Inc.

First Printing, July 2005
10 9 8 7 6 5 4 3 2 1

SIGNET ECLIPSE and logo are trademarks of Penguin Group (USA) Inc.

Printed in the United States of America

PUBLISHER'S NOTE
This is a work of fiction. Names, characters, places, and incidents either are
the product of the author's imagination or are used fictitiously, and any resem-
blance to actual persons, living or dead, business establishments, events, or
locales is entirely coincidental.
  The publisher does not have any control over and does not assume any
responsibility for author or third-party Web sites or their content.

For Terri Castoro,
critique partner extraordinaire.

Thanks for sticking with me
through thick and thin.

Acknowledgments

I wish to thank:

My editor, Laura Cifelli, for so cheerfully taking on another author and helping to make this story the best it could be; my agent, Elaine Koster, for invaluable support and career guidance; Glynnis Campbell, for calling around Napa Valley to find the elusive grape-growing information I needed (thank goodness I have such a good friend, since I am allergic to the telephone); Sara Rodger, librarian at Arundel Castle, for tracking down and sending me nineteenth-century floor plans (twice . . . thanks to a less-than-reliable postal system); Brent Royal-Gordon, for designing and maintaining my award-winning Web site; Jack, Brent, Blake, and Devonie, for being happy I sold another trilogy even though that meant I'd be disappearing back into my deadline cave; my parents, Herb and Joan Royal, as always, for everything; my official First Readers, Ken and Dawn Royal, Herb and Joan Royal, and Taire Martyn, for honest first impressions; my Awesome Publicity Engine—Rita Adair-Robison, Debbie Alexander, Dick Alexander, Joyce Basch, Alison Bellach, Diana Brandmeyer, Carol Carter, Elaine Ecuyer, Dale Gordon, Darren Holmquist, Catherine Hope, Taire Martyn, Sandy Mills, Karen Nesbitt, DeeDee Perkins, Jack Poole, Jerry Royal, Ken Royal, Stacey Royal, Wendi Royal, and Diena Simmons—for all their hard work on my behalf; my incredible Street Team (you can see all their names on my Web site) for all their enthusiastic support . . . and all my readers, whose wonderful letters and kind words make me want to sit down every day and write.

Thank you, one and all!

Prologue

Cainewood Castle, the South of England
Summer 1808

It was almost like touching him.

Alexandra usually sketched a profile in just a few minutes, but she took her time today, lingering over the experience in the darkened room. Standing on one side of a large, framed pane of glass while Tristan sat sideways against it on the other, she traced his shadow cast by the glow of a candle. Her pencil followed his strong chin, his long, straight nose, the wide slope of his forehead, capturing his image on the sheet of paper she'd tacked to her side of the glass. Noticing a stray lock that tumbled down his brow, she hesitated, wanting to make certain she caught it just right.

Someone walked by the open door, causing Tris's shadow to flicker as the candle wavered. "Are you finished yet?" he asked from behind the glass panel.

"Hold still," she admonished, resisting the urge to peek around at him. "Artistry requires patience."

"This is a profile, not oil on canvas."

True, and she often wished she had the talent to paint, like her youngest sister, Corinna. But the fact that she was missing something Corinna had—that elusive, innate ability to see things others missed and convey them in

color, light, and shade—didn't keep her from taking
pride in her own hobby.

Alexandra made excellent profile portraits.

She'd been asking Tris to sit for her for years, but
he'd never seemed to find the time before. "You promised you'd sit still," she reminded him, knowing better
than to read malice into his comment. "Just this once
before you leave."

"I'm sitting," he said, and although his profile remained immobile, she could hear the laughter in his
voice.

She loved that evidence of his control, just like she
loved everything about Tris Nesbitt.

She'd been eight when they first met. Her favorite
brother, Griffin, had brought him home between terms
at school. In the many years since, as he and Griffin
completed Eton and then Oxford, Tris had visited often,
claiming to prefer his friend's large family to the quiet
home he shared with his father. Alexandra couldn't remember when she'd fallen in love, but she felt like she'd
loved him forever.

Of course, nothing would ever come of it. Now, at
fifteen, she was practical enough to accept that her father, the formidable Marquess of Cainewood, would
never allow her to marry plain Mr. Tristan Nesbitt.

But that didn't stop her from wishing she could. It
didn't stop her stomach from tingling when she heard
his low voice, didn't stop her heart from skipping when
she felt herself caught in his intense, silver-gray gaze.

Not that he directed his gaze her way often. It wasn't
that he was unfriendly, but, after all, as far as he was
concerned she was little more than Griffin's pesky
younger sister.

Knowing Tris couldn't see her now, she skimmed her
fingertips over his shadow, wishing she were touching
him instead. She'd never touched him, not in real life.
Such intimacy simply didn't occur between young ladies
and men. Most especially between a marquess's daughter
and an untitled man's son.

The drawing room's draperies were shut, and the resulting dimness seemed to afford them an odd closeness alone in the room. She traced the flow of his cravat illuminated through the glass onto her paper. "Where are you going again?" she asked, although she knew.

"Jamaica. My uncle wishes me to look after his interests. He owns a plantation there; I'm to learn how it is run."

He sounded sad. During this visit he'd seemed sad quite a bit. "Is that what you wish to do with your life?"

"He doesn't mean for me to stay there permanently. Only to acquaint myself with the operation so I can make intelligent decisions from afar."

"But do you wish to become his man of business? Do you want to manage his properties? Or would you rather do something else?"

He shrugged, his profile tilting, then settling back into the lines she'd so carefully drawn. "He financed my entire education. Have I a choice?"

"I suppose not." Her choices were limited, too. "How long will you be gone?"

"A year at the least, probably two, perhaps three."

Everything was changing. Griffin would leave soon as well—their father had bought him a commission in the cavalry. Although Griffin and Tris had spent much of the past few years at school and university, these new developments seemed different. They'd be across oceans. It wasn't that she'd be alone—she'd still have her parents and her grandmother, her oldest brother and her two younger sisters—but she was already feeling the loss.

"Two or three years," she echoed, knowing Griffin would likely be gone even longer. "That seems a lifetime."

Tris's image shimmied as he laughed out loud. "I expect it might, to one as young as you."

He wasn't that much older, only one-and-twenty. But she supposed he'd seen a lot in the extra six years he had on her. Young men left home as adolescents to pursue their educations. They spent time hunting at country houses and carousing about London.

While she didn't exactly chafe at her own more restrictive life, she was counting the years and months until she'd turn eighteen and have her first Season. She'd spent hour upon hour imagining the balls, the parties, and all the eligible young lords. One of those titled men would be her entrée to a new life as a society wife. A more exciting life, she hoped. And she would love her husband, she was certain, although right now she could hardly imagine loving any man other than Tris.

He had never overtly indicated any interest in her, but of course he wouldn't. As well as she, Tris knew his place. But that didn't stop her from wishing she knew whether he cared.

Just whether or not he cared.

"Will you bring me something from Jamaica?" she asked, startling herself with her boldness.

"Like what?" She heard astonishment in his voice. "A pineapple or some sugarcane?"

It was her turn to laugh. "Anything. Surprise me."

"All right, then. I will." He fell silent a moment, as though trying to commit the promise to memory. "Are you finished yet?"

"For now." She set down her pencil and walked to the windows, drew back the draperies, and blinked. The room's familiar blue-and-salmon color scheme suddenly seemed too bright.

She turned toward him, reconciling his face with the profile she'd just sketched. From the boy she'd met years ago, he'd grown into a handsome, masculine man—one might even say he looked arresting. But she wouldn't describe him as pretty. His jaw was too strong, his mouth too wide, his brows too heavy and straight. As she watched, he raked a hand through his hair—tousled, streaky dark blond hair that always seemed just a bit too long.

Her fingers itched to run through it, to sweep the stray lock from his forehead.

"It will take me a while to complete the portrait," she told him as she walked back to where he sat beside the glass, "but I'll have it ready for you before you leave."

"Keep it for me."

She blew out the candle, leaning close enough to catch a whiff of his scent, smelling soap and starch and something uniquely Tris. "Do you not want it?"

He rose from the chair, smiling down at her from his greater height. "I'll probably lose it if I take it with me."

"Very well, then." She'd been hoping he'd say she should keep it to remember him by. But as always, Tris was the perfect gentleman. If he did harbor any affection for her, he wouldn't betray so with such a remark. "I wish you a safe journey, Mr. Nesbitt."

She'd called him Tristan—or Tris—for years now, but suddenly that seemed too informal.

His gray eyes remained steady. "Thank you, Lady Alexandra. I wish you a happy life."

A happy life. She could be married by the time he returned, she realized with a shock. In fact, if he were gone three years, she very likely would be.

Her heart sank at the thought.

But at least she'd have his profile. When she was finished, it would be black on white in an elegant oval frame, a perfect likeness of his face. And she'd almost touched him while making it.

As he walked from the room, she peeled the paper off the glass and hugged it to her chest.

Chapter One

RATAFIA PUFFS

Take halfe a pound of Ground Almonds and a little more than that of Sugar. Make it up in a stiff paste with Whites of five Eggs and a little Essence of Almond whipt to a Froth. Beat it all well in a Mortar, and make it up in little Loaves, then bake them in a very cool oven on Paper and Tin-Plates.

I call these my magical sweets . . . my husband proposed directly after eating only one!
—Eleanor Chase, Marchioness of Cainewood,
1728

Cainewood Castle, seven years later
June 1815

"Not all of it!" Alexandra Chase made a mad grab for her youngest sister's arm. "We're instructed to add a *little* more sugar than almonds."

Corinna stopped grating and frowned. "I *like* sugar."

"You won't like these ratafia puffs if they're *all* sugar," their middle sister, Juliana, said as she took the cone-shaped sugar loaf and set it on the scarred wooden table in the center of the cavernous kitchen.

"Here, my arm is tired." Alexandra handed Corinna the bowl of egg whites she'd been beating, then scooped a proper amount of the sugar and poured it into another bowl that held ground almonds. Stirring them together, she shook her head at Corinna. "You really are quite hopeless with recipes. If you didn't look so much like Mama, I would wonder if you were truly her child."

A sudden sheen of tears brightened Corinna's brilliant blue eyes, but she quickly blinked them away. "She always made good sweets, didn't she?"

"Excellent sweets," Juliana said in a sympathetic tone, shooting a warning glance to her older sister.

Alexandra felt abashed, and suddenly a little teary herself. She looked away, her gaze wandering the whitewashed stone walls of the castle's ground-floor kitchen. Heaven knew Corinna was the most talented of the three of them. She'd meant only to tease her sister about her lack of their family's renowned skills for making sweets, not remind her of their mother. Memories could still be painful, since Mama had been gone less than two years.

But the time for sadness was over . . . following years of mourning various family members one after another, Alexandra and her sisters were finally wearing cheerful colors and ready to face the world. In Alexandra's case, she was *more* than ready to put the sadness behind her and get on with her life.

During her first and only Season four long years ago, she'd entertained many excellent offers of marriage. But her grandmother had died shortly thereafter, and all thoughts of a wedding had been postponed. She'd missed the 1812 Season while mourning her grandmother, then her father had died. She'd missed the 1813 Season while mourning him, then her mother had died. She'd missed the 1814 Season while mourning her, then her oldest brother had died, making 1815's Season yet another one of solitude here in the countryside.

All of the marriage-minded men who'd courted her had long since found available brides. But Alexandra wasn't sure she wanted to face another Season, with all the attending games and frivolity. She just wanted to be a wife. She wanted to put her old life behind her and start over in a new place and a new situation.

As for her younger sisters, they'd yet to be presented at court and were beside themselves at the thought of finally having a Season. It seemed all Juliana and Corinna could talk of were the many parties, balls, breakfasts, dances, and soirees they were looking forward to attending.

"I can hardly wait for next spring," Corinna said, echoing Alexandra's musings.

Juliana added a few drops of almond extract to the egg whites. "If Griffin has his way, we'll all be married long before spring. We'll *never* have a Season."

"He cannot get us all married off so quickly." Alexandra idly stirred the almonds and sugar. "Never mind that he's been inviting his friends here to meet us since before we were out of mourning. You two will have your Seasons. He'll have to be content with my marriage for now."

"If the 'magical' ratafia puffs do their job." Corinna handed the bowl of eggs back to Alexandra. "Here, now *my* arm is tired. This is hard work." Mopping her forehead with a towel, she looked pointedly through an archway to where a scullery maid stood drying a towering stack of dishes. "I cannot understand why you won't ask *her*—"

"If the magic is to work," Juliana interrupted patiently, "Alexandra must make the ratafia puffs herself, not relegate the task to a servant."

"Holy Hannah!" Corinna tossed her mane of long, wavy brown hair, which she insisted on wearing down even though she had long since become old enough to put it up. "It's blazing hot in here with the coal burning all the day long. Ladies don't work in the kitchen."

Still beating the eggs, Alexandra glanced at the ancient, stained journal that lay open on the long table. "Chase ladies do. Our foremothers have been making sweets forever." The heirloom volume was filled with recipes penned by Chase females going all the way back to the seventeenth century. "It's a tradition," she added, looking back up at her sister. "Will you be the first to break it?"

"Perhaps. Unlike you, I don't put much stock in tradition."

Alexandra beat the eggs harder. "You should," she started.

"Girls." Juliana, always the peacemaker, took the bowl of stiffened eggs from her sister and dumped the almond and sugar mixture into it. "Why is there no ratafia in ratafia puffs?" she asked, adeptly changing the subject.

"Perhaps we're supposed to serve ratafia with them," Corinna suggested.

Alexandra laughed. "Griffin invited Lord Shelton to take tea, not to drink spirits. I expect they're called ratafia puffs because they taste of almonds like ratafia does."

Corinna dipped a finger into the sweet mixture and licked it off. "Do you think Lord Shelton will really propose?"

Juliana rolled her lovely hazel eyes. "Alexandra could feed him dirt and he'd propose. Have you not seen the way he looks at her?"

"Like he'd rather eat her than the sweets?"

"Oh, do hold your tongues." Alexandra *had* noticed the way Lord Shelton looked at her, and although she couldn't figure out *why* he looked at her that way—she knew she had a pretty face, but her boring brown eyes and impossible-to-control brown hair left a lot to be desired—she had to confess it was gratifying. She only wished she felt the same way about him.

But even though he didn't make her heart race, he was handsome and kind. He possessed a fortune of his own, so she knew he wasn't after her sizable dowry. And he lived nearby, so she would see her sisters often.

He really was quite perfect.

Once, at fifteen, she'd basked in the illusion of love.

But now she suspected love to be an unrealistic, childish expectation. Years of sadness and disappointment had taught her to expect less than she used to of life.

With any luck, the ratafia puffs would work their magic, she thought as she dropped shiny dollops of the batter onto a paper-lined tin baking sheet.

The Chase sisters sorely deserved some luck.

Chapter Two

For the first time in seven years, Tristan Nesbitt rode over Cainewood Castle's drawbridge and into its quadrangle. As a groom hurried from the stables, he swung down from his black gelding, his gaze skimming the clipped lawn and the four stories of living quarters that formed a U around it.

Cainewood didn't look any different, although there was no reason it should. If he remembered right, the castle had been in Chase hands—save during the Commonwealth—for close to six hundred years. He shouldn't have expected it to change in the last seven.

But *he* had changed, so it felt odd that this place hadn't.

Seven years ago, he'd been a young man of one-and-twenty on his way to Jamaica to begin a promising career working with his generous Uncle Harold. He'd had a new degree from the University of Oxford, a soon-to-be-healed broken heart, and nary a serious care in the world.

Four years ago, Uncle Harold had died, and Tristan had taken his place as the Marquess of Hawkridge.

These days, he was anything but carefree.

The young groom tipped his cap. "Take your horse, my lord?"

"Yes, thank you." Tristan handed over the reins. As his mount was led away, his gaze wandered the ancient keep—still as tumbledown as he remembered it—and past it to the old tilting yard that lay beyond. He smiled, recalling games played there as a youth, he and Griffin—and often, Griffin's charming little sisters—running through the untamed, ankle-high vegetation. Those summers spent here during his school years were memories to be treasured. Griffin's family had been a jolly substitute for the lack of his own.

"Tristan. Or I suppose I should call you Hawkridge. Whichever, it's been entirely too long."

Lost in his thoughts, he hadn't heard Griffin approach, but now he turned to see his old friend holding out a hand. He reached his own to grasp it.

"Ah, hell," Griffin said and pulled him into a rough embrace instead.

Tristan stiffened for a stunned moment. Other than the impersonal attentions of his valet or a perfunctory handshake now and then, it was the first human touch he had felt in . . . entirely too long to remember.

He clapped his friend on the back. "Yes. Entirely too long," he echoed as he drew away. "Am I supposed to call you Cainewood?"

"Strikes the ear wrong after all these years, doesn't it?" Like the castle, Griffin's slightly crooked smile was familiar. "Griffin will do. I didn't expect you until tomorrow at the earliest."

Tristan walked with him toward the entrance. "Your note sounded urgent."

Before they reached the front steps, the double oak doors opened. Cainewood's longtime butler stood between them. "Welcome back, my lord," he said with a little bow.

"Why, thank you, Boniface," Tristan returned, pleased to see him again. The man was aptly named, for he had a bonnie face—a youthful countenance that belied his forty-odd years. No matter how hard he tried to look stiff and serious, he never quite succeeded. And other than a touch of gray gracing his temples, the years hadn't changed him a bit.

Tristan couldn't say the same for Griffin. "You look older," he said as they climbed the steps. Griffin's jaw looked firmer; his green eyes looked almost world-weary. "But I expect one could say the same of me."

Griffin nodded. "We're both shouldering responsibilities we never thought to have."

"Feeling overburdened, are you?" Tristan was surprised. "Surely the marquessate is less pressure than plotting war strategy."

"You have no idea." They stepped inside. "I have three sisters to marry off, and that is only the beginning—"

"They cannot already be old enough to marry!"

Griffin's laugh boomed through the three-story-high entrance hall, all the way up to its stone-vaulted ceiling. "You expect we aged while time stood still for them?" He led Tristan up the carved stone staircase. "Corinna— the baby—is nearly twenty. Plenty old enough to find a husband."

Tristan frowned. "And Juliana and Alexandra?" he asked, deliberately mentioning her last.

Maybe she would seem less important that way.

"Twenty-one and twenty-two." They turned on the landing and went up a second level to the family's private apartments. "Four deaths in the family have kept them from the marriage mart, but I mean to see them all settled now—and soon." Griffin ushered Tristan into a dark wood study. Waving him into a leather wing chair, he went to open a cabinet.

Tristan sat warily. "Look, old man, I sympathize with your problem, but your letter indicated you were in dire straits and needed my expertise—"

"Yes." Rather than sitting behind the massive mahogany desk, Griffin chose the chair beside Tristan's. "I appreciate your response." He set two crystal glasses on the small table between them, unstoppered a matching decanter, and began pouring. "Regardless of the fact that you've hidden yourself away in the countryside all these years, you are known far and wide—"

"I am not in search of a wife!"

"—for your advances in scientific agriculture and land management." In the midst of handing Tristan a glass, Griffin blinked. "Wife? Do you imagine I asked you here to marry one of my sisters? Perish the thought!"

Tristan breathed deep of the brandy as he wavered between relief and annoyance. Never mind that he had no interest in wedding any of Griffin's sisters—or anyone else, for that matter—he wasn't sure he appreciated having his unsuitability thrown directly into his face. "Why did you summon me, then?"

"I need your help. I've heard you've worked miracles with Hawkridge's vineyard."

"I've managed to revive it, yes. We've had two excellent harvests—the wine from last year's is particularly good." Relaxing back into the cushioning, Tristan took a bracing sip of the fine spirits. "You are in need of wine?"

Griffin's sip was more like a gulp. "Charles," he said, referring to his late older brother, "had taken up growing grapes, with an eye to making wine. He planted vines some three years ago—"

"Charles wanted to make wine?"

"It's the latest thing; have you not heard? What with the prices soaring during the war against France, I suspect he thought to make a killing. But regardless, Charles always did make sure to keep up with whatever was newest."

"Yes," Tristan said dryly. "He did." He well remembered Charles, a tall, dark man with an air of superiority and an eye to owning the best. "Go on, then."

"I've been told not to expect a yield suited for production for another year at the least. But the vines should be bearing fruit by now, should they not? They're not producing anything."

"Three years with nothing at all? Not even the odd bloom?"

"Nothing beyond leaves. I fear they may be dying. And I haven't the foggiest idea what to do." Griffin's fingers tightened on his glass. "I'm trained to lead men into battle, not manage land and livestock."

"Not to mention make wine, which is another enterprise entirely." Tristan sipped thoughtfully. "With more than thirteen thousand acres, a good percentage of that productive, you cannot stand to lose the vineyard? This is your emergency?"

Griffin colored. "I apologize if my letter made it sound dire. But . . . this was Charles's pet project. He invested a fair amount of funds, and I wish to make a success of it." He hesitated a moment, then met Tristan's eyes. "I hate to think I might fail where my brother would have succeeded. I'm not comfortable with these responsibilities—they were meant to be his, and I wasn't raised to the task. But I mean to make the best of it."

The admission sounded pained, but Tristan could sympathize. He didn't imagine that military officers sat around at night baring their souls. And as for himself, it had been a long time since he'd had anyone to confide in.

"I understand," he said. He hadn't been raised with expectations of inheriting a title, either. Quite the contrary, he'd been born the son of a second son, a mere mister who'd attended the right schools only on the largesse of his uncle. "I'm trying to make the best of my life, too."

Griffin nodded, looking uneasy.

These days, most everyone was uneasy around Tristan.

"Shall I have a look at your vineyard?" He drained his glass, set it down, and began to rise.

"It will have to wait until tomorrow." Waving him back down, Griffin refilled the glasses. "It's a good hour each way by horseback, and I'm expecting another caller shortly. A very acceptable suitor for Alexandra's hand."

Alexandra. Tristan pictured long dark curls and innocent young eyes. He wondered how she'd look all grown up.

He wondered if she'd have the same effect on him she used to.

"We'll ride over in the morning," Griffin added. "You'll stay, won't you? At least long enough to evaluate the situation?"

"I'll stay as long as I'm needed." Though Griffin's problem wasn't as pressing as Tristan had imagined, it had been a long time since he'd felt needed.

And a long time since he'd seen Lady Alexandra Chase.

Chapter Three

"You look lovely, Alexandra." Standing in the high gallery, Juliana tweaked her sister's low, ruffle-edged neckline. "Lord Shelton will not be able to resist you."

"Especially after he tries your magical ratafia puffs." Corinna grabbed one of the small sweets from the tray on a marble side table and popped it into her mouth. She sighed as it dissolved on her tongue. "François said they turned out perfect."

"Lord Shelton won't be able to try one if you eat them all first." Alexandra lifted the silver tray, smiling at the little golden puffs, which had been beautifully arranged by François, their French cook. "Come along, now. Lord Shelton is surely waiting." She hurried through the gallery, lifting her blue sprigged muslin skirts with one hand while carrying the dainty tray with the other.

Her sisters flanked her going down the wide stone staircase. "Gentlemen expect to wait for ladies," Juliana said. "It is not the thing to appear too eager."

"I don't care to play those silly feminine games," Alexandra said, frowning at the top of her sister's head.

Juliana was exceedingly short—so short she made Alexandra feel tall, although she and Corinna were rather average in height. Juliana, Alexandra had noticed in the brief time Griffin had been inviting his friends to pay calls, attracted men like bees to honey—most especially the shorter ones.

Thankfully, Lord Shelton was tall.

On the first floor, Alexandra paused in the picture gallery outside the drawing room's door. Masculine voices drifted out. Griffin must have been entertaining her guest—or, more likely, trying to talk him into a proposal.

With any luck, his efforts would pay off.

She schooled her expression into a welcoming one and rounded the corner into the room. "Lord Shelton," she said pleasantly, "please excuse my tardiness. I hope these sweet confections will make up for the wait."

Lord Shelton turned and smiled, walking toward her. But her gaze shifted past him, to where another man stood beside her brother. As he turned slightly and she met his eyes—intense gray eyes she recalled from years before—her heart gave a little skip.

Tristan Nesbitt.

He still had the same strong jaw, the same long nose, the same heavy, straight brows. His skin was unfashionably bronzed, as though he'd spent much time outdoors, and his streaky brown-blond hair still looked tousled, as it used to—and still made her wish to run her fingers through it.

The mere sight of him robbed her of breath.

"Good afternoon, my dear," Lord Shelton said. "I was more than pleased to receive your invitation to take tea."

She tore her gaze from Tris. Lord Shelton looked pale in comparison, his skin a pasty white, his hair the lightest blond, his eyes an innocuous blue. Odd, his paleness had never made an impression on her before. It seemed almost as though he'd faded.

And he wasn't as tall as she'd thought. At least not when he was standing in the same room with Tris.

"Thank you for accepting the invitation," she murmured, struggling to remember her manners.

"I'm certain you girls recall Tristan," Griffin prompted.

Juliana and Corinna curtsied. "Mr. Nesbitt," they said in unison.

Dazed, Alexandra followed suit. "Mr. Nesbitt."

"The Marquess of Hawkridge now," her brother informed them. "Tristan inherited four years back."

Tris was titled now? How had that happened? And where had he been all this time? she wanted to ask. That and a million other questions. She hadn't seen him in . . . sweet heaven, was it seven years? While she hadn't precisely forgotten him in all that time, she *had* forgotten how just looking at him made her insides melt like butter.

Or maybe she'd just banished that from her thoughts.

"Lord Hawkridge," she corrected herself.

"Lady Alexandra," he returned with a vague if polite nod. "And Ladies Juliana and Corinna. My, if you haven't all grown up since I saw you last."

Of course, when he saw her last, he'd paid her little mind at all. She'd been only Griffin's bothersome younger sister.

And he didn't seem to be paying her any mind now, either.

He turned back to Griffin. "Do you know what time of the year Charles planted the vines?"

"I haven't the foggiest idea," Griffin said.

Lord Shelton stepped closer. "Lady Alexandra." There was a cloying quality to his voice that had been missing when Lord Hawkridge said the same words. Alexandra supposed Lord Shelton was trying to sound romantic. She probably would have reacted positively to that yesterday.

He lifted her gloved hand and pressed a kiss to the back. "My dear, you look exquisite."

She'd never heard anything quite so disingenuous.

Juliana elbowed her discreetly. "Perhaps Lord Shelton would like to taste one of your ratafia puffs."

Alexandra looked down to the silver tray, forgotten in her other hand. "Oh, not quite yet." Her laughter sounded forced to her own ears. "Do you not think we should pour the tea first?"

Ignoring her sisters' puzzled frowns, she walked clear across the room and put the tray on a gilt-legged table that sat against the wall.

Juliana began pouring. "The puffs can hardly work their magic from over there."

"Magic?" Lord Shelton inquired.

"Please do sit," Alexandra told him, leaving the tray safely distant while she made her way back across the room. She seated herself on one of the light blue velvet sofas instead of a chair; a tactical error, since Lord Shelton immediately took the place beside her.

That wouldn't have bothered her yesterday. But his scent—an Oriental mix—was too flowery and suddenly annoying.

When Juliana handed her a teacup, she rose and went to Lord Hawkridge where he was talking with her brother. He smelled of clean soap and starch and something else she couldn't identify—but it was decidedly male. "Tea, my lord?"

"Thank you." He took it while barely sparing her a glance. "Not every variety is suited to our climate," he said to Griffin.

"You're welcome," Alexandra murmured.

"Alexandra," Corinna called conspicuously, "since you're up, why don't you get the ratafia puffs and bring them over here?"

"Not just yet." Alexandra marched to the sofa and plopped back down, giving her sister a pointed look. "I'm not certain I wish to serve the ratafia puffs at all."

Lord Shelton glanced between them, clearly confused. "And why not?"

"Yes, why not?" Corinna pressed. "They're supposed to be *magical*."

"Precisely." Alexandra accepted another teacup from Juliana and sipped. "I've no wish to employ magic."

"Magic?" Lord Shelton repeated.

Juliana stood. "May I speak with you in private?" Before Alexandra could disagree, Juliana pulled her up by the arm and drew her out into the picture gallery, Corinna in their wake.

Juliana's hazel eyes radiated concern. "What is going on?"

"Nothing." Alexandra glanced away, her gaze landing on a solemn ancestor who glared from a canvas on the smooth stone wall, looking exceedingly disapproving.

"Nothing?" If possible, Corinna appeared even more disapproving. "Why won't you give Lord Shelton one of the magical ratafia puffs?"

"Magical?" Putting scorn into her voice, Alexandra focused on each of her sisters in turn. "Do you truly believe that eggs and sugar can be magical?"

"Of course not," Corinna said quickly. "But do you not think it's worth a try?"

Juliana laid a gloved hand on Alexandra's arm. "If they *did* work," she said gently, "you could add a notation to Eleanor Chase's entry in the recipe book, verifying her allegation. It's a tradition."

"I don't care," Alexandra said blithely. At least, she hoped she sounded blithe.

Her sisters stared at her, their eyes wide.

"You don't *care*?" Juliana breathed. "About tradition?" She pulled off a glove and reached to touch Alexandra's forehead. "Are you ill?"

"No." Alexandra drew away. "I just don't care about this silly tradition."

"But, Alexandra . . ." Juliana hugged herself. "You're the most traditional person I've ever met."

It was true. Juliana was known for her wild ideas—always meant to help, of course—and Corinna was a bit of a rebel. But Alexandra always did exactly the right thing. She ran her brother's enormous household like clockwork; she kept up with her correspondence; she visited the villagers and tenants, both healthy and ailing, always with some famous Chase sweets in hand. She could sing, play the pianoforte, make lovely profile por-

traits, and embroider—and if she wasn't exactly renowned for any of those talents, at least she was
competent.

Alexandra was a perfect lady. The best single word to
describe her was *traditional*. But right at the moment,
tradition could hang for all she cared.

She set her jaw. "I don't want Lord Shelton to eat
any ratafia puffs."

Her sisters exchanged matching looks of astonishment.
"Why?" Juliana asked carefully.

Corinna cocked her head. "Are you *that* certain he
will propose without them?"

"I don't wish him to propose at all."

Juliana dropped her glove. "*What?*"

"You heard me." Alexandra drew a deep breath, relieved the truth was out. "I've changed my mind."

Juliana blinked. "But Griffin expects you to marry
Lord Shelton."

When Alexandra only shrugged, Corinna frowned.
"You always do the expected thing."

"How very tedious. It's about time I changed, don't
you think?"

"Girls?" Alexandra's flabbergasted sisters were saved
from answering when Griffin stepped into the gallery.
"What are you all doing out here?"

"Talking." Juliana bent to retrieve her glove.

Griffin looked toward the stone-vaulted ceiling as
though praying for heaven-sent strength. "Lord Shelton
is inquiring after your presence." He lowered his gaze
to Alexandra and smiled. "He likes your sweets very
much."

"Oh!" she said, when she wanted to say "Drat!" Not
that she believed in magic, but . . . what if the ratafia
puffs worked? She didn't want to actually *turn down*
Lord Shelton's proposal. Griffin would never forgive her.

"I'm not feeling well," she told him—and suddenly, it
wasn't a fib. The thought of marrying Lord Shelton
made nausea rise in her throat. "Please give Lord Shelton my apologies," she said. "I must go lie down."

Chapter Four

Alexandra sat at her gold-and-white Chippendale dressing table, fingering the oval cameo she'd dug out of the bottom of her jewelry box. "It's pretty, isn't it?"

"Beautiful, my lady." The maid she shared with her sisters deftly pinned up her hair. "I've never seen you wear it before."

"It's been put away for a long time."

Alexandra hadn't been able to find the note that had come with the cameo that exciting day it arrived, about a year after Tris left for the West Indies. But she'd read it so many times, the words were burned into her memory. *My dear Lady Alexandra*, it said in a bold scrawl so distinct she could picture it even now,

> *Here is the gift I promised you from Jamaica. I expect it will arrive a year or two before myself, but I saw it in a shop and knew it for the perfect choice. The cameo reminded me of your profile portraits, and its subject reminded me of yourself. It is my wish that you'll wear it in the best of health and happiness.*
> *Yours,*
> *Tristan Nesbitt*

The cameo, set in a beautiful silver bezel, featured a

girl carved in profile on an oval of blue agate. She'd cherished it and been thrilled to think the pretty, curly-haired young miss on it reminded Tris of her. She must have read the words *My dear* and *Yours* a million times, wishing there were some way he *could* be hers. But after a year had passed, and then two, she'd given up those childish dreams and put both the cameo and the note away.

After another year, she'd taken his profile portrait from her wall and put that away, too.

And now, he wasn't even Tris anymore. He was Lord Hawkridge, a strange and distant man.

On the other hand, now that he was a marquess, he was no longer unsuitable. Perhaps she could—

"Are you ready yet?" Corinna called from the doorway.

"Almost. Come in a moment." As her sisters entered, she threaded a ribbon through the cameo's bale and quickly tied it around her neck. Then she lifted a little pot of clear gloss. Watching in the mirror, she slicked it on her mouth.

"A Lady of Distinction doesn't approve of lip salve," Corinna informed her. "In *The Mirror of the Graces*, she says—"

"A Lady of Distinction can go hang," Alexandra interrupted. "Do you expect Lord Hawkridge might have stayed for dinner?"

Juliana straightened Corinna's yellow satin sash. "Oh, yes. Griffin has asked him to stay the night, so he can assist him with some sort of problem at the vineyard tomorrow morning."

So that was what Tris and Griffin had been so busy discussing while Alexandra was trying to keep the ratafia puffs from Lord Shelton. If Tris would be here through tomorrow, she thought with a little frisson of excitement, perhaps she might have time to catch his interest.

But she was terribly inexperienced . . . Did she have what it would take to tempt a marquess?

"And has Lord Shelton departed?" she asked with not a little trepidation.

His presence could ruin everything.

"Of course. He was invited only to take tea, after all." Corinna sat carefully on Alexandra's blue damask bedcovering. "He hopes you'll feel better soon."

"I am absolutely recovered," Alexandra assured her. Even more so now that she knew she'd escaped the dreaded proposal. She handed her maid a blue ribbon. "Lord Hawkridge didn't seem to mind staying?"

"Not at all." Juliana smiled at her in the mirror. "I don't mind him staying, either. He's quite handsome, is he not? In a rugged way, I mean."

"He's *gorgeous*." Corinna flung herself back on the bed. "I want to paint him."

"He's mine," Alexandra said quietly.

The room fell silent.

"You cannot be serious," Juliana finally said. "You're marrying Lord Shelton."

"I am not. I thought I made that clear this afternoon." Alexandra turned from the dressing table and glanced up. "Thank you, Mary. That will be all."

As her maid slipped from the room, Alexandra squared her shoulders. "I mean to marry Lord Hawkridge if he will have me." Juliana gasped, but Alexandra rushed on. "I hope you two will support me in this. I'm aware it seems rash, but the truth is, I've been in love with him since I was fifteen. Or years earlier. I'm not sure."

Corinna sat upright again, her eyes round as blue saucers. "Does he know?"

"Of course not. Last I saw him, he was a grown man of twenty-one and I was still in the schoolroom. He wasn't supposed to even notice me."

"He noticed us," Corinna disagreed. "He talked to us quite often, and he used to tease us mercilessly."

Alexandra sighed. "That wasn't the sort of noticing I was hoping for."

"In any case, he was a mere mister then," Juliana pointed out, "with no prospects."

"I never cared."

Juliana smoothed her pink skirts. "Father would have cared."

"I know. And I accepted that then. But now everything's changed—"

"Good evening, ladies." Griffin appeared in the doorway. "Father would have cared about what?"

The sisters exchanged glances; then Juliana looked toward him and smiled. "Father would have cared to see one of us wed to Lord Hawkridge."

Griffin blinked. "Let us hear none of that. I didn't invite Tristan here as a potential suitor."

"Why not?" Corinna asked. "You've invited every other unmarried man in all of Britain."

"Not quite yet, but I'm working on it." He flashed her a crooked grin, then nodded toward a book on Alexandra's night table. "Have you been reading *The Mirror of the Graces*?"

"Oh, yes. Every night," she assured him, ignoring her sisters' muffled giggles. Griffin had given them each a copy of the etiquette manual, authored by "A Lady of Distinction," in the hope that they would learn to deport themselves in a manner conducive to winning fine husbands.

He was leaving no stone unturned in his quest to get them all married off.

"Excellent," he said. "I trust you're feeling better now?"

"Much better, thank you. Shall we go down to dinner?"

Somewhere in the house, she thought as she trailed her siblings out of the room, Lord Hawkridge was waiting. Just realizing she would see him again made a pleasant hum warm her body. And to think, only this morning she'd considered feelings of love to be an unrealistic, childish expectation.

Pretending indifference toward Lady Alexandra was one of the hardest things Tristan had ever done. And years of practice didn't seem to be making it any easier.

Dinner had been pure torture, chitchatting with Griffin about his trouble with the vineyard while all the while he could feel Alexandra's gaze on him. Now, their little party having removed themselves to the music room, he was sipping his port at an impolite pace while Griffin's sisters provided entertainment.

Corinna had a pretty voice, and the music Juliana coaxed from her harp was nothing less than exquisite. But Tristan had eyes only for Alexandra. She'd removed her gloves, and her bare fingers, long and elegant, flew gracefully over the keys of the pianoforte. Though his ears told him the resulting tune was proficient rather than inspired, her playing had him enthralled.

She was wearing the cameo he'd sent her several years earlier, and he found himself entirely too pleased about that.

"Would you care for more?"

Tristan looked up to find Griffin standing over him with the bottle of port. "My thanks," he murmured, raising his glass.

Griffin settled beside him on the small gold brocade sofa. "Civilized, aren't they?" He gestured toward his sisters, all seated primly on dainty chairs with brocade seats and gilt backs. His chuckle was low enough to not be heard across the room. "Whoever would have thought they'd actually grow up?"

Tristan smiled, but he'd always known Alexandra would turn out to be something special. A rather gangly girl, she'd grown into her looks during the years since he'd last seen her. Sweet curves now softened her slender frame. Her sooty-lashed eyes, which had always reminded him of warmed brandy, now peered out from a delicately featured face. Her chestnut hair was the same as it always had been—so springy it seemed alive, refusing to stay pinned primly atop her head.

Any man would find her alluring.

But there was something else about her—something harder to put his finger on. Even as an adolescent she'd been responsible beyond her years, accomplished and more than competent . . . and yet, underneath, he'd sensed a melting romanticism, a yearning for love that the younger, more idealistic Tristan would have given anything to fulfill.

Then, as today, he'd sometimes sensed his feelings were returned—something in the way her eyes would soften when he caught her looking at him. But there had been no sense in pursuing anything. From the start, he'd known the Marquess of Cainewood would not allow his high-born daughter to wed the son of a common drunkard.

And nothing was different now. True, his situation had changed, and the old marquess and his first son had both died, leaving Griffin to inherit the title. But Griffin had new reasons to reject Tristan's suit—reasons even more damning than those his father would have objected to all those years ago.

Alexandra glanced over at him again, watching through lowered lashes as a gentle smile curved her lips. He looked away and sipped. He would have to have a talk with her. He disliked discussing his circumstances, but honor compelled him to explain.

"What is life like at Hawkridge?" Griffin asked quietly.

Lonely, Tristan thought. He hadn't realized how lonely until now. But he wasn't looking for pity. "I keep busy," he said. "Doing very ungentlemanly things."

"Are you implying you *work*?" Griffin asked in mock horror.

"Incessantly, I'm afraid."

Griffin's laughter brought Alexandra's head up once more, and she met Tristan's eyes, her own melting in that way that threatened his resolve.

But he wouldn't allow her to pierce his armor. He couldn't stand the pain . . . especially because, as her older brother, Griffin would see that nothing ever came of it, anyway.

"Hawkridge's restored vineyards are only the beginning of my improvements," he said, turning deliberately to Griffin. "I am building a gasworks. And I've found that careful land management produces significantly larger crops."

Griffin sipped slowly. "According to rumor, you've started a new breeding program as well. Not just for horses, but common swine and sheep."

"Yes, I'm importing stock from distant estates. I ascribe to the theory that interbreeding produces weak animals."

"I look forward to learning more of this."

"I look forward to explaining it," Tristan told him with a smile.

Miraculously, it seemed that Griffin had remained his friend. Still more reason to steer clear of Alexandra. It wasn't worth ruining such a long-standing relationship over something that could never be.

The song came to an end, but instead of launching into another one, the sisters held a short, murmured conversation. Tristan saw Juliana nod before they all rose. As they started across the parquet floor, Alexandra's hand went up to touch the cameo hanging from a ribbon above her low neckline.

Yes, he had to explain things, difficult as that would be. Perhaps feigning indifference wasn't the hardest thing, after all.

"That was very nice, girls," Griffin said.

Although he knew his friend used the term with affection, Alexandra no longer struck Tristan as a *girl*. He looked away, staring blankly at the large gilt-framed mirror that hung above the white marble fireplace. The room seemed too hot. He tugged to loosen the cravat his valet had so carefully tied early that morning.

"Are you overly warm?" Juliana smiled sweetly. "Perhaps a walk along the battlements in the night air would help."

That sounded like an excellent idea. "I believe I shall take your suggestion," he said, beginning to rise. He needed to get out of here. He needed to think. He needed to plan carefully what he would say to Alexandra. Out of sight of her, and her beautiful eyes, and the cameo he'd given her dangling near her pert, filled-out breasts.

"I'm pleased you agree," Juliana said, still smiling. "Alexandra would be happy to accompany you."

Chapter Five

Alexandra was shocked at Juliana's bold suggestion, and even more shocked when Tris—Lord Hawkridge, she reminded herself—paused, then nodded rather grimly and said, "That would be delightful."

"Tristan," Griffin said in a quiet tone laced with warning. But Lord Hawkridge ignored Alexandra's brother, rising and taking her elbow, and she was too excited to pay Griffin any heed. She'd always followed the rules and obeyed authority, but it seemed she was changing more and more by the minute.

Lord Hawkridge had agreed to walk with her alone outdoors. It was almost too good to be true. Maybe she *would* prove able to make him notice her in the short time he would be here.

In silence they descended the staircase and walked outside into the quadrangle. After a while, the silence grew worrisome. After all, he hadn't exactly sounded happy when he'd agreed. Perhaps he had only acquiesced to avoid embarrassing Juliana. Maybe he would rather have stayed inside with Griffin.

There was a full moon tonight, but his gray eyes were unreadable. "My lord," she started.

"After all these years," he interrupted, "you're not going to start addressing me formally now, are you?" Having spent enough time at Cainewood to know his way around, he led her uphill toward the keep, which sat atop an ancient motte—a mound of earth built to give the castle's defenders the advantage of height. "You called me Tristan when we were younger. Or Tris. I always liked that."

Had he? Feeling her cheeks heat at the thought, she was happy for the sudden darkness as they stepped into the tower. He let her lead the way up the winding stone staircase, following close behind—as a gentleman should—in case she should stumble in the pitch-blackness.

She put a hand to the rough wall for balance. "You weren't a marquess when we were younger."

"I'm still the same person."

She wasn't so certain he hadn't changed in seven years. Braver in the dark than she'd have been in the moonlight, she blurted the question she'd been dying to ask all day. "However *did* you become a marquess?"

Behind her, Lord Hawkridge sighed. "My father was a second son—a spectacularly unsuccessful one. It was my uncle—the marquess—who financed my schooling and university."

"So I gathered over the years." She glanced at him as they stepped through the archway and back into the pale illumination. "But your uncle had heirs, did he not?"

"The requisite heir and a spare, yes." By unspoken agreement, they began strolling along the top of the wide, crenelated wall. "My uncle had married well, an heiress who came with a large plantation in Jamaica. Her family lived on other property they owned on the island, and though she and Uncle Harold had a good marriage, she pined to see them from time to time. Five years ago—while I was still there learning the ropes—she brought her sons home for a visit. None of them returned. Weeks after they were due to arrive, my uncle learned their ship had gone down in the Caribbean. Suddenly I was his heir."

"And then he died?"

"A year later, yes. That was four years ago, just after

I'd returned to England. My own father had died a scant six months earlier, and I'd inherited his estate—which was little more than a mountain of debt. I was . . . in dire straits."

He hesitated as though he wanted to say more, but she waited a while and he didn't. "That was solved when you inherited from your uncle?" she prompted.

"Yes," he said, and hesitated again. Their footfalls echoed into the night. "But there's no need to call me Lord Hawkridge," he finally added, bringing the conversation back to where they'd started.

She was certain there was something else he hadn't told her, but it wasn't her place to press. "You've always called me Lady Alexandra. On the rare occasions you noticed me, that is." She glanced toward him and smiled, a fetching smile, she hoped. "Last time you saw me I was only Griffin's vexatious younger sister."

If only she could become more than that now. His features, shadowed in the moonlight, gave her little clue to his thoughts. A lock of his tousled hair had fallen onto his forehead. His eyes looked hooded, his mouth firm.

"I always noticed you, Alexandra."

No *Lady*. She should take offense, she supposed— they weren't close enough to warrant that sort of familiarity. Not anymore, in any case. But she *wanted* to be that close. And he'd said . . .

Had he *actually* said he'd always noticed her?

"Did you?" she asked breathlessly, even knowing he couldn't have meant it the way she hoped. *I always noticed you.* "Probably because I bothered you," she said with a shaky laugh.

"Not at all. You used to talk about the most interesting things. Deep things."

She'd always been somewhat of a philosopher, even as a girl. Her sisters were forever telling her she was too serious. She turned to the ledge and stopped, gazing out over the darkened landscape, the fields and the nearby woods. The River Caine glistened in the distance.

She felt rather than saw him come up to stand beside her.

"I hadn't expected you listened," she said quietly.

"Alexandra."

Something in his voice made her turn to him. "Hmm?"

"I listened to every word." He laid a hand over hers where it rested on the ledge, and she realized suddenly that she'd forgotten to replace her gloves after she stopped playing the pianoforte.

And he wasn't wearing gloves, either. His hand felt warm and a little rougher than a true gentleman's hand should. Not that she'd ever touched another gentleman's bare hand.

The sensation was thrilling beyond words.

"Tris," she breathed, the only syllable she seemed capable of uttering.

He grinned, his teeth straight and white in the moonlight. "That's better."

Had she really called him Tris? She decided to gloss over that. "I . . . I don't think it's proper for you to be touching me."

"You're right. I most definitely should not be touching you."

But instead of removing his fingers, he tightened them over hers, and his other hand came up to touch the cameo that lay against her chest. Near his fingers, her breasts tingled and their crests seemed to tauten.

"You kept it," he said.

"Of course I did." She wouldn't tell him she'd put it away for years. "It . . . it was the best gift I'd ever received. I was so surprised when it arrived."

"I promised I'd send you something from Jamaica."

"No. You were supposed to *bring* me something."

"I couldn't," he said simply. And then, "Alexandra, there is something I must tell you."

"Yes?"

"I've listened to you, thought about you, for a long, long time. I wanted you to know that."

Had he really said those words, the very ones she'd been longing to hear? Her heart seemed to swell in her chest. She was so excited, she barely heard what he said next.

"But I also need for you to know—"

"Oh, Tris! I always noticed you, too."

He winced, as though her admission had hurt him. "I am almost sorry to hear that. For you, sweetheart. There are circumstances . . ." Sweet heaven, he'd called her *sweetheart*. But he seemed to be struggling for words. "We are not meant to be together," he finally said. "Your brother would never—"

"Oh, yes." Now that she knew Tris had noticed her, she wouldn't let Griffin or Lord Shelton stand in her way. She wasn't known for being stubborn for nothing. "I shall have a talk with my brother."

He shook his head mournfully. "Even in the unlikely event that Griffin would agree, I cannot allow—"

"Hush, Tris." She had to make him understand. She turned her hand over beneath his and gripped his fingers, hard. "I will not listen to this." She searched his eyes for a moment, looking for the agreement he couldn't seem to give. Then, without thinking, she reached up and swept that single renegade lock back from his forehead.

His breath rushed out, and all at once, something changed in that deep gray gaze.

He stepped closer, and his scent overwhelmed her— that clean-Tris scent she'd noticed earlier in the day. "Alexandra," he murmured, the pads of his fingertips grazing her cheek. His warmth enveloped her, warding off the chill night air. He cupped her face in his hand and angled his head as he pressed closer, his large, rangy body all but pinning her against the ancient stone wall. Closer, closer, until she could feel his breath teasing her lips.

She held her own breath. In fact, she wondered fleetingly if she would ever find the strength to draw breath again. Then his lips touched hers, and all thought fled for a long, glorious moment.

His kiss was tender at first, no more than a brush of mouths, his lips softer than she'd expected. Then his mouth settled on hers more firmly, demanding her response.

She sighed and leaned in to him, raising her arms to wind them around his neck, threading her fingers through his slightly too-long hair. His tongue traced the line where her lips met, and she parted them in surprise. He took immediate advantage, sinking his tongue into her mouth. Shocked, she tensed, but as he probed gently, a languid shiver rippled through her. She'd never imagined such an intimacy. He slid a hand into her hair, cupping the back of her head and tilting it to make their lips mesh more completely, and she allowed herself to relax, to lose herself in a sensual haze.

He explored her mouth as though intent on learning her, on owning her, on claiming every nook and cranny. In turn, she touched her tongue to his, tasting him and letting all the new feelings wash over her.

Had she ever been kissed before? She'd thought so . . . during her one long-ago Season, several overwrought, hopeful men had somehow managed to maneuver a few seconds of privacy, enough to press their lips to hers. But now she knew she hadn't really been kissed, not a true kiss like this.

None of those kisses had made her heart pound. None of those kisses had made heat gather low in her middle. None of those kisses had made her lean wantonly into a man as she was doing with Tris now.

Her behavior was scandalous, really. But she couldn't seem to help herself. And Tris's obvious response was her saving grace, for surely he wouldn't kiss her like this without the most honorable of intentions.

Soon, she thought dizzily, his surprising, thrilling words still swirling about in her head . . . soon, he would be her husband.

He shifted, wrapping his arms around her, one hand against her upper back and the other down lower, drawing her tight against his hard, warm body. He pressed little kisses to her cheeks and chin and neck, pausing in the hollow of her throat, making new, tingly sensations dance along her skin. Close as he was, she was certain he could hear the pounding of her heart.

"Tris," she whispered.

"Holy Christ," he grated out.

When his hands fell from her body, her eyes flew open to find his closed. It seemed an eternity before he opened them.

She gave him a trembly smile. "That was nice."

"No." He shook his head, running a hand through his hair raggedly. "It was most certainly *not* nice."

"Well, not in that way, perhaps," she said, confused. She drew a shaky breath and let it out. "But that cannot really matter so long as we . . ."

"So long as we what?"

"So long as we . . ."

He hadn't proposed, and she couldn't bring herself to do it for him. But as she watched and waited, she saw understanding dawn in his eyes. And then she saw his jaw set as he stepped farther back. "A kiss does not equal a marriage proposal, Alexandra."

His voice shouldn't sound so cold and resolute. He'd felt the same feelings she had; she was sure of it. "But I thought—"

"I'm sorry," he said, looking it. "I cannot marry you. There are circumstances . . . Damn, I knew I needed to plan out how to explain this." She watched his Adam's apple bob as he swallowed hard. "Forgive me, Alexandra. What I just did was unforgivable, but I can only promise it will not happen again. There is no chance I will ever take you for a wife."

Chapter Six

"I see," Alexandra said and immediately turned to leave.

Though he knew he should elaborate, Tristan remained silent as he walked her back to her family. Along the wall walk, down the winding steps of the tower, and across the quadrangle, he cursed himself a dozen times. Alternately, he thought about how he should word his explanation. He needed to make her understand that his inability to offer for her hand fell squarely on his shoulders and had nothing to do with any inadequacy on her part.

And in between all of that, his mind kept flashing back to that one galvanizing moment when she'd reached toward him, when her fingertips had grazed his skin as she swept the hair from his forehead.

When, if ever, had a woman touched him so tenderly?

That single gesture had, quite simply, undone him. He'd been taken by surprise, found himself lost in temptation. Holy Christ, she had never even been kissed before. The innocent sensuality of her response had devastated him. He wouldn't—couldn't—allow anything similar to ever happen again.

On the steps in front of the double doorway to the castle's living quarters, he stopped and turned to her. "Alexandra—"

The door opened to reveal Griffin. "My sister does not look happy," he said flatly.

He—or perhaps Juliana and Corinna—must have been watching them approach through one of the picture gallery's tall, narrow windows.

Alexandra stepped decisively into the stone entrance hall. "I am fine."

Griffin didn't look like he believed her.

Tristan followed and shut the door behind them. "I can explain."

"There is no need." She raised her chin. "I understand completely."

As Griffin moved closer to his sister, Tristan looked between the two of them: Alexandra, calm and composed—she would never be flustered for long, nor, Tristan expected, was she the sort of woman to succumb to fits of weeping—and her protective older brother. Theirs was a close-knit family; it seemed to make little difference that Griffin had been gone for so many years. That closeness was so foreign to Tristan's own experience as to be almost unimaginable.

He felt impotent in the face of their united front.

"I must explain," he repeated.

"You did," Alexandra said. "I shall talk to Griffin and straighten this all out. Now."

Griffin emitted a long-suffering sigh as he turned to Tristan. "There is more port in the music room. Please help yourself."

Tristan heard the delicate notes of the harp wafting down the staircase. But he didn't need liquor or entertainment. What he needed was to go back to his secluded world—the world he should never have left.

"I believe I shall take my leave for Hawkridge," he said.

"No." Griffin stopped him with a hand on his arm.

Everyone seemed to be touching him today.

"You've promised to help me," Griffin added. "Stay, please. At least until you've seen the vineyard in the morning. I need you."

It had been a long time since a friend—or anyone not a dependent—had needed Tristan. He could damn himself for his weakness, but he found that irresistible.

He nodded shortly. "I shall retire, then. It's been a lengthy day. Good night." Before he could talk himself into leaving again, he turned and started toward the great carved stone staircase.

Boniface appeared out of the shadows. "Allow me to accompany you, my lord."

"Thank you, but I know the way."

The butler handed him a lantern. "I shall send a valet to you posthaste."

Tristan didn't want a valet. He wanted to be alone. He'd been relieved to escape his own very fine and competent valet that morning and ride to Cainewood in blessed solitude, assuming this would be naught but a day trip. But he was a marquess now. Upon inheriting the title, the world believed he'd forgotten how to undress himself.

What he'd forgotten instead was his head. His manners. His bred-in-the-bone knowledge that Alexandra Chase would never be his. And he'd made a bloody damn mess of things with his bloody inability to explain the bloody scandal that made any relationship between them impossible.

Holding the lantern high, he mounted the stairs, cursing himself. He cursed himself all the way through the picture gallery, across the arched dining room, and along the impossibly long length of the hammerbeam–ceilinged great hall. At its far end, he stomped down a corridor and slammed into the room he'd been assigned.

Within Cainewood's thick stone walls, even summer evenings were chilly. The makings of a fire had been thoughtfully laid on the marble hearth. No doubt a chambermaid hovered in the passageway, waiting for his summons to start it. In an act of defiance, he set the lantern on a gilded dressing table and bent to light the logs himself.

Straightening, he looked around and groaned.

With any luck, he'd be leaving here after inspecting the vineyard in the morning. But in the meantime, this gaudy room was no place to relax.

Seemingly endless rows of guest bedrooms lined this wing, and he'd never been given this one before. Of course, he hadn't been a marquess before. The gold chamber, this room was called, and it was saved, a chatty chambermaid had informed him, for only the most honored guests. Having been decorated for a royal visit in some previous century, it was filled with heavy gilt furniture and draped in golden fabric. It dazzled the eye. And had him tiptoeing his way around.

He sat gingerly on a carved, gold-leafed chair to await the bloody valet. Hawkridge Hall, the mansion he'd inherited, had its share of impressive rooms, including one very much like this. He rarely went in there. He hadn't been raised among such valuable trappings. He was almost afraid to touch anything.

He shouldn't have touched Griffin's sister, either.

"Sit down, Alexandra." Griffin waved her toward one of the study's leather wing chairs, then settled himself behind the big desk she still thought of as belonging to her father. Establishing his authority, she thought with an internal sigh. Well, it didn't matter. Everything had changed today. She was finished being the obedient sister, and she wasn't going to let Griffin pressure her into marrying Lord Shelton—or anyone besides Tris.

He rested his elbows on the mahogany surface, steepling his fingers. "What happened out there?"

She hesitated a moment, then squared her shoulders. "Tris kissed me."

"He did *what*?"

"You heard me. We wish to marry." Pressing her advantage while Griffin still looked shocked, she rose, moving closer to slap her hands onto the desk and lean toward him. "I don't wish to marry Lord Shelton. I want to marry Tris."

"Tris," he echoed pointedly, abruptly leaning back in

the chair. She was the only one who had ever called his friend "Tris." He rubbed the nape of his neck. "He hasn't asked for your hand, has he?"

"Not exactly." Something in her brother's eyes, in the tone of his voice, was making her uneasy. She leaned harder on her palms. "He seems to think you won't approve."

"Damn right, and that's why he would never ask." He fixed her with a piercing green gaze. "The man's been accused of murder."

Chapter Seven

"Murder?" Alexandra's elbows gave out, and her energy seemed to drain on the spot. With some effort, she straightened. She couldn't have heard Griffin right. "Murder?"

"Murder. His uncle—the last Marquess of Hawkridge—died under very suspicious circumstances."

Slowly Alexandra backed toward her chair. "What circumstances?"

"The man went to bed with a mild fever and failed to awaken the next morning. Poison, it was whispered, and Tristan was with him at Hawkridge at the time. Since his father had recently drunk himself to death and left him in heavy debt, penniless and well nigh desperate, there are those who believe his timely inheritance of his uncle's title, property, and massive fortune was rather too convenient."

"Poison." She lowered herself gingerly to the cushioned leather. "I don't believe it for a moment."

Griffin sighed. "Neither do I. He was never convicted—there was no solid evidence—but there are still many who think him guilty of the deed. What we personally do or do not believe has no bearing on the fact that Tristan Nesbitt is unsuitable as a husband."

Alexandra smoothed her dress over her knees while she tried to remember to breathe. If what Griffin was claiming was true, she had to agree that wedding Tris was out of the question. Although she could live without the social whirl, if her family aligned themselves with him by any bond so strong as marriage, their own good name would be ruined. Juliana and Corinna would find it impossible to make good matches for themselves . . . and despite Alexandra's new resolve to be less blindly obedient and traditional, she wasn't selfish enough to doom her sisters to bleak futures as a consequence of her own marriage.

If what Griffin said was true.

"I don't believe it," she repeated. "I don't believe any of it. How did I never hear of this? It must have been an enormous scandal."

"It was. So major a scandal that Tristan has remained cut off from the polite world. He never claimed his seat in the House of Lords. He abandoned his friends rather than subject us to society's criticism. Did you not wonder why he ceased coming around for visits?"

"You were in Spain, Griffin. He could hardly have come around to visit *me*."

"I came home for short periods over the years."

She shrugged, though even that small movement seemed exhausting. "The last time I saw him, he was headed to Jamaica."

"For two or three years, not seven. Did you never hear the murmurings, the nasty rumors? Well, of course you didn't," he answered himself. "You were hidden away here in the countryside wearing black." He pushed himself up from the desk and came around to lean down and wrap her in a hug. "I'm sorry," he said quietly. "But you cannot marry Tristan."

When he pulled back, she took a big breath and nodded up at him. She'd never been one for tears, but she couldn't remember feeling closer to shedding some. "I don't want to marry Lord Shelton."

He sat in the chair beside her. "You wanted to this morning."

"Well, I've changed my mind. I realize now that I cannot be happy with him. Please don't make me—"

"I would never make you marry anyone. Anyone in particular, that is." Something akin to panic flooded his eyes. "You *do* still want to marry? In general, I mean."

Under different circumstances, she might have laughed. "Yes, I still want to marry." She couldn't imagine what she would do with her life if she didn't. From birth, her mother had trained her to oversee a household and its accounts, to care for an estate, to raise children of her own. She didn't have a passion like Corinna's painting, or, like Juliana, a compulsion to meddle in other people's lives.

She just wanted to live her own. "I only wish . . ."

Though her wish remained unspoken, her brother knew what she wanted to say. "Wishing won't buy you anything," he said and then added, "He shouldn't have kissed you," looking totally disgusted. "I'll send him away. Immediately. You won't have to face him at breakfast."

"No. Please don't. Juliana said you need his help."

"Yes, I do need his help." With an agitated motion, he unstoppered the crystal brandy decanter that sat on the table between them. "But I don't need him seducing my sister."

"He didn't. I swear it." She watched him pour two glasses, one much fuller than the other. "Honestly, Griffin, it was only a kiss. I'm sorry I even mentioned it."

"There is nothing *only* about a kiss. At the very least, I will have a serious talk with him." He handed her the glass with less brandy.

She stared at it stupidly. "I've never had brandy."

"Then it's about time you did. Drink up, little sister. You need it right now."

This was certainly a day for firsts. She swallowed a gulp and coughed.

Griffin laughed. "You're supposed to sip it." Cupping the glass, he took an appreciative sniff, then a small sip. "Like that."

Cradling her glass in imitation, she drew deep of the

heady scent. She sipped carefully, feeling the spirits' heat trail down her throat and warm her inside.

"Nice?" he asked.

"Very nice." She took another taste. "Go easy on Tris. Please. I asked for that kiss."

His eyes widened. "Did you?"

Not in the way he was assuming, of course, but she knew Tris wouldn't have kissed her of his own accord. Knew now, in hindsight, that he'd agreed to walk with her because he'd wanted to tell her about the scandal, the reasons why he couldn't ask her to be his wife.

But she hadn't let him talk. Instead, in her desperation to win him, she'd touched him, linked her fingers with his, skimmed his hair from his forehead. What had happened afterward was natural, not a seduction on Tris's part.

Or at least not a planned one.

She sipped again, feeling very much seduced regardless. And unbearably sad, knowing that nothing could possibly come of it.

Griffin reached to pry the glass from her hands. The empty glass. A corner of his mouth curved up in a sympathetic half smile. "I think you'd best get a good night's sleep."

She looked longingly toward the decanter, then sighed. The brandy was much stronger than the wine she was used to, and she couldn't even drink much of that. Her head was already buzzing, and more spirits wouldn't solve anything. "You're right. Just promise you won't send Tris away until he's done with what you asked him here to do."

"Very well. But—"

"And you won't make him feel uncomfortable here, either."

"I suspect he'll feel uncomfortable around you no matter what I—"

"—and you won't tell him I told you he kissed me."

"Would you let a man complete a sentence?"

She laughed. A heavyhearted laugh, but a laugh nonetheless. "Only if you're going to say what I want to hear."

"I pity the man who finally marries you." Griffin drained the rest of his brandy and set down his glass. "Of course, we have to find a man before I can pity him."

"We can wait for the Season—"

"Good God, no." He looked horrified at the thought. "Securing two husbands next year is a daunting enough task." He steepled his hands and tapped his fingers against one another, then suddenly stopped. "We shall host a ball, and I will invite every unmarried gentleman of my acquaintance. At least twice as many men as women . . . that will ensure that no man is monopolized by another female, and you'll have ample chance to meet all of them."

Feeling bold with the brandy in her, Alexandra rolled her eyes. "You've no idea the preparation that goes into hosting a ball."

"Well, of course not. We didn't host balls on campaign." He sighed and poured himself another drink. "I do know how to play the proper host, though. And I have you to do the planning—"

"Me? I've never planned a ball!"

"You cannot tell me Mother never had you assist with the planning. We shall hold it in a month, I think. The Season will be well over by then, and Charles will have been gone a full year by then, too, so no one will be able to claim we didn't wait a decent period."

"A month? I cannot plan a ball in a month! Invitations should go out more than a month in advance. Mama spent all year planning Cainewood's annual ball." Realizing she'd as much as admitted she *did* know something of what it took to plan a ball, she rushed on before her brother could make a smug comment. "We'll need two months total, at the very least."

"Six weeks, then." Griffin refilled his glass and then raised it, admiring the way the candlelight illuminated the amber liquid. "You're nothing if not efficient, Alexandra. I'm certain you can plan a ball in six weeks."

"Six weeks." Pacing the music room and shaking her head in disbelief, Alexandra popped another ratafia puff into her mouth. They certainly didn't seem to be working any magic. "He wants us to plan a ball in *six* weeks."

"We can do it." At her easel, Corinna sighed happily. "A ball! We'll all need new evening dresses."

"Alexandra isn't concerned about our wardrobes at the moment," Juliana chided. She rose from her harp and went to stop her sister's frantic pacing, placing a gentle hand on her arm. "I cannot believe Griffin is searching out another husband for you already. You haven't even recovered from the loss of Tristan yet."

Normally Alexandra would protest that she couldn't have lost Tris when she'd never had him, not to mention they'd renewed their acquaintance mere hours earlier. But it *did* feel like a loss. "I don't believe he committed murder."

"Neither do we," her sisters chimed in unison.

"He doesn't have it in him," Juliana added. "Griffin had no right to forbid you to marry him." Juliana always wanted to see everyone happy. "You should elope; you could run off to Gretna Green—"

"Don't be a goose." Alexandra moved away from her sister and back to the ratafia puffs. "For one thing, Tris has not asked me to marry him. For another, have you thought about the effect such an event would have on your own prospects? Our good name would be ruined. You and Corinna would never find suitable husbands."

"Perhaps that wouldn't happen," Juliana said. "You cannot pretend to know how society would react—"

"Oh, yes, I can. Look how they've treated Tris all these years!"

"In any case, you should not sacrifice your own happiness for us," she concluded loyally, looking to Corinna for agreement.

Corinna swallowed hard but nodded. "We shall survive, one way or another."

"Geese. I'm surrounded by geese." Alexandra resumed pacing, wishing now that there were real ratafia in the ratafia puffs. Was she forever doomed to exercising enough common sense for all three of them? "I will not marry a man if the two of you will suffer as a consequence."

The look that passed between her sisters set her teeth on edge. If they were plotting to conspire against her, it wouldn't be the first time. Juliana made a hobby of meddling in other people's lives, and Corinna had played her willing accomplice more than once. But Alexandra was determined to undermine them, never mind that their hearts were in the right place.

"Tris won't marry me in any case," she informed them. "He told me there is no chance he would ever take me for a wife."

Juliana and Corinna exchanged another glance. "He's hardly had time to propose," Juliana started.

"That doesn't signify." Alexandra could tell by her sister's eyes that her protests were falling on deaf ears. "He made his intentions—or non-intentions—perfectly clear. So don't go getting any ideas in your head. A single kiss does not mean—"

"A kiss?" Corinna interrupted. "He *kissed* you?"

Juliana jumped to Alexandra's defense. "I'm sure it was just a good-natured peck on the cheek. There is nothing so wrong with that."

"That's not what it says in *The Mirror of the Graces*," Corinna informed her. "A Lady of Distinction claims that 'good-natured kisses have often very bad effects and can never be permitted without injuring the fine gloss of that exquisite modesty which is the fairest garb of virgin beauty.' "

"Must you remember everything you read?" Alexandra asked with a huff.

"I cannot help it if I can see pages in my head after I've read them. In any case, I didn't say I believed it. *The Mirror of the Graces* is dreadfully straitlaced."

Alexandra had had quite enough of this nonsense. She was tired and brokenhearted, and she wanted to go to bed. "Well, it wasn't a good-natured kiss, anyway," she said, leaving her sisters gaping as she quit the room.

Chapter Eight

Breakfast the next morning was a damned uncomfortable meal. Tristan couldn't help but notice Alexandra wasn't wearing his cameo, and he wasn't sure whether he found that a relief or a disappointment. He spent the entire hour avoiding her eyes while feeling her gaze on him.

He'd never realized a gaze could be so heavy.

And he'd never been quite as relieved as when Griffin pushed back from the table and said, "Let's go."

Unfortunately, the relief was short-lived. After calling for their horses, Griffin waited in stiff silence while Tristan wondered what he should say. But it was a crisp, sunny morning, and once they were on their way to the vineyard, it felt good to be astride in the fresh air. Good and familiar.

"Race you," he challenged.

Griffin slanted a single look at him before digging in his heels.

They hadn't designated a stopping point, but it didn't matter. Tristan leaned over his mount, bunching his muscles along with the animal beneath him, enjoying the rush of cool wind, the pounding rhythm. Beside him, Griffin kept pace; they could both afford expensive horseflesh.

What Tristan *couldn't* afford was to feel this distant

from the only friend he had. They were neck and neck, but farther apart than when they'd lived on separate continents.

When the horses were blowing, they slowed to a walk and rode silently for a while.

"You can still ride," Griffin conceded.

Tristan raised a brow. "And I wasn't in the cavalry."

"Keep your hands off my sister."

"I will." He wondered how much Alexandra had revealed. "I'm sorry."

"I know," Griffin said.

Just like that, the tension eased. Such was the way of old friends. But Tristan felt very fortunate that their friendship had survived his indiscretion.

It had been a terrible mistake. They were all lucky the two of them hadn't been caught. In Alexandra's world, a kiss was often as good as a declaration, an *observed* kiss sometimes enough to compel two people to marry.

And Tristan had no intention of marrying—not Alexandra or anyone else.

"Thank you," he said quietly.

"It's forgotten." Griffin raised his face to the sun. "I'm certain it won't happen again."

They rode in silence a few more minutes, but it was a comfortable silence this time. Tristan felt his clenched muscles slowly slacken, the stiffness ease from his neck.

"Why did your brother plant this vineyard so damn far from the house?" he finally asked.

"You think I understood Charles? Ever?"

"He was a dandy, if ever I met one. But he left this place in decent shape, did he not?"

"Though it pains me to admit it, yes. He was good at what he did." They rode over a crest, but the grapevines still weren't in sight. "What made you decide to restore Hawkridge's vineyard?" Griffin asked. "Given its age, it must have been an arduous task."

Tristan shrugged. "It wasn't so much damaged as neglected. Grapevines are hardy, for the most part."

"Not mine, apparently."

"We shall see. In any case, I viewed Hawkridge's vineyard as a challenge. It was planted more than a century ago, in the early 1680s."

"By whom? Do you know?"

"Oh, yes, not only who, but why. The Hawkridge records are impeccable. An earlier marquess—one Randal Nesbitt—saw taxation rising under Charles II. With the extra duties imposed on French wine, he thought to try to produce his own. According to the accounting, his father-in-law was something of a gardening devotee and helped to establish the vines."

"And they survived all this time."

"Under the brambles, yes. I'll do my best to see that yours survive, too."

At last, the vineyard loomed before them, tidy rows of staked vines lining a vast hillside. Tristan gave a low whistle. "It's large."

"Charles never did anything halfway."

"He did his research. They're spaced nicely and on a south-facing slope, both of which are ideal."

"But they're not thriving."

"Let's see why that may be."

As they rode closer, Tristan could see his friend was right: The vines' tendrils were drooping, the young leaves were wilted, and there was no fruit in sight. He swung off his mount and crouched by a particularly pathetic example, digging his fingers into the soil.

"You're getting dirty," Griffin said.

"You never got dirty fighting a war?"

"I wasn't a marquess then."

"Bloody hell, you're turning into your brother."

"That didn't come out right," Griffin protested. "I only meant that I didn't ask you here to do manual labor."

"You want to grow crops, you have to expect to get a little dirty." Tristan scraped away at the roots. "I may be a marquess now, but I was a land manager first—and always will be." He stood, pulling the whole vine up with him.

They both stared at the scrawny thing.

"The roots are stunted," Tristan finally said, stating the obvious.

"Do you expect Charles planted them the wrong time of year?"

"We'll never know. You say these are three years old?" Tristan thought back. "There may have been drought conditions the season these were planted."

"Drought? Here in England?" Griffin gestured to the blue sky, where seemingly ever-present rain clouds were gathering on the horizon.

"If you're unaware of the reality of drought, you clearly weren't trained to farming."

"You can say that again," Griffin muttered dryly.

"Those clouds?" Tristan flung a hand in their direction. "They may dump several inches on the next town yet leave the ground here bone-dry. English weather is nothing if not random and unpredictable. And in any case, drought or not, it seems Charles neglected to see his new vines received enough water."

The look on Griffin's face showed plain disbelief that his brother could have done wrong. "I've never heard of irrigating vineyards."

"Established ones, no. It is commonly held that some water stress is optimal for producing fine wine. Irrigation affects both the size and the quantity of the fruit, but wine grapes shouldn't be allowed to grow as large as table grapes—the sugar concentration is more important than overall yield."

"Well, then . . ."

"That has nothing to do with cultivating young vines. The soil surrounding new roots should be kept damp until they're deep and established. My best guess is Charles neglected to do that here."

"Is it too late to do something to save them?"

Tristan considered. "Perhaps," he decided. "But maybe not. Deep watering may cure the shallow roots even now. The vines are still young—it's worth an attempt." He scanned the landscape, focusing on a glistening ribbon in the distance. "We can pipe water from the River Caine."

Griffin shook his head. "The river is lower than this hill. Even I know that water runs down. Logistically— short of carting it by hand—there is no way to get it up here."

"Have faith, my friend." Tristan grinned. "You've summoned the right fellow."

"Come again?"

"I've just built a hydraulic pump to supply my new gasworks direct from the Thames. A water ram pump. You've heard of them, I presume?"

"Of course. We often talked of mechanical pumps while on campaign."

Already deep in thought, Tristan ignored the good-natured sarcasm. "We'll need a drop," he mused, embracing the challenge. "If there's no waterfall nearby— a few feet is all that is required—we'll have to situate the pump in a pit and pipe the river water down to it."

"And the pump will force the water back up?"

"An amazing distance—thirty feet or more in height. It's quite a brilliant design; wish I'd thought of it myself."

"Will the force be sufficient to propel the water this far overland?"

He gauged the span to the river. Half a mile or so, no more. "That won't be a problem. You'll want to water very heavily, an entire day so the flow penetrates the soil to a goodly depth. Then repeat when the ground begins to dry. A week between sessions," he decided, his brain racing as he formulated the plan. "We'll run a pipeline along the top of the slope with caps every few feet. You—or your people," he amended, watching Griffin's face, "will cap and uncap different sections every day, so by the end of the week the entire vineyard has been deeply watered. Then begin again where you started."

"For how long?"

"I'm not sure. A few months, if you're asking me to

guess. You'll have to keep checking. When the taproots have reached three feet or so, you'll shut off the pump." Pleased with the plan, he nodded to himself. "I'll stay until it's all in place."

"That won't be necessary," Griffin rushed to assure him. "If you explain how to build the pump—"

"I don't believe I can. It looks like a simple enough design, but the parts must be adjusted perfectly. The first pump I built was a colossal headache. I've thought of a better design since then, so I believe this one will be easier, but for someone unfamiliar with the basic concept—"

"How long will it take to set all this up?" Griffin didn't sound happy. "Run the pipeline? Build the pump?"

Tristan hesitated, knowing Griffin's real question was the one left unstated. *How long will you be here torturing my sister?*

Old friends or not, Griffin didn't really want him to stay.

But Tristan wanted to help—this was the sort of challenge that excited him. He wanted Griffin to have the satisfaction of making a success of his brother's failure. And he wanted to prove he was a good enough friend— a strong enough man—to avoid temptation where it wasn't appropriate.

"It depends," he answered slowly. "Have you a foundry nearby to cast the pump's parts from my drawings?"

"Yes."

"A *cooperative* foundry, willing to drop everything at your request to take on this project?"

"I'm the marquess," Griffin said dryly.

"There is that." Tristan had learned he had power as a marquess as well, regardless of his state of disgrace. "Will you hire a goodly sized crew to construct the pipeline?"

"Of course," Griffin snapped.

"A week, then. We can have this in place in a week."

"I suspect it will take longer, but even a week is not insubstantial." Griffin measured him a moment, silent. "You'd take a week out of your life to build a pump and run pipeline that will be used a scant few months? Knowing it may not even achieve the desired results?"

"You want to save your brother's grapevines or not?"

Griffin hesitated only a beat. "I want to save them."

"Then we'll do what needs to be done." Tristan knelt to reseat the vine and pat the soil into place around the roots. "I'll draw up the pump design today, but I'll have to return here tomorrow to take measurements." He climbed back up on his black horse, holding the reins with muddy fingers. "And choose a spot to site the pump."

"Thank you," Griffin said.

Although he hadn't felt this needed—this wanted—in a long time, Tristan gave a casual shrug. "This is what friends are for."

Chapter Nine

"Lady St. Quentin," Alexandra said that afternoon in the drawing room, adding the name to their guest list in her careful, tutored script. "We cannot forget *her*."

"I'd like to forget her." Corinna stood and stretched and, leaving her easel, wandered over to where Alexandra sat at their mother's pretty rosewood writing desk. "She's a busybody."

Seated on one of the blue sofas, Juliana looked up from the menu she was creating. "Do you think we should serve beef or lamb?"

"Both." Corinna peered over Alexandra's shoulder. "Holy Hannah, how did this list get so long? I was unaware we even *knew* so many people."

"How many?" Juliana asked.

Alexandra pulled out a third sheet of vellum. "A hundred and thirty-eight, so far."

Juliana's eyes widened. "Griffin was away for seven years, and he's hardly had time to become reacquainted with anyone. Where did he come up with all these names?"

"Griffin has always been friendly," Corinna said in a tone that made the statement more like a complaint than a compliment. "Consider all the men he's managed to bring around to meet us already. My hand is hurting just thinking about writing all these invitations."

"Think about the new evening dress you're going to make him pay for instead," Juliana suggested.

Corinna grinned. "It's going to be yellow. With embroidery and seed pearls."

"I sent a note to the mantua-maker this morning," Alexandra said. "She should be here in a week."

"Excellent. I can scarcely wait for her to arrive." Corinna plopped onto a salmon velvet chair. "What shall we say on the invitations?"

"There is proper, accepted wording, I am certain." Alexandra pointed her quill at her youngest sister. "You're the only one of us who's finished reading *The Mirror of the Graces*. What does A Lady of Distinction have to say?"

"Nothing. A Lady of Distinction is distinctly opinionless concerning invitations. She talks only about dress and deportment. We are to choose the colors of our new evening apparel by candlelight, you know. For otherwise, she says, 'If in the morning, forgetful of the influence of different lights on these things, you purchase a robe of pale yellow, lilac, or rose color, you will be greatly disappointed when at night it is observed to you that your dress is either dingy, foxy, or black.' "

"Black!" Juliana rolled her eyes. "As though a gown of pale yellow might ever appear black."

"A Lady of Distinction is a twit," Corinna said.

"None of this is helping with the invitations." Alexandra frowned. "Mama always knew what to write."

"She had a book with proper examples of all correspondence," Corinna reminded her. "Do you not remember that slim volume with the dark green cover?"

"Oh, yes!" Juliana exclaimed. "I saw it in the library only last week."

"Will you fetch it, then, please?" Alexandra asked. "We'd best get busy writing if we're to give everyone proper notice."

"Proper," Corinna muttered as Juliana rose and left

the room. She went back to her easel and dabbed a brush in blue paint. "Everything must be proper."

Less than two minutes later, Juliana returned. "I think you'd best fetch it yourself, Alexandra. It is up too high for me to reach."

Alexandra was busy adding yet another name to the list. "Use the ladder."

"The ladder is at the far end of the room." She sat on the sofa and picked up her menu. "And it's dreadfully heavy."

"The ladder is on wheels." Corinna set aside her paintbrush. "Was there ever anyone more lazy? I shall fetch the book. Where in the library is it located?"

"Lower level, at the top of the third bank of shelves on the right. The middle bookcase." Juliana scratched something out on the menu. "But I think Alexandra should go. She's taller."

"Only by an inch."

"I *think*," Juliana repeated meaningfully, "that Alexandra should go."

"Ohhhh," Corinna said. "Is it up that high, then? Alexandra, perhaps you should go."

"We could have written a dozen invitations by now." Alexandra pushed back from the desk. "Third bank of shelves on the right? I shall return directly."

Using a long stride that A Lady of Distinction would surely disapprove of, she hurried through the picture gallery, past the music room and the billiard room. Her sisters, she thought as she entered the two-level library, wasted entirely too much time on petty disagreements.

She strode down the red-and-gold striped carpet, then stopped short. Precisely in front of the third bank of shelves on the right, at a round mosaic table, sat Tris.

She mentally revised her last thought: Her sisters wasted entirely too much time on conniving plots.

An inch taller, indeed.

Pencil in hand, Tris was engrossed and hadn't noticed her. While he erased a line and carefully sketched another, she watched. Even drawing a picture, he looked like a man of action. Lean, wide shouldered, his skin kissed by the sun. Like last night, a lock of hair flopped over his forehead.

Like last night, she wished she could push it back.

It was pointless, she reminded herself—any feeling for him was pointless. But she remembered the exquisite intimacy of his kiss. The wonderful warmth of his body. Her own body melting against that wonderful warmth.

Suddenly he looked up, then bolted to his feet. "Lady Alexandra."

Lady. So they were back on formal terms. It was for the better, she decided. "Sit, please. I didn't mean to bother you. I need only to get a book." She hoped he couldn't divine her earlier thoughts by the heat that had crept into her cheeks.

He didn't sit. "May I help you?"

"It's right behind you." She walked over and slid between him and the shelves. The books were covered by doors of brass mesh in mahogany frames. In order to open them, she had to step back. "Pardon me," she murmured, wishing he would move. Then, when he did, wishing he hadn't.

He was as warm as she remembered.

"It's just here," she said, rising to her toes to reach the top shelf.

"Let me help you." The words were soft by her ear. He reached around her and up, his front grazing her back. His very male scent seemed to surround her. Her breath caught in her throat, and it took everything she had not to lean back against him.

"This green one?" he asked.

"Yes." The single syllable came out as a breathy sigh.

"Here you go," he said, sliding it free.

She twirled around, almost in his arms. Almost.

But if she expected to see her own lust mirrored in his eyes, she was doomed to disappointment. With a polite smile, he handed her the book. Then he returned to his chair and lifted his pencil.

Apparently, while her knees had been threatening to buckle under her, he'd only been getting her a book.

"Thank you," she said from behind him, feeling schoolgirlish and silly.

"You're quite welcome." He erased another line.

She clutched the book to her chest as though it could protect her from unwelcome emotions. "What are you drawing?"

"A water ram pump. I'll be giving these sketches to the foundry so they can cast the pieces. When I've built it, it will pump water from the river to Griffin's vineyard."

Peering over his shoulder, she saw two versions of the metal contraption: a view of the outside, and, below that, a cutaway view showing the inner workings. "That's very clever," she said.

He shrugged. "I've tampered with the design some, but it's not as though I invented it. That accomplishment belongs to a gentleman in France."

"Well, it's still clever of you to be able to draw it— and build it." She waited for a response, but he only shaded a portion of the sketch. "I must get back to my sisters," she said finally. "I'll . . . I'll see you at dinner."

"Of course."

Of course. It was as simple as that. She sidled out from behind him and began walking away.

"Alexandra," he called softly.

No *lady* this time. She stopped and turned to find he'd risen again. "Yes?"

"I want to apologize for last night. I should have explained."

"I understand. And I know you tried. Your failure was as much my fault as yours—"

"Regardless, I had no right to kiss you. I beg you to accept my apology. It will not happen again."

Why did that cause a heaviness in her chest? It was the only prudent choice. But that didn't stop her from wishing things were different. From wishing the rest of society had the faith in him that she did.

"I don't believe the rumors," she told him. "You don't have it in you to commit murder."

"I appreciate your confidence." His gaze remained steady, cool. He was very good at masking his feelings. Either that, or she'd only imagined those feelings last night.

She'd never considered herself a very imaginative sort of person.

He sat again, a silent dismissal. With an internal sigh, she turned to leave—and saw Griffin striding toward her.

He glanced at Tris, grabbed her by the arm, then marched her into the picture gallery, and, for good measure, through the door to the billiard room.

"I don't want to see you alone with him. Ever."

In her current state of thwarted passion, her brother's overprotectiveness was more than vexing. She wrenched her arm free. "I was only getting a book."

"Just keep clear of him, will you? With any luck, we'll complete this project in a week or so, and then he can leave."

"And in the meantime, am I supposed to avoid entire rooms in my own home?"

"If that's what it takes."

"You could trust me a little." In a huff, she leaned against the oak billiard table.

"Stand up straight," Griffin said. "You can throw the table off balance."

She snapped upright, her fragile emotions threatening to snap, too. Following her father's death, her foppish brother Charles had enjoyed lording it over his younger sisters. And now Griffin. "Stop telling me what to do."

"I'm only trying to protect you—one of my many responsibilities, in case you've forgotten. I'd appreciate your cooperation."

"We don't need you to watch over us. After Charles died, it took three months for you to arrive. We did just fine without you then, and we can do without you now."

Matching temper lit his eyes. "You want me gone? How convenient, since I'd just as soon not be here, either." With an angry twist of his wrist, he sent an ivory billiard ball across the green cloth that covered the table's wooden surface. "My friends just defeated Napoleon without me." The ball bounced off a cushion and hit another ball with a *crack*. "Perhaps I should rejoin them."

"As you said, you have responsibilities now. Beyond me, beyond Juliana and Corinna."

"I had responsibilities then, too," he said, referring to his years as an officer. Years when, she supposed, he'd become used to everyone following his orders.

But if he was hoping for an apology, he was hoping in vain. She'd had enough of other people deciding what was right for her. "Sadly, you cannot leave."

"You want me to leave?" He raised his gaze from the table and watched her, waited for her to answer.

"No," she finally said on a sigh. Suddenly, she felt beyond weary. All the fight drained out of her. The truth was, although Griffin might be less than an ideal guardian, she couldn't imagine her life without him. She'd missed him dreadfully the years he was gone. "I don't know what I want," she said.

He sighed, too. "I don't know what I want, either." In a complete change of mood, he stepped forward and chucked her under the chin. "Life hasn't treated us well the past few years, has it?"

"Perhaps not, but I'm tired of feeling sorry for myself." She gave him a shaky smile. "As concerns Lord Hawkridge, you've nothing to fear, I promise you. Your friend has become a proper gentleman overnight."

If part of her regretted that fact, a larger part knew it was for the best.

"I'm glad to hear it." Griffin smiled back, a relieved smile, then took himself from the room.

Alexandra sent another ball across the table with a force that outdid her brother's. It bounced off two cushions and rolled neatly into a pocket.

If only her life would roll into place that perfectly.

Chapter Ten

Two days later, Griffin woke on the wrong side of the bed. At least that was what Tristan surmised, given the man hadn't strung more than three words together during their ride out to the vineyard, where they were going over the final plans prior to setting them in motion.

They walked along the riverbank, leading their horses by the reins. "We'll site the pump here," Tristan said, "belowground with a grating over the opening. Ten feet in depth. That will give us the drop we need to start the water flow through the mechanism." The day before, he'd staked off an area roughly six feet square. "Four straight walls. You'll want to line them with brick to prevent erosion, but that can wait."

Griffin nodded soberly. "I'll instruct my men to start digging the pit immediately. Is that your drawing of the pipeline?"

Tristan handed him the sketch. "It's a fairly straight shot from here to the top of the rise."

"And these dotted lines are where you've divided the vineyard into seven areas for irrigation?"

"Each serviced by a section of the pipe that runs along the ridge."

"Capping and uncapping each section as needed." Frowning, Griffin traced a finger along the path. "The water will run straight down the slope. It should work."

Tristan swung up onto his gelding. "Of course it will work. We planned it perfectly," he quipped, hoping to goad his friend out of his bad temper.

Squinting up at him in the morning sun, Griffin didn't look convinced. He held out the drawing, and Tristan leaned from the saddle to retrieve it. "We'll make it work."

"We?" Griffin asked.

"Think of it as a learning experience." Tristan folded the paper and slipped it into the pocket of his coat. "Race you back," he challenged, taking off before Griffin was mounted.

Long minutes later when their horses tired, they slowed to a walk. Their friendly competition had served to cut the time of their journey. Tristan had hoped the invigorating ride would also serve to boost his friend's brooding mood, but as they continued on in silence, it seemed instead that his low spirits might be contagious.

As the crenelated walls of the castle came into view across the downs, Griffin's fists clenched on the reins. "Impressive, isn't it?" he said in a bitter tone that contradicted his words.

"Magnificent." Tristan slanted him a glance. "But you don't feel like it's yours, do you?"

"No," Griffin said flatly. "It was never meant to be."

"Hmm." Tristan debated whether to sympathize or knock some sense into the man. The latter was tempting. "Is that why you hesitate to learn how to manage it?"

"I'm learning," Griffin protested in an ill-tempered tone. They rode a while longer in silence before he added, "Very well, damn you, I've been hesitating."

The first step was acknowledging the truth, and God knew Tristan had climbed all the steps. Dragged himself up them, one at a time. "You've not been home long. I expect I hesitated, too, when I first inherited Hawkridge."

"Four years, now. Tell me, do you feel like it's yours?"

"Yes." He hadn't felt that way at first, but he'd *made*

Hawkridge his, put his own brains and sweat into its improvement. "Cainewood will feel like yours, too, someday. You'll have a family here—"

"Whoa." Griffin held up a hand. "I need to find husbands for my sisters before I even think about myself."

"Why?"

"Why? A gentleman doesn't put himself first. Besides, I've no interest at present—"

"I meant, why are you set on marrying them off so quickly?"

Griffin shifted in his saddle, staring straight ahead. "At their ages, they're all but on the shelf already, never mind it's through no fault of their own."

Tristan just looked at him until he was forced to turn and meet his gaze.

"Very well. I want my old life back. And while I continue to be responsible for the three of them—"

"You'll never have it," Tristan interrupted.

"Have what?"

"Your old life back. Your sisters have naught to do with that, and the sooner you accept that fact, the happier you'll be. If you would find a special lady—"

Griffin's laugh was so harsh it was almost a bark. "The sort of woman I'd be interested in at present would not go by *lady*. I'm too occupied figuring out how to run this hulk of a place to entertain any thoughts of settling down. I prefer the relationships I had in my military days: quick, passionate, and not expected to last."

"Good luck finding that here in Jolly Olde England," Tristan said with an amused snort. "Unless you're willing to pay for it, that is."

"It could well be worth the blunt," Griffin muttered.

Tristan shrugged. "There's a particular house in Windsor . . ."

"I say!" his friend exclaimed with sudden good humor. "So you *haven't* been a monk these four years past."

No, he hadn't. But then, neither had he and Griffin during their university years. The two of them had always known where to find the nearest brothel.

"You'll have to introduce me," Griffin added.

"As you wish," Tristan agreed, although, he suddenly realized, he hadn't made his way to Windsor in a good twelvemonth. Or maybe longer.

As their horses clip-clopped over the wooden draw-bridge, Griffin shot him a speculative glance, his sour mood apparently vanquished. "I shall look for a special lady for you instead. One who isn't my sister."

"No ladies." Tristan hadn't courted any women at all since scandal had tarnished his name. "I wouldn't ask my worst enemy to share my current life, let alone anyone special."

"Whatever happened to that girl you left behind in Oxford?"

"We were talking about your love life, not mine." When his friend remained closemouthed, Tristan shifted uncomfortably in the saddle. "Doubtless she's married with several brats. She made it clear she had no interest in waiting while I gallivanted around the globe."

How nonchalantly he could say that now. At the time, he'd thought he'd never get over her. He'd sailed for Jamaica with a dull, empty ache where his heart should have been.

"And the woman you wrote of from Jamaica?"

"What is this, an inquisition?" They dismounted, Griffin once more expectantly silent. "She decided against leaving the islands for England," Tristan explained in an offhand manner.

The truth was, she had agreed to marry him, then left him at the altar the day before he sailed.

The women he loved *always* left him.

After a while, he supposed, as a groom took his horse and he and Griffin crossed the lawn toward the door, a fellow grew accustomed to the pain. And if not, it didn't matter—because it wouldn't be happening again.

Hell would freeze over before he gave his heart to another woman.

Chapter Eleven

"What is going on here?" Griffin asked, poking his head into the drawing room.

"We're choosing new evening dresses." Alexandra held up a swatch of fabric. "Would you care to help?"

"In the dark?" Entering, he blinked. "Why in blazes have you closed the draperies?" He strode toward one of the windows.

"No!" Juliana cried. "We must see the fabrics by candlelight."

"Whose bacon-brained idea was that?" Griffin turned to the mantua-maker.

Madame Rodale laid a plump hand on her ample bosom. "Not mine, my lord, I assure you," she said in her fake French accent.

"It was A Lady of Distinction's idea," Corinna informed him.

"A lady of what?"

"A Lady of Distinction. The author of *The Mirror of the Graces.*"

"The book you bought for all of us," Juliana reminded him as she pawed through a box of lace. "To help us catch husbands. A Lady of Distinction says we must choose our dress fabrics by candlelight, because otherwise we might select a pale yellow in daylight that appears black by night."

"A pale yellow look black? Can the woman be serious? I cannot believe I even bought a book written by a woman who is so obviously such a—" Griffin broke off, apparently unable to come up with a word to describe her that was acceptable in mixed company.

"Twit?" Corinna suggested.

"A twit, yes. Perhaps you girls shouldn't read that book, after all."

"Oh, thank heavens," Alexandra breathed.

Juliana nodded. "That twittish Lady of Distinction also says we should never paint our faces at all, and we should wear only modest clothing at all times."

"Does she?" Griffin smiled. "Keep reading, then."

All three sisters groaned.

"What do you think of this yellow?" Corinna held a square of fabric to her cheek.

"Pretty, but bright," Alexandra said. "A Lady of Distinction favors pastels."

" 'Tis called *jonquille*," the mantua-maker put in. "And it is *très* fashionable."

Corinna gave a happy sigh. "I shall have it, then."

"How can you even *see* it?" Griffin complained loudly.

"Griffin?" Tris barged into the drawing room. "We must leave soon, if I'm to—" Locking gazes with Alexandra, he cut off. "Pardon me," he said quickly, turning to leave, much to her relief.

Griffin reached to grab him by the upper arm and pull him back into the room. "Do sit down. You, too, can help my sisters choose their new evening dresses."

"Choose dresses?" Tris echoed dubiously. But he sat, arranging his rangy form on a sofa.

Alexandra would have sighed if she wasn't afraid it would draw too much attention. In the past week, for her own comfort and to mollify her brother, she'd done her best to avoid Tris. It had proved a simple matter, since he was feverishly working to solve Griffin's problem.

Tris had taken to rising at dawn and breakfasting before Alexandra, an early riser herself, even ventured forth from her room. He spent most of his daylight hours in the temporary workshop Griffin had set up for him off the quadrangle between the laundry and the dairy, effectively hidden from where her family lived on the two upper floors. And when he wasn't in the workshop building the pump, he was visiting the foundry that was casting the parts, or out in the fields directing the construction of the pump's housing and pipeline. Alexandra rarely saw him except at dinner.

That made things a little easier, but she was impatient for him to finish and return to Hawkridge. For now, she decided, she would simply ignore him.

At least he was focused on Griffin at the moment, rather than her. "Damn, it's dark in here," he said.

A twinkle in Griffin's eye was apparent even in the dimness. "Did you not know," he drawled, "that dress material is best selected by candlelight, lest something pale yellow in the daytime appear black by night?"

"Black?" Tris crossed his arms. "What sort of addlepated—"

"We can open the curtains now," Juliana interrupted. "We've all chosen our fabrics. Look at mine." While Griffin went to pull back the draperies, she held up a swatch of the palest pink. "It's called blush."

"It's lovely," Tris said. Although Alexandra was ignoring him, she couldn't help but notice he looked amused at the goings-on.

"And Alexandra," Corinna announced with a long pause for dramatic effect, "will be wearing amaranthus."

"Amaranthus?" If anything, Tris appeared even more entertained.

"A bright shade of purple with a pinkish tint." As a painter, Corinna was good at describing colors. "Show him, Alexandra."

Alexandra didn't want to show Tris anything. She wanted to smack her sister, but she suspected A Lady of Distinction would not approve. Instead she reluctantly held forth a piece of the silk, which shimmered in the newly admitted sunlight.

"Hmm," Tris said.

Corinna grinned at her sister while addressing the room in general. "Can you believe it?"

Griffin frowned. "Believe what?"

"That she would wear such a color. She always wears blue."

"Does she?"

"Her room is blue, the ribbons on her bonnets are blue, her shoes are blue—"

"Are they?" Griffin asked, looking perplexed. He stared at Alexandra's blue shoes where they peeked out from beneath her blue skirts. "I hadn't noticed."

"Oh, he's such a man," Juliana said to no one in particular.

Corinna shrugged. "Madame Rodale showed Alexandra a stunning swatch of bishop's blue—"

"I am weary of wearing blue," Alexandra interrupted. "I wish to wear a different color. *Many* different colors," she amended. "A new color every day."

The old Alexandra would have opted for blue, but the old Alexandra would have spent weeks or months languishing after Tris, as well. And she was quite over him.

She just wished he'd go home.

"You all made lovely choices," he said. "But, Griffin, we really must be off."

"Tristan has finished the pump," Griffin explained. "We spent the morning overseeing its installation. A perfect installation, I might add."

"We hope." Tris didn't look quite as confident as her brother. "Now that it's been running a few hours, I'd like to inspect it once more before I leave."

"You're leaving?" The words tumbled out of Alexandra's mouth before she had a chance to think.

"This afternoon, assuming everything continues well."

"Oh," she said. He was leaving. Her wish was coming true.

So why did she feel as though all the air had quite suddenly been sucked right out of her?

Juliana slanted her a glance. "The pump must be very impressive," she said to Tris. "May we all come along and see it?"

His gaze slid to Alexandra and back before he answered. "There is not really that much to see."

"We could bring a picnic!" Corinna gestured outside the bright windows. "It's a beautiful day."

"Yes, please." Juliana turned to Griffin. "We've not gone on a picnic in months. We've not done anything at all as a family in months."

Juliana sounded so sincere, Alexandra wondered for a moment if perhaps she really did want to picnic, as opposed to using the request as a ploy to get her and Tris together for an afternoon.

But both her sisters looked entirely too animated and expectant. It was a ploy.

A ploy their brother was falling for. "Perhaps," he said, looking to Tris.

Tris raked a hand through his hair, messing it up as usual. "I was planning a quick ride out, a quick look, and a quick ride back. I was hoping to get home before dinner."

A picnic would mean a carriage, considering they'd have to bring baskets and blankets and other assorted paraphernalia. None of which brought to mind the word *quick*.

"You could have dinner back here before you leave." Griffin shot his friend a look halfway between pleading and apologetic. "The days are long this time of year, so your ride home later should still be by sunlight." When Tris shrugged, Griffin turned to Alexandra. "What do you think?"

Her poor, misguided brother was just trying to make his sisters happy. Which meant there was no way she could get out of this without looking like a cantankerous crab, even though agreeing would mean hours shut up in a carriage with Tris. At least they wouldn't be alone, she told herself, forcing a smile to curve her lips. "It sounds delightful."

"Mesdemoiselles." Madame Rodale cleared her throat and held up a large scrapbook filled with fashion plates. "You have yet to select your designs."

Griffin strode over and took it from her hands. "They can choose during the drive. You won't mind, will you?" He smiled, turning on the charm. "If you'll but wait a few hours, I'll make it worth your while."

Madame, who was old enough to be his mother, blushed to the roots of her graying hair. "Very well," she murmured, forgetting her fake French accent.

Griffin's charm could be lethal. No wonder he had so many friends.

"It's all settled, then." He turned his smile on the rest of them. "Girls, you have half an hour to wheedle a picnic lunch out of François and change your clothes should your feminine sensibilities require that. What does one wear to a picnic? A carriage dress? A walking dress?"

"A garden dress," Alexandra informed him, forgiving him his masculine ignorance.

When he was nice like this, she wanted to kick herself for telling him he should leave.

Chapter Twelve

In the shade of a large elm atop a rise overlooking the grapevine-covered slope, Tristan leaned back on his elbows, stretching his legs out on the red blanket Griffin's sisters had packed along with the picnic lunch. "That was delicious." He glanced into the empty basket and feigned good-natured surprise. "What, no famous Chase sweets to complete the meal?"

Sitting across from him, Corinna finished her last bite of cheese and licked a finger. "Griffin didn't give us enough time."

"Don't go blaming me," Griffin protested. "As though you, of all people, would volunteer to spend hours in the kitchen."

"My talents do not lie there." She put her dainty nose into the air. "A Lady of Distinction said that whatever it is worthwhile to do, it's worthwhile to do *well*."

"She was talking about dancing," Juliana said with a roll of her eyes. She looked to Tristan. "May we see the pump now, please?"

"Certainly, at least what little there is to see of it." He rose to his feet and stretched, gazing down to where Alexandra had her own dainty nose buried in Madame Rodale's book of fashion plates. She'd barely looked up to eat; in fact, she *hadn't* looked up at all during the long drive out here in the carriage. She'd positioned herself safely between her sisters and kept her eyes on the scrapbook, discussing each engraving in such detail that he'd wanted to scream.

While it was true he'd done his best to avoid finding himself alone with her, that shouldn't mean they must ignore one another while in company. Once, years ago, he'd considered her a friend, one of the few girls he could relate to as a person as well as a female. Perhaps she hadn't seen it that way—she seemed to think he hadn't noticed her when they were young. But he'd always watched her, and listened, and responded—in a completely appropriate, respectful way, of course. And he'd thought of her as a friend.

Though they'd never be together in the way his body craved, he wanted that friend back.

He leaned down and shut the book. "Are you coming along?"

She looked up, startled.

"We're leaving," he elaborated, his face still close to hers.

"Oh." Her pupils grew large and dark in her brandy-brown eyes. Clearly flustered, she glanced around him as if noticing for the first time that everyone else was standing. Her sisters were donning their hats. "Oh, yes."

"Excellent," he said, straightening and offering a hand to help her up.

She hesitated before putting hers into it, and when she did, he thought he felt a tremble run through her. He knew for a fact that something disturbing hit him— right in the gut. Thankfully, the contact was brief.

It was a good thing he was leaving tonight.

The walk from the vineyard to the river was pleasant in the sunshine. Alexandra hurried ahead to join her sisters. From Tristan's vantage point behind them, the three women were a study in contrasts, with tiny Juliana in the middle flanked by her taller siblings. Juliana's straight, dark blond hair was swept up in a flawless style, and Corinna's mahogany waves draped elegantly down her back, while Alexandra's springy dark curls seemed determined to escape their pins.

They all looked graceful, making their way across the downs in high-waisted frocks, Juliana and Corinna in white and Alexandra in pale blue. From the fragments of chatter that drifted back, he surmised they were once again discussing their evening gown selections. Although she'd always dressed and groomed herself beautifully, he'd never known Alexandra to be so obsessed with clothing.

In fact, he was certain she wasn't. A competent woman like Alexandra had more important things to occupy her mind.

"The men are almost finished testing all the stations that will water the different areas," Griffin said, tearing Tristan's attention from the renegade curls on the back of Alexandra's neck. "Everything seems to be working perfectly."

"You're not surprised, are you?"

"That it would work? No. You always did a thorough job of it, even back in school. But I *am* surprised it came together so quickly. I didn't truly believe you when you said you could do it in a week. I owe you my apologies—and my thanks."

"You had a cooperative foundry."

"Regardless, I appreciate your attention to the matter. And your . . . shall we say *lack* of attention to my sister."

Tristan's gaze went to Alexandra's slender form. Her laughter drifted back to him. "I made a promise," he said.

A promise to keep his hands off. But he hadn't promised to abandon their friendship, and he was determined to renew it.

By the banks of the River Caine, all five of them gathered around the square pit that Griffin's men had dug, staring down through the grille at the noisy, gray metal pump. Rhythmic, hissing sounds shimmied up through the air.

"I told you there's not much to see," Tristan said.

"The workings are all inside. I hope you're not too disappointed."

"It's very impressive," Juliana disagreed tactfully. "How does it work?"

He couldn't imagine she really cared, but he explained anyway. "That pipe there runs from the river down to the pump." Everyone stepped back while he opened the hinged grating. "It provides the water, and the downward motion of that water flowing into the pump provides the energy that the pump uses to send it back up." He descended a ladder into the pit and stood there looking up at the rest of them. "This slender valve took me longest to adjust," he said, pointing to a shank that moved up and down with rapid precision. "It pulsates fifty to seventy times per minute—roughly once per second. Each of those pulsations provides half a pint of water."

With each pulsation, a bit of water squirted out. "It's losing water," Corinna said.

"Not much, and that's part of the design, not a leak. The vast majority of the water is sent into the main chamber here." He laid a possessive hand on the vibrating machine. "Inside, there's a flap to keep the water that goes up from coming back down, and air in the top forces it through the outlet and into the pipe that runs uphill to the vineyard."

Tris kept talking, but Alexandra wasn't really listening anymore. The pump looked exactly like the pictures he'd drawn in the library. He'd created this, and it worked to get a job done even when no one was there watching it. Awed, she stared down at him in the pit and thought about how he was so very intelligent. Intelligent and handsome and hardworking. And honorable, too—never mind that he had kissed her.

She wished so very much that he could kiss her again.

It was a good thing he was leaving tonight.

"Your lordship?" When a gravelly voice interrupted her thoughts, she looked up to see a man addressing her brother.

"Yes?" Griffin replied.

"The caps on one of the stations aren't working properly."

Griffin looked inquiringly at Tris.

"Go on," Tris said, climbing back up the ladder. "I won't be here to solve any problems tomorrow."

Griffin nodded. "I'll meet you all back at the blanket."

Alexandra watched her brother head off toward the vineyard, the other man explaining as they went. "Griffin can handle it," she said when their voices had faded away.

"I have no doubt." Tris hopped out of the pit and turned to lower the grille. "Your brother is a very competent man. He led troops all over the Peninsula."

"Sometimes I forget that," Juliana said as they started back at a leisurely pace. "Sometimes he makes me furious."

"Sometimes you make him furious, too, I'd wager." Tris softened that with a smile. "Did you ladies finally choose your dress designs?"

"Oh, yes." Corinna gave a little skip. "Mine will be covered with embroidery and pearls."

Juliana hugged herself. "Mine will be off the shoulder, with puffed sleeves and silk flowers tacked along the hem."

"And yours?" he asked Alexandra.

"Oh, it will be very pretty."

Suddenly, she didn't feel like discussing her dress. A dress Tris would never see.

Other men would see it. Wearing it, she would smile and flirt and dance, and one of the other men would end up her husband. She knew she should be excited about that, but she could hardly think straight with him here walking beside her.

It was a good thing he was leaving tonight.

Juliana met her gaze, her eyes sympathetic. Alexandra looked away. To the north across the hedgerows, fields were planted, but the rolling land beneath their feet was covered only by untamed grass. The air smelled fresh. A kestrel hovered overhead in search of prey.

"Will there be a famous Chase sweet to finish mý last dinner?" Tris asked.

"Perhaps." Corinna looked to be considering.

"Strawberry tarts." Suddenly enthusiastic, Juliana turned to him. "Do you fancy strawberry tarts?"

"Very much so—"

"François rarely keeps strawberries in the larder," Alexandra pointed out.

"No matter," Juliana said cheerfully. "There's a patch of them over there."

Corinna looked to where she indicated. "Wild strawberries!" Perhaps she had little talent for making sweets, but she certainly enjoyed eating them. "And this late in June, they ought to be perfectly ripe." She sighed, looking down at her white garden dress. "A pity we have nothing to put them in." Their skirts would surely stain should they use them to carry fresh fruit.

"We have the empty picnic basket." Juliana grabbed Corinna's hand. "Let us hurry and fetch it."

Disconcerted, Alexandra watched her sisters run ahead. "That's not very ladylike," she muttered to Tris. "A Lady of Distinction would not approve."

"Is that why you're not going with them?"

"No. I'm . . . I cannot pick strawberries. They make me itch."

"Even if you just touch them?"

She nodded. "If I eat them, my tongue swells and my throat starts feeling tight."

And Juliana had known that, of course. Juliana had taken advantage of that to leave her alone with Tris. Juliana, who always knew what was best for everyone—one had only to ask her to be informed of that—had been trying to maneuver the two of them together all week.

Tris touched her arm on the bare skin below where her blue puffed sleeve ended. When she jumped, he dropped his hand. "I am glad you cannot pick strawberries."

Her arm tingling, she stopped walking and turned to him. "You're glad they make me itch?"

"I wanted to talk to you."

The little hairs on her arm were standing on end. "Talk to me about what?"

"Although we cannot ever be together as we might wish—" He cut himself off when she opened her mouth to interrupt, raising two fingers to briefly touch her lips. "There is no sense in denying what we both know."

Now her lips tingled, too. "There is no sense in discussing it, either."

"But that doesn't mean we cannot talk at all, about anything. I always considered you a friend, Alexandra. I don't want to lose that, too."

Tristan watched her fight with herself, watched her swallow hard, watched her eyes go from glassy to clear as she came to a decision. "I'll be your friend," she finally said. "Always."

He took her hand and squeezed it. "I am very, very glad."

He expected her to pull her hand away. Instead she squeezed his back, so hard he wondered if her slim fingers might break. Then she left it in his as they continued walking back to the abandoned picnic site.

They strolled silently for a while, simply holding hands. Such a small, innocent connection. But although he'd shared his whole body with many a willing woman, he was more aware of Alexandra's hand in his than he remembered being aware of any physical sensation, ever. And he knew, as well as he knew his name, that it was the same for her.

"Tris?" she finally said.

"Hmm?"

"Do you believe there is only one perfect person for each of us in this world?"

He smiled to himself. This was the sort of philosophical question she used to bring up when they were younger. "Perhaps some of us have no perfect person."

"Be serious," she said.

He had been, but obviously she didn't want to hear that. "No. My father believed there was only one for him, though. I don't think I ever quite forgave him for that."

"What do you mean?"

"He wasn't always a drinker and a gambler," he said, wondering vaguely why he was telling her this, "although I barely remember him as anything else. But my uncle assured me he'd once been a kinder man, and responsible."

"What happened?"

"When I was seven, my mother left us."

Her eyes widened. "She just left?"

"Yes, she just left. Went to America—"

"With another man?"

He shrugged. "I don't know. I expect there is more to the story, but no one bothered telling a lad of seven." And over the years, he'd never asked. Perhaps he'd feared the truth. And when his father and uncle died, the facts had died along with them. "One day my mother was gone, and Father said she had gone to America. She took my older sister with her. Susan."

"Tell me about her," she said softly.

She must have heard the wistfulness in his voice—an unintended wistfulness that had taken him by surprise. After all these years, he'd figured he was past feeling pain from old memories.

He took comfort from her fingers laced with his. "Susan was my half sister, really—from my mother's previous marriage. The odd thing is, though I missed Mother something fierce, missing Susan hurt even more."

"Sweet heaven." She squeezed his hand. "You must have loved her very much."

"With all my heart. Worshipped her, to tell you the truth," he admitted sheepishly. "She was more a mother to me than my own mother, and I couldn't understand why she would leave me. Now I realize she probably wasn't given a choice."

"Have you ever tried to find her?"

"They both died. Of smallpox. We received a letter a year later. That was when my father became blue deviled and never recovered. It reached the point where he eventually squandered all of his inheritance, endangering the viability of his estate and the people who depended upon it. Who depended upon him."

"You were one of those people."

"I wasn't talking about myself, but yes, I suppose I was." He didn't like to think of himself as a victim—there was nothing to be gained by placing blame; it was better to get on with life. "You see—to get back to your original question—he'd loved my mother, and I collect that until he saw that letter, he hadn't given up hoping she might return. But once he learned of her death, he was so convinced love would never happen for him again that he never bothered trying to find it."

"Did you want another mother?"

The sympathy in her tone all but killed him. "Desperately, when I was young—all the other boys had one, after all. But perhaps it is as well my wish never came true," he added to make her laugh. "With my luck, she would have turned out to be a mean stepmother like Cinderella's." She did laugh, and his heart warmed. "Do *you* believe there is only one perfect person for each of us?"

"No," she said in a way that made it clear she had thought on the subject before. "I've seen many of my family's acquaintances lose spouses and find someone new. Ofttimes they seem happier."

"Maybe the first person wasn't the right one and the second one was."

"Perhaps, in some cases. But I still don't think there's only one in the world for each of us. What would be the odds of finding him or her? God wouldn't make it that difficult for us to be happy."

He knew she was thinking about finding someone besides him. The stab of hurt he felt at that was unexpected and entirely inappropriate. He hoped she'd find her one true love—or two or three should she think that possible. With all the grief she'd suffered in the past few years, she still saw happiness in her future. Bless her for that.

Life had taught him to be more cynical.

As they came in view of the vineyard where her brother knelt by the pipeline in the distance, she slid her fingers from his and gave him a soft, apologetic smile.

He was very glad they were friends again.

But it was a good thing he was leaving tonight.

Griffin made dinner that night into a celebration, toasting Tris and their success with champagne. Conversation flowed along with the bubbly wine. Her tongue loosened by spirits and Tris's offer of friendship, Alexandra was very much a part of it.

But while she watched everyone else eat Juliana's strawberry tarts, a maudlin mood started settling in. When Tris's horse was saddled and waiting, she defied her brother's wishes and walked Tris downstairs.

The stone entrance hall felt cold this evening; the carved beasts that topped the newel posts looked fierce and forbidding. Although it was still light out, the sun had shifted, throwing shadows through the open oak doors.

They both paused on the threshold. "I don't know when next I'll see you," she said.

"I wouldn't count on it being soon. I don't go about in society."

"You could visit again. You and Griffin are still friends."

Tris's gaze flicked to that friend, who stood on the staircase watching them like a hawk, his fingers gripping the gray marble handrail. "I won't be visiting for a while, I expect."

"Not until I'm married," she said to the floor.

In spite of Griffin's vigilance, Tris reached out and lifted her chin, forcing her eyes to his. "I wish you a happy life, Lady Alexandra."

He'd said the same thing years ago, she remembered, captured in his intense gray gaze.

And as then, she had no answer.

Chapter Thirteen

The next month passed in a whirl of preparations for the ball. Though Alexandra had spent the first few days in a melancholy blur, she'd long since recovered from that. She wasn't the sort of woman to mope around. After all, a mere four days from now, the great hall would be filled with the most eligible men in all of England. Surely one of them would sweep her off her feet and make her forget Tris Nesbitt.

In fact, due to her own determination, she'd half-forgotten him already. She was hardly thinking about him at all as she slogged through the household bills and prepared them for sending to Griffin's solicitor.

"Mrs. Webster is overpaying for meat again," she muttered, referring to their housekeeper.

Corinna mixed two colors of paint on her palette. "Griffin can afford it."

"That's not the point." Alexandra pushed back from her mother's rosewood desk and wandered pensively to one of the drawing room's windows. The morning outside was gray and dreary. Her reflection in the glass looked rather dreary, too. "I shall have to have a talk with her and set her straight."

Juliana looked up from her copy of *La Belle Assemblée*. "You should be paying attention to other matters now, Alexandra."

"Everything for the ball is in place."

"I meant personal matters."

She turned from the window. "Like what?"

"You'll want to present yourself—"

"Your skin, yes. A Lady of Distinction says a flawless complexion is key." Adding a dab of white to the hue she was creating, Corinna nodded toward Juliana's magazine. "I read in there that if you hang a sprig of tansy at the head of your bed, a few inches above the pillow, you shall not be bitten by any bugs as you sleep."

"Not her skin. Her skin is beautiful." Juliana shook her head. "Her deportment. She needs to practice enticing men."

"Practice?" Alexandra scoffed. "I've never had trouble enticing men—I simply haven't been afforded the chance." She certainly hadn't had any trouble enticing Tris into that kiss. But since Juliana seemed to draw men like moths to a flame, she couldn't help but be intrigued. "What sort of practice?"

"For example, smiling in the mirror. You should have many smiles, you know, for many different occasions. And if you wish to make men fall at your feet, you need to practice the look."

"The look?" Alexandra and Corinna asked together.

"The look." Juliana set down her magazine and stood facing them. "First you locate the man you wish to entice. Then you command his gaze."

Her sensual, blatant stare had both her sisters swallowing hard. "Then?" Alexandra prompted.

"Look down, bowing your head slightly to display your lashes against your cheeks—lashes you will have darkened, no matter what that twit lady says—and then sweep your eyelids up, gaze at the man full on again, and curve your lips in a slowly emerging smile." She demonstrated.

Both her sisters sighed. "Where did you learn that?" Corinna asked.

"I was born knowing it." She plopped back down on the sofa and picked up the magazine, idly flipping pages.

"But I have no doubt you can master it with enough practice."

Corinna stared hard at Alexandra, shut her lids, opened them again, and grinned.

"Not like that!" Alexandra rolled her eyes. "She's right—you need practice."

Likely they both needed practice. There were no mirrors in the drawing room, so while Corinna gave up and frowned critically at her painting in progress, Alexandra walked back to the window to use her reflection there.

Command his gaze, look down, then sweep your eyelids up—

She blinked at the scene beyond the glass. Astride a black horse, a man was galloping toward the castle. A man she'd have recognized at any distance.

Juliana heard her soft gasp. "What is it?"

"He's here again." As he rode around the side of the castle out of view, Alexandra turned from the window. "Tris has returned."

"Did you bring the pump?"

"Good morning to you, too," Tristan said.

"I'm sorry." Griffin had the good grace to look chagrined. "I'm a mite distracted these days." He ushered Tristan inside, letting Boniface shut the door behind them. "I appreciate your response," he said, then waited a beat before repeating, "So, did you bring the pump?"

Tristan followed his friend up the staircase. "I've not started building it yet."

Griffin glanced openmouthed over his shoulder. "I sent the note to you a full week ago."

"I received it only yesterday, since I wasn't at Hawkridge. I do have other properties." As they approached the first floor, something drew Tristan's gaze over the gray marble handrail.

Alexandra, watching from the picture gallery.

Suddenly he remembered why he hadn't wanted to return.

In the month since he'd last seen her, she had come

to him in his dreams, and there he'd touched her as he hadn't in life. He'd danced with her, their bodies pressed close. He'd released the pins from that mass of curls to comb her hair with his fingers. He'd tasted her skin and breathed in her scent and explored her sweet curves with his hands. Her laughter had lifted his heart, and her smiles had soothed him, and when she'd grown serious, as she was sometimes wont to do, she'd seemed to understand him as no woman ever had.

And here, in the flesh, she was even more appealing than that woman who haunted his dreams.

And every bit as unattainable, he reminded himself fiercely.

Her sisters were with her. "Good morning, ladies," he called from the landing.

"Good morning," they replied in chorus, looking shocked to see him there.

Griffin wasn't allowing time for pleasantries. "Come on up to the study."

Demonstrating a deplorable lack of resolve, Tristan's gaze lingered on Alexandra before he resumed his climb. "Did you not tell them I was expected?"

"I hadn't the foggiest idea when you'd arrive," Griffin hedged. "Particularly when I failed to hear from you. I figured it would take you at least a week to build the pump—"

"Quite a bit longer to do it from home. The foundry here has the molds from my newest design." In the study, Tristan claimed his favorite chair. "Were your sisters unaware you even contacted me?" he pressed.

"The ball is only four days from now," Griffin said in an apparent non sequitur.

But Tristan understood. "Ah," he murmured. Obviously Griffin hoped as well that, in only four days, Alexandra would be betrothed and therefore safe.

Safe from him.

She was safe from him already. He'd spent a month apart from her and had survived just fine. Perhaps he'd dreamed of her sometimes, but his life was tranquil and productive, and he had no intention of upsetting hers by trying to be anything more than a friend.

He accepted the glass of brandy Griffin offered, but didn't drink. "I am not here to seduce your sister."

Griffin busied himself pouring another glass. "No. You're here, once again, to help me solve a problem." He sat and met Tristan's gaze. "Thank you."

"You're welcome." Tristan took a sip. "Why do you need a second pump? Your note was more than vague as to your requirements. Ram water pumps are known to be very reliable, but if the first one malfunctioned, most likely I can repair it. And instruct you—or one of your men—how to do so as well. I should have demonstrated the workings before I assembled it. I will not make that error again."

"The first pump is working fine. Read this." Griffin rose momentarily to swipe a letter off his desktop. "It's from my cousin upriver."

Tristan set down his glass and took the paper. Judging from the careful, fancy script, Griffin's cousin was decidedly female. *Dear Lord Cainewood,* Tristan read silently,

> *I write on behalf of my brother, Lord Greystone, who finds himself in London and unable to communicate. In his absence, his estate manager approached me concerning flooding in our southernmost fields. Upon investigating the matter, I have discovered this is a result of water runoff from your property, apparently due to an irrigation program you have initiated. I must insist that this irrigation cease, as the resulting marshland is detrimental to our crops.*
>
> *My thanks for your immediate attention to this matter.*
>
> *Yours Sincerely,*
> *Lady Rachael Chase*

Tristan remembered Griffin's cousin Rachael; she was a quite distant cousin, if he recalled correctly, her family several generations removed from where their line intersected with Griffin's. But as they shared the same surname and lived close by, Rachael and her younger sisters had been great friends with Griffin's sisters and spent many a day here at Cainewood.

"So formal," he murmured. "Could she not come to you directly?"

"I've not seen her in seven years."

Tristan looked up in surprise. "Have you not paid calls since returning from the Peninsula?"

"The Greystone Chases were in London for the Season; they've returned only recently." Griffin rubbed the back of his neck. "Upon receiving Rachael's letter last week, I rode out to assess the problem. Her conclusion was not in error. The way the land is contoured, all the runoff from my vineyard is creating a stream that drains onto Greystone's estate. Twenty-four hours a day, I am essentially pumping water onto his land. The only solution I could see—short of ceasing the irrigation—is to direct all that water into another pipeline and pump it back to the River Caine."

"It's downhill. You should be able to dig a simple canal to direct it back to the river."

"Unfortunately, from where it's collecting, the only way to avoid running it through Greystone property is to direct it uphill before it can go down. Hence the need for the second pump."

"Sounds as though you've investigated this fairly thoroughly. But before I invest time in building another pump, I'd like to ride over and inspect it myself."

"Naturally. How quickly do you think you can build the pump and have it delivered?"

"Are you suggesting I build it at home? That could easily take a month." Perhaps that was a bit of an exaggeration, but Tristan realized Griffin wanted him gone well before the ball, and building the pump at Hawkridge wasn't the best solution. "The foundry there is deucedly slow compared to yours, plus they would have to start from scratch to cast my newer design. As I said earlier, the foundry here has the correct molds. Assuming they haven't destroyed them, that is—we shall have to check on that."

"How long if they saved them?"

"Depends more on their schedule than mine. But given the correct parts, I can build and adjust the thing in a day, two at the outside. I know this design inside out now. How fast can your men construct another pipeline?"

"Depends on how much I pay them," Griffin said with a pragmatic smirk. "If you think the pump can be ready and installed by Thursday, I will see that the pipeline is finished then as well."

"The ball is Friday?" At Griffin's nod, Tristan stood and started to leave. "Let us go look at the site and have a word with the foundry," he said, opening the study's door.

Three startled faces were on the other side. The sight of one of them—Alexandra's, to be precise—robbed his breath like a punch to the gut.

Not a proper reaction to a friend.

Griffin snorted at his sisters. "You can hear better if you put an empty glass to the door."

"We weren't listening," Corinna protested in entirely too innocent a tone. "We were just . . . on our way to change our dresses."

"Yes," Juliana said. "We're wearing morning dresses, and we need our walking dresses now."

Tristan couldn't help but notice Alexandra wasn't saying anything. With her mouth, at least. Her eyes, focused on him, spoke volumes. Clearly she found his unexpected visit unsettling.

Hell, so did he.

"Where are you planning to walk?" Griffin asked.

"To the village," Corinna said.

"We baked lemon cakes earlier this morning," Juliana added, "planning to make some calls."

"Go on, then." Griffin waved a hand. "As I expect you heard, Tristan and I are likely to be gone for the next few hours."

Tristan watched Alexandra accompany her sisters through the high gallery, her skirts swaying gracefully to match her gait. When she disappeared into the corridor that led to their bedrooms, he released a silent sigh.

Or maybe it hadn't been silent. "What?" Griffin said, looking at him sharply.

"Nothing." He shouldn't have come back here. "What the devil is the difference between a morning dress and a walking dress?"

"Damned if I know." Griffin started down the stairs. "You think I understand anything to do with women?"

Chapter Fourteen

SMALL LEMON CAKES

Take half a pint of milk and heat to boiling, then pour over a like amount of bread crumbs and leave until heat has abated. Melt 8 spoons of butter and to this add grated rind of lemons, a fair measure of sugar and three eggs well beaten. Mix all together and pour into buttered cake-cups and bake until browned.

Medicine for the heart. These cakes will brighten the most melancholy of days.
—Belinda Chase, Marchioness of Cainewood, 1811

Tristan's assessment of the drainage problem had proved in concert with Griffin's, and they were both relieved to find the foundry had saved the molds. If all went to plan, the pump would be installed by Thursday, and Tristan would be well gone before the first guests arrived for Friday evening's ball.

Riding home beneath gray skies, they congratulated each other. For once, everything seemed to be going right.

But no sooner had they passed under the barbican than Cainewood's big double doors opened and Boniface stepped out. He hurried down the steps and toward them across the quadrangle. "You've a caller, my lord. Lady Rachael Chase."

Griffin swung down from his mount. "She must have come to see my sisters. Have they not returned yet?"

"No, my lord, they've not. But she specifically asked to see you. Something about an unanswered letter?" The stern frown didn't sit quite right on the butler's pretty face. "She's been waiting for well over an hour."

As Boniface returned to his post, Griffin swore under his breath. Tristan dismounted and followed him toward the doors. "You must have received Lady Rachael's letter a week ago or more. Did you never reply?"

"I wanted to make certain my solution would work before I explained it."

Tristan had to take the steps two at a time in order to keep up. "So you simply ignored her?"

"Her brother, the owner of the land that is affected, is currently away in Lon—" Griffin stopped short as they stepped inside. "Good afternoon, my lady."

"Lord Cainewood?" Perched on one of the entrance hall's heavy walnut chairs, Lady Rachael rose slowly to her feet, gazing slack-jawed at Griffin, as though he looked quite different from what she'd expected.

Or much better.

Tristan hadn't thought much on it, but he supposed his friend had filled out and gained a few inches in height during the last few years. Not to mention honed some muscles in the military. But then, Lady Rachael didn't look much like Tristan remembered her, either. Although she wasn't his type—he preferred a subtler sort of beauty—he did have eyes in his head, and he could see that she had grown into a stunning example of the fair sex.

She finally closed her mouth, then opened it again. "I trust you received my letter?"

"I did, indeed." Griffin blinked at her, looking rather entranced himself. "Did Boniface not fetch you refreshment?" he asked, neatly sidestepping the topic at hand.

He released an elaborate sigh, as though his servant's lack of hospitality far outweighed his own neglect. "It's so difficult to get good help these days, is it not, Tristan?"

"Mr. Nesbitt," Lady Rachael said graciously while still staring at Griffin. In fact, it looked as though the two had locked gazes permanently. She licked her lips. "It's a pleasure to see you again after all these years."

Amused, Tristan executed a small bow. "The pleasure is mine, my lady."

"Mr. Nesbitt is Lord Hawkridge now," Griffin informed her. "The Marquess of Hawkridge."

"Of course." She finally turned to Tristan, her expression an odd mixture of apology and curiosity. "I'd forgotten about that."

Tristan would just as soon she hadn't remembered, since he was certain it was the scandal she was recalling. He wished she'd go back to staring at Griffin. "It's a long story—" he started.

"My sisters will explain everything, Lady Rachael," Griffin interrupted. "You came to visit them, did you not?"

"I came to see you, as your butler has informed you." Recovering her composure, she lifted her reticule off one of the ornate iron treasure chests. "Shall we discuss this somewhere private?"

Griffin guided her up the staircase, his feet obviously dragging. Tristan had some trouble dredging up sympathy, given his friend had brought this on himself. Besides, he figured there were worse things than having to answer to a gorgeous woman like Lady Rachael.

"I shall arrange for refreshment to be brought to you in the study," he called after them lightly. And with that, he took himself off, leaving his friend to the mercy of his lovely cousin.

There were no servants hovering about, so Tristan made his way toward the side door that led to the household offices and kitchen, hoping to find Boniface, or perhaps the housekeeper or cook. Then, hearing footsteps and feminine voices drifting from the quadrangle, he turned back.

Boniface reappeared from nowhere and opened the door to admit Alexandra, Juliana, and Corinna. "Welcome home, my ladies."

"Good afternoon, Boniface," they chimed in chorus, belying the gray day in cheerful straw bonnets and pale pastel dresses. Walking dresses, Tristan presumed, though for the life of him he couldn't figure what made them such. They were high-waisted and slim-skirted, like all the other dresses he'd seen them wear this summer.

"Lord Hawkridge," Juliana said in surprise. "Have you and Griffin returned already?"

"No, you're seeing a mirage," Corinna quipped.

Juliana laughed. Alexandra did not.

"What have you there?" Tristan asked, indicating the baskets they all carried.

"Lemon cakes," Juliana said. "Or what's left of them."

"We've just come from the village," Corinna elaborated. "We were visiting with the ill and infirm."

"All of the tenants and villagers look forward to our sweets," Juliana added. "Would you care for one?" Her gaze flicked from him to Alexandra and back as she reached into her basket and handed him a cake. "They're reputed to cure melancholy."

Did he look that distressed? "How kind of you, then, to bring some to the ill." He bit into the lemony confection and smiled, wishing Alexandra would say something. "I was just on my way to procure some refreshment for your cousin, Lady Rachael. Perhaps she'd enjoy some of these."

"Rachael is here?" Corinna squealed. "Where is she? Did Claire and Elizabeth come along as well?"

"I don't believe she brought her sisters with her. She's in with Griffin, now—"

"Griffin?" She frowned. "Whatever does she want with him?"

"Oh, it has to do with some flooding on her land. I

think." He laughed, remembering the way they'd interacted. "Has Lady Rachael previously shown an interest in your brother? Or he in her?"

"What sort of interest?" Juliana looked intrigued. "She was little more than a child when he left for Spain."

"She's not a child now."

"Of course she isn't." Juliana handed Alexandra her basket. "Take this, will you? We shall see that refreshments are brought to the drawing room for when Rachael is finished with Griffin."

After a silent moment, she nudged Corinna with her elbow.

"Oh, yes," Corinna said. "Do take mine as well." She shoved her basket at Alexandra and followed Juliana upstairs.

Alexandra shifted the three baskets awkwardly. "Well," she said as her sisters disappeared.

One word, Tristan thought. It was a start. "They do have a habit of leaving the two of us alone together, don't they?" Doing his best to appear nonchalant, he polished off the rest of the cake.

She crossed to one of the iron treasure chests, set down the baskets, and busied herself combining the remaining sweets into one of them. "They mean well," she said, facing away.

Walking closer, he watched her in the large, rectangular looking glass that hung above the chest. "What do you expect they're hoping will happen?"

Her cheeks went pink, but she met his gaze in the silvery surface and answered in her forthright way. "I expect they think you might kiss me again."

"I won't," he said quietly.

"I know," she said and turned to search his eyes.

They were steely and determined as always. Alexandra supposed she should be grateful for that—it meant at least one of them would keep a clear head. Since she'd spotted him riding to their door earlier that morning, she'd suffered a riot of emotions: surprise, happi-

ness, annoyance, and confusion. Confusion reigned
supreme. She'd been looking forward to the ball, to
meeting new—eligible—men. In the past month, she'd
thought she'd succeeded in relegating him to that role
in her life labeled *friend.*

But a single glimpse of him had cured her of *that*
illusion.

Though she knew it was wrong, her lips fairly ached
for the caress of his. Her gaze left his eyes and wandered
down to his mouth, which she remembered as being
softer than she'd expected. A lock of his hair had
flopped over his forehead as usual, and she reached to
sweep it away.

He caught her gloved hand. "That won't work this
time."

"I know," she repeated.

Their hands dropped together. Slowly his moved up
her arm until he was touching bare skin. He grasped her
there. "You don't *want* me to kiss you, do you?"

"Of course not," she said quickly, knowing that was
what he wanted to hear.

"Good," he said. "Because I cannot marry you, Alexandra. I cannot marry anyone."

She couldn't marry him, either—not and live with herself when her sisters would pay the price. But surely
there were ladies available who didn't have families to
consider. She couldn't bear to think of Tris alone all of
his life. "Do you not wish for an heir?"

His fingers gripped her forearm tighter. "There are
other ways a man can leave his mark—perhaps mine
will be made in agriculture or mechanics. Marriage and
children are not my fate."

"Fate." He was standing so close, his very scent
seemed to surround and overwhelm her. "Do you believe in fate?"

"Absolutely. One cannot be happy until one accepts
one's lot in life."

She wondered if she'd ever be happy, then. *He* certainly didn't look happy. "Is it so wrong to hope for more? To work for more?"

"Of course not." Absently, it seemed, he slipped a thumb beneath the edge of her glove and caressed the delicate skin on the inside of her wrist. "But it is wrong to expect more as your due."

She could scarcely think straight with him touching her like that. But she remembered how, after completing university, he'd felt he had no choice but to work for his uncle. And now, it seemed, he felt he had no choice but to accept loneliness as his lot in life.

That fact made a lump rise in her throat.

"I don't believe in fate," she told him. "Or settling. I believe in striving to make things better." She laid her free hand over his on her arm, and he glanced down, looking startled to find he'd been touching her. But he didn't pull away. "Promise me," she said, "as your *friend*, that you'll search for a way to be happy."

"I am—"

"*Promise* me."

He didn't. Instead, following a tense silence, he leaned closer and kissed her on the forehead. "You're too sweet for your own good," he said and walked away.

Chapter Fifteen

Rachael certainly seemed more businesslike than he re-membered, Griffin thought, facing her from behind the safety of his heavy desk. Businesslike and beautiful, standing there with one hand firmly on a cocked hip, her silly little reticule dangling from her other wrist.

Why the devil didn't women wear pockets?

He picked up her letter and stared at it, then back to her. "When I read this, I was picturing you as a twelve-year-old with a plait hanging down your back."

She raised one perfectly arched brow. "I never wore plaits."

He certainly couldn't picture her wearing plaits now. Rachael was half a year younger than Alexandra, which meant she'd been fourteen the last time he laid eyes on her. The transformation from that girl to this woman of almost twenty-two was nothing short of astonishing.

The lavender dress she wore clung to her body, made of some thin fabric that did nothing to disguise her wom-anly curves. Her eyes were large and the color of a cloudless sky—a hue Corinna would describe as cerulean—and beneath that startling blue gaze, her lips looked like she'd just licked them. Her chestnut hair was done up in a ladylike style, but the loose tendrils around her face weren't tightly curled as was fashionable, instead falling in long, soft waves that hinted at tresses he imagined were heavy and luxuriant.

His fingers itched to unpin the mass so he could see if he was right. He had never seen a woman in a day dress manage to look so . . . sultry.

"Did you bother reading that letter?" she asked in a voice much huskier than Griffin remembered.

He swallowed hard. "Of course I read the letter. I invited Lord Hawkridge here as a result. He is assisting me in rectifying the problem."

"In what way?"

"We're diverting the water back to the river by means of pipes and a pump. The new system should be in place by Thursday."

Her eyes narrowed. "Why?"

"Why?" He frowned. "Because I am flooding your brother's land."

"I meant, why did you begin irrigating in the first place? Have we not enough rain on this blessed island?"

"I am attempting to save my brother's vines."

Her forehead crinkled, and even that looked charming. "Vines?"

"Grapevines, to be precise. I'm raising grapes, with an eye to starting a winery. Or perhaps I should say Charles was raising grapes, and as his successor, I am doing my best not to kill them."

"Oh." She sobered. "I was sorry to learn of Charles's passing."

"So was I," he said dryly.

She moistened her lips, watching him speculatively. "You don't fancy being the marquess?"

"I wasn't trained for it. Given the trouble I have sustaining the lives of mere grapes you may pity the unfortunate tenants and villagers who rely on me for their keeping. Sit, please," he added, indicating one of the leather wing chairs.

She did, setting her reticule on the small table beside

it. He sat, too, with some relief, as he had begun wondering if his knees might give out.

He leaned his elbows on the desk and steepled his fingers, watching her over them, his jaw tense. If she dared to lick her lips just one more time, he might be tempted to leap over the desk and kiss away that delicious sheen.

But he couldn't, because she was his cousin. And cousins were offered marriage proposals—not indecent proposals. One didn't kiss one's cousin unless one were prepared to ask for her hand.

Which was completely out of the question. He had no intention of marrying anyone until after all of his sisters were settled.

Years after they were settled.

"I'm sorry about your parents," he said.

"It's been six years."

"That doesn't mean it cannot hurt."

Rachael felt tears spring to her eyes and ruthlessly blinked them back. "I haven't cried in forever," she said. "Damn you for making me start now."

If Griffin was shocked at her language, he didn't show it. He just kept gazing at her—no, she decided, *devouring* her with his eyes. It was infuriating. He was an irresponsible scapegrace, and she wasn't sure whether she wanted to slap him or kiss him.

She couldn't remember ever being so attracted to someone who made her so spitting mad. She couldn't order her thoughts. Her mind kept bouncing back and forth, one second thinking about how unreliable he was and the next second noticing he was as handsome as sin personified.

The reckless, gangly youth she remembered had grown tall, dark, and sleekly muscled. His eyes were a pure leaf green; his jaw was strong and square; his smile was slightly crooked and entirely too engaging.

And he was her *cousin*.

"I'm sorry," he finally said. "I didn't intend to bring up old feelings."

"It is time for me to deal with them," she admitted.
"None of us have, if you want to know the truth. We
lost Mama and Papa so quickly—a carriage accident is
such an unexpected shock. Even the staff seems loath to
believe they are gone. A chambermaid cleans their
rooms every day just the same as if they still lived there.
Nothing of theirs has been touched."

"If keeping part of them with you makes you feel
better—"

"No. It doesn't, not truly. It just keeps us from facing
the truth." She drew a deep breath. "I've decided to
empty their suite before Noah comes home in Septem-
ber. He was so young at the time—only fourteen—that
it never occurred to us to move him into their rooms. It
was too early for him to accept the responsibilities of
an earl."

"You were only fifteen," Griffin pointed out.

"But I felt much older than Noah. It seemed natural
for me to take over for him while he finished growing
up. Now, though, he's twenty, and it's past time for him
to come into his own. The master suite should rightfully
be his. It is time to let go of the illusion. They're only
things, anyway, yes? Not so significant."

She couldn't believe she was asking for his opinion,
his approval. Griffin, of all people.

But something loosened in her chest when he gave
her one of his gentle, lopsided smiles. "Yes, they're only
things. You won't forget your parents, Rachael. You can
keep some of their more special items . . . and regardless,
they'll always live in your heart."

Damn if the tears weren't threatening again. "When
did you get so wise?"

"Oh . . ." He pulled out a very old gold and sapphire
pocket watch that she remembered had belonged to his
father. "About two minutes ago."

He'd always been able to make her laugh.

Damn him.

Chapter Sixteen

"Rachael!" Alexandra and her sisters rushed across the drawing room to welcome their cousin.

"Whatever did you want with Griffin?" Juliana asked after they'd hugged.

"It's not important." Graceful as always, Rachael slid onto a sofa. "He's already solving the problem."

"We've been wondering when you'd return." Alexandra sat beside her. "How was the Season?"

Rachael shrugged. "I'm still unmarried. Not for lack of offers, mind you," she added with a grin.

Sitting next to Juliana on the sofa opposite, Corinna frowned. "Were none of the men suitable?"

"Indeed, there were an earl and a baron among them. Worry not, dear, you will find no shortage of adoring gentlemen when you head for London next year. It's only that none of them seemed right . . . for me."

All four of them released heartfelt sighs.

Juliana poured tea and handed Rachael a cup. "Is Noah getting frustrated?"

"Noah?" Rachael laughed. "If Noah had his way, I'd never marry at all. Who would run his household while he's out playing the rake? Not Claire or Elizabeth, I can assure you!" She turned to Alexandra. "Who will run *your* brother's household when *you* marry?"

"Juliana and Corinna." Alexandra looked to her sisters. "Mama trained us all in the housewifely arts."

Corinna paled; evidently she hadn't considered the ramifications of Alexandra marrying. "But we haven't the aptitude that you—"

"We shall do whatever is necessary," Juliana interrupted. "Besides, we shall not have to concern ourselves if we find Griffin a wife."

"As usual, Juliana knows what is best." Rachael's eyes danced with good humor. "If she wasn't here telling everyone what to do, the entire world would go to hell."

"Rachael." Juliana heaved an ever-suffering sigh. "It's not the thing for a lady to talk like that."

Rachael sipped, looking every inch the lady despite her language. "For all intents and purposes, I've been an earl for the past six years—with all the aggravations and frustrations thereof. I'm entitled to curse should I care to."

Juliana never allowed anyone the last word. "A potential husband may not think so."

"I'd have no respect for a man who couldn't look beyond a spot of unconventional language."

Alexandra hid a smile behind her own teacup. "Griffin wouldn't care about that."

"Pardon me?" Rachael's lovely sky-blue eyes widened. "Whatever compelled you to say such a thing?"

"Tris. Lord Hawkridge. He told us you and Griffin seemed quite taken with each other."

"Well, Tris—Lord Hawkridge—is wrong!" A telltale flush stained Rachael's cheeks. "Why, Griffin might as well be my brother. We grew up together."

Corinna passed her a plate of sweets. "You haven't seen each other for years, though, have you? I'd say you finished growing up apart."

"He's my cousin."

"There is nothing in the marriage laws to prohibit the union of cousins," Juliana said quite reasonably. "Cousins wed one another often."

"I would *never* marry a cousin."

The words were stated with such vehemence, Alexandra's teacup rattled as she set it back on her saucer. "Whyever not?"

"Do you remember my cousin Edmund?"

"The monster?" Corinna asked.

"Do not call him that!" Rachael closed her eyes for a moment, then opened them and sighed. "Edmund was a very sweet child. He just . . . didn't look right."

"He didn't think right, either," Corinna said. "He couldn't even really talk. He only . . ."

"Grunted," Rachael finished for her. "Yes."

Alexandra poured more tea. "Edmund died when we were young."

"Yes. Yes, he did." Rachael moistened her lips. "Perhaps you never knew that he was my aunt's child. My mother took Edmund when her sister died. Aunt Alice's husband didn't want his son."

"How dreadful," Juliana said.

"Yes. Everything concerning Edmund was sad. Aunt Alice lost many children before having him, and the doctors told her that the miscarriages, and poor Edmund's condition, were most likely because her husband was also her cousin."

The sisters were silent a moment. "Her first cousin, I'd wager," Juliana finally said. "Griffin isn't nearly so close a relation."

"That doesn't signify." Rachael bit into a lemon cake and changed the subject. "What does your family cookbook claim these are supposed to do?"

"Cure melancholy," Corinna said. "But to look at Alexandra, they aren't working."

Rachael turned to Alexandra. "Are you melancholy, dear?" She looked relieved to have the attention focused elsewhere. "According to the last letter I received from you in London, you were expecting to soon be engaged. Has Lord Shelton still failed to propose?"

Juliana took a cake for herself. "He'd propose in an

instant if she'd let him within speaking range. But one look at Tristan, and she banished Lord Shelton forever."

"Tristan?" Rachael echoed, looking shocked. "You cannot be seriously interested in *him*."

"Why not?" Alexandra asked cautiously, afraid she knew the answer.

"He's tainted with scandal! Everyone knows he's been accused of murdering his uncle."

"*I* didn't," Alexandra pointed out. "How is it we never discussed this?"

"I don't know." Rachael reached for another cake. "It happened years ago, did it not? It must have been one of those Seasons when I was in town and you were stuck here . . . but that doesn't signify, does it? Whether we discussed the scandal or not, it *did* happen—and in light of that, you cannot consider Lord Hawkridge's suit."

"There is no suit." Alexandra clenched her hands in her lap. "Tris refuses to even entertain the thought of marriage."

"Good for him. He's retained *some* honor, at least."

Alexandra's eyes widened at her cousin's tone. "You cannot think he committed murder? He wasn't convicted."

"Not in the House of Lords. But in the hearts and minds of the people who matter—"

"Rachael! You know Tris. He cannot have done something so heinous."

"I don't know him. Not anymore. It's been years—"

"He hasn't changed," Alexandra insisted. "Not that much."

Rachael's lips curved in a faint smile. "You always have been the most loyal person I know."

"My loyalty is not misplaced. Not in this case, anyway."

Rachael considered, then nodded. "Very well. But that still doesn't make him marriageable."

"My sisters don't seem to agree." Alexandra turned

to Juliana. "You left us alone again. You're trying to push us together, and don't try to deny it."

Juliana didn't. "Is it working?" she asked instead.

"Yes," Alexandra admitted miserably. "But he hasn't kissed me again."

"He *kissed* you?" Rachael breathed. "And you allowed it with no intention of marriage?"

Alexandra measured her cousin for a long moment. "You've had four Seasons. Have you never been kissed?"

"Well . . ." Rachael's cheeks flushed a delicate pink, then deepened when Alexandra looked pointedly at the fourth finger of her left hand. "No, I didn't marry any of them."

"Any?" Corinna burst out. "How many men have you kissed?"

Rachael fisted the hand with the ringless finger. "They were only kisses!"

"Exactly," Alexandra said with not a little satisfaction.

Corinna snatched another lemon cake. "I must be the only unkissed girl in all of England."

"Not the only," Juliana disagreed with a sigh.

Alexandra sighed in sympathy. "You'll both have your Seasons. But only if I *don't* marry Tris. So it is in your best interests to let him finish what he came here to do and leave . . . without being caught in a compromising position with me, thanks to you."

"But what about *your* interests?" Juliana insisted. "You don't care so much for society—you'll be happier married—"

"I won't be happy if you're not. And how many times do I have to tell you that Tris has no intention of marrying me regardless of your plans?" She took a lemon cake, too. "Perhaps at the ball I will dance with someone who will sweep me off my feet."

Rachael smiled. "Waltzing always makes me fall halfway in love."

"Waltzing?" Alexandra repeated, alarmed. "There will be no waltzing. We don't know how to waltz."

"Of course there will be waltzing! There hasn't been a society ball without waltzing since 1812."

"We've had no dance lessons since 1812—people in mourning don't dance." Juliana looked panicked. "There is no time to send for a dancing master—the ball is in only four days. Good gracious, how will Alexandra find a husband if she doesn't know how to waltz?"

"This isn't just about me," Alexandra snapped.

Rachael bit into another lemon cake and shrugged. "One way or another, you will all have to learn how to waltz."

Chapter Seventeen

The gray day had finally delivered on its promise, and rain pattered on the drawing room's windows. "Lord and Lady Charlford will be delighted to attend," Alexandra read off a sheet of heavy cream-colored paper. Seated on one of the blue sofas, she set the acceptance note facedown on the empty space beside her.

At the desk, Juliana flipped through the guest list. "Charlford," she murmured. "Ah, here they are." She made a mark. "Next?"

"Is she gone?" Griffin peeked into the room before entering.

Alexandra looked up. "Who?" she asked innocently. Her sisters snickered.

"Rachael," Tris clarified, walking in. He moved the stack of responses aside so he could sit beside Alexandra. "Griffin would just as soon avoid her."

Griffin grunted as he plopped down on a chair.

"Rachael? You're afraid of little cousin Rachael?" Juliana walked over from the desk to hand her brother the last of the lemon cakes. "Here, this will cure your melancholy."

"I'm not melancholy," Griffin growled before biting into it anyway.

Tris's thigh pressed alongside Alexandra's skirts, and

she could swear she could feel his heat burning through them. Not only that, she could still feel the imprint of his lips on her brow from earlier. Right in the center above her eyes.

This would never do. The euphoria she'd experienced upon sighting him this morning was rapidly turning to despair. If only he hadn't returned! She should be looking forward to the ball, not fighting this impossible attraction.

Rubbing her forehead hard, she rose and wandered over to see Corinna's latest painting. On the unfinished canvas, two lovers lounged, sharing a cozy picnic. Corinna often painted landscapes, but Alexandra couldn't remember her ever including people. She watched her sister create the dappled shade beneath a tree. "That's not one of your usual subjects."

Corinna looked up from her easel. "Do you like it?"

"Very much," Tris said, suddenly standing beside Alexandra.

Corinna glanced at the two of them before focusing on her scowling brother. "Griffin's in love," she teased.

"I am not," he mumbled around a mouthful of lemon cake.

She swirled her brush in gray paint. "Rachael took a fancy to you, too."

He swallowed, half choking. "She did?" They all burst out laughing while Griffin slowly turned red. "I am sure she said nothing of the sort."

Alexandra started inching her way back to the sofa. "Of course she didn't, but we could tell."

"We're girls," Juliana added.

"As though I hadn't noticed with all your dressmaker's bills." Griffin swallowed the last of the sweet. "It doesn't signify in any case. I cannot have an affair with Rachael."

Leaning against the painted stone chimneypiece, Juliana crossed her arms. "Of course you cannot. That would ruin her. You'll have to marry her instead."

"I don't intend to marry anyone at present." He gestured to the pile of letters Alexandra had left on the sofa. "Are those the responses?"

"Yes," she said, grateful to have an excuse to move farther away from Tris.

"How many have accepted our invitation?"

She reclaimed her seat and picked up the acceptance notes, straightening the stack on her lap. "More than a hundred."

"Including Rachael," Corinna added with a mischievous smile.

Alexandra thought her sisters had meddled quite enough. "Oh, do leave him alone. Rachael made it clear she would never marry him, anyway."

Though Griffin looked curious, he remained stubbornly mute. The rain sounded louder as they all waited.

"What did she say?" Tris finally asked for him.

"She will never marry a cousin."

"Just that?" Griffin burst out, apparently unable to help himself. "Just she will never marry a cousin?"

Juliana took the chair beside him. "Do you remember her cousin Edmund?"

Griffin shook his head.

"The monster," Corinna reminded him.

"Don't call him that!" Alexandra burst out at the same time Griffin said, "Oh, yes," wincing at the memory. He looked to her. "We all called him the monster."

"Well, he wasn't one. He was a sad little boy. And Rachael will get very upset if you call him that in front of her."

Tris sat once more by Alexandra. "Tell me about him."

Heat seemed to be radiating off him again. "Edmund looked very odd," she said, scooting away a little bit.

"Ugly," Corinna elaborated. "Malformed."

"I was trying to be nice, but yes. And he couldn't talk. He only grunted." Alexandra rubbed her forehead. "He died very young."

"His mother and father were cousins," Juliana said.

"The doctors suggested perhaps that was to blame for Edmund's condition. And Rachael said that is why she will never marry a cousin."

Griffin nodded thoughtfully. "When we were young, Edmund scared me out of my seven senses. I can understand why Rachael would be frightened of giving birth to such a mon—such a child." He released a tense breath, looking relieved. "Obviously, marrying her is out of the question. I don't know that her fears are founded, but given her feelings, that hardly makes a difference."

"There are others who believe close marriages aren't wise," Tris added in support. "I concur with the theory that interbreeding produces weak animals."

Corinna snickered. "Griffin and Rachael are not animals!"

"But they are . . . in the strictest definition."

"Look at our own Mad King George," Griffin pointed out. "A product, you must admit, of copious interbreeding."

"What a picture," Corinna said. "You and Rachael interbreeding 'copiously'—"

"Do shut up," Griffin interrupted in a tone that was dangerously polite. "Tell me what you've planned for the ball."

Alexandra rubbed her forehead again. "The invitations went out last month, requesting guests arrive at eight. We have procured a band of music from Chichester, and we'll place them in a corner of the great hall—"

"Not the minstrel's gallery?" Griffin broke in.

"No," Juliana said. "That is too far removed from the dancers. We want the musicians to take requests and interact with the guests. We shall have dancing until one o'clock, when a handsome supper shall be served. After supper, the dancing shall resume until dawn, and, for those who stay the night, we shall serve breakfast between eleven and twelve."

"And how many of our hundred-plus acceptances are from men?"

"Most of them!" Corinna cried. "There shall be a much greater number of unmarried men than unmarried ladies."

"Excellent." Griffin looked pleased.

Tris reached for some bread and cheese, leaning against Alexandra in the process. "Your ball sounds like quite an ambitious undertaking."

Juliana turned to him with a smile. "We've yet to receive *your* response, Lord Hawkridge."

"I don't attend balls," he said quietly, sitting back and brushing Alexandra again.

"Tristan will be leaving before the ball." Griffin stretched his long legs and crossed them at the ankles. "Everything is all set for Friday night, then?"

"No." Alexandra rose abruptly and went to the desk, bringing the response notes with her as a pretense. She sat and tucked them away in a drawer. "Rachael alerted us to a problem. We don't know how to waltz."

"Then we won't waltz," Griffin said easily.

"We can*not* not waltz," Juliana said. "Everyone who is anyone waltzes. It's the thing."

"*The thing* is, we don't know how. One of you shall simply have to explain to the musicians—"

"I know how to waltz," Tris interrupted. He stood and walked over to the desk. "I can teach you all," he offered, absently rearranging items on the surface.

"Wonderful!" Juliana clapped her hands. "Tonight?"

"Griffin and I must finish planning the pipeline tonight—we have men arriving first thing in the morning for instructions. We can dance tomorrow, while I'm waiting for the parts to arrive from the foundry."

"What will we do for music?" Corinna asked. "If we're all dancing at once—"

"We can hum," Juliana said.

"We cannot all be dancing at once," Alexandra pointed out, moving the inkwell back to where she liked it. "Tris is the only man."

"I take offense to that," Griffin said in a tone laced with pretended outrage.

"You don't know the dance."

Tris lifted a quill. "He can dance while he learns. But we'll need a third man." Looking contemplative, he stroked his chin with the end of the feather. "I know. Boniface."

"Boniface?" Juliana scoffed. "Butlers don't dance."

Tris raised a brow. "Butlers do as they're told." He reached with the quill to tap Griffin on the nose. "Go inform him. You're the lord around here."

Griffin batted the feather away and stood. "I'm doing this only because I want to see Boniface's expression when I tell him," he claimed in a transparent attempt to retain his dignity.

"I want to see his face, too," Juliana said and quickly followed him. "Corinna?"

"Wouldn't want to miss this." Corinna dropped her palette and ran after them both.

A Lady of Distinction would find her sisters quite vulgar, Alexandra thought. Releasing a long sigh, she rubbed her forehead.

"Have you the headache?" Tris asked, looking solicitous.

"No."

"But you keep—"

"No." She wasn't going to tell him she felt phantom lips caressing her brow.

He shrugged and smiled. "They left us alone again."

"I was just leaving." She rose and started toward the door, then, sensing him on her heels, whirled to face him. "Would you please stop following me around?"

"I've not been—"

"Yes, you have. All afternoon, you've shadowed my every step."

"Have I?" He looked puzzled, as though he truly hadn't noticed.

"Yes. And you keep touching my things." *Not to mention touching me*, she added mentally, plucking the feather from his fingers.

Rain pattered while he stared at his empty hand as

though he hadn't noticed he'd been holding the quill, either. Taking it with her, Alexandra left him there and hurried off to the solitude of her room.

Men could be so oblivious.

Chapter Eighteen

CHOCOLATED SPONGE CAKES

Take a measure of sugar and a like amount of butter and mix together well. To this add two beaten eggs and then flour in the same amount as the butter and sugar. Put together with a little milk to make soft and pour into your pan. Put in your oven for half an hour until well risen, then cut into little squares, cover with chocolate icing, and decorate with white icing strands to make them look like little presents on a plate.

Mere acquaintances have been known to call on me hoping to find these offered . . . They look like tiny gifts and are reputed to be irresistible!
—Katherine Chase, Countess of Greystone, 1769

Boniface's pretty face was even prettier with red cheeks.

"Take her hand, Boniface," Tris said patiently, demonstrating with Corinna. "You can do it."

Even with their hands gloved, the butler held Alexandra's fingers so hesitantly she had to cling to his to hold on.

"Put your other hand around her back."

Boniface complied, but Alexandra could barely feel his fingers grazing her spine.

"Music, please."

All three sisters started humming.

"The basic figure is a full turn in two measures using three steps per measure. Like this." Tris swept Corinna into the dance, the two of them turning so fast she was forced to rise to her toes. She stopped humming. Her laughter echoed through the cavernous great hall.

Alexandra hummed through gritted teeth.

Griffin and Juliana took a few tentative steps, then seemed to grasp the idea. "Oh, this is fun!" Juliana cried, leaving Alexandra humming alone.

She changed to la-la-la's. Boniface still stood there, limply attached to her, his blue eyes wide with apprehension. Unlike most families, the Chases did not ban their servants from marrying, and Alexandra had sometimes wondered why he chose to remain a bachelor.

Now she knew. By all appearances, he was terrified of women.

"Shall we dance?" she prompted, abandoning the music. It was still raining—it had rained all night—and the drops sounded louder in the sudden silence. "Hum!" she commanded her sisters, turning back to Boniface when they took over. "Well?" she asked.

He nodded mutely, but remained riveted in place.

Tris frowned as he twirled past. "Go on, man. Give it a try."

"It's delightful!" Corinna called encouragingly.

Seeing her sister in Tris's arms, a stab of jealousy caught Alexandra by surprise. Boniface took a few jerky steps, and she lurched with him, trying her best to stay attached. She hardly noticed the three times he trod on her feet, so busy was she watching Tris guide her sister in whirling circles around the planked wood floor. He danced with admirable grace, looking handsome and debonair and absolutely delicious.

She could pretend that she didn't want him following her or touching her or talking to her. But that didn't make it true.

She wanted him as much as ever.

"Enough," he finally said, saving Alexandra's toes.

They all stopped humming. "Change partners. No, wait—allow me to fetch another sweet first." He walked over to where Alexandra had set up a few refreshments on a side table, taking his sixth bite-sized chocolate-covered cake. "These are truly excellent."

"So you've assured me," she said with a little smile.

He snatched another one and ate it quickly before returning. "Now we switch partners." To Alexandra's disappointment, he went to Juliana. "Griffin, you take Alexandra. Boniface, I think you'll find Corinna an accomplished waltzer already."

Corinna beamed. Boniface's face turned even redder, if that were possible.

Alexandra and her sisters resumed providing the music, and everyone started dancing. Griffin held her a bit awkwardly, but at least his hands were firmer than the butler's. Tris shouted occasional words of encouragement and correction. He and Juliana glided by, making the dance look effortless—and sparking envy that seemed to spread from Alexandra's heart clear out to her fingers and toes.

She wondered if she'd actually turned green.

"Stop watching him," Griffin muttered.

She focused up at the hammerbeam ceiling. "La-la-la."

His fingers gripped hers tighter. "You think I don't notice the way you look at him?"

"La-la-la."

"Three days from now, this room will be full of eligible men, all vying for your hand."

"La-la-la."

"I hope you'll fall in love with one of them."

The great hall looked plain and empty today, but on Friday evening it would be crammed full of people, blazing with torchlight, and twinkling with the jewels adorning their guests. Guests who had been invited expressly to provide her with the chance to meet someone special.

And her brother wanted her to find love. He wasn't bent on marrying her off to the first man who offered.

She stopped singing. "I hope so, too."

"I'm glad to hear it." Griffin smiled . . . until her gaze wandered again to Tris. "Pay attention to your dancing, will you?"

"I think I'm improving." Reluctantly, she looked back to her brother. "You're a great deal better than Boniface."

"That's not saying much," he muttered as the butler stumbled by with Corinna.

"Switch!" Tris called, heading toward the cakes. While everyone else shuffled partners, he ate two more.

Then finally, just when Alexandra felt like she'd been waiting forever, he slipped an arm around her waist and took her hand. As he locked her body into the proper position opposite his, he locked his eyes on hers, too.

Pure lust rippled through her. And through him, too—she'd swear it. He couldn't look at her like that and not feel as she did, not sense the current that ran between them.

And then he began to dance. He moved so smoothly, she didn't even have to think about what her feet did. All by themselves, they seemed to know the steps. She forgot to hum.

His smile seemed as intimate as a kiss—that second kiss she was craving but knew she would never get. "Now you can follow me around," he said playfully, "instead of me following you."

"I'm sorry about yesterday. I was in an odd mood."

"I understand."

The fact that she believed he *did* understand didn't make her feel any better.

His gray eyes watched her so intently, she feared she might lose herself in their depths. She couldn't have torn her own gaze away if she'd wanted to. She fit perfectly in his arms, the two of them moving in tandem as though they were born to share a dance floor. Where his hand rested on her back, heat seemed to penetrate his glove and her dress, warming her all over.

The song came to an end. Corinna and Juliana stopped humming. The incessant rain pounded on the hammerbeam roof. Tris kept dancing, his gaze still fastened on Alexandra.

She felt rather than saw Griffin's glare. "Switch!" he called, shoving himself between them. He handed Tris a sweet. "Time for another chocolate cake, is it not?"

"Thank you," Tris said stiffly. He stepped back, allowing Boniface to take his place.

For the next minute or two, Alexandra danced in a daze. Boniface had improved slightly. He actually held her hand, and he only trod on her toes once.

"Switch!" Tris called. Alexandra noticed Juliana sweetly hand him a cake as she joined him.

Sometimes her sister grated on her nerves.

"Why are you frowning?" Griffin asked, holding her a little too tightly. "You're supposed to pay attention to your partner."

"Thank you for the advice. You could write a book and call yourself A Gentleman of Distinction."

"Stop watching him," he growled low.

"I'm studying his technique. He's good, is he not?"

"How would you know?" He swung her to face away. "You've never seen anyone waltz before in your life."

"Switch!" Tris called. Not to be outdone by Juliana, Alexandra rushed to grab one of the little cakes before meeting him.

Her sisters laughed, but the smile Tris gave her made her knees turn to jelly. Yet when his arm came around her, his sure guidance kept her twirling in perfect rhythm. She felt giddy, light-headed. As their gazes held, she wondered whether to attribute that to the motion or to him.

Him. Definitely him.

Wishing he'd never let go, she searched for a neutral topic of conversation. "If you never go out in society, when did you learn how to waltz?"

"Directly after my uncle died, when I first inherited the marquessate."

Before the scandal broke out, then. "Did a dancing master teach you?"

"No." When she just looked at him, he added, "A woman taught me."

If she hadn't turned green before, she surely did now. "A woman? Who?"

It was possibly the rudest question she'd ever asked.

"It doesn't signify," he said, somehow managing to sound both evasive and blithe. "Just someone who hoped to dance with me at many balls."

He spoke in past tense, Alexandra consoled herself. Quite obviously, that woman's hopes had ultimately been dashed.

But she hated her, regardless.

"Switch!" Griffin yelled, sounding so annoyed she was glad her next partner was Boniface instead of him.

She gave the butler a big smile. "You're surely improving, Boniface."

"Thank you, my lady." He stumbled. "Pardon me."

"No, no, you're doing fine." Since he didn't seem to be leading her, she led him instead. "Just think, you'll be able to waltz at the next servants' ball."

"I think not, my lady. I don't believe waltzing is my forte."

"Oh, bosh," she said, although she agreed. "You're doing just fine."

"Switch!" Tris called.

Griffin started twirling her with a little more gusto than necessary. "What were you two talking about so intently?"

"Boniface fears that waltzing is not his forte."

"Not Boniface. You and Tristan."

"Goodness, Griffin. That was a good two minutes ago. I cannot remember the conversation, but I'm certain it wasn't anything significant."

"He was holding you too close."

"No, he wasn't. You're not holding me close enough. There's a reason some people think the waltz is a scandalous dance, I will have you know."

"Switch!" Tris called. While Alexandra headed to

fetch him a chocolate cake, he added, "You're all doing splendidly."

"Good," Griffin said. "Because we're all finished."

Alexandra turned to protest, her gaze swinging past her brother and over to Tris. As she met his eyes, she felt that connection slam into her once again.

Her knees started shaking.

Sweet heaven, Griffin was right. Tris *had* been holding her too close. And she'd been cooperating—no, encouraging it—not to mention flirting and acting jealous.

That was all wrong, so wrong. Tris was wrong for her, wrong for her family, wrong for her sisters.

She took the plate of remaining cakes, holding it before her like a shield. "I'll go put these in the dining room," she said, keeping her tone as casual as possible. When Tris gave the sweets a longing glance, she released a tense laugh. "Don't worry; we'll save them for you. They'll go well with your port after dinner."

She didn't breathe until she'd escaped, leaving the sweets on one of the dining room's side tables and her heart in the great hall.

Chapter Nineteen

With only a day and a half left before the ball—and less than that before Tris departed—Alexandra was finding it hard to sleep. Still lying awake in her bed well after midnight, she sighed and lit a candle, leaned back against her pillows, and slid a copy of *Mansfield Park* off her night table.

Then sat with it unopened on her lap.

It had been almost two days since the dance lesson, but unless one could count fleeting glances, she hadn't seen Tris in all that time. He'd ordered his meals brought to the workshop, where he was building the second pump. But his rush to finish didn't really explain his avoidance.

Nor did it explain why, the few times she'd caught sight of him, she'd walked the other way.

It seemed silly and childish—and *wrong* somehow—and each time it happened, she swore to herself it would be the last. But after all, it took two to play the game. She suspected that, like she, he'd been surprised by the strong connection they'd felt while waltzing. Surprised and dismayed. For both their sakes, nothing like that must ever happen again.

If only things were different. According to Griffin, although the incessant rain had delayed completion of the new pipeline, the pump was ready, and Tris would be leaving after they installed it tomorrow. A full day before the ball, just as planned. Griffin was jubilant, but her feelings on the matter ran to melancholy mixed with relief.

Well, she told herself sternly, staring into space was not going to change anything. With another sigh, she opened her book. But she hadn't read two paragraphs when her attention was claimed by the prolonged creak of a slowly opening door.

Apparently she wasn't the only one finding sleep hard to come by this night.

She heard furtive footsteps, followed by a soft knock and murmured conversation. Her sisters, she was sure of it. Puzzled, she waited for them to fetch her, too, but instead their voices receded down the corridor, leaving her feeling very much alone.

In the next quarter hour, she read the same page of *Mansfield Park* countless times while wondering what Juliana and Corinna were up to and why they hadn't invited her to their middle-of-the-night rendezvous. Now hurt warred with all her other emotions. Only pride kept her from seeking them out.

Until she heard movement in the dining room, which was directly below her chamber. A thud, as though perhaps someone had stumbled. And other muffled noises.

Curiosity overcame pride.

Without thinking too much, she set aside her book and climbed from her blue-draped bed. She tied a wrapper over her nightgown and, taking the candle, tiptoed from her room past her sisters' open doors and downstairs.

Walking through the picture gallery toward the dining room, she considered what she should say when she found Juliana and Corinna. Should she act wounded or surprised? Disapproving or conspiratorial? Would she join them or suggest they return to their beds?

She'd play it by ear, she decided, depending upon

their attitudes. Hopefully, they would all have a good laugh. That could go a long way toward releasing some of her tension.

Anticipating a little sisterly mischief, she rounded the corner into the dining room.

And stopped short, bobbling the candle in her hand.

Her sisters weren't there. Instead, Tris stood with his back to her, barefoot, wearing a long dressing gown of rich burgundy brocade belted loosely around his waist.

Though he was more than decently covered, the sight of him in such intimate clothing made her mouth go unnaturally dry.

Standing by a gothic mahogany side table, he was devouring what remained of the little chocolate cakes she'd left there yesterday morning. The embroidered cloth she'd laid over them sat crumpled on the floor.

He had yet to notice her. Recovering her composure, she laughed softly and walked closer, determined this time not to flee in the opposite direction. "Sneaking sweets, are you?"

The last cake in his hand, he turned to her. "Alexandra."

Placing the candle on the side table, she knelt to retrieve the cloth. "We missed you at the last few meals. But you could have asked if you wanted more." She straightened, setting the cloth on the table, too. "I'd have sent them to you in the workshop."

He tilted his head, giving her a look so calculatedly innocent—his smile vague, his eyes deliberately blank—that she laughed again. "I'm going to tell everyone you're a sweet thief."

The cake fell from his fingers and landed with a little *plop* on the carpet. "Alexandra," he repeated and reached for her, dragging her into his arms.

Though stunned, she went willingly. Her heart seemed to roll over in her chest as his mouth came down on hers. His lips were soft, but also demanding, insistent. His tongue sought hers in a gentle dance of desire, and a shiver of pure want rippled through her.

Although she hadn't thought it possible, this kiss was even more thrilling and intimate than their first one. It wasn't new to her, so she didn't hesitate this time. Instead she allowed herself to sink into the experience, responding to his desperate tenderness with breath-stealing explorations of her own. His mouth felt like hot, wet silk. He tasted of sugar and chocolate and Tris, a sweeter combination than she'd ever imagined.

One of his hands cradled the back of her head and the other splayed flat against her back, pressing her against his hard body. She wrapped her arms around him, scandalized to discover he wore nothing beneath the dressing gown—nothing besides skin so warm it radiated heat through the fine fabric. She skimmed her hands over his back, feeling muscles earned by the hard work of a man who was much more than an idle aristocrat.

Much too much for her.

Reluctantly, she pulled away. "We cannot," she whispered.

The look he gave her was so odd and intense, it seemed to go right through her.

"I—I need to go back to my room," she stammered. When he didn't reply, she added, "I'm sorry," even though she wasn't sure what she was apologizing for.

He nodded, his lips curving in a sad almost-smile.

"We should both go back to our rooms," she said more firmly. "Good night."

"'Night," he echoed and turned to exit the far end of the room.

Almost against her will, she followed him to the doorway and watched him slowly traverse the long length of the torchlit great hall, standing there until he disappeared into the dark corridor that led to the guest chambers.

He didn't look back.

She released a long, shuddering breath before retrieving her candle and starting upstairs. All the way down the picture gallery, the little flickering light reflected off the canvases on the walls—all her solemn, disapproving ancestors. She shouldn't have allowed Tris to kiss her again.

But now that he had, all she could think was that she wanted more.

She didn't remember actually going upstairs, didn't remember walking through the high gallery or down the corridor past her sisters' rooms. She was settled beneath her covers before she realized their doors had been closed and they must be safely back behind them.

So much for some sisterly mirth to release her tension and allow her to relax. She blew out the candle and listened to the rain, wondering if she'd ever sleep well again.

"There's our thief!" Alexandra proclaimed loudly when Tristan arrived late for breakfast the next morning.

Spreading marmalade on toast, Juliana tittered. "What can you mean?"

"Do you see the plate of chocolate cakes that is *not* on that sideboard? Tris sneaked in here and finished them in the middle of the night."

Though Tristan was weary and distracted—thinking about how to fix the pump he'd discovered damaged this morning—he vaguely wondered why Alexandra was suddenly so friendly and cheerful when they hadn't so much as talked in a day and a half. He dropped onto the chair a footman pulled out. "I did what?"

"Don't try to act the innocent," she accused gaily. "I caught you red-handed. Or perhaps I should say brown-crumbed."

"You did?" He raised a hand to his mouth and absently wiped away nonexistent crumbs. "Very well, I confess. I cannot resist your sweets."

Her sisters both laughed. Griffin frowned. And Tristan racked his brain.

Despite his "confession," he had no memory of leaving his room in the middle of the night. While plastering a smile on his face, he groaned inwardly, more distressed by this news than he'd been by the broken pump.

Apparently, he was sleepwalking again.

All of his life, Tristan had been an occasional sleepwalker. For years, he'd suffered through mornings where people informed him of his own doings the night before—often comical doings, none of which he ever remembered. After some of these episodes, his schoolmates—Griffin included—had teased him mercilessly.

As he'd grown, the episodes had become fewer and farther between—eventually far enough between that he was able to discern a pattern. He was most likely to sleepwalk when under pressure of some sort. As an adolescent and even more so as an adult, the infrequent occurrences seemed to be brought on by emotional stress.

After several years of peaceful nights, he'd decided he must have outgrown the odd habit. But now it was back. Since he wasn't personally affected by Griffin's irrigation problems and had no great concerns of his own, that could only mean one thing . . . he was more attracted to Alexandra—and frustrated by his inability to do anything about it—than he'd allowed himself to believe.

He really needed to install this pump and go home. For good. Social isolation had its drawbacks, but it had afforded him a peace he could only hope to reclaim.

"You rose late," Griffin commented.

"To the contrary, I've been awake for hours." Tristan held out his cup for coffee. "I've been in the workshop. We won't be installing the pump today."

"Why not? It operated perfectly during the test last night—"

"Well, someone—or something—bent the shank. The valve no longer works. I don't expect you have any wild animals about the premises?"

"Nothing capable of—"

"Juliana and I are finished," Corinna interrupted.

"May we be excused? Madame Rodale has already arrived for our final fittings."

Obviously distracted, Griffin waved a hand. "Go." When Alexandra didn't follow, he turned to her. "Are you not going with them?"

"I'll join them in a moment," she said quietly and looked to Tristan. "Are you feeling quite well this morning?"

He noticed she was wearing his cameo again and wondered about that. "As well as I expect one can when one's work has been destroyed." Not feeling hungry, he put down his fork. "The piece will have to be recast, and the entire pump taken apart to reinstall it. This will set us back a day, if not more. I've thought of going home and returning, but . . ." He trailed off, not wanting to sound selfish.

"That would cost you another two days of your life," Griffin finished for him. "Besides, I promised Rachael the job would be finished."

"Then you shall be here for the ball," Alexandra said, looking dazed.

"I may still be here at Cainewood, but I won't be attending." Tristan hadn't attended a ball in four years, and he didn't intend to start now. He rose and turned to Griffin. "You might think about placing a guard at the workshop when I'm not there—being a lumber room, it has no proper door. However this came about, we'll want to make certain it doesn't happen again."

In a dark mood, he headed off to the foundry.

Chapter Twenty

In contrast to Tristan's mood, the atmosphere in the drawing room was jubilant. The rain had finally stopped, and summer sunshine streamed through the windows; if the weather held but a day, they'd have a beautiful evening for the ball. Madame Rodale and her two assistants swarmed about, making last-minute tucks here and tiny adjustments there. While Alexandra slipped into her new dress, Juliana and Corinna chattered excitedly, admiring each other's choices.

"You look beautiful." Corinna tweaked one of Juliana's short, puffed sleeves, which were decorated with knots of pale pink ribbon. "That blush color is so becoming on you."

"A Lady of Distinction would approve." Juliana grinned. "Now, as for your bright *jonquille* . . ."

"I adore it." As Corinna twirled, her skirts belled out, pearls shimmering all over the sheer top layer. Entwined with strings of yet more pearls, a drapery of lace went all around the bottom. "Doesn't Alexandra look lovely, too?"

Trying to smile, Alexandra settled her skirts into place. The dress was certainly not blue; shimmering in the morning light, the pinkish-purple amaranthus hue looked almost shocking. The hem was embellished with white velvet roses and a wide rouleau of amaranthus.

Below that, a row of dangling white tassels alternated with sparkling white beads, nearly skimming the floor.

She'd never felt so pretty. But she could no longer hold her tongue.

"You two did it, didn't you? I heard you leave your rooms last night, so don't try to deny it."

"Deny what?" All innocence, Corinna adjusted her tiny, tight yellow bodice.

"That you ruined Tris's new pump." Alexandra didn't wait for confirmation. "And all for naught, as it turned out. He is determined to avoid the ball, and nothing you do will convince him otherwise. You ought to be ashamed of yourselves."

Juliana didn't try to play coy, but she didn't look ashamed, either. "We did it for you. We thought if Tristan attended—"

"Our other guests will not welcome him. Stop dreaming, will you? I'm not going to marry him, and nothing you do will change that." Nothing Tris could do would change that, either. Not even middle-of-the-night kisses that made her melt. "Now, Griffin is paying for this ball for the express purpose of finding me a husband. I'm planning to do my best to have a proper attitude and make the most of it."

The sound of applause came from the doorway. "I missed the majority of that speech," a voice came from behind them, "but I heartily approve of the last part."

They all turned to see Griffin.

At the sight of them, his eyes all but popped out of his head.

"Aren't our dresses exquisite?" Performing a few happy waltz steps, Corinna turned in a circle.

"Um, yes. Pull your sleeves up, Juliana, will you?"

She tugged at them, but the dress was designed to be off the shoulder. "They won't go."

One by one, he eyed their dresses' waistlines—as high as possible to enhance pert young busts—and their low-cut, cleavage-baring necklines—if one could call them that, since they weren't anywhere near their necks.

"You are all going to cover"—at an apparent loss for words, he patted his own chest—"with one of those scarf things, right?"

"A fichu?" Madame sniffed. "I think not. These are evening gowns, my lord."

"They don't look like the pictures my sisters showed me."

"Those pictures were naught but a starting point, my lord. By the time the fashion plates make it here from France, they are already somewhat out of style."

"We wouldn't want to be wearing last month's fashions," Juliana added. "These dresses are the thing."

"Am I to understand that this month's *thing* is for fashions to display your entire—"

"Griffin. Good news. The foundry will have the new part cast by the end of the day." Tris walked in, scanned the room with a low whistle, and settled on Alexandra. "Holy Christ, you ladies will put every other woman to shame."

"My sisters will not be wearing these dresses," Griffin said.

"Of course they will." Tris tore his gaze from Alexandra and turned to his friend. "While I take apart the pump, you'll want to head out to the vineyard and see that work on the new pipeline is resumed."

"Very well." Griffin turned to leave, then swiveled back. "I'm not paying for those dresses," he warned. "Not until they're made decent."

Madame Rodale gave a little French-sounding "hmmph."

"You'll pay for them," Tris disagreed. "Do you not want men to find your sisters attractive? Irresistible? *Marriageable?*"

"Not if they're men like . . ."

"Like us?" Tris suggested helpfully.

Griffin's "hmmph" put the mantua-maker's to shame. "I need to get to the vineyard," he muttered and left.

"Madame has finished with my dress and Corinna's," Juliana announced. "We'll just go to our rooms and take them off." Grabbing Corinna's hand, she pulled her out the door.

Madame's two pasty-complexioned assistants fluttered around Alexandra, pinning her dress here and there. Tris stood watching. She shifted uncomfortably, wondering what she should say now that he'd kissed her.

Wondering if he'd kiss her again.

"Stand still," Madame said. "Lest Mariette poke you."

She stiffened and met Tris's gaze. "Do you not need to work on the pump?"

"You're beautiful."

"Thank you," she whispered.

"Of course, you're always beautiful—it has nothing to do with the dress." He spoke almost conversationally. "You'd be beautiful in a shapeless burlap bag. And you'll be beautiful when you're a hundred years old, because your beauty comes from inside. It's what makes me want to be your friend."

She didn't say anything, because she didn't know what to say.

"I want to apologize," he continued, "for the way I treated you the last time we were together—"

"Are you finished yet?" she interrupted, addressing the assistants. The two girls were standing back, watching her and Tris as though they were performing a most fascinating play.

"Oui," Madame said briskly. "Remove the dress carefully, please, and bring it down the corridor to the armory, if you will." Since the armory was just an empty room with rusty weapons all over the walls—Alexandra figured it hadn't been renovated since before the Civil War—Griffin was allowing them to use it as their sewing room. "Come along, Mariette, Martina. We have much to do before tomorrow."

Tris waited until their footsteps had receded down the corridor. "Do you expect their names are really Mariette and Martina?"

She laughed, loving his irreverence. "No, I think their names are Mary and Martha."

They shared a smile before he sobered. "As I was saying . . ."

"Yes?" She'd never seen him look quite so uneasy.

"The last time we were together, I didn't treat you much like a friend."

"No, you didn't," she agreed quietly. He'd treated her as much more.

And he'd kissed her.

"I didn't look at you the way one looks at a friend."

"I didn't look at you like a friend, either." They'd looked at each other like lovers; there was no other way to put it.

And he'd kissed her.

"I held you too close."

He certainly had; she could still feel his body against hers. His almost-naked body.

And he'd kissed her.

"I'm sorry for all of that," he concluded. "I still wish, more than anything, to remain friends."

She blinked. That was it? He still wanted to be friends? For him, nothing had changed last night?

Of course, nothing had changed for her last night, either—on the surface, that was. Marriage still wasn't an option. But clearly they'd crossed a certain line. Surely, regardless of the fact that they couldn't act on their mutual feelings, they could acknowledge them and admit that they were more than simple friends.

"I can scarcely even imagine going back to a distant, polite friendship," she said carefully.

"I'm so pleased you agree," he said, looking relieved. "The hours and days we've spent avoiding each other . . . I should not like to go back to that ever again." He released a pent-up breath. "There are many definitions of friendship. We're both adults. Certainly we can control—"

"What about the kiss?" she burst out.

"That was weeks ago. More than a month. I thought we'd agreed to forget it." His gray gaze narrowed warily. "What about it?"

"What have you been talking about, then?"

"What do you mean, what have I been talking about? The dance lesson, of course. I held you too close, and that precipitated our latest—"

"What about last night?"

"What *about* last night?"

"You kissed me again last night," she said, exasperated. "Am I expected to forget about that, too? Or shall I assume kissing is part of your definition of friendship?"

He visibly paled, his jaw going slack. "Are you sure?" he asked.

Evidently he *had* expected her to forget it.

"What do you mean, am I sure?" She remembered each moment of that kiss like it had ended a mere instant earlier. Just thinking about it, she could feel his arms around her, his lips slanting over hers. She could taste the hint of chocolate. "How could I forget such a thing?"

"I meant . . ." He hesitated, apparently fumbling for words. "I meant, are you sure you wish that to be part of the definition? Because frankly, I don't think it should be." The color had returned to his face, and unlike a moment ago, he sounded quite certain. "I don't think I could handle that. I don't think I could stop with kissing."

Part of her was shocked at the implication, but she couldn't help being flattered, too. And although she'd never considered kissing to be part of friendship, she had to admit the idea was tempting. After all, despite his stated opinion, kisses didn't *have* to go further. Hadn't she told her sisters they were "only kisses," not meaningful in and of themselves? And Rachael had said the same thing.

"I'm sorry," he continued, interrupting her musings. "I seem to be apologizing quite often these days, but I assure you, I mean it. I hope to remain friends, but I won't be kissing you again."

"I wish you would," she said under her breath as he walked out.

*   *   *

Holy Christ, he'd kissed her in his sleep.

Descending the stairs two at a time as he headed for the workshop, Tristan couldn't decide which was worse: the fact that he'd done such a thing, or the fact that he'd missed out on really experiencing it.

The only thing he was certain of, he thought as a footman threw the front doors open wide, was that he needed to go home. He'd take the pump apart today and put it back together with the new piece tomorrow. Adjusting the damn thing again would eat up the better part of the day, but that would keep him busy while everyone else was occupied with the bloody ball. Saturday morning he'd install the pump and leave with a sigh of relief. He was counting the hours.

And hoping he'd find the strength not to kiss her again.

I wish you would.

Had she meant him to hear that? No matter—he had. And—friendship be damned—the thought that she might want him regardless of his reputation was enough to make him run in the opposite direction.

Anything beyond friendship would prove a disaster for them both—he was sure of it.

"My lord? Are you in need of something?"

Tristan blinked, realizing he was standing stock-still in the middle of the quadrangle. Servants crisscrossed the lawn, carrying baskets of laundry and buckets of water, slanting him curious glances as they went about their business.

"No," he told the footman. "Thank you for your concern."

He headed for his temporary workshop, a dim, doorless room meant for storing lumber, but empty this time of year. After lighting a few candles around the pump, he stood waiting for his eyes to adjust.

No wonder she'd put on his cameo this morning—she thought something had changed. To her, that kiss had been meaningful.

He wished he could remember it.

And he wished, for the hundredth time—or maybe the thousandth—that their circumstances were different. That he wasn't a social outcast. Because he wanted her in the worst way, but he knew, without a doubt, just how much their association would affect not only her sisters, but herself.

She was sweet and loyal, but also so damned idealistic. And naive. Idealistic and naive the way only a sheltered female raised in a peer's household could be. All the sorrow she'd faced in her young life didn't change the fact that she'd grown up in the bosom of a large, loving family—a family that was unquestionably part of society's elite. She'd never known isolation, never faced disapproval, never walked into a room and felt the chill of icy gazes that stared right through her. Never had whispers behind her back sound louder than the voices in her own head.

And now that he'd kissed her again, he feared the voices in her head might be telling her an alliance between them could be possible.

Cursing under his breath, he set to removing the first bolt. Damn this ridiculous affliction. Not only had it suddenly reappeared, it seemed to be getting worse. He'd never before kissed anyone while sleepwalking—at least as far as he knew. Usually he just ambled around for a bit—at least as far as he knew—although he'd been known to dress himself and go outdoors on occasion. Once in a while he'd had reports of other activities, but he'd never done anything in his sleep that wasn't a trivial, everyday action.

At least . . . as far as he knew.

Sometimes he wondered.

Chapter Twenty-one

MARCHPANE FRUITS

Take a Pounde of almonds, Blanched and Beaten in a stone mortar, till they begin to come to a fine paste, and then add a Pounde of sifted Sugar and make it into a perfect paste, putting to it now and then the white of an egg and a spoonful or two of rose-water. When you have Beaten it sufficiently, separate into balls and colour as for fruit, red for apples and cherries, yellow for lemons, orange for oranges, purple for grapes, and the like. Shape small pieces of your coloured Paste into fruits and leave out to dry.

These festive fruits are lovely for parties and elegant enough for a ball. Or anytime at all. For like all sweets, they are truly delicious.
—Kendra Chase Caldwell, Duchess of Amberley, 1690

There were no wallflowers at Cainewood Castle's ball.

Griffin's strategy had proved an unqualified success. So many more men than women were in attendance that even the plainest girl had barely a moment to sit and rest. And in their new dresses, the Chase sisters were anything but plain.

The three of them had been claimed for every dance, and though it was barely two hours into the long evening—only ten o'clock—Alexandra's feet were already beginning to ache. Since she was now involved in a rather staid country dance, she tried her best to ignore the pain—and the dull gentleman who was her partner—and take a moment to savor the results of her hard work.

The great hall hadn't looked so beautiful since before her parents died. The enormous Gobelin tapestries on either end of the hall had been cleaned and rehung, their colors more vibrant than Alexandra remembered ever seeing them. The ancient, planked floor gleamed with polish, and the huge chamber was ablaze with light from torches mounted between each of the arched, stained-glass windows. But what really made the room glitter was the people—all the guests in their gorgeous dresses and handsome evening suits. The ladies' necks, wrists, and hands sparkled with jewels, and diamonds winked from many a man's cravat.

The music came to an end. "Thank you for the dance," the gentleman said with a bow. Lord Haversham, or Haverstock, or Haversomething . . . she really couldn't remember.

She smiled and curtsied. "It was my pleasure."

A row of red velvet chairs beckoned along the oak-paneled wall. She was heading toward one of them when Lord Shelton intercepted her.

"May I have this dance?"

"I would be delighted," she told him, ordering her feet to stop complaining. After all, she'd been dreadfully rude the last time she saw Lord Shelton, refusing to serve him ratafia puffs. She could hardly dismiss his request of a dance. But when he offered his arm to lead her back to the dance floor, she took it and felt nothing. *Nothing.* She could scarcely believe she'd once contemplated marrying him.

Thankfully, the musicians didn't strike up a waltz, but another country dance. As she took her place across from Lord Shelton, she had to admit he looked handsome in his formalwear. Pale and blond and very, very English. But she still thought his scent was too flowery.

"I am pleased to see you have recovered," he said. "You suffered from quite a lengthy illness."

Was that the excuse Griffin had used to keep him away? Bless the man. He was a fine brother, indeed. "I'm feeling quite myself now," she assured her former suitor.

"May I call on you Monday morning, then?"

Oh, drat. "I'm afraid I have prior plans." Surely she'd need to wash her hair.

"I should like to resume our courtship."

So she had surmised. "I expect you should speak with my brother," she said, mentally composing her apologies to Griffin already.

"I shall," Lord Shelton replied.

The steps then separated them for a spell, and when they came back together, Alexandra launched into a lively discussion of the weather. After she'd exhausted that fascinating topic, she steered the conversation to talk of the latest fashion in gloves and the best way to keep household account books. When the dance—which seemed to last at least half an hour—mercifully ended, she headed toward the chairs again, only to be stopped by Griffin this time.

"Alexandra, I have an old acquaintance for you to meet."

"My feet wish for me to sit. They are protesting my treatment."

"You can sit tomorrow."

She groaned inwardly, but put a smile on her face. The purpose of tonight, after all, was for her to meet men. Just because she hadn't fallen head over heels for the last dozen didn't mean the next one might not catch her fancy.

Besides, she owed Griffin, though he had yet to learn it. "Lord Shelton will be approaching you. He wishes to resume his suit."

"What am I to tell him? You're obviously in the bloom of health."

"Oh, you'll come up with something." She smiled as a man approached. "Is this the gentleman you wish me to meet?"

Griffin scowled at her, then switched on the famous charm as he turned to greet his friend. "Lord Ribblesdon, I'd like you to meet my sister, Lady Alexandra."

"A pleasure," the man said, bowing over her gloved hand. "Would you honor me with this dance?"

"I'd be delighted," she assured him.

Though Lord Ribblesdon wasn't as handsome as Tris, he was attractive, his hair dark and his eyes a pleasant blue. The musicians were starting a quadrille, so they formed a square with three other couples.

From another square nearby, Juliana grinned. "The look," she mouthed silently.

Alexandra had completely forgotten. Now she dropped her gaze and then raised it, curving her lips in a slight smile as she met Lord Ribblesdon's eyes.

Looking a bit dazzled, he smiled in return. "Your home is beautiful."

"I like it. I've always felt Cainewood is a special blend of old and new."

"You would like my estate, too," he said, and proceeded to describe it in exquisite detail as they danced.

After a few minutes, she glanced at the tall-case clock that sat against a wall. Ten twenty.

Lord Ribblesdon droned on, describing his octagonal breakfast room, which apparently boasted an unusual chandelier. Next he waxed enthusiastic about a pond on his property that was filled with notable fish.

Why did these dances have to go on so very long? An hour passed, and she glanced at the clock again.

Ten twenty-five.

She caught Griffin's gaze across the hall and gave him a tight smile. He shrugged and nodded, looking around for another candidate. She figured he'd been successful when he positioned himself at the edge of the dance floor to wait for her.

"I need to sit," she told him when the dance that

would never end finally did. This time she headed for
the small room where they'd set up refreshments and
took a chair there. "Ahh," she breathed as she dropped
onto it.

He snatched a few marzipan fruits and brought them
to the table with two cups of punch. "What was wrong
with him?" he asked, sitting beside her.

"The same thing that's wrong with every other man
here tonight. They have nothing to say of significance."
She munched on a miniature apple, hoping the sweet
almond paste confection would revive her. "They talk
only about themselves. Or their property."

He devoured a piece of marzipan in two bites. "Their
goal is to impress you. What else should they talk
about?"

"Why should they think I'll be impressed by the number of acres they own or the new horse they just bought
at Tattersall's?" She drained the cup of tepid punch,
telling herself it was refreshing. "I trust you wouldn't
introduce me to anyone of insufficient means or a man
after nothing but my dowry. I don't particularly care
what these gentlemen own; I'd much rather know what
they think."

"About what?"

"Life. The state of the kingdom. Walter Scott's latest
book. Anything."

"Have you asked them?"

"No," she admitted to both her brother and herself.
She hadn't. She'd let the men lead both the dances and
the conversations, but perhaps it would be best to take
the latter into her own hands. "I'll try that. Thank you."

"You're welcome. Ah," he added, rising. "Here comes
Lord Sandborough now."

The next dance was a waltz, and Lord Sandborough
was a superb waltzer. If it felt a bit odd to be held by
a strange man, at least he was a dashing one. He had
golden hair and merry green eyes, and his evening
clothes hung nicely on his well-proportioned frame.

As they glided over the floor, she decided that, yes,

she could imagine marrying this man. She considered giving him "the look," but instead she cast about for a good question, finally remembering one she'd asked Tris. "Do you believe there is only one perfect person for each of us in this world?"

"Indeed." He smiled, displaying nice teeth. "And I'm certain my person is you."

He didn't even know her! Suddenly he wasn't so dashing. Stupidity—not to mention insincerity—had a way of tarnishing a person's appearance.

Griffin introduced her to five more men, one after the other, and she danced on her aching feet with all of them. Three of them claimed she was their perfect person. Lord Jamestone said yes, he believed there was only one perfect person for each of them in this world, but alas, his lady had died. Though he assured her he was willing to settle for second best, for some reason she couldn't see herself in that role.

The fifth man apparently couldn't wrap his mind around the question. He simply declared that his mother had often assured him nobody was perfect. Alexandra assumed that was because he was very imperfect indeed.

She couldn't recall his name, but privately christened him Lord Sapskull.

Though the long great hall could be accessed from the dining room on one end and a corridor leading to the guest chambers on the other, it also had its own impressive entrance in the middle, complete with a grand staircase from the quadrangle. As the dance with Lord Sapskull came to its blessed end, three late guests appeared at the top of the stairs.

"Rachael!" Alexandra cried, hurrying to meet them. "And Claire and Elizabeth!" One by one, she wrapped them in welcoming hugs.

Her own sisters appeared, too, and the hugs were repeated.

"We're sorry," Rachael apologized. "I was certain we'd be your very first arrivals, but a carriage wheel broke on the way."

Though their estates adjoined, Cainewood Castle was at one end of Griffin's property, and Rachael's home was at the far end of Greystone. It took more than two hours to ride between them in a carriage, even one with all its wheels intact. "I understand," Alexandra assured her. "You'll stay the night, won't you?"

"Absolutely." Rachael's smile was impish. "We wouldn't want to miss the breakfast. Seeing how everyone looks in the morning is much more amusing than the actual ball."

They all shared a laugh. "All of you look lovely," Juliana said.

Claire, the middle sister, grinned. "Since Noah wasn't home to consult, we decided he would want us to have new dresses." She twirled in hers, white lace over pale violet satin with a neckline every bit as low as Alexandra's. Her unusual amethyst eyes danced, and she'd teased some of her curly raven hair into little ringlets that framed her face. At nineteen, Claire was already an accomplished flirt. "Do you like it?"

"How about mine?" Elizabeth, a year younger, wore blue and green stripes. They went well with her green eyes and the sleek dark hair she'd swept up into her feathered headdress. She dipped into a deep curtsy worthy of royalty. "My lady."

Alexandra laughed as she took her hand to help her rise. "You're more than ready for presentation at court." Along with Alexandra's own sisters, Elizabeth would be coming out next year. "And you're both stunning."

But neither of them could match their eldest sister. A dress of poppy-red muslin sprigged with gold clung to Rachael's slim curves. Double rows of gold lace embellished the bodice and hem, and a broad band of gold lace circled the high waistline. Her hair was tucked into a headdress of gold and poppy satin, and the loose strands that framed her face weren't curled like her sisters', but left to fall in soft waves.

"May I paint you in that dress?" Corinna asked reverently.

"When Noah gets home, perhaps I'll be able to find time to sit."

"By the lake, I think," Corinna said, staring into the distance in a way Alexandra knew meant she was envisioning a painting.

Alexandra glanced around, smiling to herself when she spotted Griffin staring at Rachael. He swiftly turned away, making her laugh again.

"What?" Rachael asked.

"Nothing." Alexandra knew she wouldn't appreciate his interest. "I expect dozens of men are waiting to dance with you all, so let me take your reticules and put them in the ladies' retiring room."

She took their three pretty little bags and started across the hall toward the small side room they'd designated for the ladies' use. A succession of feminine gasps followed by the low hiss of whispered murmurings made her stop and look over her shoulder. Her gaze swept the great hall, searching for the cause of the commotion.

At the far end of the room, Tris stood, his chin held high.

Her first thought was that he'd look better in gray, to match his eyes. Her second thought was that he couldn't possibly look any better.

His tall, lean form was breathtaking decked out in clothes for the ball. The formal suit was rather dated—the dark blue tailcoat was classic, but his white knee breeches were five years out of fashion, as were the ruffled white cuffs that peeked from beneath the coat's sleeves. Tris wouldn't have brought evening apparel along with him, so the outfit had likely belonged to her father or her brother Charles. He must have asked a valet to scare it up. But since several other country gentlemen hadn't bothered to update their wardrobes to the latest London offered, he didn't really look out of place.

Yet if the reaction of their other guests was any indication, he didn't belong here—and his clothing had nothing to do with it.

It was not that anyone confronted him. To the contrary, they all backed away, clearly snubbing him by keeping their distance. By the time she reached him—at the same moment as Griffin—he stood very much alone.

"You'd best turn up your noses," he drawled in a dry tone, "else your guests may conclude you think me worthy of more than the cut direct."

"You *are* worthy," Alexandra returned hotly.

Griffin was much more composed. "I thought you were determined not to attend."

Tris shrugged his elegantly clad shoulders. "I changed my mind. Quite obviously a dismal decision." His steely gaze skimmed the disapproving crowd. "It seems they have long memories."

Alexandra seethed at the sight of so many women whispering behind their fans. "How can they 'remember' something that never happened?"

"Regardless of the events leading up to it—or the lack thereof—the scandal happened, I can assure you." Tris managed a cool smile, which Alexandra imagined was for the benefit of their other guests. "It was very real."

"It was very wrong." She wasn't sure which made her more angry: her rude guests or Tris's nonchalant acceptance of their attitude. "Come dance with me. I wish to show them we are not swayed by their misplaced disapproval."

The slight shake of Griffin's head clashed with his plastered-on smile. "I don't expect that would be wise."

Tris nodded in agreement. "I shall take my leave before the two of you—and your dear sisters, by association—are tainted by my tarnished reputation." He swept them a proper bow. "Good evening."

The guests turned, almost as one, to watch him leave. Instead of escaping down the corridor to his room, he walked, head held high, across the great hall and out the grand entrance. Alexandra supposed he wanted everyone to think he'd left Cainewood, rather than guessing he was staying. But what would he do? Hide in the workshop all night?

The noise level rose as the other guests gossiped in

earnest now—behind Tris's back. Alexandra looked to Griffin, gripping the three reticules so tightly her knuckles turned white. "They're all going to think we sent him away."

"All things considered, that is not such a bad thing."

"He's the best man here tonight."

"You wound me," Griffin said, clutching his chest as though she'd just put a knife through his heart.

Normally that would make her smile, but she was too frustrated. "He's your oldest friend. Where is your sense of loyalty?"

"Right here," he said, pointing down at the planked floor. "In this very room, with you and your sisters and your futures. Sometimes," he added between gritted teeth as he smiled at two guests approaching them, "we are forced to rank our loyalties, whether we like it or not."

"Lord Cainewood!" Lady St. Quentin, a rail-thin older woman who was a fixture at every country party, hurried closer. She had a pinched face, and her brows were too arched, making her look perpetually astonished. Her beady gaze swept curiously over both of them. "Could you believe the nerve of that man? You did the right thing sending him packing."

When Alexandra might have opened her mouth, Griffin shot her a look of warning. "Let us forget this unpleasantness, Lady St. Quentin. It is over. And I see you've brought your son."

"I was hoping for the honor of a dance," her son said in a quiet voice, almost as if he were making up for his mother's loud one. Pale and long-faced, with a knife-edged nose and small eyes, he didn't compare to Tris.

But then, no one in the great hall compared to Tris. The more men Alexandra danced with, the more she realized that although they were all perfectly acceptable, none of them were ever going to measure up to the man who held her heart.

Yet she had to keep an open mind, because anything more than friendship with Tristan Nesbitt was impossible. If she wanted to be a wife and mother, she was going to have to settle, like Lord Jamestone, for second best. And if the thought of that made the marzipan congeal in her stomach, she was determined to ignore it. This was, after all, her family's ball, their long-awaited reentry into society. It should be a happy occasion.

She put a smile on her face and looked up at Lady St. Quentin's son. She wouldn't marry him—it was rumored the St. Quentin finances were poor, and in any case, the thought of Lady St. Quentin as a mother-in-law was enough to make her quail. But she didn't want the old prattlebox questioning her manners, either. The son seemed nice enough, if a bit of a milksop; certainly she could be polite. "I should be delighted to dance with you," she told him with a wider, more determined smile. "Let me just dispose of these reticules, and I shall return posthaste."

Chapter Twenty-two

When the elegant supper was all but finished and the majority of the guests had forsaken the dining room to resume dancing, Rachael moved to an empty chair beside Alexandra's. "Are your feet thanking you for sitting?"

Alexandra drained the final sip of the half glass of wine she'd allowed herself. "I've danced with so many men, my feet are numb now."

"How fortunate."

"How about yours?"

"I've danced with my share of your guests, but you had a three-hour head start. Mine still hurt." Rachael reached to touch Alexandra's cameo. "This is very pretty."

It wasn't nearly as pretty as the diamond necklace that graced Rachael's neck, Alexandra thought, or the glittering jewels that adorned the other ladies. But she'd wanted to wear it tonight. "Tris sent it to me from Jamaica."

"You used to wear it all the time, didn't you? I remember it now." Rachael's smile was a little too understanding for Alexandra's comfort. "Have your numb feet led you to a future husband?"

"Not yet. Have your aching feet led you to anyone special?"

"Alas, they haven't."

"Alexandra!" Juliana hurried into the room, followed by Corinna. "Griffin is looking for you. Several more men have requested introductions." She turned to Rachael. "Have you danced with Griffin yet?"

"I'm not a whit interested in dancing with Griffin. But I will say he's managed to bring together an impressive array of eligible men for your sister's consideration." Rachael's eyes twinkled as they shifted to Alexandra. "You don't mind sharing with the few other ladies here, I'm hoping?"

Alexandra laughed. "No, I don't mind. I need only *one* for myself."

And that one, she feared, was outside tinkering in a lumber room.

"Griffin hasn't found time to dance at all," Corinna said.

"That's a pity." Rachael leaned forward and pulled off her poppy red shoes. "My feet are killing me."

Juliana frowned. "You should go into the ladies' retiring room to do that. A Lady of Distinction would not approve."

"A lady of what?" Rachael asked, rubbing one of her stockinged feet.

"The author of *The Mirror of the Graces*. Griffin gave us all copies so we can learn manners that will win us husbands."

"I've never heard of that book." Rachael switched to her other foot. "If a man won't take me the way I am, I expect I wouldn't want him anyway."

"Rachael would spit on A Lady of Distinction," Corinna informed her sister with some relish.

Figuring she'd better go find Griffin, Alexandra groaned as she got to her feet.

"Not numb anymore?" Holding her shoes in one hand, Rachael rose with an exaggerated wince. "I'd best see what Claire and Elizabeth are up to," she said as they all moved toward the door. "I don't think they ate three bites between them; they couldn't wait to get back to the dancing."

Griffin spotted the four of them the minute they entered the great hall. "There you are," he said, leading a handsome, dark man toward his oldest sister. "Alexandra, this is Lord Shipworth."

As Alexandra made the appropriate responses and went off with the prospective suitor, Rachael tried to sidestep away. Juliana caught her by the arm. "Rachael thinks it's a pity you've not found any time to dance," she told Griffin. "She wishes to rectify that situation."

"I do not—" Rachael started before catching herself. Although the last thing she wanted was to dance with her cousin, refusing to his face would be dreadfully rude. "I do not . . . want to put on my shoes."

"Then don't," Juliana said gaily, taking the red slippers from her limp fingers. "Just dance in your stockinged feet. You've never feared scandal before."

"I damn well have."

"Such language only proves my point. Ah, a waltz." Grinning, she grabbed Rachael's hand and put it right into Griffin's. "Enjoy yourselves, will you?"

"I'm not very good at this," Griffin muttered as he guided Rachael onto the dance floor and took a few tentative steps. "I learned to waltz only this week."

He was certainly holding her awkwardly. And at arm's length, as though he could hardly bear to touch her. But at least he wasn't trodding on her stockinged toes. "You're doing very well for a beginner," she assured him. "Especially considering you didn't want to dance with me."

The pink flush that crept up his neck clashed with his green eyes. "I never said that."

"Liar." She laughed. "I'd wager you told Juliana you're not a whit interested in dancing with me."

A crooked half smile curved his lips. "I said nothing about a whit."

"Well, I did. I told her I wasn't a whit interested in dancing with you, but it seems she ignored us both completely."

"That was a brave confession." The smile turned full-blown now, revealing creases in his cheeks that matched the slight dent in his chin. "I promise not to hold it against you."

"Do you expect I would care if you did?"

"Not at all. That's what I love about you. In a strictly platonic way, of course," he hurriedly added.

"Of course," she echoed pleasantly. Now that he'd relaxed, he was proving a much better dancer than he'd given himself credit for. He held her a little closer. He smelled of spicy soap.

It was really too bad he was her cousin.

"Juliana deserves to be beaten," he said.

"You won't do it," she returned confidently.

"You're right. I'm an excessively ineffective father. And I never *dreamed* I'd be a matchmaking mama."

"A mama?" she echoed with a laugh. A more masculine man she'd never met. "That sounds more like a nightmare than a dream." She smiled as they twirled around the room, noting all the women were on the dance floor while many extra men waited around the edges. "Given that you're a beginner at matchmaking as well, I'd say you're doing an excellent job."

"But I have only"—he glanced at the tall-case clock—"four more hours to match Alexandra."

"Four hours? I hesitate to dash your expectations, but it's likely to take longer than that. I've been searching for a husband for four *Seasons*."

Four Seasons, Griffin thought. Good God. If it took his sisters that long, he'd be well into his thirties before he could concentrate on his own life. "Have you had no offers in all that time?"

"Oh, only about a hundred." She laughed with him for a moment, but then sighed, the tip of her tongue sneaking out to moisten her lips. The sight generated a ball of heat that smacked him in the chest and spread down, making his body stir in areas it had no business stirring. "My parents shared a special love," she said softly. "I wish for no less. I will wait until I find it."

"I see." Griffin danced silently for a few measures,

wondering if his sisters were that idealistic. He wanted them to be happy, but four Seasons was a long time. Of course, Rachael had been busy overseeing the earldom during that time, too. Perhaps she hadn't paid enough attention to her courtships. "Have you made progress preparing the master chamber for your brother's arrival?"

"Yes, much." Her good cheer returned. "It hasn't been as difficult as I expected. I haven't gone through anything very personal yet, but packing Mama's and Papa's clothes away has actually recalled many pleasant memories."

"I'm glad," he told her with a smile. She smiled back—a smile that lit up the entire great hall as they whirled across the crowded dance floor. No one else smiled like Rachael—she put her whole soul into it. He couldn't imagine why, in four Seasons, no man had managed to snatch her up. She was so open and refreshing.

The music stopped, but he held her a little longer, a little closer, thinking that if he were in the market for a wife, he'd want one exactly like her.

Had he really thought that? he wondered, pulling back. He must be getting soft in the head. This match-making business was entirely too much pressure.

She looked bemused, her cerulean eyes wide and opaque. "Um, thank you for the dance."

"Thank you," he said, "for being such a sport. I shall have a talk with Juliana. It won't happen again."

Chapter Twenty-three

"What do you think of my son?"

"He seems a fine young man." Casting about for a way to redirect the conversation, Alexandra lifted a silver tray off a nearby table and held it out to Lady St. Quentin. "Would you care for another marzipan fruit?"

"Why yes, dear, I would." She chose a miniature bunch of grapes. "These remind me of your sweet mother."

"There you are!" Corinna barged into the refreshment room. "You must see something, Alexandra."

"One moment, Corinna." Alexandra smiled apologetically at Lady St. Quentin. "Indeed, Mama made these most every time she held an entertainment. We could but do the same. It's one of our traditions."

"I admire a traditional woman. Do you expect you and my son might suit?"

"Alexandra—"

"I'm pleased the marzipan brought back good memories, Lady St. Quentin. If you'll excuse me." Still carrying the tray, Alexandra hurried off with Corinna. "What could be so important?"

"Did you really want to answer her question about her son? Just come with me."

Huffing out a breath, Alexandra lifted her skirts and followed her sister to the far end of the great hall, into the corridor, and up a dark, narrow flight of stairs. "You know what a gossip Lady St. Quentin is. I danced with her milksop son, hoping she'd think well of us. Now she'll be telling everyone we're rude."

"Oh, do stop being such a fusspot," Corinna said as they stepped onto the landing.

Juliana waited there by a door. "What are you worried about now?"

"Nothing," Alexandra said.

"Not nothing," Corinna disagreed. "She's fears Lady St. Quentin might think her less than a perfect hostess."

"If you stopped worrying about what everyone thinks, maybe you could find happiness." With that annoying proclamation, Juliana slowly opened the door. Music floated up and through it from the great hall. "Look," she whispered.

There, in the minstrel's gallery, stood Tris. He leaned on the balcony's rail, his back to the door, staring down on the festivities below.

Alexandra didn't know whether to be angry with her sisters or grateful to them. She wasn't sure whether she should go to Tris or leave. Juliana solved her dilemma with a little push. By the time Alexandra turned around, the door had been quietly shut behind her.

The torches in the great hall threw light and shadow into the high, empty space. For a moment, she just drank him in. His shoulders looked tense beneath the fine, dark blue tailcoat; his hair grazed the collar in the back. He'd be leaving before nightfall tomorrow. This might be the last time she'd ever be alone with him.

She drew a deep breath and walked closer. "Would you care for a sweet?" she asked over the music.

Tris started, then turned to face her. "No. Thank you."

He looked different tonight. Perhaps it was the formal clothing, or perhaps it was because his hair was combed neatly for once. Or perhaps it was because the more time she'd spent with other men, the more she'd become convinced he was the only one she wanted.

As he met her eyes, an odd tingle erupted in the pit

of her stomach. She held his gaze for a moment, but could find nothing encouraging there, nothing to lead her to believe anything had changed. But over the course of the evening, everything had changed for her.

She was just now realizing how much.

Although he was stone-faced, she gave him a little smile. "How did you get back inside?"

"One of the servants' entrances, a few passageways, a set of back stairs. I learned my way around long ago, playing hide-and-seek with Griffin."

Of course. He had history here. It just wasn't with her.

"I thought you were determined to avoid this ball at all costs." The wooden structure held no furniture, so she balanced the tray carefully on the rail. "Why did you put in an appearance?"

"To make a point." His gray gaze remained steady, resolute. "To prove to you, once and for all, that life with me would be a living hell."

The music swelled as she gestured over the edge of the balcony. "That is not life. I don't need those people." She swallowed hard. "I need you, Tris."

"You don't."

"I do. But I cannot ruin my family's good name." Here she was, in the most beautiful dress she'd ever owned, and she'd never felt worse in her life. "I don't know what I can do."

"You can go back down there and find another man."

"I tried, damn you."

He looked startled at her language, or perhaps at the fact that she'd been pushed to it. A long silence stretched between them, and the music from below failed to fill it. Despite his stated resolve, she watched his gaze rake her form, then focus on his cameo. The steel in his eyes dimmed and softened.

She moved closer and laid a gloved hand against his blue-and-white patterned waistcoat. "I think I'm in love with you," she confessed quietly.

The steel hardened as he stepped back. "*Think* is the operative word. You cannot be in love with me."

"I know my feelings, Tris."

"You don't."

She fisted the hand that had fallen from his chest. "Stop telling me what I do and don't feel."

"Stop pretending you can change our circumstances by wishing."

"I know I cannot." She heard tears in her voice and cursed herself for them. "But I cannot change my feelings, either."

He sighed, a sigh burdened with age-old memories. "I've thought I was in love before, too. But it was never more than an illusion, and I won't make such an error again. Neither will you, once I leave and you come to your senses. Day after tomorrow, Alexandra, you'll wake up free of me."

She'd never be free of him, not in her heart. "Will you tell me about the ladies you loved?" she asked carefully.

He turned to stare blindly over the dancers. "There was a girl in Oxford who wouldn't wait for me when I had to leave. And a girl in Jamaica who wouldn't come back with me to England." His fingers gripped the rail. "More recently, there was a woman named Leticia. Miss Leticia Armstrong."

When he stopped there, she laid a hand over his on the rail. "What happened?"

"She was the daughter of a local baron. I met her around the time I inherited, when everything in my life seemed charmed. She seemed charming, too, and I was certain she returned my feelings. In fact, she swore her undying love. I asked her to wed me, and she accepted happily enough. But then scandal broke out, and when I suggested her reputation might suffer should she stand by my side, she readily agreed and fled."

Leticia. She must have been the woman who had taught him to waltz. Although Alexandra supposed she should be grateful for that, instead she hated Leticia— and the others—for hurting him. For turning him into a cynical man who refused to believe in love.

She studied his shadowed profile—so like the portrait

she'd done of him years ago. Except his jaw looked harder, and his heart had hardened, too. "Leticia never loved you, or she'd have stayed with you. Perhaps she loved who you were—a marquess. She loved the life she imagined you'd give her. But when that life was threatened, her love disappeared. It wasn't true love."

"And neither was my love for her. Or the others. Each time, it dissipated easily enough. As will yours. You'll make a nice life for yourself—with another man." He finally turned to look at her, but it wasn't to offer hope. "I won't marry, Alexandra, neither you nor anyone else."

She'd heard that from him before—too many times before—but he couldn't fool her any longer. While she understood that he didn't want to be responsible for a wife being ostracized by society, she also knew he didn't want to open himself up for more hurt. She knew he wanted her, in a physical sense, at least—he'd admitted as much more than once. But those three women had damaged him more than he'd admit. He'd built a wall around himself.

She wished she could figure out how to scale it, even as she knew that, for her sisters' sakes, she couldn't.

Unless . . . "What if you're proven innocent?" she asked, stunned that she hadn't considered this angle before. Should he be exonerated, society would welcome him—and his wife—with open arms. "Did you ever search for the real killer?"

He looked defeated before he even opened his mouth. "I'm not convinced there was a killer—my uncle had not been himself since his family was lost. Men often die in their beds naturally, from hidden illnesses or a broken heart. He *was* ill—a mild chill, we all thought, though it might have been something more serious. But yes, I tried to find a culprit. And no, I am not going to reopen the investigation now."

"Why not? Perhaps we can find new evidence."

"We?" Something like panic filled his eyes. "Stay out of this, Alexandra."

"But I could help—"

"No. No, you cannot." Below, the musicians struck up a waltz. "The matter is closed and has been for years. No one murdered my uncle. Forget it. Dance with me instead."

He pulled her into his arms, and they started moving together to the music, twirling across the wide, empty balcony. She found herself buffeted with emotions: frustration that he flatly refused to try to clear his name, sadness that they would probably never dance together again, happiness at finding herself this close to him if only for the space of a dance.

He drew her even closer, much closer than he had during their lesson. She felt his hard chest against her soft bosom, and her breasts seemed to ache in response. His large hand rested against her back, pressing her closer still. They whirled faster. A lock of his carefully combed hair came loose and flopped over his forehead. Her heart seemed to beat directly against his, quick and unsteady.

She couldn't remember ever being so happy and so distressed all at the same time.

As for Tristan, *distress* didn't begin to describe his feelings. Her declaration had thumped into his midsection like a well-aimed fist.

I think I'm in love with you.

He'd never heard anything more horrifying.

In the aftermath of Leticia leaving him, he'd made firm decisions, the main one being he would never again believe a woman's claims of undying love. To do so left him too vulnerable, his emotions too close to the surface, his heart too open to pain.

But to disbelieve Alexandra might very well be impossible.

She couldn't be in love with him—she just couldn't. She was too loyal, too sincere, too difficult to heartlessly deny. He couldn't cope with her love, with the guilt of leaving her, with the thought of her going to another man. His only saving grace was his certainty that she was wrong. She didn't know love any more than he did.

And *he* wasn't even certain it existed.

The waltz was sweet torture, her yielding body against his, her gloved hand squeezing his so hard he wondered how the blood could make its way through their veins. Beneath a fussy little bonnet, her hair was piled atop her head in a loose, sensuous arrangement, and he buried his nose in it, inhaling the fragrance as though it could sustain him.

"I'm getting dizzy," she breathed as he spun her faster. "Dizzy on lo—"

"Don't say it." There was no point, and it wasn't even true. "Just dance with me."

She leaned away from him, just far enough to meet his eyes. "Why?" Even as she asked, her grip tightened on his hand, her other arm tugged him closer. "What made you ask me to dance?"

Sheer terror. He'd have done anything to stop her from continuing her line of questioning. The only thing more frightening than love was the murky uncertainty surrounding the mystery of his uncle's death.

But he couldn't tell her that. "It was our last chance," he said instead, not wanting to encourage her but unable to come up with another explanation.

"And Griffin isn't watching."

"No," he agreed, "he's not."

When the music stopped, he twirled her once more before reluctantly releasing her.

"Will you kiss me?" she whispered in the hush that followed. "It's our last chance for that, too."

He shook his head. "I cannot." His reputation might be in shreds, but he still had his honor.

"You kissed me before."

He couldn't tell her he'd been sleepwalking. That would be humiliating, not to mention somewhat of an insult. "I cannot trust myself to only kiss you. I thought I explained—"

"Never mind." She started pulling off one of her gloves.

Below, the musicians struck up a cheerful country dance. But Tristan was feeling anything but cheerful. He stared at her busy hands. "What are you doing?"

"I just want to touch you." She dropped the glove to the floor and started on the other one. "Do you remember when I made your profile portrait? Years ago, before you left for Jamaica?"

"Yes, but—"

"I wanted to touch you then. I pretended I was touching you while I traced your face. I've loved you for all that time, Tris. Maybe longer."

"You cannot have." As her second glove hit the wooden planks, he started backing away toward the rail. "Young girls often have crushes on their older brothers' friends. You never let go of that. Now I understand."

"No. You don't understand." Following him, she raised a hand to his forehead, swept the hair from his brow. Her fingers were gentle, and she smelled warm and sweet, and it took everything he had not to drag her back into his arms.

"That won't work," he said unsteadily.

She only shrugged and reached for one of his hands, tugging to loosen the glove, slowly and deliberately, fingertip by fingertip. As she slid the silk free and dropped it to join hers on the floor, a tremor ran through him, leaving a queasy ache in his gut and a more urgent ache down lower.

Damn if she wasn't seducing him—and successfully, at that. His body was sending him all sorts of messages his brain didn't want to accept. He should leave. Now.

Before he found himself lost in temptation.

The door was right there in front of him, but he backed away some more instead. A smile curving her lips, she followed again, giving his second glove the same rapt attention as the first. When it hit the floor, she linked her fingers with his—both hands—and sighed so prettily it made her breasts rise and fall in the tiny bodice Griffin had said she couldn't wear. "I just wanted to touch you."

He just wanted to kiss her. He couldn't. As she swayed toward him, he took one more step toward the rail—

And knocked the silver tray clear off of it.

"Drat!" Alexandra cried, twisting sideways to lean over the rail. They both watched in horror as the tray hit the floor below with a resounding metallic crash, scattering miniature colored marzipan fruits all over the polished wood. A few dancers screamed, scattering along with them, while the rest of the dancers froze. The musicians stopped playing midnote.

Alexandra wrenched her hands from his and pushed hard against his chest. Her harsh whisper rent the silence. "Run!"

She turned and fled, clattering down the stairs before he could even reach the door.

Chapter Twenty-four

Before any servants could arrive to help, Alexandra skidded into the great hall and dropped to her knees on the floor, scrabbling for the marzipan fruits. A Lady of Distinction would surely disapprove, but she couldn't bring herself to care at the moment.

"We'll have this set to rights in a minute," she announced to anyone who would listen, "and the dancing can resume. No need to panic."

Never mind that she was panicking herself. Her stomach was in a knot. Her breath was quick and unsteady. Her pulse was racing faster than it had when she'd tried to coax Tris into kissing her.

Tris. Sweet heaven. If anyone had glanced up and seen them there together . . .

Rachael knelt beside her, adding a tiny apple, orange, and strawberry to the dented tray. "What happened?" she whispered.

"Later," Alexandra muttered out of the side of her mouth. She stood, holding the tray with one hand while smoothing her skirts with the other. With a deliberate smile, she addressed the little crowd that had gathered around them. "Pray, continue." She waved a hand at the musicians. "If you will?"

The music resumed, and the guests began dispersing. A few ladies whispered behind their fans, but it seemed the worst was over. Alexandra's heart began to calm; her breath began to slow; the knot in her stomach began to unravel.

"Lady Alexandra." Someone tapped her on the arm with a folded fan.

She turned to see Lady St. Quentin. "Yes?"

"Where are your gloves?"

She forced a light laugh. "Oh, silly me. I must have left them up in the minstrel's gallery."

"Well, then," Lady St. Quentin said, a keen glitter in her eyes, "shall we go recover them?"

"I'd be pleased to do that," Rachael offered quickly.

But Lady St. Quentin was already heading for the corridor, as unstoppable as a battleship under sail. A very narrow one. Alexandra shoved the tray at her cousin and ran to follow.

"I wonder what we'll find up there?" Lady St. Quentin asked.

"Nothing much," Alexandra said, knowing exactly what the woman would find: *two* pairs of gloves, one of them quite obviously a man's. But she seemed helpless to stop the meddlesome harridan. "I was overly warm," she babbled at the woman's bony behind as they climbed the stairs. "I was . . . yes, I was overly warm, so I went up to the minstrel's gallery and removed my gloves, and I was watching the ball from up there—so beautiful, it was—just resting a bit and cooling off, when I very unfortunately dropped—"

Alexandra broke off, fearing her heart might stop as the harridan marched through the gallery's door.

But there were no gloves. None at all. The floor was as bare as when she and Tris had danced on it.

Her knees weakened with relief.

"What happened to your gloves?" Lady St. Quentin turned on her, a predatory look in her eyes. "Do you suppose your lover took them as a souvenir?"

"Wh-what?" Alexandra stammered. Her knees weakened still more, but now it was with fear. "I have no lover."

"You were up here with a man," the woman accused in a low voice. "I saw you, so don't try to deny it." She smiled, the mean smile of an undeserving victor. "You're ruined, my girl. Fortunately, my son is willing—"

"Your son is willing to do what?" Griffin interrupted from the doorway.

Alexandra turned in time to see Rachael arrive behind him; perhaps she had alerted him to the trouble. But however he had come to be here, Alexandra had never been happier to see him in her life.

Lady St. Quentin lifted her pointy chin. "My son is willing to marry your sister."

"Would her sizable dowry have anything to do with that?"

"Does it matter? She should consider herself lucky. She was seen up here with a man."

"Was she?" He turned to Alexandra. "Were you up here with a man?"

"No. Of course I wasn't." Alexandra gave him a grateful—if shaky—smile. "That would be very improper."

"She wasn't up here with a man," Griffin calmly told Lady St. Quentin.

Two bright pink spots appeared on the woman's cheeks. "She was."

"She was not. Now, would you care to return to the ball? Or shall I have a footman escort you to your carriage?"

"I saw them," the harridan insisted.

Griffin gave a long-suffering sigh and crossed his arms. "Let me put this another way, Lady St. Quentin. Should you spread the falsehood that my sister was seen with a man, neither you nor your son will ever receive another invitation to Cainewood . . . or anywhere else south of London. Do I make myself clear?"

All the color drained from her face, which looked even more pinched than usual as she sucked in her cheeks. The widow of a baronet with little land was no match for the Marquess of Cainewood. "Indeed," she said stiffly.

"Excellent." His smile failed to reach his eyes. "I trust you know your way back to the great hall?"

Alexandra hadn't known her brother had it in him to be so commanding. She supposed it could be his experience as an officer, but whatever the reason, he seemed to be growing into his role as a marquess. As she listened to Lady St. Quentin make her muttering way down the stairs, she felt like applauding.

Rachael did applaud. "Bravo!" she said softly, her eyes shining as she turned to Griffin. "You were magnificent."

Alexandra wondered if she looked at Tris like that. It really was a shame Rachael was so dead set against marrying a cousin.

"Thank you," she said to them both. "I hope she won't spread lies."

"She won't," Griffin said, sounding very sure. "Whom were you up here with, Alexandra?"

She swallowed hard. "Tristan. Juliana noticed him watching the ball, and she and Corinna suggested I come up and keep him company for a short while." That was close enough to the truth. "He's leaving tomorrow."

He gazed at her for a long moment, then nodded. "There are six more men waiting to dance with you. We'd best go downstairs." He flipped open his pocket watch, looked at it, and closed it again with a *snap*. "You have two hours left to see if any man catches your fancy."

"And if no one does?"

He shrugged. "We'll have to plan another ball."

Another brother might have said that in a threatening tone, Alexandra thought as she preceded him downstairs. But from Griffin, the statement had sounded good-natured and matter-of-fact. So good-natured, in fact, that she felt terrible about dallying with his best friend and thereby possibly damaging their relationship.

Many handsome, eligible gentlemen waited in the great hall. She renewed her resolve to be open-minded when meeting them.

But two hours later, when she'd said her good-byes to the guests departing for home, when she'd settled the people staying overnight in the rooms down the corridor, when she'd finally fallen exhausted into bed . . . she'd come no closer to finding anyone who could make her forget Tris Nesbitt.

Chapter Twenty-five

Alexandra was having the most extraordinary, most incredible, most delicious dream.

Tris was kissing her. Slow, sensuous kisses. Cherishing kisses. Kisses that made her senses spin and heat gather in a molten ball low in her middle.

But that wasn't all.

He also had his hands on her body.

On her *breasts*.

Even in her dream, she was scandalized, but as it was only a dream, she decided to lie back and enjoy the luscious experience. Just lie back and pretend that in real life he would touch her in such a tender, forbidden way. Just lie back . . .

Oh, yes, she realized . . . she was lying on a bed. Her bed. Her eyes were closed, but she knew it was her bed regardless, perhaps because it was her dream. The drawstring ribbon that secured the neckline of her nightgown had been untied, and the garment was pulled down beneath her breasts, and Tris was touching them, tracing feathery circles around their fullness and cupping them in his warm hands, and—oh!

It felt so wonderful, her very breath caught in her throat.

He captured the crests in his fingers, gently squeezing, rolling, pinching. They contracted under his attentions, sending pleasure sprinting along her nerves, throughout her body, centering in a tingling place between her thighs. She'd always known that place was there, of course, but it was as though she hadn't quite known what it was for . . . and now, in her dream, she did. It was for making her feel languid and achy and altogether decadent.

She squirmed, wanting something, needing something, unsure exactly what but craving it with every fiber of her being.

"Tris," she murmured against his lips. She felt him smile before his mouth left hers, a warm, lingering parting. He bent his head, trailing his lips across her cheek, down her chin, to the hollow of her throat, where he dallied, teasing the sensitive skin. And then lower, dusting little kisses all over her upper chest, kisses that made her whole body squirm with pleasure.

And then lower still, until his mouth closed over a breast.

A hot stab of lust lanced through her. She gasped and sighed and arched, offering herself to him like a wanton tart. She could barely conceive of acting so forward in real life, but this was a dream . . .

And if some small part of her wondered how she could dream of things she didn't know, the rest of her silenced that question, reveling in all the marvelous new sensations.

Warm, damp breath feathered over her skin as he licked and nipped and then lavished her other breast with similar attention. More feelings were building in her, amazing feelings. Sparks skittered along her veins as her heart pumped furiously. She couldn't remember consciously breathing in a dream, but she did now, each ragged inhalation making her head swim.

His mouth returned to hers, kissing her senseless, a mating of lips and teeth and tongues . . . and he slipped his hand beneath the hem of her nightgown. His fingers inched up her legs, teasingly, excruciatingly slowly, tracing patterns on her calves, behind her knees, across her thighs. His touch felt divine. He seemed to be worshipping her with his fingers, and every inch of her tingled in response.

Oh, this dream was glorious!

Breaking their kiss, he wiggled her nightgown farther up her body. She eased away, lifting herself to help him pull it off over her head, then scooted close again, wrapping her arms around him and nestling her body against his.

He felt large, strong, his muscles contoured under taut, hot skin.

Dear God in heaven, he was *naked*.

And the glorious dream was no dream at all.

She tensed at the realization, her hands stilling on his body. Tris Nesbitt—a *naked* Tris Nesbitt—was here in her very real bed.

Such sweet scandal, she thought as her heart stuttered and restarted.

Things had already gone far past the point of propriety, but she couldn't bring herself to be sorry. Though this wasn't a dream, the man of her dreams was making her feel as no other man ever had. With all her heart, she was grateful for this unexpected gift. Never had she imagined such exquisite pleasures. And if she was fated to settle for marriage to another man, she couldn't regret experiencing this intimacy just once with the one who owned her heart.

Besides, it was not as though he'd taken her virginity. Tris was a gentleman—surely he would stop as soon as she asked.

No one else would ever know this had happened.

She knew she should ask now, but she couldn't resist moving yet closer, molding her soft curves to his firmer form. Just a few seconds more to savor these incredible sensations. To commit them to memory.

She concentrated on all the wondrous things she was feeling. Pressed against his chest, her breasts felt heavy and sensitive, their crests still tight from his touch. She felt his lips locked on her mouth, his tongue a sweet, thrilling invasion. Felt her heart race, felt her breath hitch. Felt the hard ridges of his back, the heavy weight of his legs intertwined with hers.

She really should ask him to stop. But as he stroked her inner thighs, his fingers inching ever higher, her breathing grew so shallow and short she didn't think she could ask him anything at all.

Then he maneuvered his hand between her legs and cupped the tingling place where her pleasure was centered, and a jolt of aching desire made her shudder from head to toe.

"Tris!" she cried.

"What?" With a jarring suddenness, he pulled away, going rigid beside her.

Her lids flew open. In the dim light from the dying fire, his eyes looked wide.

"Don't stop," she whispered desperately, although she knew, without a doubt, that was the exact wrong thing to say.

"Don't . . . what?" When he made no move to comply, her first impulse was to grab his hand and put it back where she wanted it. But though her body still reminded her just how wonderful he had made her feel, her head cleared a bit. Thank heavens he had more sense than she did and had saved her from her folly.

She could scarcely believe she'd become that lost in temptation.

"Where am I?" he asked, and she felt foggy, confused. He struggled to rise to an elbow, his gray gaze swiftly scanning the room. "How the devil did I come to be—" He broke off as he focused on her beside him, then gasped at her naked shoulders and half-exposed chest. Slipping a hand beneath the covers, he skimmed her bare side briefly, as though needing confirmation before he jerked back his fingers and dropped his head to the pillows.

"Oh, bloody hell," he ground out through a groan.

Chapter Twenty-six

His thoughts still mired in a haze, Tristan watched Alexandra snatch the counterpane higher to cover her bare breasts. In the pale, flickering light, her eyes were pools of brandy mist. Her cheeks were rosily flushed. Her breath sounded heavy and uneven. She looked passionate, sensuous, beautiful.

The mere sight of her was horrifying.

Because beneath those same covers, he was as shockingly naked as she. His breath was as ragged as hers. His body trembled with the aftereffects of recent arousal.

He had never been more appalled in his life.

He'd done the unthinkable—made love to his best friend's sister. And having done the unthinkable, now he could barely think.

"Bloody hell," he repeated more vehemently. His heart was pounding from much more than lingering lust. He would have to make amends. Damn his traitorous body, or brain, or whatever it was that compelled him to commit unforgivable acts in his sleep. In his waking hours, like now, he still had his honor. Perhaps it was hanging by a thread, but he was determined to maintain it.

"We shall have to marry," he declared stiffly.

She stared at him, her breathing slowing to something approaching normal while her eyes cleared. "I'd love nothing more," she finally said in her considered, calm way. No temper tantrums for Alexandra, no matter how much she deserved to throw one. "But we cannot. Nothing has changed. My sisters—"

"Everything has changed," he snapped.

Her brow crinkled in confusion. "I thought you were dead set against marriage."

"I cannot believe you are arguing." As romantic proposals went, he knew his had fallen far short of ideal. But her reaction was incomprehensible. "You could even now be carrying my child."

"Carrying your child?" If anything, she seemed even more confused. "Have you changed your mind and now think to trick me?"

"No, I have not changed my mind." To the contrary, after tonight's doings, he was more fearful of marriage than ever. If he could make love to Alexandra while sleepwalking, what else might he be capable of while unaware? Would he be a danger to his own wife? "Unfortunately, under the circumstances, I don't see where we have a choice."

She shook her head. "I might be a bit hazy on the details, but I've known the facts of life since the age of twelve. My mother was not remiss in my education. What just happened in this bed—nice as it was—could not possibly result in a child."

Could she mean . . . had he not followed all the way through?

The possibility hadn't occurred to him. He'd assumed, since he wasn't aroused, he'd completed the act. Before he'd fully awakened, could the shock have stolen his desire?

"Are you certain?" he asked.

Her brow crinkled again. "Are you not?"

"No," he said simply.

The single word hung in the air. She waited, just looking at him, expecting an explanation.

Holy Christ. Humiliating though it might be, there was nothing for it but to confess the truth. "I have no mem-

ory of our encounter," he said. "I don't even know how
I got to this room."

"How can that be?"

"I was sleeping. Or rather, sleepwalking." He braced
for her reaction. "The last thing I remember before waking here in your bed was going to sleep in my own. I
realize that's difficult to believe—"

"Were you really sleepwalking?" she interrupted, the
confusion in her voice replaced by curiosity. He'd been
certain she'd think him addled, but that didn't seem to
be the case. "I thought that only happened in books."

"It's happened to me all my life, on and off. I'm sorry.
I know that's a pathetic excuse for stealing your
virginity—"

"You didn't," she said in her usual, straightforward
way. "Perhaps you stole some of my innocence, but my
virginity is intact."

Most women, Tristan imagined, would be furious regardless. "Are you certain?" he asked again.

She laughed. At a time like this, she laughed. "I'm
positive. You only . . . touched me, Tris. In . . . very
nice ways. With your hands and your mouth—but not in
any fashion that would compromise my virginity, let
alone leave me with child."

He couldn't remember ever being more relieved, both
by that news and her reaction to his confession. She
really was a very special woman.

It was almost too bad he couldn't marry.

"Thank you," he said, "for your honesty. This won't
happen again. As far as I know, I've never sleepwalked
twice in a night." He started to rise, the covers falling
to his waist.

She stopped him with a hand on his arm. "Please, stay
for a while." Her eyes wide, she stared at his bare chest.
"I know it's frightfully improper, but what is a few more
minutes? I want to hear more about the sleepwalking.
And you're leaving tomorrow."

He hadn't ever seriously talked to anyone about this.
The thought was alarming, but also strangely appealing.

He drew a steadying breath and gestured to his dressing gown at the foot of the bed, vaguely wondering when he'd donned it, let alone taken it off. "Shall we . . . put something on?"

Her gaze flicked to her nightgown, a crumpled white ball beside her. She clutched the covers tighter beneath her chin, clearly unwilling to relinquish them in order to dress. "Just relax. I promise I'll not attack you."

With a strained chuckle, he resettled himself on the sheets, on his side, facing her but carefully separated by a space. The fire was dying, and with it the light. He briefly considered rebuilding it, but he thought the darkness might make talking easier. And he wasn't cold. Having her this close—and the both of them undressed—made a fire of another kind altogether.

A fire he was determined to resist.

"What do you want to know?" he asked.

"Everything. When did you first sleepwalk?"

"As a small child. I used to do it quite often, but as I grew older, I seemed to outgrow it. The episodes tapered off. Now it seems to happen only when I'm under pressure of some sort. The occurrences have really become quite infrequent. In fact, I was hoping they had stopped altogether. Until this week, I hadn't sleepwalked in three or four years."

"Since your uncle's death," she mused quietly. "What is it like?"

"I don't know. I never remember." He'd guessed right that the darkness would help. Answering a disembodied voice was so much easier than responding to an expectant face. And yet more intimate somehow. "What does it look like to you?"

"My eyes were closed," she murmured. "I wasn't looking."

Her tone made him imagine that if the room were lighter he'd see her blush. "How about the other night? When you caught me 'stealing' the chocolate cakes. What were your impressions then?"

"You were sleepwalking then?" Her voice was suffused with wonder. "Of course," she answered herself. "That's why you didn't remember our kiss. I can see it now. See you, I mean. You seemed a bit . . . distant—well, other than during the kiss—and you didn't respond well to my questions. I thought you were being deliberately evasive."

He nodded beside her although she couldn't see it. "Others have said the same. A blank look in my eyes, responses that don't quite make sense." He sighed. "I never, ever remember. It's rather frightening, if you want to know the truth."

"No, it isn't. I would think it should be, but it isn't."

Bless her for that. But that wasn't what he had meant. "I've never kissed anyone in my sleep before, let alone climbed into another's bed. It's frightening because I don't know what I might do next." And for some unknown reason, he felt compelled to add, "And what else I might already have done."

"Like what?" she breathed.

His voice dropped to a low, almost-whisper. "Like possibly—though I don't remember it—poisoning my uncle."

There. He'd said it out loud. He prepared for her shock and imminent departure, but she didn't run screaming from the room.

Instead, she reached across the mattress, rooting beneath the covers until she found one of his hands and took it in hers. "You don't really believe that."

The simple statement stole his breath, like an unexpected blow to his midsection. Her unquestioning belief in him was a force all its own, a sort of acceptance he'd never experienced or expected. He couldn't see her in the dark, but her hand squeezing his told him all he needed to know.

She had more faith in him than he had in himself.

"You don't believe that," she insisted. "Tell me you don't."

"Sometimes, in the dark of the night, when I wonder what I did to deserve my life going so dreadfully wrong . . ."

He'd never told anyone this. Not even, he suddenly realized, himself.

He wasn't the sort to brood over life's inequities, and until recently—very recently—he hadn't felt particularly deprived. Even taking his isolation into consideration, he had so much more than so many other people in this world. A magnificent ancestral home that he enjoyed updating and improving, several estates to occupy his time and challenge his talents and ingenuity, and more money than he knew what to do with. Considering the misery most people endured on a day-to-day basis, he knew he had no right to complain.

It was only lately that he'd realized he was lonely. But that shouldn't be so much to bear.

"My uncle died in the middle of the night," he said. "I had recently arrived from Jamaica to find my own father had passed on. Uncle Harold hadn't been himself since the deaths of his wife and sons, and I was staying with him at his request." He knew he'd told her some of this before, but he needed to put it in context. "As I was now his heir, he wished to instruct me, and I wished to cheer him. Truly, I did. He was only in his early fifties; I expected him to live a long, long time. I had no wish for his death."

"I'm sure you hadn't," she said quietly.

"But can you not see? I was there, sleeping in his house, that morning when he failed to awaken. And I'd been sleepwalking—after three years of peaceful nights in Jamaica, I'd come home to find my father dead and my financial life in a shambles, and I'd begun sleepwalking again. I don't remember murdering my uncle, and I felt nothing but love for him, I assure you. I don't consider myself capable of killing anyone, let alone the man who had fathered me more than my own father. But the fact remains that I was under great pressure at the time, and I'd already sleepwalked once or twice . . . so a part of me has always wondered."

"A very small part of you, I'm sure."

He wasn't sure it wasn't a large part. It was something he tried not to think about.

"That's what's kept you from digging too deeply to clear your name," she said suddenly. "You're afraid you might discover the opposite, that you were responsible for your uncle's death."

His first reaction was knee-jerk denial, but she sounded so reasonable he felt obligated to mull it over a moment. "Perhaps," he finally conceded. He'd never clarified that in his mind; he'd always thought of it as putting the past behind him and getting on with his life. But he had to admit that what she said might be true.

And that she must understand him very well to surmise it.

"That's ridiculous." She pulled her hand from his, leaving him feeling very alone in the dark. "There is absolutely no way you could have murdered your uncle."

He recoiled from the certainty in her voice, the anger she so very rarely displayed. "It's a possibility," he disagreed stiffly. "Only a possibility, but—"

"It is *not*." He felt her fingers brush his face, and her voice gentled, but not much. "You're a good man, Tris Nesbitt. And I am positively certain that, as such, you would never do anything while asleep that you didn't wish to do while awake."

It was an interesting theory, but he couldn't quite buy it. "How about *this*?" he returned, reaching to skim a hand over her bare hip, still horrified that he'd all but ruined her.

She hesitated rather than answering, releasing a little moan before she closed the distance between them. Her arms went around him and held him snug. Damning his own weakness, he melted in her embrace, wrapping his own arms around her to hold her close.

"You wanted to do this, too," she whispered into the night.

He couldn't argue with that. He'd been craving her for weeks, months . . . years, if he were to be honest. Just having her so near was a torture he could barely endure. She felt too warm, too giving, too damn sweet in his arms. And even though he couldn't remember so much as a moment of their earlier encounter, she somehow felt familiar in his arms, too.

As though she belonged there. But she didn't.

No one belonged in his arms.

Her protestations of his innocence had done nothing to ease his worry. God only knew what he might do next in his sleep. Though he hesitated to wed before, now he was absolutely determined never to subject a good woman to his menace.

And every fiber of his being was aware of her against him. Dangerously aware. "I must leave," he said, trying to pull away.

She held him tighter, her curves melding to match his contours, the soft pillows of her breasts crushed against his chest. "Stay. Please. A few minutes longer."

She didn't say why. She didn't need to say they would never be like this again.

"Just hold me," she added. "Just hold me for a little while."

So he just held her. It was, perhaps, the most difficult thing he'd ever done. His entire body was rock hard. Her skin was so silky beneath his hands, her loose, long hair so fragrant. He buried his face against her neck, and he could feel the pulse in the slim column of her throat, rapid and unsteady, just like his.

And when she fell asleep in his arms, he knew he'd never known a moment sweeter.

He wouldn't succumb to sleep. He'd just lie here a little longer, imprinting this moment in his brain so he could relive it in the long, lonely years ahead.

He wouldn't sleep.

Chapter Twenty-seven

There was an empty space at the breakfast table.

True, it had taken a good half hour for the family and all their guests to make their bleary-eyed way to the dining room. But now it was almost noon. And Alexandra—normally the earliest riser of them all—had yet to appear.

"Do you expect she's had a relapse?" Lord Shelton asked, his pale brow wrinkled in concern. "Could the evening have been too much for her in her current, fragile state?"

Griffin shrugged, secretly pleased. "Perhaps." With any luck, this would provide an excuse to put the poor man off another month or so.

"Alexandra is the veriest picture of health," Juliana declared, to his annoyance. "I shall go fetch her." She started to rise.

"I expect Lady Alexandra is still sleeping," Lady St. Quentin said in her superior, all-knowing way. "I do believe she had a late night."

The low buzz of conversation ceased as all eyes in the room turned to her.

"We all had a late night," Griffin said into the sudden silence.

Lady St. Quentin blithely buttered a slice of toast. "Do you know," she continued conversationally, "I was rather restless during the night. All the excitement, I expect.''

Juliana reseated herself. Griffin narrowed his gaze. "Go on," he said. She would in any case, the old gossip.

"Well, I took a little stroll down the corridor, and what do you suppose I saw?" Enjoying her rapt audience, she paused to take a delicate bite, chew it leisurely, and swallow. "None other than the Marquess of Hawkridge, coming out of another room."

"Mother," her son interjected halfheartedly.

She waved him off, turning to Griffin. "I thought the marquess had departed after learning he wasn't welcome."

"You were mistaken," Griffin said with a forced smile.

"I'll go fetch Alexandra." Juliana rose again.

Lady St. Quentin raised her cup of chocolate to her lips, watching Griffin over the rim. "You'll want to go with your sister," she said pointedly.

He barely resisted huffing out a sigh. "Why?"

"Because when the marquess left his room, *he went upstairs.*" She paused to let the significance of that sink in. "And he left his door open, and it still isn't closed, *and* he isn't inside. So I suspect he has yet to come back down."

"Why the hell would you surmise that?" Rachael snapped.

Lady St. Quentin raised one of her overly arched brows. "My dear, you must learn to watch your language."

"Mother," her son repeated hopelessly.

She didn't even bother waving him off this time, ignoring him as she focused on Rachael. "I do believe Hawkridge is the man I saw in the minstrel's gallery with your cousin last night."

Several gasps were heard around the table.

"I'm going to fetch Alexandra," Juliana stated and headed from the room.

"I'm going with you." Corinna pushed back her chair and ran after her.

"So am I," Griffin added through clenched teeth.

Several more chairs rasped along the carpet as various guests rose to trail them. Griffin hurried after his sisters, refusing to look back. Gobble-grinders, all of them. Let the whole world follow, he thought as he took the stairs three at a time, passing Corinna and then Juliana handily. The St. Quentin woman would be red-faced before this was over. Alexandra was the most proper girl he knew.

Long-legged strides carried him rapidly through the upper gallery and down the corridor past Corinna's and Juliana's rooms. The two of them had to run—decorously, of course—to keep up. Reaching Alexandra's door before them, he twisted the knob and pushed it open.

Then slammed it closed.

He turned to his sisters. "Get rid of them," he gritted out, referring to the nosy guests making their leisurely way up the stairs and through the upper gallery. "Now."

"Why?" Corinna asked.

"Just do as I say for once, will you?"

Juliana's hazel eyes were as round as saucers. "They're both in there, aren't they?"

"Brilliant deduction. I'll give you your prize later. Now, go—"

He whirled to face the door as it opened again, from the inside this time, revealing a sleepy-eyed Tristan wearing a dressing gown. An improvement over a moment ago, when all Griffin had seen of the man was a head and bare shoulders peeking from under the blankets.

The blankets on his sister's feminine Chippendale bed.

"Get back in there!" Griffin whispered, reaching to pull the door shut again, quietly this time.

"Aha." Lady St. Quentin's triumphant voice was unmistakable. "I knew it!" Elbowing past the other approaching guests, she made her way to the door and pushed on it.

It reopened with an ominous creak. Inside, Alexandra cowered in her bed.

"You're ruined, girl," Lady St. Quentin crowed. "Ruined!"

"She is not," Corinna protested, throwing Griffin a desperate, apologetic glance.

But it was too late. The crowd rushed to see, forming a loose semicircle in front of the door. Alexandra *was* ruined.

"I sleepwalked in here," Tristan said quietly, as though he and Griffin were the only ones there. A nerve jumped in his clenched jaw. "Unaware of my own actions."

"Balderdash!" Lady St. Quentin exclaimed. "I've never heard such a pathetic excuse. It won't save her reputation; that I can promise."

"Stubble it," Griffin said dangerously. All the whispering behind him wasn't helping him think straight. He glared at Tristan. It was some consolation to learn Alexandra hadn't invited the man into her bed, but of all the damned, unexpected . . . "You *still* sleepwalk?"

"Infrequently, but yes."

"You didn't have to stay," he bit out.

"You're right. My sincerest apologies. I'll leave now." Tristan started from the room.

"You will not." Griffin stopped him with an outstretched hand flat against his chest. "You stayed the night, you'll stay now. You'll marry my sister. By special license. Tomorrow."

Gasps rose from the onlookers. Tristan glanced down at Griffin's hand, then stepped back. "If that is what you wish."

Griffin's arm dropped to his side. "It is not what I wish, but it is what must be."

"Nonsense," Lady St. Quentin cut in. "You cannot marry your sister to a murderer." She reached back into the cluster of spectators and pulled her son stumbling through to the front. "My Roger will be happy to marry her."

Her Roger looked mortified.

"For her dowry?" Griffin asked Roger's mother pointedly.

"Does it matter?" she returned.

Griffin's gaze flicked to where his white-faced sister sat motionless on the bed, her blue covers clutched under her chin. "Do you wish to marry Sir Rog—"

"You cannot let the chit decide this for herself," Lady St. Quentin scoffed.

Was there another woman in England as irritating? "As a matter of fact, I can should I choose to do so. And I can certainly solicit her opinion." He drew a calming breath and turned back to Alexandra. "Do you wish to marry Sir Roger St. Quentin?"

She shook her head infinitesimally.

"No," Juliana said for her. "She most certainly does not."

Griffin and Lady St. Quentin sent her matching glares.

"I'll marry her," came another voice. Lord Shelton stepped out of the clutch of gawkers.

Despite his own distress, Griffin felt sympathy for the man. If he knew Alexandra's mind, Shelton was about to be publicly refused. He looked back to her. "Do you wish to marry Lord Shelton?"

"No," Juliana started at the same time Alexandra said, "I'm sorry."

Thin and shaky, her voice barely carried from the room to the corridor. "My apologies, Lord Shelton. I am honored by your offer, but I do not think we would be happy together." Suddenly, her eyes flashed—Griffin would swear he saw red in the medium brown. "And Lord Hawkridge is no murderer," she added loudly and perfectly clearly.

Griffin stood silent, cursing the fates that had put *him* in charge of his siblings. Two perfectly acceptable men had offered for his disgraced sister. If he forced one of them on her, this scandal would eventually blow over. She'd be miserable all her days, but their sisters would be able to marry well. If he allowed her to wed Tristan . . .

He felt everyone's eyes on him while his own vision swam. Never in his life had he found it so hard to make a decision. Thank God he wasn't on a battlefield with the enemy bearing down . . . although, given the antagonistic mood of some of those around him, that analogy wasn't so far off.

Rachael stepped close and laid a hand on his shoulder, drawing him away and down the corridor. The guests all turned to watch as she walked him to the end so they wouldn't be able to overhear.

"Your first instinct was good," she said quietly. "Let her marry the man she loves."

His gaze flicked to the curious onlookers. "But—"

"I, too, once thought this union inadvisable. But now that I've seen them together—"

"What they feel for each other has little bearing on the repercussions of this match."

"Have faith in her. She has faith in him."

Griffin had faith in Tristan, too—but that wasn't the point. "The *ton* doesn't mirror that faith."

"Will you allow that to influence your decision? That isn't the Griffin I remember. The one I imagined riding into battle with his principles held before him like a shield."

That idealistic youth, Griffin feared, was long gone. He stared at her. "You never thought of me that way. You thought I was a reckless rascal."

"Perhaps. I do recall you once telling me to ask for forgiveness, not for permission. But you were also stubborn as hell. You never let anyone else's opinions stand in the way of your goals."

His gaze swept the assembled guests, landing on the odious Lady St. Quentin. He could see her straining to hear.

Damnation. Rachael was right. He was not going to let that despicable, fortune-hunting woman decide his sister's fate. He could not consign Alexandra to a life of utter misery, even to save the rest of them from suffering society's disfavor. Not and live with himself, anyway.

With a sigh, he surrendered to the inevitable, marching back to face his old friend—damn the barefoot bastard—in his sister's doorway.

"Get dressed," he said tightly. "The Archbishop of Canterbury is half a day's ride, and you're in need of a special license."

Chapter Twenty-eight

Alexandra sighed as she watched the last of their guests' carriages roll out of the quadrangle. "Why do I think they're all going to gather at the end of the road and have a good gossip?"

"Because they will," Juliana said.

"The repercussions have begun already." Alexandra turned to follow her siblings back inside. "They didn't even stay long enough to finish breakfast."

"That is only because it was stone-cold," Corinna said, sitting on an old, ornate treasure chest.

"No, it wasn't." Tired and demoralized, Alexandra plopped onto one of the walnut hall chairs. "No one wants to associate with us. Dear God in heaven. What am I going to do?"

"You're going to marry Tristan tomorrow." Griffin sat on the third step of the staircase, leaning forward with his elbows on his spread knees, his hands dangling between them. "And you're going to be happy. I demand it."

"How can I be happy when the rest of you will be miserable?" A single tear rolled down her cheek.

An expression of horror came over his face. He sat up straighter. "You are marrying the man you claim to love. There is no crying allowed. You hear me?"

"She's not crying for herself," Juliana said, moving to

pat Alexandra on the shoulder. "She never cries for herself. She's crying for *us*."

"I am *not* crying," Alexandra said, swiping at the rogue tear with a frustrated motion.

In truth, she wasn't sure why she was crying. She was a bundle of emotions. One moment she was elated to be marrying Tris, the next racked with guilt that it meant making pariahs out of her siblings. And she was humiliated beyond belief—absolutely mortified that half of society had seen her naked in her bedroom.

"I'm sorry." She gave a long, wretched sniff. "I've ruined all your lives."

"Good God," Griffin said. "Cheer up, will you? You don't see any of us crying."

"We're *thrilled* for you," Juliana put in.

Alexandra looked around at all the grim faces. "Indeed."

"We are," Corinna insisted. "We're just a little . . . shocked. You've always been the *good* sister."

"Well, I've been changing, in case you haven't noticed. It seems my transformation is now complete. From a paragon of traditional femininity to an utter tart, and all inside of a single summer."

"No one thinks you're a tart," Juliana said.

Corinna nodded. "A little fast, perhaps, but—"

"She's about to be a married matron," Juliana interrupted, glaring at her younger sister. "There is nothing fast about that. Griffin, you did exactly the right thing."

"Thank you," he said dryly.

Alexandra sighed. "There *was* no right thing."

"Does Tristan really sleepwalk?" Corinna asked her brother.

He nodded. "All of his life." His jaw clenched. "I'm going to kill him."

Alexandra jumped up. "You wouldn't dare!"

"Sit down. I was jesting." He rubbed the back of his neck and added, "I'd *like* to kill him, but I'll restrain myself. For your sake."

"Thank you." She plopped back down.

"Just be happy. That is all the thanks I require."

But she couldn't be happy—not when she'd ruined her family's reputation. She wouldn't be happy until she fixed that. Until her sisters could win any men they wanted. Until Griffin didn't have to defend his friend or his decision to allow her to marry him.

Until, she realized, the seeds of an idea taking root in her brain, she found the evidence that would clear Tris's name.

"Just give me a week or two," she said slowly. "Then we'll all be happy."

Corinna's blue eyes narrowed. "What do you mean?"

"I'm going to find whoever murdered Tris's uncle." She could do it. She had to do it. "Then Tris won't be shunned anymore by society, and you'll be able to make a brilliant match. After all, your older sister will be married to a handsome, popular marquess who is well-known for his expertise in machinery, animal husbandry, and land management." Alexandra tried for a brave grin.

"You're going to find his uncle's murderer," Griffin said flatly. Disbelievingly.

She raised her chin. "Yes. I am."

"How?" Juliana asked.

"I don't know. I'll need to investigate matters at Hawkridge Hall."

"Tristan doesn't think there *is* a murderer," Griffin reminded her. "He thinks his uncle died in his sleep."

"Well, we'd best all pray he's wrong, because a natural death will be much harder to prove. But I'll find a way, because it's the only hope for us all."

"Surely it's not as dire as all that," Juliana said.

But no one spoke up to agree with her, because it *was* as dire as all that.

Alexandra sighed into the silence.

"Holy Hannah!" Corinna exclaimed after a long moment.

Juliana turned to her. "What?"

"She's going to investigate matters at Hawkridge Hall. She's going to *move* to Hawkridge Hall."

"Tomorrow," Griffin said matter-of-factly. "I expect Tristan will want to leave directly after the wedding."

"She cannot leave tomorrow!" Juliana shook her head. "She's made no preparations, she has no trousseau, she—"

"She has no choice." Griffin stood, one hand on the staircase's marble rail. "I'm going to change my clothes and head out to the vineyard. Since Tristan has abandoned me, I'll need to install his pump." He started upstairs, gazing down at them as he went. "You'd better pack your things, Alexandra. And choose a wedding dress. With any luck, I'll be finished and back for dinner."

"A wedding dress," Alexandra breathed.

Corinna nodded. "A Lady of Distinction suggests a white one."

"I don't even *own* a white dress."

"You can borrow one of ours," Juliana said. "And you'll need a veil. We'd best get busy."

The sun was sinking in the sky by the time Tristan returned, special license in hand, to learn that Griffin was at the vineyard. A change of horses and a brisk gallop got him there just before dark. Griffin's crew was completing the pipeline, lighting lanterns to provide illumination while they finished. As Tristan rode up, one of the men approached him, holding two of the lamps.

"I was just taking these to Lord Cainewood, my lord." He nodded in the direction of the newly dug pit.

"I'll take them for you," Tristan offered, sliding off his mount. He tethered the horse and headed toward the pit, both lanterns in one hand. Slipping his other hand into his pocket, he toyed with the ring he'd detoured to Hawkridge to pick up. A simple gold band, wide but worn thin from centuries of use. A family heirloom for traditional Alexandra. Though it was plain, he hoped she would like it.

Curses were coming from the square pit. Colorful ones. Still holding the lanterns in one hand, he started down the ladder, his eyes widening as he saw what was going on inside. "What the hell do you think you're doing?" he said as he reached the bottom.

"Installing your damn pump." Griffin's wrench slipped, eliciting another burst of foul language.

Tristan set the lanterns in a corner on the dirt floor. "I would have done it if you'd waited."

"When? In the middle of my sister's wedding night?" Griffin mopped his brow with the back of a grimy hand. "I think she'd have my head. Besides, it's time I learned how to do this myself. Given the way my luck has been running, I'm likely to need another pump or a dozen soon."

"Let me give you a hand." Tristan took the wrench.

"One of the hands you couldn't keep off my sister?" Griffin snatched it back. "No thanks."

Heedless of the dirt, Tristan leaned against the wall, crossing his feet at the ankles and his arms across his chest. The whole pit exuded the pungent scent of recently turned earth. As fresh and sharp as his friend's mood. "You're angry with me."

"Give the man a prize."

"I didn't compromise your sister on purpose."

"No, you were sleeping. Just waltzed in there unaware. Or so you said—"

"Hey—"

"All right, I believe you." Griffin banged the wrench against a pipe, then winced at the sharp *clang*. "That doesn't mean I have to like it." He whacked the pipe again.

"You want to hit me?"

He looked all too intrigued by that idea. "No."

"Go on. Hit me. It'll make you feel better."

"It'll make *you* feel worse."

Tristan just shrugged. "You cannot but admit I deserve it."

Tapping the wrench against his palm, Griffin stared at

Tristan for a few long, tense moments. Then he dropped the tool to the dirt, drew back a fist, and rammed it into his friend's shoulder.

Though pain exploded, Tristan didn't flinch. "You can do better than that."

"You're right." Griffin hauled off and punched him in the mouth.

Tristan saw stars. His friend looked wavery through his watering eyes. Tasting blood, he flexed his jaw. "Feel better?"

"Not yet." Gritting his teeth, Griffin took half a step forward, then drove his fist full force into Tristan's gut.

The wind rushed out of him, and he doubled over in pain and surprise. When he came up, gasping for air, he returned the favor with a blow to Griffin's face that sent him careening into the wall.

"Hey!" Griffin said.

"That's enough."

"I think not," he ground out, coming back swinging. "You compromised my sister. It will never be enough."

Tristan took two punches but ducked the third, straightening to throw a left-handed jab that landed solidly in his friend's midsection. Griffin retaliated with a right-handed hit that was even harder. From there, Tristan lost track. The blows flew fast and furious until finally they both stood there, panting and exhausted, neither of them possessing enough energy to continue.

Griffin dropped to sit on the dirt floor, his legs sprawled out before him, his face cradled in both hands. "I think you broke my nose."

"No, I didn't. You're such a widgeon." Leaning against the wall above him, Tristan spit out blood. "I think you loosened my teeth."

"I hope so." Griffin grinned up at him, then winced. "You feel worse now, don't you? Just as I predicted."

Tristan slid down to sit beside him, groaning at new assorted aches. "Nothing you do could make me feel worse. Believe it or not, I'm more upset at this turn of events than you are."

"I don't believe it. You didn't just ruin two of your sisters' lives."

"No, I ruined three of *your* sisters' lives instead."

"Three? Alexandra was dying to marry you."

But the way Tristan saw it, she could die *because* she married him. Who knew what he might do the next time he sleepwalked? He was scared stiff.

"Besides," Griffin added, "she's going to clear your name, and then no one's lives will be ruined."

"She's going to *what*?"

"She's determined to find your uncle's killer."

"My uncle didn't have a killer. He died in his sleep."

Griffin started to shake his head, then apparently thought better of it. "I told her you'd say that."

Chapter Twenty-nine

CORIANDER BISCUITS

Take eight eggs, a little Rose water, some Madeira, and a pound of fine Sugar; beat them together for an Hour; then put in a Pound of Flour and half an Ounce of Coriander seeds; then beat them well together, butter your Pans and put in your batter, and set it into the Oven for half an Hour; then turn them, brush them over the Top with a little of the Eggs and Sugar that you must leave out at first for the Purpose, and set them in again for a quarter of an Hour.

These biscuits are perfect to take visiting. My mother always brings some when we're to meet someone new.

—Lady Elspeth Caldwell, 1691

"What the devil are you doing up so late? It's three o'clock in the morning."

"Is it?" Startled, Alexandra turned to see her brother standing in the shadowed entrance to the kitchen. "I'm making coriander biscuits to bring along to Hawkridge." She beat Madeira into a bowl of eggs, sugar, and rose water. "I cannot arrive there with nothing."

"You don't have to bribe Tristan's people to accept you. You'll be their marchioness."

She shrugged, adding flour to the mixture and dumping half of it onto her shaky hands in the process. "Chase women always bring sweets."

"Tomorrow will be a big day for you. For God's sake, go to bed. If you truly feel a need to bring something, you can ask François to make it in the morning."

Not bad advice, except she was too excited—and nervous—to sleep. "We missed you at dinner," she said, changing the subject. "And afterwards." As he walked closer, she blinked and set down the bowl. "What on earth happened to your face?"

He touched it gingerly. "Your soon-to-be-husband happened to it," he informed her dryly.

"Tris? Whyever would he hit you?"

"Perhaps because I hit him first?" He looked around the cavernous kitchen. "Is there anything to eat in here besides raw biscuit dough? We just finished installing the pump. It works beautifully, but I'm about to expire from starvation."

"And Tris?"

"Said he's not hungry. Went straight to bed."

"I meant, does he look like you?"

"Not much." He crossed to where François had left out some bowls covered with cloths. "His hair is lighter, and his eyes—"

"Griffin!" She walked over and playfully punched him on the shoulder with a flour-coated fist.

"Ouch!" He waved at the white powder flying in the air. "I hurt everywhere, so keep your hands off."

"How much did you hurt *him*? Will I have to keep my hands off my husband as well?"

Her brother's face flushed red beneath the bruises. "I prefer not to discuss you touching that man at all. Or any man, for that matter." He rooted in a bowl of fruit and came out with an apple. "Do you know," he added, polishing it on his grimy shirt, "I think I'm just as happy you've been ruined. Saves me from having to explain all about the wedding night.''

"I wasn't ruined, Griffin."

"What?" He bit into the fruit with a juicy crunch. "Of course you were ruined. Why else would I marry you to someone completely unsuitable?"

"Don't talk with food in your mouth." She dabbed at his chin with a dish towel, wincing in sympathy when he winced. "In society's eyes, yes, I was ruined. But not in truth."

He swallowed this time before responding. "What do you mean?"

"Nothing really happened in my bed." Perhaps that was an understatement, but the gist of it was true. "Tris kissed me and touched me, but that was all. Mostly we just talked. And then we fell asleep."

The apple sat forgotten in Griffin's hand. "You just talked," he said. "Naked."

Heat flooded her face. "Well, our clothes came off while Tris was still asleep. He took them off, I mean, while I was half-asleep. But after we both awakened . . . yes, we just talked." Turning away, she started putting dollops of batter on one of the two pans she'd prepared. "You believe me, don't you?"

"I'm not certain I do. I have never in my life just *talked* to a naked woman."

"I'm so glad to hear that," she said toward the biscuits.

She heard the crunch of another bite. "Why?"

"Because, being unmarried as you are, I wasn't precisely sure you had experience. In matters pertaining to the bedroom, I mean. But I'm glad that you do, because that means you'll be able to explain everything to me." Hearing choking sounds, she turned to him. "Are you all right?"

He nodded wildly. She wondered whether his red face was a result of the choking, the bruising, his embarrassment at her request, or all three. Since there was nothing she could do about the second two, she only waited for him to stop choking before she continued.

"You will explain what will happen on my wedding night, won't you? Because I'm dreadfully nervous." She almost wished Tris had finished what he'd started, because then she'd know. "I think I will stay up all night making coriander biscuits if you don't tell me what will happen."

"Can I have some of that Madeira first?" He gestured toward the half-empty bottle.

"Certainly." She handed it to him, looking around for a glass.

"Don't bother," he said and drank directly from the bottle.

She watched him take several gulps. "Madeira should be sipped," she said as tactfully as she could.

He chugged another swallow and wiped his mouth with the back of his hand. "Oh, yes?" Avoiding her gaze, he took a deep breath. "You see, there are birds, and then there are bees, and—"

She laughed. "You don't have to start there, you goose. Mama taught me all of that. Did she not explain it to you?"

"Father did. When I woke one night in a wet bed."

"What?"

"Never mind." He raised the bottle again, but took a more normal sip this time.

"Were you twelve? I was twelve when I started bleeding, and—"

"Stop," he ordered, holding up his free hand. He took a bigger swallow, then set the bottle on the table with a *thunk*. "Men don't care to hear of those female things."

"No?"

"No. You'd best keep that in mind for the future. And if Mother told you everything, what the devil do you need to hear from me?"

"I want to know what will happen on my wedding night." She turned back to the table, placing more dollops of batter on the second pan. "Mama told me the basics, that the man plants his seed in the woman. And I know about the body parts it takes to accomplish that. But *how*? I've seen horses—"

"It's not like horses," Griffin interjected quickly. "You will do it face-to-face."

"Oh." That alone was somewhat of a relief. "We'll be able to kiss, then."

"Yes."

"Excellent. I like kissing."

"I don't want to hear this." He took another swallow.

"What will happen, Griffin? Tell me."

He set down the bottle again. "He will probably leave you alone to change into a nightgown—"

"My nightgowns are rather plain." She licked some batter off a finger. "I've packed one that Juliana lent me—hers are much prettier."

"Why does *Juliana* have pretty nightgowns?"

She turned to him. "She likes them. She says they make her feel more womanly."

"I don't want to hear this," he repeated, lifting the bottle for another sip.

"Then why did you ask?"

"Will you be quiet and let me explain? When you're all ready and waiting in bed, he will come to you, probably wearing a dressing gown. To make things easier."

"Easier?"

"Easier to get undressed. Do I have to spell out everything?"

"I think so. I am really quite innocent though the world thinks me a fallen woman." She handed him one of the pans and took the other herself. "I just want to know what will happen."

"So I've gathered." He followed her over to the brick oven and shoved his pan inside. "After he joins you in bed, he will probably kiss you and touch you—"

"I find touching to be very enjoyable."

"Splendid. You would not believe how happy I am to hear that." He didn't sound happy at all. "After that, he will open his robe and lift your nightgown."

"I think he will take them both off," she disagreed. "When he was sleepwalking, after all—"

"He may take them off," Griffin conceded wearily. "Will you stop interrupting? Let me finish."

"All right." She wiped her hands on her apron, then clasped them together in front of her. "I'm listening."

"He will ask you to open your legs." His face was turning all red again, and she didn't think it due to the heat from the oven. "He will climb on top of you with his legs between yours, and sort of lie on top of you—"

"Ah." She could see it now. Almost. "But he's much heavier than I am," she said dubiously.

"Stop worrying. He'll support himself on his elbows. The part of him that will, um . . ."

"Plant the seed?" she supplied helpfully.

"Yes. That part will be hard so he can slide it into you. Don't ask how; it just happens. It's all quite simple, really." He looked relieved, like he was finished.

She took two thick mitts off hooks on the wall. "And then what?" she asked, shoving her hands into them.

"That's it, for the most part." When she stared at him, he raised the bottle for another long swallow. "He will, um, rub against you, more or less, and it will feel good— for you both—and he'll release his seed and it will be over."

"All right." It really did sound quite straightforward, if a little strange. And somewhat boring. "Thank you." She took the first pan out of the oven and set it on the big wooden table. The biscuits looked golden and smelled heavenly. "Would you like one?" she asked. "Just one, mind you, because they're for Hawkridge's—"

"It might hurt," he blurted out. "But just a little. And only the first time. I . . . I thought you should know."

Taking the second pan out, she froze. "Just a little? Are you sure?"

"I'm sure," he said. "In Spain, I slept with—oh, never mind. I'm sure. I'm sorry I even told you, because it's truly nothing to concern yourself with." There was only a tiny bit left in the bottle. He drained it, looking like he wished there were more, and set it down. "Do you believe me? Please say you believe me."

"I believe you." She did. He'd never lied to her before. Teased her and misled her, perhaps, but never lied.

"Are we finished? Can you sleep now?"

"I think so." She put the second pan on the table and slid the mitts off. "Let's have some biscuits first, though. *Two* each. You've earned them."

And then she let him have three.

Chapter Thirty

Tristan could scarcely believe he was a married man.

The wedding had been a simple affair, held in the old family chapel, witnessed not only by Alexandra's siblings and three female cousins, but the effigies of her ancestors dating back to the fourteenth century. When the minister asked if anyone present could show just cause why he and Alexandra should not be lawfully joined together, Tristan had half expected a five-hundred-year-old marble statue to pop up, sword and shield in hand, and take exception.

After all, it took a lot of nerve for a disgraced man like him to wed a lovely, proper Chase daughter.

He'd practically held his breath until the ceremony was over, until they'd shared a kiss that was decorous and chaste but set his blood on fire nonetheless. And then he *still* didn't quite believe she was his wife. And he couldn't decide whether their marriage was a dream come true, or—under the circumstances—a nightmare gone bad.

The wedding breakfast—which was actually a luncheon—had been a haze of delicious food mixed with feminine chatter and laughter. Alexandra, he'd been unable to help noticing, had spent a lot of time looking at him and very little time eating her meal. The latter wasn't all that surprising. His own stomach felt a bit sour from worry paired with exhaustion.

And anticipation.

His gaze kept drifting to the low, square neckline of Alexandra's simple wedding dress. She looked beautiful in the white lace, but he could barely wait to untie the pale blue satin sash and get her out of it.

Tonight he'd make her his.

That truth didn't quite hit him until they were in the barouche he'd borrowed from Griffin, making their way toward Hawkridge and hoping to arrive before dark.

It was a warm day with no threat of rain, so they'd left the top down to enjoy the setting sun. It was fortunate there were only two of them traveling, since Alexandra's luggage took up all the remaining room. In fact, Tristan couldn't even stretch his legs out. But with her seated beside him, snuggled against him, he decided that was but a minor inconvenience.

She yawned, daintily covering her mouth with a gloved hand.

He took it to draw off the glove. "You're sleepy," he said, keeping his voice low so Griffin's coachman couldn't hear.

She swallowed nervously as he slipped the silk from her fingers. "I was up most of the night." With her free hand, she motioned toward a covered basket perched carefully on top of her other belongings. "I made coriander biscuits for your staff."

Removing her second glove, he stifled a smile. Such a gesture was all but unheard of, but so very Alexandra. "They're certain to be surprised."

"Pleasantly surprised, I hope."

"I have no doubt." He pressed a kiss to her bare palm. Carefully. His bottom lip was still tender where Griffin had bashed him in the teeth. But he'd have endured any pain to hear the rough hitch of her breath.

Smiling into her palm, he kissed it again. "I wish I'd known you were baking. I would have kept you company."

"Griffin did, instead," she told him, obviously struggling to appear unaffected. "He was rather cheerful for a bloody and bruised man."

He nodded, completely understanding. "In an odd way, it felt good to fight."

"'Odd' is an apt description. How can hurting each other feel good?"

"I cannot explain it. You'd have to be a man to understand." He kissed her palm once more, then flicked it gently with his tongue, smiling to himself when he felt her shiver.

Recovering her composure, she slanted him a curious glance. "He said he hit you first."

His smile spread into a grin so wide it hurt. "But I got the better of him, did I not?"

"You look rather the worse for wear yourself." She ran gentle fingers over his bruised jaw and across his sore lip, then blinked and snatched back her hand, apparently surprised to find herself touching him so boldly in public. "Although the black eye Griffin woke up with this morning was more colorful."

"He was suffering from the headache this morning, too, I do believe."

"*That* was because he drank half a bottle of Madeira." Her smile was the fond smile of a sister. "Why did he hit you?"

"Because I told him to."

She blinked up at him. "Whyever would you do that?"

"Another thing you'd have to be a man to understand."

Shaking her head, she looked back toward the road. Her hair, which had been covered by a lace veil for the ceremony, was very simply dressed. Several strands had blown loose. Sweeping the baby hairs off her neck, he leaned closer to kiss her nape.

She shivered again, not hiding it this time. He laid a hand on her cheek to turn her face toward him and brushed his lips across hers.

"The coachman," she whispered.

"He's not watching." He wished they had taken a closed carriage. This ride was beginning to seem like the longest of his life.

"He has only to turn his head."

"We're allowed to kiss. We're married."

She blushed and looked down. "Yes, we are," she said, twisting the wide gold band on her finger. "I didn't expect you'd have a ring on such short notice."

"On the way back from Canterbury, I stopped home to pick it up."

"It fits me perfectly." She rubbed the plain surface, burnished from years of wear. "Is it old?"

"Very. A family heirloom," he said, reaching to gently pull it off. "There are names and dates inside." He handed it to her so she could see.

"So many!" She held it up to the setting sun, squinting at the tiny engraved letters. "Henry and Elizabeth, 1579. James and Sarah, 1615. William and Anne, 1645. Randal and Lily, 1677." She looked up at him, her eyes shining. "And more. So many generations."

Such a long, noble line whose reputation he'd destroyed. And now, Alexandra's and her family's, too.

He wouldn't think about that, he decided as his gaze drifted to her lips. Maybe tomorrow he would think about those things, but not now. He wanted her, and she wanted him . . . Before reality intruded, the least he could do was give her a lovely wedding night to remember. The wedding night she deserved.

He would be kind and gentle, and he would do his best to put her at ease. Perhaps this marriage was ill fated, but they would both have tonight.

When she clenched the ring in her fist, he smiled. "I'll have our names and date added the next time we're in London. You don't mind that it's old?"

"Sweet heaven, no." She slipped it back on her finger possessively. "I cannot imagine a ring more wonderful."

Knowing how she valued tradition, he'd hoped she'd feel that way. But he hadn't been sure. "I'm glad," he told her, pleased.

She leaned her head on his shoulder. "Do you suppose all the other wearers were happy?"

He shrugged. "I haven't the faintest idea."

"I think they were," she said decisively. "And we will be, too," she added through a yawn.

He wished he could be so confident.

He wasn't at all sure that she'd adjust well to his isolated life. That she wouldn't come to resent him. That she'd retain her calm assurance without the stamp of society's approval.

That he wouldn't unknowingly do her harm.

That, in the long run, he wouldn't lose her.

Her family would always be there for her, and eventually she could decide to run back into their comforting arms. There she could make a different life for herself, perhaps including a discreet affair or two. Husbands and wives living apart were all too common among the aristocracy.

Her head felt heavy against his sore shoulder. He reached up to stroke her hair, welcoming the dull ache, because it meant that she was his, at least for now. Because frightened as he was, he couldn't bring himself to be sorry. Not now—not with the sun sinking quickly and their wedding night just over the horizon.

"Tris?" she murmured sleepily.

"Hmm?"

"I love you."

His stomach clenched. His fingers tangled in her tresses and stilled. Not *I think I'm in love with you*, but *I love you*. Three simple words said with a quiet conviction he would never, ever have. Such deep emotion was beyond him.

She fell asleep waiting for the response he couldn't give.

Chapter Thirty-one

"We're almost home," Alexandra heard softly in her ear.

She startled awake, lifting her head to look around. The road they were on followed the Thames, and as they turned off it and started up a wide drive, Hawkridge Hall came into view. Although it wasn't a castle like Cainewood, the symmetrical H-shaped building looked large and imposing, three stories of red brick.

The very sight of it brought the truth crashing down. She'd spent the past day in a haze of disbelief, but now her new home loomed before her. A new place. A new situation . . . one that had cost her family their reputation.

Tris squeezed her hand as they approached. "What do you think?"

Sweet heaven, she loved him. She swallowed hard, resolving to put the negative thoughts away—for tonight, at least. It was her wedding night. How long had she dreamed of this night with him, never daring to hope it might actually happen?

Besides, she was determined to prove Tris was innocent so her sisters wouldn't be affected.

"Very impressive," she replied with a smile. She was *not* taking her happiness at the expense of her family.

Not in the long run, anyway. She just needed a week or two to set everything to rights. "Is the house very old?"

"Seventeenth century, down to the furniture." He smiled at her puzzled expression. "You'll see when we get inside."

As they skirted the stone figure of a river god in the center of the circular drive, the arched front door opened. Servants poured out onto the two sets of stone steps, their expressions a mixture of curiosity and welcome.

Alexandra watched as they arranged themselves carefully, men along the left and women on the right. "They knew we were coming?"

"I told them yesterday, when I stopped by to get your ring and my wedding clothes. I suspect they've been in a frenzy since then, getting the house all ready for a new mistress."

She disengaged her hand to reach forward and grab her basket. "I hope they'll like me."

"They'll love you." He turned her face toward him and pressed a kiss to her lips, quick but heartfelt. "They won't be able to help themselves."

Seeing grins spread on several of the staff's faces, she blushed wildly. And wished he'd said *he* wouldn't be able to help loving her. She'd have to give him time. She was determined to knock down that wall around him, but it looked like she'd have to do it brick by brick.

Another project for the coming weeks.

Directly in front of the door and all those smiling faces, the carriage rolled to a halt. A footman rushed to help Alexandra down. "Welcome to Hawkridge Hall, my lady."

"Thank you, . . . ?"

"John," Tris provided as he climbed out behind her. "Uncle Harold called all the footmen John."

"Well, that's just plain silly." Here, finally, she felt in her element. She knew how to handle a household staff. She reached into her basket. "Would you care for a coriander biscuit? And pray, what is your given name?"

"Ernest," the man said, looking at the biscuit in his gloved hand as though he'd never seen one before. "Thank you, my lady."

"Thank *you*, Ernest." She started up the wide stone steps, where the butler waited, looking very stiff and serious.

Tris came up beside her, taking her arm. "This is Hastings," he said by way of introduction. "I couldn't run this place without him."

Gray-haired Hastings was older than Boniface and not nearly as pretty. But hearing Tris's praise, his stern features relaxed, revealing a pleasant face with brown eyes. "Welcome, my lady."

"Why, thank you, Hastings." She smiled, handing him a biscuit before heading for the first of a half-dozen footmen lined up beside him, all dressed in blue livery. "And your name is?"

"Will. Welcome, my lady."

"I'm so pleased to be here, Will." She handed him a biscuit and moved on. "And you are . . . ?"

"Ted. Welcome to Hawkridge Hall."

She reached for another biscuit. "Thank you, Ted."

"John," the next man said. When she gave him a dubious glance along with his biscuit, he added, "It truly is John, my lady. My father was John, and his father before him."

"A fine name," she assured him. "So long as it belongs to you."

It turned out there were *two* Johns among the footmen. After Alexandra met the rest of the butler's staff and a complete set of outdoor servants, another man stepped out of the house. Dressed like a perfect gentleman, he was tall and big boned. He had a wide nose, full lips, and skin the color of a moonless night.

"My valet," Tris said quietly, obviously noting her surprise.

Though she'd never spoken with a black man before, she went up to him unhesitatingly. "Would you care for a coriander biscuit, Mr. . . . ?"

"Vincent. Just Vincent. I have no second name." His deep voice and musical accent made her think of palm trees swaying on a beach. "Welcome to Hawkridge Hall, my lady. My master is bound to be in better spirits with you here."

"I hope so," she told him, mentally filing the interesting tidbit that Tris's valet thought he'd been in poor spirits of late. "Thank you."

Vincent smiled, displaying a mouth full of large, white teeth. He was impeccably groomed and well mannered, and she liked him very much. But although it was common for servants to call their employers master and mistress, his use of the term, coupled with his lack of a surname, made her wonder if he was a slave.

She turned to Tris, unable to picture him as a man who would own another. With a cryptic smile, he took her arm to cross her over to the women's side.

Her questions would have to wait for later.

"My indispensable housekeeper," he said. "Mrs. Oliver."

A short, slight older woman with pink cheeks and sparkling chocolate eyes, Mrs. Oliver bobbed Alexandra a curtsy. "If you don't mind me saying so, my lady, we are so pleased that Lord Hawkridge has wed."

"He was lonely," Alexandra said softly.

Mrs. Oliver darted Tris a glance. "Yes."

"Thank you for taking such good care of him."

She beamed. "I expect you'll do that now."

"I'm going to try my best." Alexandra handed Mrs. Oliver a biscuit and moved on.

Although the housemaids had all been called Mary, only one bore that actual name. There were so many that Alexandra despaired of remembering them all as she worked her way down the line, smiling and exchanging pleasantries.

A middle-aged maid named Peggy bobbed a curtsy as she accepted a biscuit. "Will you be needing a lady's maid, my lady?"

She looked kind and friendly, with pale green eyes

and a mop of slightly graying brown curls beneath her starched cap. Alexandra returned her smile. "Why, yes, as a matter of fact. I shared my maid with my two sisters." She looked to Mrs. Oliver for approval, and when the older woman nodded, turned back to Peggy. "Would you like the position?"

"I should be honored, my lady. I served the last Lady Hawkridge. I am very good with hair."

"I'm very pleased to hear that," Alexandra assured her and moved on to meet everyone else.

When the introductions were finally complete, she handed her basket to the cook, a plump woman in her forties with a button of a nose and pale blond hair pulled back in a severe bun. "Will you all share the rest, Mrs. Pawley? And I hope you won't mind me invading your kitchen now and again. I do adore making sweets."

Mrs. Pawley's merry blue eyes looked surprised, but she quickly hid that with a smile. "I do adore eating sweets, my lady."

"Then we should get along famously," Alexandra said.

Tris took her by the hand. "Shall I show you the house?"

She'd forgotten to replace her gloves, and her fingers tingled in his, reminding her of what was to come tonight. The servants hurried past them, returning to their jobs, as she stepped into her new home for the first time.

The entry led straight into the great hall, a beautiful rectangular room with a floor of black and white marble squares. Above Alexandra's head, a large octagonal opening in the ceiling was railed all around, so those standing above could see down to where she stood. It lent a height and grandeur to the room that made it that much more impressive.

Before she could say as much, though, a huge dog came bounding down the stairs. It slid across the marble floor, jarring their hands apart as it rammed straight into Tris.

"Oof!" he said with a laugh. "This is Rex. Rex, your new mistress. Shake."

Fawn colored with a black mask and ears, Rex obediently raised the most enormous paw Alexandra had ever seen. She shook it, wondering if it were her imagination or if the canine looked mistrustful. "He must be twice my weight! You never said you had a dog."

"He's not my dog. He came with the house."

Rex was trotting happy circles around him. "He seems to have adopted you. Did your uncle name him, then?"

"Yes. But it's not as though he had a choice. According to family lore, there has always been a mastiff named Rex at Hawkridge Hall."

"And why is that?"

"I asked the same question, but Uncle Harold didn't know. That didn't stop him from naming this one Rex, though. The Nesbitts are big on tradition."

Looking around the room, she could see what he meant by that as well as his earlier comment that the house was seventeenth century "down to the furniture." Indeed, although the various tables and chairs were lovingly cared for—beautifully carved, polished to a high sheen, and reupholstered in rich fabrics—they were heavy pieces compared to modern furniture. And the gorgeous paneling on the walls, though recently refinished, obviously dated from earlier times as well. "Goodness. Is everything just the same as when the house was built?"

"Tradition," he repeated with a smile. "Though if you look carefully, you'll see some recent improvements."

Alexandra's gaze followed his gesture to a lamp attached to the wall, containing a yellowish open flame protected from drafts by a glass chimney. Her mouth dropped open in astonishment. "Gas lighting? Indoors?" Although in recent years gas was increasingly being used to illuminate London's streets, she'd never seen it in a house.

"Yes," Tris said proudly. "Installed it myself. With help from two of the Johns." He shook his head. "Make that one John and Ted."

She smiled, appreciating his willingness to adapt—not

just his attitude toward the servants, but to the latest advancements. She supposed she shouldn't find it surprising that a man who employed progressive farming techniques, a man who built things like pumps, would also implement gas lighting. "Did you design the lamps yourself, too?"

"No, but I believe I've improved on the original design some." He showed her the key mechanism by which she could turn the gas on and off or adjust the height of the flame, and he watched her practice until he was satisfied she understood. "You catch on quickly."

"It's not difficult. Where does the gas come from?"

"I'm burning coal in a closed iron vessel outdoors, a safe distance from the house. The resulting gas is piped inside."

"How very clever."

He shrugged. "This is a small system, conceived as an experiment of sorts. Since it proved successful, I am currently building a large gasworks that will be used to supply the entire village. When it's finished, all the streets and businesses—and homes, should people like— will be lit by gas. And once that is complete, I hope to form a group to pursue an enterprise wherein we approach larger towns and cities to build gasworks and supply them via gas mains."

He was so different from the other men she knew. "A gentleman does not aspire to enterprise," she teased. "Such an undertaking would limit his time for amusements."

Too late she realized he wouldn't be welcome in any gentlemen's clubs or the other places such men went to amuse themselves. But he seemed as determined as she was to avoid thinking of such unpleasantness tonight, because he just shrugged again in a genial manner. "I'm afraid I am tainted by my common roots."

She loved his dry humor, but her smile was at least half due to relief. "You do like having the newest, don't you?"

"Tradition is fine, but progress can also be good. And progress will march on, so we may as well be part of it." He took her hand again. "Let me show you the rest of the house."

With Rex following at their heels, Tris led her through the ground-floor rooms, teasing her palm with his thumb all the while so she could hardly pay any attention. She gleaned little more than general impressions, and even those were muddled. The main parlor looked pretty and comfortable, the dining room had a beautiful two-toned parquet floor, and the study—which, oddly enough, was accessed through the dining room—had a heavy, ancient-looking desk. There were also some lovely guest rooms and Tris's uncle's rooms—which Tris seemed reluctant to go into.

"I can see them later," she told him. "Where am *I* going to sleep?"

For truly, beautiful as the house was, having blanked her mind of worrisome concerns she could think of little else besides sharing one of these rooms with him tonight.

Finally he led her up the massive oak staircase, a feature clearly built to impress. Rex bounded up ahead, his huge body taking the wooden steps with amazing ease. Alexandra skimmed her free hand along the polished wood handrail, the panels beneath composed of boldly carved cannons, muskets, lances, and other trophies of war, all highlighted by sparkling gold leaf.

"Goodness," she asked Tris, "were your ancestors very savage?"

He laughed as they reached the landing. "Not that I'm aware." He rubbed the dog's giant head. "Although I understand this house was used as a base of operations to plot against Cromwell in the Civil War."

The next room looked to be a gallery of sorts. "The round gallery," Tris clarified.

It wasn't really round, but more oblong. It was a room mainly used to access others, sort of a very wide corridor with a hole in the middle of the floor—a large, railed octagonal opening where one could see down to the great hall below. But she didn't take time to look, as she was staring at the paintings on the walls.

"Corinna is going to die when she sees this," she said.

He brushed a loose strand of hair off her cheek. "Hmm?"

"You know she paints." She gestured to the many gilt-framed canvases. "Rembrandt, Van Dyck, Rubens—"

"That one was painted by one of Rubens's students."

"Regardless. She'll sit here and study these for hours. She'll forget to eat."

"Like you at our wedding breakfast?" he asked with a tender smile. "What were *you* studying, sweetheart?"

You. But she wouldn't say that, even though he'd just melted her heart by calling her sweetheart. "I simply have a ladylike appetite," she informed a staid Dutch woman in one of the paintings.

He laughed and took her elbow, guiding her into a corridor, Rex following close behind.

Peggy was in the next room, already unpacking Alexandra's things. "Enjoying your tour, my lady?"

"Very much." Alexandra blinked at the sumptuous furnishings. Behind a balustrade in the French style, an enormous state bed sat on a raised parquet dais. Hangings of rich turquoise were heavily embroidered with gold thread, and great poufs of matching ostrich feathers crowned the bed's four corner posts. The ceiling was elaborate painted plasterwork, the walls hung with heavy, old tapestries.

"It looks fit for a queen," she breathed.

"Queen Catharine of Braganza, Charles II's wife," Tris confirmed. "It was decorated for her visit."

That was all too easy to believe. The streaked marble fireplace was adorned with gold crowns. "Is this to be my room?"

"Hell, no," Tris said.

Peggy didn't even hesitate, let alone stop unpacking. "My lord, Mrs. Oliver wanted your new lady to have the best Hawkridge has to offer. The last Lady Hawkridge enjoyed this room very much."

What a saucebox, Alexandra thought, although she supposed that if Peggy were a shy one, she wouldn't have so boldly asked for the position of lady's maid. But although the chamber was gorgeous, she couldn't imagine being comfortable here. Goodness, what if she spilled something on Queen Catharine's antique counterpane? "It's lovely," she said tactfully, "but—"

"Lady Hawkridge will be sharing my rooms," Tris interrupted. "While we dine, please move her things."

"But—"

"You may ask two footmen to assist you with the trunks. While you're downstairs, please inform Mrs. Pawley that we'd like a light supper in half an hour." He took Alexandra's hand to draw her from the room.

"That was a bit harsh," she said once they were out of earshot. "I know she defied you, but—"

"I've never liked that one."

"Why have you kept her on, then?"

"She came here as a young girl. What kind of man would I be if I turned her out?" He drew her down the corridor, Rex trotting by his other side. "Are you certain you want her for your maid?"

"Since I've already given her the position, I'll wait and see how we get along. As long as you don't mind."

"Whatever makes you happy," he said, squeezing her hand. "Stay, Rex." As they entered another chamber, he closed the door behind them. "My rooms," he announced. "And yours, too, as soon as Peggy moves you in here."

A huge bed dominated the space—an old-style four-poster hung with dark blue velvet bordered in yellow silk. The walls were hung with blue velvet panels on a yellow background, and, set before the fireplace, two cushioned armchairs were upholstered in blue-and-yellow striped fabric. "It's beautiful," she said. "And much cozier than the queen's bedchamber."

"I didn't want you in a separate room," he said low, making butterflies flutter in her middle. Then he grinned. "Although I was half tempted to leave you there as revenge for putting me in your gold chamber."

"Thank you for resisting." She heard the heavy thumps of Rex padding away down the corridor. "If you don't allow him in here, where does he sleep?"

"Given his size, I'd say anywhere he wants. But a man is entitled to a bit of privacy, don't you think?" He pulled her closer. "Besides, he snores something terrible."

She laughed, then suddenly stopped when he gathered her against him. Heat erupted inside her, spreading through her body as his lips descended on hers. He brushed her mouth with aching tenderness, then settled into place like he belonged there.

Clearly he did.

He'd kissed her before, of course—several times. But until today, they'd been stolen, forbidden kisses. And the two today—during their wedding and in the carriage afterward—had been barely more than a whisper of lips.

This time there was no one watching. This time there were no nagging feelings telling her it was wrong. This time there was blessed solitude, the sanctity of marriage, and the thrilling, compelling pressure of Tris's mouth claiming hers.

She sank into his arms, into his kiss, into the impossibly wonderful truth that he was hers.

He kissed her lower lip, her upper, then traced a line with his tongue between them. She sighed and opened her mouth, inviting him in. His hands wandered down her back and settled on her bottom, feeling oh so scandalously warm as he drew her more snugly against him.

A brisk knock sounded, and the door swung open. She and Tris jerked apart, her head swimming with desire.

"In here," Peggy directed. Alexandra struggled to steady herself while four footmen marched in carrying two large trunks. "Through the sitting room to the dressing room," Peggy added briskly.

Alexandra had been so focused on Tris, she hadn't even realized there *was* a sitting room or a dressing room. She stared at him now, breathless, her body still yearning for something she couldn't put a name to.

Her new husband's eyes reflected her own frustration. He sighed and took her arm. "Shall we have supper while she puts away your things?"

Chapter Thirty-two

Light supper at Hawkridge turned out to be a three-course meal. But for the second time today, Alexandra found herself unable to much.

Still reeling from the hasty events, hunger was the last thing on her mind. She sipped sparingly from a glass of Hawkridge's surprisingly fine wine and managed a few spoonfuls of the delicious shellfish soup, but she surreptitiously fed Rex bites of her cornish hen and carrots, reaching under the dining room's long cedarwood table and praying his huge jaws wouldn't snap off her fingers along with the food.

While she picked at her potato pudding—which, unfortunately, she had no way to feed to the dog—she and Tris discussed the staff. She learned Peggy wasn't the only servant long in residence at Hawkridge Hall. To the contrary, many of the staff had been born here. The butler, Hastings, had inherited the post from his father; Mrs. Oliver's mother had held the housekeeper's keys before her; and the groundskeeper's great-great-grandfather had first laid out the gardens. Likewise, many of the lower servants' families had served Hawkridge for years.

"Tradition," Alexandra said with a smile.

"Mrs. Pawley is Hawkridge's first female cook in generations, however." Tris, of course, was eating like the proverbial horse. Nothing—not even the upheaval of a hasty marriage—affected a man's appetite. "Her father was the cook, and his father before him. When Pawley failed to sire any sons to whom he could pass his culinary skills, he trained his daughter instead. Uncle Harold was a mite uneasy about that."

So Mrs. Pawley wasn't married, Alexandra reflected as a footman removed her plate and replaced it with the sweet course. The cook still bore her father's name, the "Mrs." only a courtesy often extended to upper servants. "Your uncle eventually accepted her, though?"

"During the Peace of Amiens in 1802, when it became evident her father's retirement was imminent, Uncle Harold sent her to Paris to study under an acknowledged master." Tris dug into his strawberry trifle. "Male, of course. Apparently, being French-trained made up for being the wrong gender."

"Her food is delicious."

"I'm sure Rex thinks so," he teased with a grin.

The mastiff was snoring contentedly in a corner of the dining room. Alexandra pushed her trifle around on her plate, trying to make it look smaller so as not to offend the cook.

"I shall have to tell Mrs. Pawley you cannot eat strawberries," Tris said.

"It doesn't matter. I'm not hungry, in any case." He was almost finished, and she still hadn't brought up the servant she found most curious. "Tell me about Vincent."

He sipped his wine, raising one brow at her over the glass's rim. "Do I strike you as a man who would own a slave?"

Her cheeks heated, but she lifted her chin. "You cannot blame me for wondering." Though new slave trade had been outlawed since 1808 in all British territories, there was nothing in the law to prevent one man from owning another. Many in England still did, particularly those who had plantations in the West Indies and brought their slaves with them when they came home.

With a sigh, Tris set down his glass. "Vincent served me well during the years I spent in Jamaica. I bought him and freed him before I left."

She released the breath she hadn't realized she'd been holding. "That was a wonderful thing to do."

"Merely decent. He was the best valet I'd ever had, and I cannot countenance one man owning another."

"But your uncle could."

He shrugged, clearly ambivalent. "Uncle Harold inherited the plantation—and its slaves—as part of his wife's dowry. Under his ownership, the slaves were treated well, and during the time I spent there and after I returned, we talked many times of freeing them. He wasn't particularly comfortable owning men. But he feared the financial repercussions of setting them free, and he was of the opinion that it was only a matter of time—a short time, in the scheme of things—before legislation was enacted that would emancipate them all and take the decision out of his hands. I agreed with him on that point."

"There has been no legislation."

"There will be. Soon." He polished off the last of his trifle and sat back, lifting his glass. "Uncle Harold wanted to wait. He felt sorry for the slaves' plight, but he feared they'd be in a worse situation as free men on a plantation that could no longer compete successfully in the marketplace."

"And you agreed."

"In theory, perhaps. In practice, no." He paused for a long swallow of the rich wine. "The first action I took upon inheriting the marquessate was freeing all our slaves in Jamaica. I wished the ship carrying the missive strong winds and smooth seas. I could not stand the thought of owning men—regardless of the consequences."

She'd known he was a good man. Feeling a tightness in her chest, she reached across the corner of the table to take his hand. "And what have those consequences been?"

"Making a profit has proven difficult," he admitted quietly. "But does it matter? There are more important things than property values and income. My honor and integrity come first." He squeezed her fingers. "A man has to live with himself if he's to sleep at night."

Sleep. She'd wager he hadn't noticed his own reference, but this, she knew, was not a man who would murder his uncle. Not even unknowingly in his sleep.

He drew a deep breath and released it, setting down his wineglass. "Are you finished?"

She nodded, wondering why she felt so unsettled. She knew she'd made the right choice in marrying this man. She'd firmly put off any thoughts of the repercussions it would have on her family. And she couldn't be worrying about the evening. Griffin had made what would happen sound very simple and straightforward.

But she found herself unaccountably relieved when Tris stood and asked, "Would you like to see more of the house?"

"That would be lovely," she said with a grateful smile.

As they exited the room, Rex rose with a gigantic yawn. He trotted after them across the great hall, up the stairs, and through the gallery with the open floor. Alexandra resisted pausing to gawk again at the famous paintings. At the other end of the gallery, a door led to a large, square room with gilded paneling on the walls and various chairs and sofas set about.

"The north drawing room," Tris said.

"It's beautiful." She walked over to an exquisite harpsichord, its case inlaid with multicolored woods. Sitting on the petit-point stool, she hit a few keys experimentally. "Johannes Ruckers," she read out loud from where the maker's name was painted above the keyboard.

"Has he a good reputation?" Tris asked from behind her.

"I haven't the slightest idea. This looks very old. I don't expect his company is making instruments anymore."

"Can you play it?"

"Probably." Since the harpsichord was much narrower than a pianoforte, the keyboard was split in two, with one half over the other. She swiveled on the stool to face him. "I shall enjoy trying it, but is there no pianoforte?"

He shook his head. "I will get one for you."

"There's no need—"

"I want you to be happy here." He raised her to stand and pressed a warm kiss to her lips.

Rex barked. His tail thumped the wooden floor, sounding much like a slap.

"I don't think he likes me kissing you," Tris observed.

"He's jealous. Until now you were all his."

"He's not mine. I told you—"

"That's not what *he* thinks."

Tris stared hard at the dog, opened his mouth, then shut it. "Well, he's going to have to get used to sharing me. Come see the long gallery."

Rex followed them through another door into a long tunnel of a room. A room that called for quiet. Woven matting on the parquet floor muffled their footsteps. Large paintings in heavy gilt frames were spaced evenly along the dark paneled walls.

Even Rex kept quiet as they walked along slowly, gazing at the pictures. The painters here weren't important; it was their subjects that gained them entry. Gentlemen in silks and velvets, ladies in stiff, white neck ruffs.

"Some are older than the house," Alexandra observed softly. "Are they family?"

"Nesbitts, one and all."

A few of the names were familiar from inside her ring. Henry and Elizabeth. James and Sarah. She stopped to study a canvas whose brass plaque read "William and Anne." The painting showed that particular Lord Hawkridge standing behind his seated lady, who held a white kitten on her lap. Her blue eyes looked kind, and Alexandra could almost see her graceful fingers stroking the silky, purring cat.

"They look happy," she decided.

The next couple, Randal and Lily, looked happy as

well. "1680," she read off the plaque. The man had gray eyes, like Tris's. His hair looked like Tris's, too, but longer, and a huge dog that looked just like Rex sat at his feet. A small child stood at his side, still in skirts so she couldn't tell its gender. The man's hand rested on the shoulder of his pretty, dark-haired lady, who beamed a smile at the baby in her arms.

Alexandra smiled in response. "Everyone here has been happy. I can feel it, can't you? This is a good house. A real home." History and tradition fairly oozed from the walls.

"My uncle wasn't happy," Tris disagreed quietly.

"Not after his family died, of course. But before?"

"He was happy," Tris conceded. He smiled and gave her another kiss, short but heartfelt, clearly unwilling to promise that they would be happy, too.

She would swear she heard Rex snort.

"The library is through here," Tris said.

It was a lofty, two-story chamber with dark shelving crammed with important-looking books. Alexandra walked over to pull one out and flip idly through it, the old pages crackling as she turned them.

"You don't want to read now, do you?" Stepping up behind her, Tris bent to kiss the side of her neck.

"Not really." Tingling warmth spread from where his lips met her skin. He reached around her to take the book from her hands and set it on a small table, and she turned in his arms to meet his mouth.

Rex's bark echoed up to the laurel wreath in the center of the high white ceiling.

"See why I lock him out of my rooms?" Tris asked with a sigh.

"I hope it's not because you like to kiss women in there."

"Only one," he said with a soft smile that made something kindle deep in her belly. "Shall we escape the beast and go there now?"

Her heart thumped harder than Rex's tail. "Are there not more rooms I haven't seen?"

"None that cannot wait until tomorrow." He skimmed his fingertips over her cheek, ignoring Rex's protest. The pad of his thumb brushed her lips. "And *I* cannot wait any longer."

That simple statement made her heart give a little leap so sudden it made her press a hand to her chest. A faint smile curving his bruised lips, he lifted that hand and brushed his mouth over the knuckles, then laced his fingers through hers.

Rex dogged their steps all the way back through the long gallery, the north drawing room, and the round gallery. Tris quickened their pace into the corridor and past the queen's bedchamber. By the time they reached his rooms, they were running. Alexandra laughed at the absurdity. When they finally darted through his bedroom door and he whirled and practically slammed it in the dog's face, she laughed even harder.

Rex whined once, barked three times, then padded away, his big feet thudding with each step.

"He knows when to give up," she observed with more giggles.

"You find this humorous?" Tris returned with mock severity. Without waiting for her to answer, he dragged her into his arms and silenced her with a kiss.

It was a kiss of desperate tenderness, a kiss that quickly escalated, igniting heat with its demand. She wondered if the pressure hurt his swollen mouth, but she couldn't bring herself to care. The scent of him filled her senses: fresh air and soap and that elusive something she thought of as him. He tasted of Tris and the wine he'd drunk with dinner, and she thought she'd like to taste him, to kiss him, forever.

When he finally released her, she just stood and stared at him, unsteady on her feet.

"You're not laughing anymore," he said with a smug smile.

"Laughing? I think I forgot to even breathe."

The smile widened as he walked away to turn down the gas lamps. There were four of them mounted on the walls, two on each side of the room. Even battered and bruised, he moved easily, with an innate grace, so tall and handsome in the wedding outfit his valet had cobbled together, the white breeches hugging his muscled thighs.

She could scarcely believe he was hers.

"There," he said when the room was bathed in a softer, hazier glow. "Is that not nicer?"

"Yes." Watching his gaze roam over her, she smoothed the white lace skirt of the dress she'd borrowed from Corinna. "Thank you."

He shrugged out of his black tailcoat and draped it over the back of one of the striped chairs before he started untying his cravat. As his long fingers worked at the knot, she noticed his tanned hands, their backs lightly sprinkled with hair that glowed golden in the gaslight. She wanted to walk closer and help him, but she didn't trust her knees. She was forgetting to breathe again. After all those years of hopeless dreaming, to think he was really hers . . .

It was unbelievable. She swallowed hard—so hard she feared he had heard it.

"Are you nervous?" he asked, sitting on the chair.

He *had* heard it. And misunderstood. "Not really. Griffin told me what to expect."

He looked a bit startled at that news. "Did he?"

"Oh, yes."

He tugged off his black pumps and peeled off his white stockings, leaving his feet and well-defined calves as bare as the day he was born. Sweet heaven. If she had to watch him anymore in the act of undressing, she wouldn't be responsible for her actions. "When are you going to leave so I can get ready for bed?" she asked a little shrilly.

He gave her a puzzled smile. "I was planning to get you ready for bed myself."

"Pardon?" That wasn't the way it was supposed to happen. He was supposed to leave her, so she could change into Juliana's pretty nightgown, and then return wearing a dressing gown himself. One that went to the floor and covered all of him. Including his legs, where her gaze seemed to be permanently fastened. "You're supposed to leave so I can prepare myself and wait for you in the bed."

He rose and came close, his silvery eyes narrowed. "Says who?"

"Griffin. Griffin told me—"

"Griffin is a muttonhead." He put his hands on her shoulders. "Turn around."

She did, her gaze falling on the bed. It looked big and soft, and by all indications, he was not going to let her get in it without him. After he untied her sash, she felt his fingers freeing the buttons down her back. Practiced fingers. "You've done this before."

"I have buttons on my own clothes, you know." He managed to sound both evasive and amused. "What else did Griffin tell you?"

"He said it's not like horses—we will do it face-to-face."

"Yes, usually," he said, and before she could ruminate on that, added, "What else?"

Her bodice loosened, and she crossed both hands over her bosom to hold it in place. "He said it would hurt. But just a little, and only the first time."

He swung her back around, his eyes searching hers. "Are you worried about that?"

"Not really."

"Good. I'll go slowly, I promise. If it hurts, just tell me, and I'll stop."

"Thank you," she whispered, caught in the intensity of his gaze.

He raised her hands from her chest to his mouth and placed a warm kiss to the back of one and then the other.

And her dress fell to the floor, revealing her sleeveless linen chemise.

He stepped back, his gaze roaming hungrily over her

half-clothed body. The possessive look in his eyes was more exciting than she could have imagined.

The shiver that ran through her was not from a chill. When he reached for her, she moved closer, raising her face for his kiss. As his mouth claimed hers, she pressed herself against him, feeling all the hard small buttons that ran down the front of his waistcoat.

He was entirely too clothed compared to her. It wasn't fair. Maybe she should do something about that. But that would mean drawing away, perhaps even breaking their kiss, which was making her head swim in the most lovely manner.

She sighed into his mouth as he ran his hands over her back, learning her body through her chemise. Her skin prickled pleasurably everywhere he touched. When his hands drifted lower, skimming her bottom, it took everything she had not to squirm in response. His fingers molded themselves to her rounded curves, cupping to pull her closer—

And froze.

"Tris?" she murmured against his mouth.

"Holy Christ." His voice a husky whisper, he moved his hands experimentally. "Sweetheart, what happened to your drawers?"

Chapter Thirty-three

Obviously shocked at the question, Alexandra pulled away. "I . . . drawers would ruin the lines of my dresses. I never wear them."

"Never?" Tristan imagined all the times they'd been together the last months, going all the way back to their first kiss up on Cainewood's wall walk. Had she not being wearing drawers then? He remembered all the meals when she'd sat beside him, bare bottomed and mere inches away. That time in the library when he'd reached around her, her backside against his front. Walking alone together after the picnic, teaching her to waltz, dancing with her and almost kissing her in the minstrel's gallery . . . Had she never been wearing drawers?

His body reacted to that thought with such violence, it took all he had not to throw her on the bed then and there.

"How about your sisters? Your cousins? The other women of your acquaintance. Do they never wear drawers, either?" He raked a hand through his hair. "Never mind. I don't want to know."

The last thing he needed now, when he'd promised to take things slowly, was visions of being surrounded by women and none of them wearing drawers.

No, forget being surrounded—the thought of Alexandra alone was enough. More than enough. Forget the recollections of the past—how about all the times they'd be together in the future? Would he ever be able to think straight again in her presence?

"A lot of ladies don't wear drawers," she said. "Current fashion being as it is, they would show. And they're still rather new, you know. Some women consider them scandalous. And—"

He stopped her with a kiss. He couldn't stand hearing any more about drawers. Not without finishing this evening a lot sooner than he'd expected.

Her mouth, warm and willing, soon claimed his attention. He'd never known anyone to put as much of herself into a kiss as Alexandra. When she was kissing him, he was convinced she was thinking of nothing and no one else. She matched his every move and made some bold moves of her own. Recalling her shocked hesitation the first time they kissed, he found it hard to reconcile that innocence with the way she was kissing him now.

His pulse quickened as he wondered whether she'd take to lovemaking as rapidly.

He trailed his lips to her delicate chin and continued down the slim column of her throat, lingering in that sensitive place where neck met shoulder. He smiled when he sensed her shiver, then pulled back when he felt her fingers go to the line of tiny buttons on his white waistcoat.

By God, she was learning fast. "You're undressing *me* now?"

Her fingers fumbled. "It seems so." She finally got the waistcoat open and slid her hands underneath and up. The white garment fell down his back to join her frock on the floor. "Shall I fetch you a dressing gown?" she asked, watching avidly as he divested himself of his braces.

"Hmm?"

She skimmed her hands over his thin cambric shirt, making his muscles twitch underneath. "Griffin said you would put on a dressing gown."

"For what, five minutes? I would only take it back off."
She nodded knowingly. "I told him that."

He wasn't at all sure he liked his friend discussing his love life. He did, however, like his friend's sister running her hands all over his torso, even when she grazed bruises that still hurt. "You feel good," she said, her eyes filled with wonder.

He ran his own hands down her sides. "You feel good, too," he told her, his gaze dropping from her intent expression to the swell of her cleavage beneath the plain, low-cut chemise.

The rosy tips of her lovely breasts tightened under his perusal, and her cheeks turned a delicate pink. "I suppose you're not going to lift my nightgown then, either?"

"Pardon?"

"He said when you were ready, you would lift my nightgown."

"What nightgown?" he asked, gesturing at her half-clad form.

"Never mind."

Alexandra swallowed tightly. This wasn't going at all the way Griffin had led her to expect. Despite what she'd said earlier, she was starting to feel a bit nervous. Her legs were trembling. She was grateful when Tris led her to a chair—until he pulled her sideways onto his lap.

She hadn't sat on a man's lap since she was about four years old. Tris's fragrance surrounded her, filling her head with the scents of soap and starch and warm man. He started plucking the pins from her hair. "Do you know," he said, "how long I've dreamed of doing this?"

"How long?" she whispered.

"Too long." He lowered the heavy mass, finger-combing the curls down her back to her waist. "It's beautiful."

"It's terribly unruly."

"I like it."

Somehow he got her shoes and stockings off, and when he rose with her in his arms, cradled against his chest, she was glad of it. For surely she couldn't have walked to the bed, considering her knees had dissolved.

He drew back the covers and laid her gently on the sheets, then straightened to remove the rest of his clothes. As he pulled his shirt over his head, she gasped and reached to touch him, her fingertips brushing the bruises. "Do they hurt?"

He flashed her a wicked grin. "I think you need to kiss them to make them better."

She nodded, thinking that sounded like an excellent plan. In fact, now that he'd given her the idea, she was dying to kiss him all over. Just as soon as he joined her in the bed—

He pushed down his trousers, and she lost her train of thought. She also lost her breath. Her heart stuttered in alarm.

She stared.

Griffin had said that part of Tris would get hard so he could slide it into her, but he'd neglected to say it would also get *big*.

"Sweet heaven," she started—and Tris jumped into bed, pulled the covers over them both, and cut off her sentence with a kiss.

It was a lovely kiss, but it failed to erase her trepidation.

"You're nervous now, aren't you?" he said.

"No. Well, maybe. A little."

"It will fit, sweetheart." He ran a hand down her side and back up. "And remember, I promised to stop if you hurt."

"Yes, you did. Thank you."

He continued slowly stroking her all over through her chemise, which she found rather soothing. Her brother would have warned her if there were a chance of it not working, wouldn't he? And she trusted Tris. Now that she couldn't see that part of his body, she was certain it wasn't as large as she'd thought.

She released a shaky breath. "Are you going to ask me to open my legs now?"

His hand stilled. *"What?"*

"Griffin said that after you kissed me and touched me, you would ask me to open my legs."

"Would you leave Griffin out of this? I really must have a talk with him. He is singularly unimaginative." Heaving a giant sigh, he reached for the hem of her chemise. "Let us get rid of this, shall we?"

"I told him you'd take it off," she said smugly, raising her arms to cooperate.

He dropped the chemise to the floor beside the bed. "Told who?"

"Griffin."

"Enough with Griffin," he demanded, snuggling closer beside her.

"All right." She really couldn't think straight when Tris was this close, anyway. Especially when he was running his hands all over her naked body, leaving a trail of warm goose bumps in their wake. Especially when he licked his way down to her breasts and swirled his tongue all over them and fastened his mouth on an aching peak. Especially when he suckled and nipped and made her wonder if anyone had ever died of too much pleasure.

She wasn't thinking of Griffin then. Nor could she think of him long minutes later, when Tris abandoned her tingling breasts and recaptured her lips with his. Just then, it seemed she couldn't think at all.

Especially when he was brushing his fingers up and down her legs.

Especially when he found a sensitive spot behind her knee.

Especially when he was drawing circles on the insides of her thighs, tiny circles that moved ever closer to that place between them where she felt a hot, growing ache.

He didn't have to ask her to open her legs, because somehow they opened all by themselves. And his hand slid between them, to cup her like he had the night he'd sleepwalked. She gasped, feeling such an exquisite need, she found herself straining against his hand in hope of easing it.

And then he moved his hand, stroking her. The pleasure grew, and the urgency grew along with it, until she heard little mewling moans and realized they were hers. For long, languid minutes he played her body, slick slides of his fingers that brought forth bursts of sensation.

Then he slipped a finger inside her. "Tris!" she cried.

"Hmm?"

That *hmm* was a hum inside her mouth that seemed to spread throughout her body. And it didn't seem to require an answer. Not that she could have answered him, anyway. Not when he was stroking her inside, and her body was responding by *clinging* to his finger. His thumb found a spot so sweet she feared she might scream from sheer excitement. He rubbed that spot as he thrust his finger deeper and kissed her at the same time, his tongue exploring her mouth with movements that matched what he was doing below.

She'd never felt anything like it. She'd never even *imagined* anything like it. Her heart raced, and little spurts of pleasure sprinted all over her body. Tremors shimmered through her, the sweet torture continuing until she thought one more velvet stroke might be her undoing. But she wanted something more. *Needed* something more.

She wasn't sure what, but she suspected it was him.

"Now," she whispered, tearing her mouth from his. "Come inside me now."

A low groan escaped his throat. He moved over her and fit himself between her legs, and she felt him there, poised to enter her, felt him trembling as he tried to hold back. He finally pushed inside, but only a little. Just enough so where their bodies were joined there was a feeling so urgent it made her whimper with anticipation.

"Now," she repeated.

"I don't want to hurt—"

"Now!" She shoved her hips against him, taking him in.

Then froze, still as the stone figure of the river god in the center of their circular drive.

"I'm sorry," he grated out, staying still with her.

"No. It doesn't hurt." It *had* hurt, but only for a moment. Now she was immobilized by sheer wonder. He was large, but he fit, and he felt incredible filling her.

He was *throbbing* inside her.

She shifted, raising her knees a little. He sucked in a breath. Her own breath caught as well, because she'd felt him move within her body, creating a cresting wave of heat.

"You're supposed to move," she informed him.

He released a strangled laugh, pulling out of her a bit. "I suppose Griffin told you that?"

"Forget Griffin," she said and lifted herself to meet his thrust.

The sensation was exquisite. The sheer beauty of it made something tighten in her chest. "Dear God," she whispered, "I hadn't the slightest idea."

"This is only the beginning," he said and moved again.

It seemed awkward at first, but she soon learned how to move with him, gasping when he pulled out and sighing as he settled back in. Gradually their motions gained speed, until she was lost in the rhythm, awash in pure pleasure. The pleasure built and built, and built some more, until, quite suddenly, her body erupted. She arched against him, holding on for dear life as wave after wave swept through her, the sensations so intense they stole her very breath. The sheer release of it was stunning, and became even more so when she felt him shudder within her and heard his low groan of surrender.

He collapsed against her, but his was a warm, welcome weight. It seemed a long time before she managed to come to her senses, to breathe a languid sigh. "I feel very sorry for Griffin," she said at last.

She felt Tris smile against her neck. "Why?"

"He said it would feel good. Can you imagine describing that as *good*?"

"No," he said with an exhausted chuckle as he eased off her. "That is a very insufficient word."

"It was glorious. No, that isn't strong enough to describe it. I don't think the right words exist." Feeling drained and yet somehow better than she ever had before, she snuggled against him, her head on his shoulder.

He pressed a slow, warm kiss to her brow.

"I love you," she whispered.

He squeezed her close and kissed her forehead again much harder, but he didn't respond in kind.

It didn't signify, she decided. He'd shown her how he felt with his body, with his hands, with his cherishing kisses. His experiences in the past had left him reluctant to trust love, and she was sure he wasn't the first man who found it hard to say those three words. She'd just keep telling him, assuring him, and he'd respond in time. Soon.

This marriage may have been precipitated by scandal, but everything was going to work out fine . . . especially after they cleared his name.

In the meantime, she'd content herself with the wonder—the pure pleasure—of simply lying here, skin to skin. She'd never felt another sensation so sublime . . . except perhaps the events of the past hour.

As she drifted off to sleep, she replayed every exquisite moment in her head.

She never had worn Juliana's nightgown. And she'd forgotten to kiss his bruises.

Chapter Thirty-four

GINGERBREAD CAKES

Take three pounds of flour, one pound of sugar, one pound of butter rubbed in very fine, two ounces of ginger beat fine, a large nutmeg grated, then take a pound of treacle, a quarter of a pint of cream, make them warm together, and make up the bread stiff. Wait a while and then make round balls like nuts and bake them on tin-plates in a slack oven.

These are reminiscent of home, and excellent with a good gossip.
—Helena Chase, Countess of Greystone, 1783

Alexandra woke first and watched Tris sleep in the dim early light. His lashes lay dark against his cheeks, making him look young and sweet and vulnerable. His chest rose and fell in a slow, even rhythm, his breath drifting in and out between slightly parted lips.

She breathed along with him. She wanted to do everything with him, but for now, breathing would have to do.

When he opened his eyes, she smiled. "Good morning."

He closed the inches between them and kissed her. A long, sleepy kiss. "A good morning indeed." His seductive smile didn't look young, sweet, or vulnerable in the least. He raised his head to peek at the clock on the oak mantel. "Do you always wake before six? I thought ladies all slept until noon."

"I had a house to run for my brother. And now another one for you."

"For us," he corrected, making her heart turn over in her chest. He reached for her.

"Wait," she said. "I owe you something."

He only raised a brow. Then laughed when she threw back the covers and began kissing every one of his bruises, slowly, one by one.

His skin tasted divine, tinged with a hint of salt and the faint, musky scent of last night's coupling. When her lips brushed a fading mark that sat above his heart, she could hear it beating wildly in a rhythm to match her own. By the time she was finished, they were both short of breath.

"Better?" she asked, her voice thick and unsteady.

"Immensely," he assured her, gathering her close.

Then he kissed her again, his body still overwarm from sleep. He skimmed a hand down her naked back, over her bottom, between her legs, where she was already slick and ready. But he took his time, matching lazy kisses with slow, gentle caresses. When he finally slid into her, she sighed with relief and let him carry them both to bliss.

She'd never slept nude, but she thought she could get used to it. She'd always risen immediately upon awakening—but she thought she could get used to lingering, too.

He rang for Vincent and Peggy, and by seven they were both dressed and in the dining room.

Alexandra smiled at him across the breakfast table. "I cannot believe how happy I am."

"I am glad." His smile more tentative than hers, Tris sipped from a steaming cup of coffee.

"What shall we do today?" She lifted the pretty little jam pot that matched the crested breakfast service, hoping for marmalade but setting it down when she saw the contents were red.

"I believe those are cherry preserves. I asked Vincent to tell Mrs. Pawley you cannot eat strawberries."

"Oh!" She dipped her knife and happily coated her toast. "Would you care for some?"

"I cannot abide anything sweet in the morning." He spread butter on his own toast, then speared a bite of eggs. "In answer to your earlier question, I'll need to make a circuit of the estate today, having been away for a while. There are matters that will require my attention. And I must spend some time at the new gasworks; I've left the builders long without my supervision. Would you care to accompany me?"

Alexandra hesitated, realizing suddenly that what happened in the bedroom was the easy part of marriage. Finding the rhythm of their days was going to be more difficult. She had no right to expect a honeymoon following such a hasty wedding, and she suspected Tris would rather not be distracted as he went about his business. And although she wanted to see everything at Hawk- ridge, this house was her domain.

"If you wouldn't mind," she finally said, "I'd prefer to stay here. I have much to learn to run this household."

"You have Mrs. Oliver for that."

"It is still my responsibility to oversee everything properly." She set down her teacup. She had another matter to broach, and there was no sense putting it off.

But as he bit into his toast, she found herself putting it off anyway and looking about the room instead. "How unusual to see wood gilded in a mosaic pattern like that," she said inanely, referring to the walls.

"It's not wood." He set down the toast and lifted his cup. "It's gold-stamped leather."

"Is it? I've never seen anything like it."

He sipped and gave her a wry smile. "It was all the rage a hundred and fifty years ago. I'm told it's supposed to absorb the smells of food, but it doesn't seem to me that it works."

"Well, thank goodness for that. A century and a half of accumulated food scents would be a bit much, don't you think?"

He chuckled, and she drew a deep breath. "How long will you be gone today?"

"I'm not certain. It depends upon what I encounter. Perhaps a few hours, perhaps until evening." He sipped again, watching her over the cup's rim. "My offer is still open for you to come along."

Although it sounded like a sincere invitation, he didn't look like he particularly wanted her to accept it. "I think I should stay here," she repeated and squared her shoulders. "But when you return later, perhaps we can discuss a strategy."

"For removing scents from the walls?"

"For mounting a new search for your uncle's murderer."

His cup clattered back to its saucer. "No."

The bruises on his face were fading, but it seemed nothing else had changed. "We must clear your name, Tris," she said carefully. "For my sisters' sakes if not your own."

His gray gaze was resolute. "I told you before, I have no wish to reopen that coil of a case. There can be no good outcome. Either my uncle died in his sleep, in which case there is nothing to find, or . . ." His voice trailed off.

The haunted look in his eyes broke her heart. "You cannot think the only other alternative is that you killed him."

But clearly he *did* think that. "Just leave this alone, Alexandra."

She swallowed hard. She had to make him understand. "Does my happiness mean so little to you?"

"Not five minutes ago, you assured me you were happy beyond belief. Have your feelings changed that quickly?"

"For myself, I am happy. But there are others involved."

"You had alternate offers," he reminded her. "Perhaps you should have accepted Lord Shelton or Roger St. Quentin."

A lump rose in her throat. The thought of marriage to either of those men made her breakfast sour in her stomach, but had she doomed her sisters as a result of her selfishness?

"I apologize," he said stiffly, watching her. "That was unfair."

"No, you're right. I wanted you," she said, suddenly fearing she'd made a terrible mistake. "But I also want your name cleared. And, Tris . . . you are *not* responsible for your uncle's death. There is no reason not to investigate."

His jaw tight, he sat silent a long moment. "I must be off," he finally said in a neutral tone. "We shall continue this discussion tonight."

After giving her a perfunctory kiss, he left.

She sat stunned for a while, her wonderful mood from the morning shattered. She tried to finish her tea, but she couldn't swallow past her tight throat. Finally she rose, fed the rest of her toast to Rex, and went upstairs to grab her family's cookbook.

Then, as she often did when she was upset, she headed for the kitchen.

Unfortunately, she had no idea where it was—Tris's tour last night hadn't included anything as mundane as the servants' quarters. But this morning she'd noticed a back passageway off the great hall, so she decided to try there first. No sooner had she wandered into the gray-painted corridor than she almost bumped into a housemaid hurrying the other direction.

"Pardon, my lady!" The girl's cheeks turned bright pink.

"Goodness, it was my fault entirely." Alexandra racked her brain for the girl's name. "I wonder, Anne, if you could direct me to the kitchen?"

Anne beamed. "Right this way, my lady." Carrying a mop, broom, and bucket, she led Alexandra down another chilly corridor to a staircase. "It's in the basement. Shall I show you?"

"I'm certain I can find it. Thank you."

"Thank *you*, my lady." Still smiling and holding everything, Anne gave an awkward curtsy and walked off while Alexandra went down the stairs.

A row of leather buckets hung overhead, pointing the way to the kitchen—always the biggest fire hazard in any house. Busy plucking a chicken, Mrs. Pawley looked up when Alexandra entered her domain.

"Good morning, my lady! I wasn't expecting you to 'invade my kitchen' quite so soon." She wiped her hands on her wide, white apron. "Did you enjoy your breakfast?"

"Very much." The room was a hive of activity: kitchen maids chopping and slicing while scullery maids scurried here and there, hauling pans and implements off to be washed. A small boy stood turning a spit. Alexandra sighed. "I thought to perhaps make some gingerbread, but—"

"Come in, come in." Mrs. Pawley shooed two kitchen maids away from the large central table. "Show me your book."

Alexandra handed it over. "It's been in my family for well over a century."

The cook flipped several pages. "This sounds delicious. And this." She looked up. "Are all the recipes for sweets?"

"The Chases do all share a sweet tooth." Despite her blue mood, Alexandra smiled as she reclaimed the old book. "Each lady in the family adds a recipe every Christmas. I'll have to return it to Cainewood, where it belongs. I've only borrowed it to copy my favorites, as Lord Hawkridge and I were married, ah . . ."

"In a hurry?" Mrs. Pawley's blue eyes danced.

"You could put it that way, yes. Have you flour and sugar?"

Beneath her starched white cap, the blond bun at the nape of the cook's neck bounced as she nodded. "We have everything you need, my lady. You've only to give me your list."

Half an hour later, they stood companionably side by side, their hands coated in flour, forming small balls out of the gingerbread dough. Mrs. Pawley, as it turned out, was not only an accomplished cook, but also an unrepentant gossip. "I did notice where your ancestor claimed these cakes are excellent with a good gossip," she said with a laugh.

"I expect she meant eating them, not making them." Alexandra sneaked a taste of the sweet-spicy dough. "Though I do confess some curiosity about the happenings here at Hawkridge."

"I remember when your husband first arrived here from Jamaica. The man was in a bad way, he was, his father dead and not a penny to his name. The last Lord Hawkridge took him under his wing, but he weren't in a good way, either."

"Yes, I've heard that. He was ill, was he not?" Alexandra scooped more dough. "Do you remember the morning the last Lord Hawkridge was found dead?"

"Oh, most vividly." Having filled the first pan, the cook dusted flour on another. "We all loved the last Lord Hawkridge. Not that we don't feel the same toward your new husband. Do you know, 'twas he who suggested Lord Hawkridge send me to France for training. Saved my position here, he did. Couldn't have been more than fifteen at the time; even as a boy, he knew the way of things. Your husband has a business head on those wide shoulders."

A vision of herself gripping those wide shoulders made Alexandra's blood heat, but she wasn't sure she wanted her servants taking notice of Tris's anatomy. "When the last Lord Hawkridge was discovered dead, was poison suspected immediately?"

"Good heavens, no! Who would poison a fine man like the last Lord Hawkridge?" Mrs. Pawley plopped another ball on the pan. "He died of a broken heart, I tell you. We all know that here. No matter what the outsiders say."

Alexandra was relieved to hear that Tris's staff didn't suspect him. "Were there any outsiders here at the time? Anyone suspicious?"

"No one a'tall. Lord Hawkridge was in the dismals—he weren't taking visitors. Excepting your husband, of course. The house was still draped in black—"

"No one? A concerned neighbor? A salesman or tradesman?"

"Not that I remember." Rolling dough between her plump hands, the cook eyed Alexandra speculatively. "Why all the questions, my lady?"

Alexandra made another ball before she answered. She knew Tris wouldn't be happy she was asking questions. But did she have a choice? His fear that he'd killed his uncle was completely unfounded, and her sisters' happiness was at stake.

She set the ball on the pan. "I'm hoping to clear my husband's name, Mrs. Pawley. If I can prove someone else killed his uncle, he will be welcomed back into society."

The cook nodded as if she'd thought as much. "I'd like to see Lord Hawkridge's name cleared as well. But there's no one here thinks the last Lord Hawkridge was poisoned. He died in his sleep, plain and simple."

"Do you find it upsetting to answer questions?"

"I suppose not. I didn't see anything that night to help you, though. 'Course, I'm stuck down here in the basement; I'm not aware of all that goes on upstairs." She reached over to pat Alexandra's hand, puffing flour into the air in the process. "If it's that important to you, perhaps you should ask the others."

Exactly what Alexandra wanted to do. Perhaps she'd be risking her husband's anger, but she couldn't see where either of them would be happy with this cloud hanging over their heads. And it was not as though she'd be combing the countryside for clues—she'd only be talking to her own staff. People she should be getting to know anyway.

If a little voice told her that was a rationalization, she decided to ignore it. With any luck, she could uncover important information and solve the mystery before Tris even arrived home.

Chapter Thirty-five

An hour later, Alexandra and a large platter of ginger-bread cakes sat in the main parlor, which had a lovely trio of windows looking out toward the Thames. The walls and upholstery were sage green damask, the ceiling painted with fat, cavorting cherubs to oversee the proceedings. Hastings—who'd had no new information to add to her investigation—showed the next servant in, bowing as he backed from the room.

"Sit, please, Ted." She waved the footman onto the sofa opposite hers, reaching to the low table between them to pour tea, in hopes of making him comfortable. "Would you care for a gingerbread cake? They're still warm from the oven."

The footman seated himself carefully. "The others told me what you are asking, my lady. I regret that I have nothing to add. But we all know our master is innocent, and we do admire your efforts to clear his name."

"I'm determined." How ironic that everyone here thought Tris was blameless—except Tris himself. That only cemented her resolve to prove his innocence in spite of his protests. Since Ted hadn't reached for a cake, she put one on a small plate and handed it to him. "Are you certain you saw no one suspicious around Hawk-ridge that night or the morning after?"

"None that I recollect."

"And was there anyone here—living here, I mean—whom you feel could have possibly had motive to harm the last Lord Hawkridge?"

"I'm afraid not. Lord Hawkridge was a fair man, much admired by all."

"So I keep hearing." She sighed. "If you think of anything that might help me, please let me know immediately. You may go. And feel free to take your refreshments with you," she added with a smile. "I suspect there may be a small party in the servants' parlor."

And so it went. She questioned all the footmen and other manservants, the housemaids, the chambermaids, the kitchen staff, and everyone in the stables and on the grounds. Over and over she heard the same answers, the same insistence on everyone's innocence. Four hours later, the platter of gingerbread cakes had dwindled, and there were only the upper servants left to interview.

"Good afternoon, my lady," Peggy said when Hastings ushered her in. She had put aside her maid's uniform and wore a clean but very outdated dress. "I've been wondering when I might be summoned."

"This is nothing for you to fret about," Alexandra assured her, thinking she'd fetch her a few dresses the next time she went home to Cainewood. Lady's maids generally expected to wear their mistresses' cast-off clothing. She poured tea and set the cup and saucer on the low table between them, along with a gingerbread cake. "Please make yourself comfortable. I just have a few questions, is all."

Peggy sat and fluffed her skirts. "You're looking for evidence to clear Lord Hawkridge's name."

"Yes. Word does get around." Peggy had done an excellent job unpacking and arranging Alexandra's things last night—even pressing her wrinkled clothing before putting it away—and this morning she'd worked wonders with her often unruly hair. So far, Tris's opinion notwithstanding, Alexandra was very pleased with her.

"Do you recollect anyone visiting the evening or morning of my husband's uncle's death?"

"No, my lady. No one." Peggy calmly sipped her tea. "And I know what you're going to ask next," she added, setting her cup back on the saucer. "I don't believe anyone here had any reason to harm Lord Hawkridge, either. He was well liked and respected, and we had all known him a long time—many of us all of our lives."

"I'm aware of that." Alexandra sipped a bit of her own tea to be polite, although she'd long ago had quite enough. "Is no one new ever hired here at Hawkridge?"

"There are rarely any openings and usually young people waiting to fill them." Peggy bit into a gingerbread cake, chewed, swallowed, and smiled. "Delicious, my lady."

"Thank you. It's an old family recipe." But the "good gossip" the cakes were purported to inspire was not netting her much in the way of results. "So you don't remember anyone who might have been new at the time? Anyone who could possibly have been less than loyal to the last Lord Hawkridge?"

"No, we're all here from way back." Peggy reached for her cup again, then stopped. "Wait." She frowned, narrowing her pale green eyes. "There was Vincent, of course. He had recently arrived with your husband." She shook her head, her mop of brown curls bouncing. "But Vincent is a big sweetheart. He'd never kill a fly, let alone a man."

"I'm sure you're right," Alexandra said, hiding her surprise that she hadn't thought of Vincent herself. It was obvious that at the time he'd have been a new arrival. "Thank you, Peggy. I'll be calling on you to help me change before dinner. Would you inform Hastings that I'm ready for Mrs. Oliver?"

"Of course, my lady." Peggy smiled and left.

While Alexandra waited for Mrs. Oliver, she stared blankly out toward the peaceful river, her mind racing. Could Vincent have killed Tris's uncle? He didn't seem the type; she had liked him on sight. But Uncle Harold, after all, had owned Vincent when he was a slave. It was certainly possible for resentment to build under those circumstances. And Vincent had to bear Tris a strong loyalty, considering he'd bought and freed him.

Seeing the man to whom he owed his freedom destitute and desperate, might Vincent have been willing to kill his former owner in order to see Tris inherit?

She didn't think so. But she owed it to Tris—and her sisters—to at least consider the possibility.

When Mrs. Oliver arrived, she brought news. "Lord Hawkridge has sent word, my lady. He's been detained at the gasworks and may not make it home until after dinner."

"Thank you, Mrs. Oliver." Alexandra forced a smile. The news was disappointing, but not altogether unexpected. And if this was to be her life, she might as well get used to it. "Please do take a seat. I hope you won't mind answering a few questions."

But although they had a nice conversation, Mrs. Oliver had nothing new to add to Alexandra's investigation.

And at long last, she had only one servant left to speak with: Vincent.

Vincent wore an impeccable black suit, a crisply tied cravat, and a wide, bright smile. He entered the room with such an easy manner that she couldn't imagine he was afraid of anything, much less worried he'd be arrested for murder.

"My lady," he greeted her in that musical voice that reminded her of faraway islands, "I have never seen your husband as happy as he was this morning. I can only thank you for entering his life."

"Surely you exaggerate." How could she suspect such a charmer? "Have a seat, please, and tell me what you remember of the night my husband's uncle died."

"The man was feeling poorly, and one morning he failed to wake up." He seated himself, seeming to take up the whole sofa across from her. "I saw nothing to suggest there was foul play involved and nothing to rule it out, either. However," he added, his deep voice brooking no argument, "Lord Hawkridge had no part in his uncle's death. I'll hear nothing of that nonsense."

"I agree with you entirely." When she handed him a cup and saucer, they looked like toys in his big hands. "I hope to find the real culprit, to clear my husband's name and restore his place in society."

"He's aware of your investigation?"

Was it her imagination, or did he know Tris would disapprove? "I've told him of my intentions."

He sipped, regarding her over the cup's rim. "Most here believe there was no culprit. That Lord Hawkridge's uncle died in his sleep. They are convinced no one here had any reason at all to consider murder."

"You don't agree?"

He shrugged his brawny shoulders. "I don't pretend to know. I had come to Hawkridge but recently, so I wasn't as well acquainted with the rest of the staff as they were with each other. Four years later, I still don't know many of them well."

He wouldn't. Upper servants rarely fraternized with those lower, and she couldn't picture him becoming fast friends with Hastings, Mrs. Oliver, or Mrs. Pawley. He struck her as the sort that would keep to himself. Which doubtless suited Tris just fine.

She offered him a small smile. "If you think of anything that could help me, please let me know."

"I will," he said, draining his tea before rising to his feet. "Your husband is a good man, Lady Hawkridge. The best. If there is anything I can *ever* do to help him, you can wager I will."

He bowed to her from his lofty height, and she watched him walk from the room.

After he left, she thought about him for a long time. She was usually a good judge of people, and she couldn't imagine him a murderer. He seemed friendly and open, and she liked him. But he'd made it clear he'd do anything to help Tris.

Could that *anything* extend to murder?

Chapter Thirty-six

It had started raining around sunset and hadn't let up since. Dripping wet and miserable, Tristan was surprised when Vincent met him at the door. Predictably, Rex met him at the door, too, bounding down the stairs and sliding across the great hall to greet him.

"Welcome home, my lord," Vincent said. Rex barked, his equivalent of a welcome.

Tristan stepped inside, immediately making a puddle on the black and white marble floor. He rubbed the dog's head, then shrugged out of his sopping greatcoat and handed it to the valet. "Where is Hastings?"

"Sleeping." Vincent took his soaked hat, too, holding both away from his own pristine clothing. "Everyone is sleeping. It's half past one in the morning."

"Holy Christ. I had no idea." Tristan dug out his pocket watch, but of course his valet was right. "Problem with the construction at the gasworks," he explained, snapping it shut. "I shall have to return first thing tomorrow. I expect Lady Hawkridge is abed, too?"

"I imagine so. Haven't seen her for hours. Should you like some dinner, sir?"

He suddenly realized he was famished. "Yes, and my thanks. Bring it to my study, if you will. I have weeks of paperwork to catch up on."

Boots squishing all the way, he headed across the

great hall to the dining room and through to the study, Rex at his heels. He briefly considered changing out of his damp clothes, but decided he couldn't spare the time. He'd waded through less than half the mail when Vincent showed up with a platter of cold roasted chicken, sliced cheddar, and a small round loaf of bread.

From where he was snoozing in the corner, Rex perked up and sniffed.

"Just leave it here on the desk," Tristan said, reading a letter from his steward in Jamaica. "And take yourself off to bed. I can undress myself."

"Thank you, my lord." Vincent hesitated.

Tristan looked up. "Yes?"

"Since your lady is asleep, I just thought you might like to know that she questioned everyone, but I don't believe she uncovered any new evidence."

He set down the letter. Slowly. "What do you mean, she questioned everyone?"

"About the circumstances surrounding your uncle's death." Vincent peered at him in the yellowish gaslight. "She assured me you were aware of her intentions."

"She did make her intentions clear, yes." And he'd thought he'd made his clear as well. "Thank you, Vincent. I'll see you in the morning."

"Good night, then, my lord."

Tristan waited for his valet's footsteps to fade from his hearing, then counted to ten. Then counted to a hundred. Then told himself he'd be better off eating his dinner and waiting for his anger to ebb, rather than stomping upstairs immediately to wake his new wife.

He ate two bites of chicken, tossed the cheese to the dog, and took a hunk of the bread with him.

Chewing savagely as he squished up the stairs, he considered the best way to wake Alexandra. A light tap on the shoulder? A whisper in her ear? Perhaps he should jerk the sheets up and thereby dump her out of the bed.

Though he'd never actually do such a thing, simply considering it was satisfying in itself. He savored the mental picture as he squished through the round gallery and down the corridor. Having wolfed down the cheese, Rex caught up to him just in time to get the door slammed in his huge, hopeful face.

Seated in one of the armchairs, Alexandra looked up from her book. "You're home."

Tristan slumped back against the door. "You're not sleeping." Damn, he couldn't dump her out of the bed. "You're not even undressed." All she'd removed were her shoes and stockings.

She set her book on the side table and smiled. "I thought *you* liked to do the undressing."

"I thought—" Bloody hell, she looked gorgeous with that beckoning smile, her eyes glazed from lack of sleep, her cheeks rosy in the gaslight, her body's soft curves evident in the slim dress she'd no doubt donned for dinner. His own body reacted as he wondered whether she was wearing drawers.

Gritting his teeth, he yanked his thoughts back to the matter at hand. "I thought I told you to stay out of my business."

Her rosy cheeks went white. "You've heard."

"Of course I've heard. Every servant here is loyal to a fault."

"So I learned today. They were all loyal to your uncle while he lived, and they're all loyal to you now. No one thinks you poisoned him, and no one believes any of the others were responsible, either. They all stand together and behind you, Tristan Nesbitt." She rose and crossed the distance between them. "It's extraordinary, when you think of it. Servant turnover is an enormous problem on most estates. Yet everyone here, it seems, has been here forever."

Rain pattered against the windows while he considered her brave speech and fought to control his anger. Perhaps all was over and done with; perhaps now the matter would be closed. "You didn't learn anything incriminating."

"Incriminating to whom? We both know you're not

at fault. But no, I learned nothing to incriminate anyone here. Not even Vincent."

"Vincent?" he snapped. "Why should you mention him?"

He saw her swallow hard. "He was the only one new to the staff. The only one who hadn't a long-standing loyalty to your Uncle Harold. The only one, in fact, who had a reason to resent him."

The anger surged anew. "Whatever do you mean by that?"

"Your uncle *owned* him, Tris. Do you not think that could have made a difference? After you freed the man and then found yourself in dire straits, do you not think he could possibly have considered murder a way to both revenge himself and solve your problem?"

He hadn't. Not for the barest moment. "I'd sooner believe I murdered my uncle myself. Just because the man has dark skin—"

"This has nothing to do with his skin." Outrage brought color back to her cheeks. "I cannot believe you would think that of me. I happen to like Vincent very much. We had a nice chat. He cares about you—"

"Then why? Why would you accuse—"

"I've accused him of nothing! Shall you fault me for simply considering the possibility? For looking everywhere I can to find someone to blame so we can clear your name and get out of this mess?"

He realized they'd both raised their voices, but he didn't give a damn whom they might wake. "I do not want this 'mess,' as you put it, stirred up again. I thought I'd made that perfectly clear. Do you understand me this time? Or do I need to write it down on a goddamn piece of paper?"

"What are you afraid of, Tris? That you'll find yourself a murderer? I *know* that won't happen." She looked beautiful in her righteous fury, her cheeks red as rubies now, her hair escaping its pins and curling about her face. "All I wanted was to ask around and see what I might turn up."

"And all *I* want is for you to stop!"

"Well, then, you have your wish," she said, suddenly sounding defeated. "I've talked to every single person on this estate, and no one had anything the least helpful to contribute. There's no one else to go to." She drew a deep breath, her breasts heaving with the effort. "It's over," she added in a voice so dead and quiet it was startling following all the shouting.

The silence reigned for a space of time, stretching awkwardly between them.

"I'm sorry," she finally said. "But I confess I'd do it again. It's over, but if it wasn't, I'd do anything I could to find a way to clear your name."

He couldn't summon any more anger—what he felt edged closer to guilt. After all, it was his fault—his sleepwalking, his failure to leave her room—that had landed them in this impossible marriage. Maybe a tiny part of him had hoped she'd be successful. Hoped she'd find a way to erase the stain on the Nesbitt name. Hoped she'd prove able to keep that stain from spreading to her own family.

Of course, a much larger part of him—the part that was scared stiff of what she might have found— overshadowed that tiny part. But it was there. Maybe.

"I'm glad it's over, then," he said. "And I'm sorry, too." He wasn't quite sure what he was sorry for. Given the chance, he'd try to stop her all over again. But he did feel sorry. And guilty. And a little angry still, and he didn't know what else.

She sighed and moved the few inches between them to lay her head on his chest. "You're damp."

"I had to ride home through the rain."

She snuggled closer anyway. "I guess we've had our first fight."

"I didn't know you had it in you," he said, wrapping his arms around her. "You're always so composed."

"When something matters to me as much as this does—as much as you do, as much as my family—I will fight for it all the way."

"I'll keep that in mind," he said dryly.

She felt warm and yielding in his arms. Soft and alluring. Though his emotions were still running high, he'd never been able to resist her pull.

Never.

His hands wandered down lower. "Are you wearing drawers?" he whispered.

"I don't own any drawers," she murmured against his chest, wiggling her bottom against his hands in a way that kicked his pulse up a notch. "If you want me to wear them, you're going to have to hire a seamstress to make them."

"Bring another servant here for you to question?" he said bitterly. "I think not."

She tilted her chin up to see him. "Was there a seamstress here at the time?"

She looked dead serious, which he found less than thrilling. Very much less than thrilling. Whatever had calmed in him flared again. "I thought you said you were finished."

"Only because there's no one left to interview."

"It's over. You said it was over."

"If there was another person here at the time—"

He silenced her with a kiss. Exasperated, he could think of nothing else to do.

He half expected her to protest, but she opened her mouth instead, immediately inviting him in. Their tongues tangled in a dance that made heat flash through him. He backed her toward the bed. She smelled like heaven and tasted like sin, and he would never get enough of her.

He was mad for her. It seemed he'd spent his entire life mad for her. He wanted to bury himself deep inside her, and there was just enough anger swirling in him to make him too selfish to treat her like the almost-virgin she was.

Their mouths still bonded, his fingers worked frantically to unfasten the back of her dress as he inched her ever closer to the bed. He dragged the frock down her arms, together with her chemise, breaking their kiss to shove them both over her hips and legs and clear down to the floor. While she stood slack-jawed in shock, he yanked off his boots and tore a seam in his coat in his hurry to get out of it.

Unbuttoning his falls with one hand, he pushed her onto the bed with the other, noting the surprise in her eyes. But there was passion in her eyes, too—utter, unbridled passion. Unable to wait a moment longer, he climbed up to cover her gloriously nude body with his.

A gasp escaped her lips before he crushed her mouth beneath his once again. He wedged a hand between her legs to test her with a finger and then another. He knew he should take his time, treat her gently, but she felt slick, sleek, throbbing around his fingers, inciting desire so raw he was helpless to hold back. She gasped again as he widened her thighs and plunged home where he wanted to be.

Hot. Impossibly tight and hot as her legs locked around him, the unschooled sensuality of that driving him to distraction. He couldn't wait. He didn't *want* to wait. He wanted to lose himself in her, and she seemed to be losing herself as well. Her hands gripped his damp shoulders, and she cried out his name, shuddering, dragging him over the edge to join her in oblivion.

When he regained his senses, he kissed her hair, her cheek, her mouth. Part of him was mortified at his lack of control, but another part, a larger part, simply marveled at the emotions she was able to rouse in him.

No other woman had ever been capable of making him lose control. But all the anger, the raw passion, had somehow transformed into softer feelings when he'd felt her respond to him. When he'd felt her join him in the madness. And that had made all the difference.

He hadn't ever made love before Alexandra, he realized all of a sudden . . . he'd only found release.

"Sweet heaven," she whispered as he eased himself off of her, both of them still shaky, her breath coming in shallow gasps. "I cannot move."

He came up on an elbow beside her, ran a finger alongside her face, kissed the wide expanse of her forehead. "Give it time."

"I think I need until tomorrow."

Alarmed, he wondered whether she was serious or jesting. "I'm sorry I was so quick and . . . ah, rough."

"I liked it." Her eyes drifted shut. "It was exciting."

Jesting, then. Although she couldn't see him, he smiled. "And last night wasn't? And this morning?"

"Every time is exciting. Every time you kiss me, touch me. Every way . . ." She lifted her lids and met his eyes. "I love you, Tris. Even though we don't always agree, I love you."

The only answer he could give her was a kiss. He poured his heart and soul into it and still knew it wasn't enough. Anything more, though, was beyond him.

He couldn't say words he didn't believe.

"I'll get the lights," he said finally and rolled out of bed.

He quickly finished undressing and then walked around the room, dousing the gaslights one by one, his gaze fastened on her as he went.

She still hadn't moved. Sprawled atop the sheets, ravishingly bare, she was every man's dream. He still didn't quite believe she was his.

He still didn't believe he wouldn't lose her.

If he woke in the night, he wanted to be able to see her. He left the last light burning.

Chapter Thirty-seven

Tristan woke in his study.

At first he just blinked, disoriented. Slowly he noticed the light coming in through the shutters, the ticking of the clock on the desk. The dog snoring in the corner, rattling the windows.

He swung himself upright on the leather sofa and rubbed his face. The sofa was too short, and his legs ached. He stretched them out before him, wondering how many hours he'd slept cramped in that position.

Hours. Hours. Holy Christ. He must have sleepwalked into here during the night.

Thankfully, his sleeping self had drawn a dressing gown around his naked body. He wrapped it tighter and tied the sash. Yawning, he stood and left the study, intending to head upstairs.

No sooner had he stepped foot in the dining room, however, than Hastings popped in. "Good morning, my lord. Will you be wanting breakfast?"

"What time is it?"

"Half past eight."

Bloody hell. He needed to get back to the gasworks. He had promised to arrive with the sun. "Yes, breakfast, please. Is Lady Hawkridge up and about?"

Hastings looked at him curiously. "No, my lord. She's yet to make an appearance."

"I'll let her sleep," he decided, amused. He must have worn her out. Rather than risk waking her, he'd have breakfast now and then quickly dress after she'd arisen.

When he'd downed his last bite of eggs and drained his second cup of coffee and she still had yet to appear, he returned to his study to finish going through his mail. An hour later, he sent a footman to the gasworks with a note. An hour after that, he hurried upstairs, concerned.

No matter how wild the night, a woman who habitually rose at six did not sleep until after eleven.

"Alexandra?" He knocked softly. "Alexandra?" He opened the door.

Curled up under the covers, she looked so peaceful he had to smile. He walked closer and shook her shoulder. "Alexandra, it's time to wake up."

She slumbered on.

"Alexandra." He shook her harder. "Alexandra!" Still no response.

At his wit's end, he drew a deep breath. And suddenly felt light-headed.

For a moment he just stood there, a vague prickling in his brain suggesting the woozy feeling should mean something significant. Shifting uneasily, he glanced around the room. And noticed the gas lamp he'd left lit.

Only it wasn't.

His pulse stuttering, he rushed over and twisted the key, hoping it wouldn't move.

It did move. The gas line had been open. It had been open with no flame, and Alexandra had been breathing gas for God only knew how long.

He prayed to God as he scooped his wife and the covers from the bed, ran down the corridor, and turned into the queen's bedchamber.

"Alexandra!" He laid her on the turquoise and gold counterpane and crawled up beside her, his heart pounding so hard he had to yell over the roar in his ears. "Alexandra, wake up!" Kneeling on the mattress, he gathered her into his arms. "Oh, God, please, wake up." He rocked her back and forth. "Wake up, God damn it!"

Her lids fluttered halfway open, then closed.

He held his breath. "Alexandra?"

"Just . . ."

Had he imagined that single, breathy word? He'd had to strain to hear it.

"Just . . . wait a moment."

A moment. Wait a moment.

He'd wait, right here with her in his arms, for minutes, hours—*days*—if only he knew for certain she would be all right.

He waited.

"You're holding me too tight," she finally said.

His heart started again.

He was shaking all over.

"I mean it," she murmured, her eyes opening at last. Warmed brandy. He'd never seen anything so beautiful.

She blinked up at him. "Let go of me, Tris."

"I can't." He did loosen his hold, though even that small compromise seemed difficult. "I think I'm going to hold you for the rest of our lives."

Her little chuckle was the most wonderful sound he'd ever heard. "What happened?"

"God, I could have lost you." He sent a little thank-you up to heaven.

"What *happened*, Tris?"

"The gas. The lamp I left burning last night. The flame went out, so gas leaked into the room, and you were breathing it."

"You're shaking."

"I know. You were breathing it, and you could have died."

She struggled to sit up on his lap. "Don't be so melodramatic. I'm fine."

"Thank God that room is not airtight. It may have been leaking for hours."

"I've never heard you talk so much of God," she said

with a little smile. "Christ, yes, especially Holy Christ. But—"

"Hours," he repeated, feeling the blood drain from his face.

"Tris?" She levered off his lap and turned to face him on the bed, drawing the covers over her shoulders and around her. "Are you all right?"

"Yes. No." His heart was pounding again. "Oh, God, I must have extinguished the flame."

"What are you talking about?"

"I sleepwalked again last night. Woke up this morning in my study. Before I left the room in the night, I must have extinguished the flame in my sleep."

"That's ridiculous." The blanket slipped off a bare shoulder, and she pulled it back up. "It was stormy last night. A draft blew it out."

"The glass chimney is there to protect the flame. A draft cannot blow it out. It had to have been put out deliberately."

"Anything can happen, Tris."

He wanted to believe her. He didn't want to believe he was capable of harming his own wife in the middle of the night. What kind of man would that make him?

A dangerous one.

What would that do to their marriage?

"I know what you're thinking." She sighed, sounding so much like hale-and-hearty Alexandra he wanted to hug her despite his distress. "Even if you did put out the flame—which I am not at all convinced is the case— surely it wasn't intentional. For heaven's sake, you did it in your sleep. You must have meant to turn it off and mistakenly extinguished it instead."

"Maybe," he said—because he knew that was what she wanted to hear.

"Absolutely." Having settled the matter—to her mind, in any case—she scooted to the edge of the high bed and slid off, swaying a bit on her feet.

He landed beside her and caught her by the elbow. "Careful."

"I'm *fine*." Hitching the blanket back onto her shoulders again, she peered up at his face. "Better than you are, I'd wager. What are your plans for today?"

He winced. "I need to ride out to the gasworks. I was supposed to be there hours ago. But I cannot leave you—"

"Don't be a goose. I told you I'm fine. I'm going to make some sweets and take them with me to meet the villagers." He'd barely opened his mouth when she added, "I know what you're thinking. I won't be asking anyone any questions about your uncle's death."

"That's the second time you've said you know what I'm thinking."

She shrugged prettily and smiled. A smug smile.

He kissed that smug smile off her face. It was a long, deep kiss, and when he finished she was swaying on her feet again, and he wasn't at all worried it was due to gas poisoning.

While they were still gazing at each other, Rex plodded in, nudged Tristan with his huge head, and barked.

"He doesn't like me," Alexandra said.

"He just wants some attention. Which I cannot give him right now." He rubbed the dog's head. "I need to get dressed." He turned to leave, then turned back and pulled up the blanket that had slipped off her shoulder again. "Make certain to take Peggy with you."

"Of course I will."

"And a footman for good measure—and a carriage. I shouldn't like to see you walking or riding after what happened here this morning. You may not be as fine as you believe." He gave her one more short, hard kiss, ignoring Rex's bark, then headed off to find Vincent.

No matter what Alexandra claimed, he knew she didn't know what he was thinking. Because when he'd stepped back from that final kiss, he'd been thinking that if he'd poisoned her with gas while sleepwalking, then it was that much more likely he'd also poisoned his uncle.

If she could read his mind, she'd surely have responded to that.

Chapter Thirty-eight

SUGAR-CAKES

Take Sugar and half again as much Butter, Beaten together, and add Eggs, as much Flour as sugar, a little Cream, some Sherry, a generous amount of Currants, and a spoon of shaved nutmeg. Shape into thin round cakes and Prick all over, then bake in a warm oven. Cover with icing of Sugar mixed with the white of egg and return to oven until Crisp.

These travel well and are good for visiting.
—Lady Diana Caldwell, 1692

It took a lot of sugar cakes to feed a village. At half-past noon, barely an hour after Tris left, Mrs. Pawley took the fourth pan out of the oven and brought it over to where Alexandra was spreading glaze on top. "Might I pour you more sherry?"

"No, thank you, Mrs. Pawley." The small glass Alexandra had drunk was quite enough—just enough, in fact, to take the edge off her disappointment that she wouldn't be able to clear Tris's name. Just enough so she could smile and laugh and pretend that everything was all right.

Although, of course, it wasn't.

More than half a glass of anything alcoholic made her very giggly or put her to sleep. When the cook had suggested they should have a wee taste of the sherry before adding it to the recipe, she hadn't expected to finish the bottle. But Mrs. Pawley was making a good dent in it.

"I'll just have another myself, if you don't mind." The cook filled her glass for the third time and sipped, watching Alexandra swirl the sugary mixture onto the cakes with a knife. "You do that very prettily, my dear."

"Thank you. My mother taught me how to do this. And my father's mother taught her, I expect, considering the age of the recipe."

Mrs. Pawley smiled and sipped again, one eye on all the activity in the kitchen. Alexandra wouldn't normally approve of Hawkridge's cook drinking wine while she worked, but Mrs. Pawley seemed unaffected, and she couldn't argue with the woman's results. Her meals were exquisite, and her kitchen was spotless.

The woman did, however, have a smudge of flour on her little button nose that Alexandra itched to wipe away. "I know your father was Hawkridge's last cook," she said to distract herself, "but did your mother work here as well?"

"Bless her, she did. Started as a scullery maid before she caught m'father's eye." The cook's blue eyes danced. " 'Course she became his assistant in short order."

Alexandra smiled. "I imagine she did like that better than scrubbing dishes."

"No one aspires to stay a scullery maid long. If a girl cannot expect advancement—"

At the sudden silence, Alexandra looked up from the pan of cakes. "What is it, Mrs. Pawley?"

"I just remembered. There was a scullery maid—Beth, she was called—went to Armstrong House a few years ago for a better position. She was here that night—the night his lordship's uncle died. Will you be wanting to ask questions of her as well?"

"Goodness, yes." The news lifted Alexandra's spirits

more than an entire bottle of sherry. "How far is Armstrong House?"

"An hour or less on horseback. You'll just need to follow the river."

"Lord Hawkridge would prefer I take a carriage." There was no reason to ignore his wishes completely. He'd doubtless be angry she'd gone at all, but she couldn't very well ignore an opportunity to solve their problems, could she?

Not and live with herself.

"May I prevail on you to finish these?" She shoved the pan toward the cook. "I have to change my dress, and have a carriage brought 'round, and find a footman to accompany Peggy and myself." She was already headed toward the door. "They need only a few more minutes in the oven; when the icing has hardened, they are finished."

Half an hour later, plans for her journey in place, she returned to fetch a few sugar cakes to bring along with her to Armstrong House. She couldn't very well arrive empty-handed.

After yesterday's rain, the day was beautiful. She opened the carriage windows to let in the sunshine and fresh air. Ernest, the footman she'd recruited to accompany her, rode up on the box with the coachman, and Peggy sat with her inside. No sooner had they started rolling than Peggy pulled a basket out from under the seat and began filling plates for them both.

"What is this?" Alexandra asked.

"Luncheon. You missed breakfast. I won't have you wasting away from starvation."

Alexandra laughed, suddenly realizing she'd forgotten to eat. She supposed she'd been too upset to really care. But now that her investigation was open again, she felt famished.

Peggy truly was a dear for taking care of her so well. She piled cold meats, cheese, pickles, and fruits on both their plates. "No strawberries for me," Alexandra told her. "I cannot eat them."

Peggy handed her a plate before adding a few strawberries to her own. "Why is that?"

"They make my tongue swell and my throat feel tight. It's really quite dreadful. The last time it happened, I thought I might perish from a lack of air."

"That *is* dreadful," Peggy said, her eyes wide.

Throughout the drive, Peggy kept up a running conversation that required little more than nods and murmurs from Alexandra. Sooner than she expected, they arrived at Armstrong House. Although smaller than Hawkridge, it was still obviously the home of a wealthy man. It looked to have been extended many times over the years and was now a sprawling mishmash of styles—medieval, Tudor, Stuart, and more modern.

"Wait here," she told Peggy. "I shouldn't think this will take long."

"Oh, but I've not seen Beth in years," Peggy said in a pleading tone.

"Very well, then. Come along."

Alexandra put a smile on her face as she approached the door with her sweets. "Lady Hawkridge," she told the green-liveried manservant who answered, her new name sounding strange on her tongue. "Here to visit with the lady of the house, if you please."

"Pardon me, but there is no lady. Lady Armstrong breathed her last in the spring."

Only then did she notice his black armband. "I'm so sorry. Is there no one to whom I may pay my respects?"

"Lord Armstrong has gone up to London. Only Miss Leticia is at home."

Miss Leticia Armstrong. Sweet heaven, was that not the name of the woman who had once been engaged to Tris? Alexandra hadn't put two and two together when Mrs. Pawley mentioned Armstrong House, but now she was dying of curiosity.

She reached into her basket. "Would you care for a sugar cake?" The footman looked startled but took it, having little choice if he wasn't to be rude. "Could you please tell Miss Armstrong that I'd appreciate a few moments of her time?"

The man walked off, cake in hand, looking dazed. Alexandra heard Peggy try—and fail—to suppress a snort of laughter behind her. She looked back and gave her a small smile. She knew it was a bit odd to offer sweets to all and sundry, but the Chase ladies had always done so and been well loved for it, so she wasn't about to stop now.

"He should have invited us in," Peggy said disapprovingly.

"You're right, of course, but I believe he was a bit flustered."

Wearing a fashionable black dress—as befitted a daughter in mourning—Leticia appeared a minute later, approaching with small, graceful steps that A Lady of Distinction would surely approve. Tall and willowy, she had clear green eyes and beautiful flaxen hair swept up in a sophisticated style.

Try as she might, Alexandra couldn't bring herself to hate her. She knew what it felt like to lose a mother, and Leticia looked like a perfectly lovely young woman.

Until she opened her mouth.

"John told me you are Lady Hawkridge?"

"Yes." Alexandra wondered why Leticia's voice should sound so cold. "It's a pleasure to meet you, Miss Armstrong. Please accept my condolences on the loss of your mother." Curious whether all the footmen here were called John, too, she reached into her basket. "May I offer you a—"

"You are not welcome here."

The sugar cake dropped from Alexandra's fingers. "I beg your pardon?"

"You heard me. The Hawkridge name has been disgraced. Please leave." Leticia started closing the door.

"Wait." Alexandra shoved a hand against the wood. She was reeling with shock, but she had come here for a purpose. "Have you a maid here by the name of Beth?"

Leticia stared right through her.

"Beth is a dear friend of mine," Peggy said, stepping out from behind Alexandra. "My mistress brought me here to see her." Her voice dropped an octave, sounding pained and sympathetic. "I . . . have news concerning her family."

Peggy, Alexandra thought, was a consummate actress. She almost had *her* convinced the invented news was dire.

Apparently Leticia did have something approximating a heart, since she nodded at Peggy. "Come inside. I'll fetch Beth."

She pulled Peggy in by the arm and closed the door in Alexandra's face.

Alexandra stood there for a stunned moment, then walked slowly back to the carriage. There was nothing else to do. She climbed inside and waited, her stomach contracted into a tight knot that made nausea rise in her throat.

Although she'd known it wouldn't be easy to be the wife of a suspected murderer, she hadn't realized how it would feel to be disregarded. Stared through as though she wasn't even there.

Her heart ached for her sisters. This was the way they would be treated. And, unlike her, they had no husbands to love, no one to hold in the night to make facing it a little easier.

It seemed forever before Peggy finally came out. "Beth knows nothing," she reported even before she entered the carriage.

"You asked her all the questions?"

"Everything you asked everyone else, my lady." She sat down across from Alexandra. "Beth believes Lord Hawkridge died in his sleep."

"Thank you for trying," Alexandra said, her heart sinking even more. It seemed Tris's uncle *had* died in his sleep. And that was going to make it very hard—if not impossible—to prove Tris's innocence.

Very hard—if not impossible—to make life better for Juliana and Corinna.

In her dejected state, the ride home seemed twice as long as the ride out. Peggy, at least, was quite solicitous. "I'm sorry it didn't work out, my lady."

"It's not your fault." Alexandra tried for a grateful smile. "I truly appreciate the way you managed to worm your way in there."

Peggy shrugged. "Miss Armstrong is a witch."

Although Alexandra agreed, she didn't think it would be seemly to say so aloud. But though she knew it was wicked of her, she couldn't help being pleased that Miss Armstrong was still *Miss* Armstrong . . . still unmarried in all the years since she'd abandoned Tris.

"I don't like to see your heart in your boots," Peggy said. "Is there anything else I can do?"

She really was a dear. "I don't think so. Unless you can remember anyone else who might have worked at Hawkridge and since left."

Peggy frowned for a moment, then shook her head. "I cannot recollect anyone else."

"I think I will talk to everyone again, though, and see if anyone remembers any departed staff members. The possibility hadn't occurred to me before, so I never asked the others."

The maid was silent a moment. "If you don't mind my saying so, my lady . . ."

"Yes?" Alexandra knew Peggy had her best interests at heart. "Please, feel free to say anything."

"Well, it's just that I overheard you and his lordship discussing this the other night. Not that I was listening, you understand."

"We did raise our voices," Alexandra admitted, embarrassed.

"Yes. Well, and don't you expect he might be upset if you talk to everyone again?"

"I'm sure he will be." She sighed. "But I must do this. There is too much at stake." She ran her fingers along the ribbon that held her cameo. "I shall just have to face his wrath and try to make the best of things."

Peggy folded her competent hands in her lap. "I could do it for you."

"Pardon?"

"I could ask all the others and make a list of any departed servants and their current whereabouts, if known. That way you will have the information without angering his lordship by asking more questions."

"Oh, Peggy, would you?" It was a perfect solution. "I'd be forever grateful."

"Consider it done." Peggy smiled. "It might take me a day or two, mind you, since I'll have to work around my other duties."

"I understand," Alexandra assured her. "I shall be very undemanding until you are finished."

Once again, Peggy passed the time with a constant stream of chatter. Although she had regained a shred of hope, Alexandra felt exhausted by the time they returned home. Perhaps the gas had affected her more than she'd thought, though she was inclined to think it was all the emotional ups and downs of the past few days. In either case, though she never slept in the daytime, she went straight upstairs, changed into Juliana's nightgown, and took a nap.

Chapter Thirty-nine

Tristan arrived home that evening eager to see Alexandra. It wasn't raining. The problem at the gasworks was finally solved. And he was starving.

After poking his head into the most likely ground-floor rooms and failing to find his wife, he took the stairs two at a time, anxious to see how she was faring after this morning's mishap.

If it *had* been a mishap.

But right this moment he didn't want to think about that. He wanted to kiss his wife and hear about her day and share the success of his. Preferably over dinner.

Vincent appeared, as he oft did, to meet him outside his bedroom door. "Your lady is sleeping," he said quietly.

Concern—and guilt—slammed into him. "Is she not doing well?"

"Peggy says she is well, my lord, only weary. Shall I arrange for a tray in your room? She may not wish to dress for dinner."

As usual, Vincent knew instinctively what was right.

"An excellent idea." Tristan paused with his hand on the doorknob. "Do you know if she went visiting today?"

"She did. She took the carriage."

That was a relief. If she had been well enough to carry

out her plans to meet the villagers, she couldn't be feeling too poorly. But he wondered how her visits had gone. While the villagers were dependent on him and therefore didn't snub him outright, his relationship with them was rather strained. They didn't like having their lord steeped in scandal.

Then again, Alexandra had his servants eating out of her hand—literally—already. Perhaps she could bring the villagers around, too.

"Did Peggy go along with her?" he asked.

"And Ernest as well, my lord. And John Coachman, of course. I mean Charlie," Vincent corrected himself. They shared a smile. "Your lady is making a lot of changes around here, isn't she?"

"Positive ones, I believe." Tristan was very happy to hear Alexandra had followed his directions. He didn't know if he could handle any more excitement today. Now that her damned investigation was over, he just wanted to see if they could settle into something resembling a marriage.

He turned and twisted the knob.

"She's not questioning anyone, either," Vincent added. "I know you were concerned about that, so you'll be pleased to hear that Peggy is doing it instead."

Tristan turned back. "Doing what?"

"Questioning the staff. Peggy came to me an hour ago, asking if I recalled anyone who might have worked here four years ago but has since left. She's compiling a list for your lady."

"Is she?"

"Yes. Is that not clever of your wife to widen the search?"

"Quite." No one had ever accused Alexandra of being dullwitted. To the contrary, it seemed she was too bright for her own good. "She's not going to find anything, though. My uncle died in his sleep. Of a broken heart."

"Of course he did. But I find it endearing that your lady wishes so much to prove otherwise."

Endearing, Tristan thought as he cracked open the

door and slipped inside. That was not the word he would have chosen. *Exasperating* was more like it.

Could she not understand that he wanted her to stop poking around where she didn't belong?

She still slumbered, huddled on her side beneath the covers, a small lump in his big bed. It occurred to him that now was his chance to dump her onto the floor. But he couldn't do it. Upset as he was to learn she was still pursuing her damned investigation, after almost losing her this morning he couldn't summon the anger he'd felt last night.

But dread of what she might find . . . that he could summon well enough.

The room was dim but not yet dark. He walked over and stood beside the bed. Her even features were outlined against the white sheets like the profile portrait she'd made of him so long ago.

"Alexandra," he called softly, half expecting her to sleep on like she had earlier. A hint of that panic came back, the blind fear he'd felt when he couldn't awaken her.

This time, though, she opened her eyes and yawned. "Tris?" she said in a sleepy murmur.

She would never know how endearing he found it when she called him that. *Endearing.* He was so relieved to see the gas hadn't seriously harmed her.

"Are you hungry?" he asked.

"Not really." She struggled to sit up against the pillows. "How did everything go at the gasworks?"

"Very well. The construction is back on track." He sat beside her on the mattress, his weight on the featherbed making her tilt toward him. "How was your day, then?"

"Disappointing." She sighed. "Mrs. Pawley recollected a scullery maid who'd left for Armstrong House to take a better position. I went—"

"You went to Armstrong House?" He blinked. "I thought you were going to the village."

"I *was* going to the village—I even made sugar cakes to take with me—until I learned about Beth." He thought he saw guilt cloud her features, but it was immediately replaced by other emotions he couldn't read. "Then, when I got to Armstrong House, Miss Armstrong wouldn't let me in the door. Peggy had to talk to Beth instead." She swallowed hard. "I must confess, I didn't like your Miss Armstrong much."

"I don't care for her much anymore, either," he assured her, noting her furrowed brow and haunted eyes. She was more upset by the rejection than she was letting on. It was on the tip of his tongue to soothe her by suggesting Leticia's attitude could have stemmed as much from his past history with her as from true outrage at his disgrace, but he decided there was no point. This would happen over and over, and he wouldn't be able to shrug off the next incident as easily.

Though he'd known the isolation and disapproval would hurt her, seeing her suffer ripped him up inside. It was why he hadn't wanted to marry. And why he feared she would leave him when she decided she couldn't take it anymore.

"You shouldn't have gone there," he said.

Guilt flashed again, this time replaced by determination. "I had to find out if Beth had any information, Tris, don't you see?"

He didn't see. Or rather, he saw all too well that she wouldn't stop digging in his past, threatening his hard-won equilibrium. He scooped a hand through his hair, fighting to maintain his even temper. "I thought you said it was over."

"You cannot expect me to ignore new information. I've asked Peggy to find out if there are any more servants who have left as well. If there is any chance—"

"I want you to stop this."

"I cannot." She sighed. "I'm sorry. It's too important. This is our *life* and the lives of my sisters. We are married for better or worse, but I cannot help trying to make it better."

He sat silent for a moment, trying to accept that. It wasn't easy. If she continued asking questions, neither of them were going to be happy with the answers. But he consoled himself that at least she had told him the truth. He hadn't known she'd been to Armstrong House, and she'd volunteered the information. She wasn't trying to hide anything, to sneak around behind his back.

Of course she wasn't. She was Alexandra.

"I don't want to fight," he said finally, determined to regain his earlier mood. When he rode up to the house, he'd been so eager to see her. There was no sense ruining the entire evening. If she was going to leave him someday—when society got the best of her—he wanted to enjoy their time together. "I'm disappointed—very disappointed—that you're not willing to let this go. But I don't want another fight."

Her eyes grew misty, which cut him to the core, because he'd never seen Alexandra cry. "I don't want to fight, either."

A knock came at the door, and Vincent entered with their dinner tray. Or rather, two trays. And then he brought in a third. Mrs. Pawley had sent up a veritable feast. Alexandra composed herself and Tristan lit the gas lamps while Vincent put everything in the sitting room. The valet ducked back into the corridor to fetch a fourth tray holding a bottle of Hawkridge's wine, two glasses, plates, and utensils. "Will there be anything else, my lord?"

"Thank you, Vincent." Tristan saw him back to the door. "This will do."

"This will do?" Alexandra asked when they were alone again. "Enough food marched through here to feed the entire household!"

"Well, come fix yourself a plate."

Shaking her head, she slid out of bed and started for the sitting room.

He stared, incredulous. "*What* are you wearing?"

"I borrowed it from Juliana." She stopped and twirled in the monstrosity, making yards and yards of white fabric and lace bell out and swirl about her. "Do you like it?" she asked, sounding a bit hesitant. "I know it's a little short on me, but my own nightgowns are so plain, I thought you would find this much prettier."

His gaze traveled from the frilly ruffle under her chin to the four rows of tiered lace skimming her ankles. The wide sleeves were gathered at the wrist with a six-inch spill of froth that completely concealed her hands. But the worst of it was the body of the gown—there was so much material, he wondered if he'd even find it possible to work his way under it.

Still, it wouldn't do to tell her how much he hated it. "I like you better in nothing," he said tactfully.

She blushed. "Oh. I'm not certain that's proper."

"There hasn't been much proper about our relationship, has there?" She looked so flustered he couldn't help but smile as he led her through to the sitting room. "Here's a plate."

There was fish, roast duck, lamb cutlets, artichoke bottoms, mushrooms, green peas, boiled cauliflower, plum pudding, apricot fritters, and bread. Alexandra took an artichoke bottom, three mushrooms, a small piece of bread, and some butter.

"That's all?" Tristan asked.

"I told you I'm not hungry."

Setting his plate aside, he laid a hand on her forehead. "Are you ill?"

"No. Just tired."

"Get in bed."

"With my food?"

"People eat breakfast in bed, don't they? Why not dinner?"

After she was settled against the pillows, he poured two large glasses of wine and handed her one. She sipped it while he undressed.

"I'm going to stay home tomorrow," he said, divesting himself of his coat and cravat.

"Hmm," she said pleasantly, sipping again.

He unbuttoned his waistcoat and shrugged out of it. "I have a lot of paperwork to catch up on. And journal entries to record." He made short work of removing his braces, then loosened his cuffs and undid the buttons at the top of his shirt. "I'm weeks behind on that sort of business."

She licked her lips as he stripped the shirt off over his head. "I suppose that's Griffin's fault."

"I'm not placing blame." He couldn't help but notice her watching him. Smiling to himself, he sat beside her on the bed to remove his boots and stockings. "It's just something I need to do."

"It shall be nice to have you here," she said while he unbuttoned his falls and untied the ribbon securing his short drawers.

He felt, rather than saw, her avid gaze on him as he stood and pushed everything down and off. His body reacting to that gaze in a very obvious way, he turned to her and grinned. She gulped the rest of her wine, licking her lips again while he took the glass from her hand and set it on the night table.

"Eat," he said, pointing to the untouched plate in her lap. She nodded and reached blindly for her fork.

He knew she watched as he walked through the sitting room to the dressing room. A man appreciated that admiring look on a woman's face. Assuming he could find his way under her hideous nightgown, this promised to be a fine evening after all.

But first things first. His stomach was rumbling, and Mrs. Pawley's lovely dinner was going cold. Tamping down his ardor, he hurried into a dressing gown and returned to the sitting room to fill a plate for himself. A little of everything, with some extra meat for good measure. It was supposed to lend a man sexual strength.

He turned and walked toward the bedroom, thinking to tell Alexandra as much and enjoy her reaction.

She was sound asleep, her head lolling on the pillows.

"Alexandra?" She slumbered on. He took the tray off her lap and set it aside. "Alexandra?" She was out so cold, if he didn't know better, he might fear gas poisoning again.

He ate his dinner and tried again, shaking her shoulder a little this time. "Alexandra?" Still no reaction.

He turned off all the gaslights. Then went back and double-checked them all. And a third time. "Alexandra?"

Quite obviously, she was out for the night.

He couldn't remember the last time he'd gone to sleep this early—to bed perhaps, but not to sleep. Yet he climbed up beside her, pulled her into the curve of his body, wrapped an arm around her . . . and held her all night.

Chapter Forty

"Sweet heaven, *what* is that noise?" Alexandra asked the next morning at breakfast.

"Rex. I left him asleep in the study." Her husband gestured toward the connecting door. "I told you he snores."

"He's louder than your ram pumps," she marveled as a footman poured her tea. "I'm surprised he hasn't wakened me in the night."

"Nothing would have wakened you *last* night." She'd never before seen Tris roll his eyes. "I will never again serve you wine at bedtime," he declared in a failed attempt to sound serious.

"I cannot blame you for that." She couldn't remember falling asleep, and she'd awakened to an empty bed. But the sheets had still held the faint scent of him, and she'd been aware all night of him holding her, curled against her back like two spoons nestled together. "I was sorry to see you gone when I woke."

He sipped his coffee, looking disgusted. "I woke to find myself in the kitchen."

"On the floor?"

"No. Just standing there, eating one of your sugar cakes."

"Stealing sweets in the night again?" she teased over

the continuing rumble of the mastiff's snores. "See, you sleepwalked, and nothing bad happened."

Tris ignored her subtle dig. "We were talking about you falling asleep on me," he said instead, his tone implying he wished she hadn't.

She felt her cheeks warm. From time to time during the night, she'd been aware of the aroused state of his body pressed against hers. But for the life of her, she'd been unable to bestir herself enough to take advantage of it. "I can only drink half a glass of wine. Any more and I—"

"Fall asleep?" he provided with a raised brow. He cut a bite of ham.

"Or get very, very silly."

He looked thoughtful as he chewed and swallowed. "I cannot imagine you silly; that would truly be a sight. However, I am not sure I am willing to risk you falling asleep in order to see it."

Two thunderous snorts came from the adjoining room, followed by blessed silence. Rex must have rolled over. Smiling, Alexandra reached for the jam pot. "Did you make a dent in the work in your study this morning?"

"A rather large dent, as a matter of fact. I may even find time to get out and take care of some business later in Windsor." He sprinkled salt on his eggs, watching her spread jam on her toast. "It won't take long. I promise to be back in time for dinner."

"I'm not passing judgment on you. I know you have much to do, thanks partially to my brother."

She also knew she wasn't offering him much incentive to remain home, given the way she insisted on going against his wishes. It was almost as though she could feel him pulling away, distancing himself from her emotionally.

She set down her knife. "I have much to do as well," she said, watching him pick up the jam pot and wondering why he was frowning. She was trying her best to be cooperative. "I am meeting this morning with Mrs. Oliver to go over—"

"No!" He dropped the jam pot, reached across the table, and snatched the bread from her hand.

She blinked. "Tris?"

"It's strawberry." He swiped a finger across her toast and licked, turning ashen as he confirmed it. "Strawberry preserves, not cherry."

"Dear God in heaven." Her heart pumping wildly, she realized the skin on the side of her index finger felt prickly. Looking down and spotting a telltale streak of red preserves there, she quickly wiped it off. "I should have looked," she said, searching her hands for other traces of jam. Finding none, she released a tense breath.

When she glanced up, Tris had gone even whiter beneath his tan. "I must have switched the preserves in the jam pot." He scraped tense fingers through his hair. "I've done it again. I am harming you in my sleep."

"You are *not*." She didn't know which she found more disturbing: discovering strawberries on her toast, or his assumption that he was at fault. "It's a long way from eating a sugar cake to switching the contents of a jam pot. I'm certain this was an honest mistake. A kitchen maid who didn't know better must have refilled the pot."

"No. Mrs. Pawley assured me she would tell everyone you cannot eat strawberries. It was no mistake. I—"

"Do you even know where the jam pot is kept?" she interrupted. "Or the preserves?"

He paused a moment. "I must have hunted around."

"In your sleep? I think not. Mrs. Pawley must have neglected to inform someone—not deliberately, of course, but in error." Who knew how often the woman nipped from the sherry bottle? "Let us call in the kitchen staff and get to the bottom of this."

A few minutes later, the dining room was crowded with kitchen maids, scullery maids, and the small boys who did odd jobs belowstairs. Mrs. Pawley looked perfectly sober—and extremely concerned. Hastings stood solemnly in the back, watching the proceedings. Mrs. Oliver did the questioning.

"Did you know Lady Hawkridge cannot eat strawberries?"

"Yes, Mrs. Oliver."

"I did, Mrs. Oliver."

"Mrs. Pawley made that clear, Mrs. Oliver."

"And did you refill the jam pot or see anyone else do so?"

"No, Mrs. Oliver."

"I didn't, Mrs. Oliver."

"Absolutely not."

It went on and on, so long that Alexandra began to suffer from the headache, especially because all the denials weren't solving anything. When at long last everyone shuffled out, she breathed a sigh of relief.

"I must have done it," Tris said in a dull, resigned tone.

"Don't be ridiculous," she returned crossly, rubbing her temples. "One of them refilled the pot. I'm not surprised no one would own up to it and risk being dismissed."

Someone else *had* to have done it. She knew, deep in her bones, that a man as good as Tris couldn't do anything to harm her—or anyone else. Not even in his sleep.

Struggling for composure, she reached across the table to lay her hand over his. "You're only sleepwalking because you're under pressure. You said that's when it happens, did you not? It's a pattern. And I think there is another pattern at work here as well. You do things when you sleepwalk that you wish you could do while awake. Like make love to me"—she blushed—"or steal more sweets than you're entitled to."

It was a pretty theory, but Tristan wasn't convinced, let alone at all mollified. "You can argue that I went to the kitchen in the night for sweets. But your pattern theory doesn't explain why I would leave a gas line open."

"You didn't. Or at least, not on purpose. You got up—and perhaps dealt with the gaslight in some way since it had been left on—and took yourself downstairs to sleep in your study. I had angered you by questioning your staff when you didn't want me to, so you were separating yourself from me in the night."

Had he really wanted to get away from her that night? He hadn't thought so. But even if her concept of a pattern were valid, there was another way to explain everything: a pattern of mayhem in his sleep. Violence.

Murder.

He couldn't shake his growing suspicion of that terrifying possibility.

"It's the pressure," she said, her hand tightening over his. "As soon as we clear your name, you'll be fine. I'd wager you'll never sleepwalk again."

He just looked at her for a long moment, searching her eyes while a strained silence stretched between them. His gaze finally dropped to the cameo she wore on a ribbon around her neck.

She'd take it off someday. Maybe someday soon.

"I'd feel a lot less pressure if you'd call off this investigation," he said at last, pushing away from the table. "I'm going back to work."

Chapter Forty-one

There were times in a woman's life when she wished she could confer with her sisters. Even though she already knew exactly what they would say.

Juliana, the peacemaker, would tell her to abide by her husband's wishes. "Your marriage ought to come first," she would say, and advise Alexandra to be the dutiful wife and put Tris's happiness and their relationship before her own wishes to right past wrongs.

Corinna, on the other hand, the rebel, would cheer on her efforts. "You are entitled to your convictions," she would say, and advise Alexandra to stand to her guns and let no man, not even her husband, sway her from doing what she thought right.

And Alexandra would be right back where she had started. But at least she would have some hugs and sympathy to bolster her. Here in this strange house, with Tris seemingly occupied most of the time, and no neighbors of her class and age willing to welcome her—a point Leticia had driven home yesterday—she was feeling rather lonely.

Still, the first part of her morning had been very productive. She and Mrs. Oliver had gone over the household budget, reviewed the cleaning and repair schedules, and discussed all the lower female servants. Everything seemed well in hand. She'd left their meeting convinced that Mrs. Oliver was a fine housekeeper indeed.

Afterward, she practiced on the harpsichord in the north drawing room for a while. It wasn't hard to play, but the double keyboard was difficult to get used to. In addition, the sound seemed thinner than a pianoforte's, and there seemed to be no way to play louder or softer. Although she wasn't a concert-quality pianist, she did enjoy putting some emotion into her pieces. But there were no pedals, and no matter how she hit the keys— tentatively or with much force—the resulting notes sounded the same. She wearied of it rather quickly.

Next she considered visiting in the village, but she wanted to take Peggy along to introduce her to everyone, and she'd prefer to have Peggy here, talking to the rest of the staff and compiling the list. The villagers would be there to meet tomorrow. Pursuing her investigation was much more important. Her attempts to convince Tris he wasn't guilty seemed to be futile, but he would never be happy as long as he believed he might be dangerous. She had even more reason to continue her efforts now.

Yet she knew those efforts were harming their relationship, and she hated that. She wanted to fix it. To that end, she decided to peek into the study and see if he wanted to join her for luncheon.

But he wasn't there. Disappointed, she sat at his desk, idly straightening piles of papers and stacks of journals. He *had* told her he had business that might take him away for a while. It would have been nice, though, if he'd sought her out to let her know he was leaving.

She shrugged philosophically, turning the chair to stare out the study's windows. Quite obviously, she still hadn't scaled that wall Tris had built, and she'd probably doubled the height with her own actions.

The study was in the back of the house, and through the windows the gardens beckoned—colorful formal gardens nearby, and then, behind them, an area of grass walks lined with hornbeam hedges and field maples that seemed to enclose smaller, private gardens. It was a glorious day, and she'd yet to explore them. She would, she decided, take her luncheon out there. And bring along some paper and her family's cookbook, so she could copy her favorite recipes while she enjoyed the sunshine.

A few minutes later, having grabbed a bonnet and asked Peggy to arrange for luncheon, she made her way out the front door and down the steps, following the cobbled path that curved around the back of the mansion. A flash of motion made her pause. She stared toward the river, watching Tris toss a stick and Rex jump into the water to retrieve it. Mere moments later, the big, wet mastiff scrambled up the bank and shook violently, spraying Tris with water that left splotches on his buff pantaloons.

Thinking she'd be tempted to laugh if she wasn't so uncertain of his feelings, she hurried toward him. "What are you doing?" she called.

To her surprise, Tris looked over and grinned. "Playing with the poor beast. He's been dreadfully neglected of late." He eyed the book and paper in her hands. "What are *you* doing?"

"I was going to take luncheon in the gardens and copy some of my favorite recipes. Would you care to join me?"

"I'm sorry, but I cannot." Rex was panting at his feet. He bent to grab the stick and tossed it arcing out over the water, watching as the mastiff gleefully splashed in to fetch it. "I have business in Windsor."

She wondered vaguely what he needed to do. She knew Windsor was the nearest sizable town, but did he have his bank there? His solicitor? She'd expect those would be in London. She needed to learn these things if he wanted her to assist with the household finances as she had for Griffin, but they had yet to discuss anything like that.

And now was not the time. "I thought you had gone already," she said.

"Without telling you I was leaving? I'm hurt you

would think me so thoughtless." Obviously reading her face, he reached to pull her close. "And you were hurt thinking I had. I'm sorry." He tilted her bonnet back and bent to give her a soft kiss.

Emerging from the water, Rex barked. "He hates me," she said.

"He does not." Tris took the stick from the dog's teeth and tossed it once more, farther out this time. "If he hated you, he'd have taken a bite out of you by now."

While Rex bounded back into the river, Tris took the book and papers from her and set them on the grass, then wrapped his arms around her and brought his mouth to hers again. "I wanted you last night," he murmured against her lips. Then the kiss turned hot and needy, and the whole of her responded. She slipped her hands under his coat and pressed herself close, mindless of his damp, dog-splashed clothes. Her heart raced, and the blood rushed through her veins. And she knew it was the same for him.

She was confused and unsure of his feelings from one moment to the next, but one thing she knew for certain: Nothing would ever change the physical pull that held them both in thrall.

Rex barked until they stopped kissing, then sprayed them both this time. Alexandra laughed. Tris brushed ruefully at his damp coat. "I really must be going, and I fear Vincent will not let me off the property without a bath and a change of clothing. I promise to be home in time for dinner." He gave her another quick kiss, eliciting another bark, then started toward the house, the dog following at his heels. "Enjoy your afternoon."

Feeling warmed all over—especially inside—Alexandra retrieved her things and wandered around the house and through the formal gardens. Gravel crunched under her feet as she followed the paths bordering beds planted with brilliant colored flowers. Finally she reached the area of grass walks that she'd seen, lined with hedges that enclosed many small, private compartments. She smiled as she peeked into them, glimpsing not only a variety of rather wild-growing plants, but also a surprise in each area. Some hid copies of famous statuary, one a sundial, another a cozy bench for two. Choosing one with a tiny round white gazebo, she slid inside.

The structure's roof offered welcome shade, so she removed her bonnet and set it, along with her book, paper, and pencil, on the bench that curved against the back edge. No sooner had she taken a seat, though, than a warm, motherly voice carried through the still summer air. "Lady Hawkridge?"

Alexandra rose and went to the opening. "Here, Mrs. Oliver!" she called, surprised that the housekeeper was bringing her luncheon instead of Peggy. "In the gazebo!"

A moment later, Mrs. Oliver entered the tiny garden. But she didn't have any food. Instead, she carried a small stack of letters. "I brought these for you, dear. I thought you might want them right away."

Alexandra took them and flipped through the pile. There were six, one from each of her siblings and female cousins. Thrilled, she smiled at Mrs. Oliver. "Thank you so very much."

"Enjoy them, dear," the housekeeper said and walked away.

With a happy sigh, Alexandra went back to the bench. She opened the two letters from her sisters first. Juliana and Corinna had both written cheerful notes, wishing her well and relating several amusing anecdotes as well as telling her all about a lovely picnic they'd shared with their cousins. Griffin's letter was shorter, mostly saying he missed her very much and threatening bodily harm to her husband should he fail to take good care of her. Rachael told her all about the goings-on at Greystone and her preparations for her brother Noah's return. Claire's letter mentioned the picnic again. And then Alexandra opened the letter from her youngest cousin, Elizabeth.

> *We all miss you very much. It was Rachael's idea we should have the picnic, and also her idea*

*that we should all write to you so you won't feel
lonely in your new home. Wasn't that so very nice?*

Alexandra had been wondering how it was that six
letters had arrived on one day. Grinning, she read on.

*I suppose you've heard that Juliana and Corinna
were DISinvited to Lady Cunnington's garden
party. I vow and swear, that made me so livid I
wrote to Lady C posthaste with my regrets—and a
piece of my mind. Worry not, dear cousin, your
sisters have much support. Rachael and Claire
have said they will not attend, either.*

The letter fluttered from her fingers to the grass. Dear
God in heaven, it was happening already. And not only
affecting her sisters, but her cousins, too.

Her throat tightened like it did when she ate strawberries. She couldn't seem to breathe.

A high-pitched voice snapped her to attention.
"Lady Hawkridge?"

She quickly gathered the letters. "Here, Peggy! In
the gazebo!"

Peggy hurried into the little garden, tray in hand.
"Your luncheon, my lady." She squeezed into the tiny
structure and set the tray on the bench, then pulled a
folded paper out of her bodice. "And the list you asked
for, completed."

"Oh!" Alexandra started breathing again as she took
it. Once she cleared Tris's name, her sisters would be
just fine. But she was disappointed to see only four entries. "Is this all?"

"Not many people leave Hawkridge, my lady. Kinder
employers are difficult to find."

"I know." And she knew she should be happy about
that. She *was* happy. Just seeing the list was a huge relief. "Thank you. And for writing down everyone's direction as well. They all live close by."

Peggy shrugged. "Not many travel too far from the place of their birth."

People, common people especially, always were more comfortable with the familiar. Which was a lucky thing, Alexandra thought, because she should be able to pay calls on these four in short order. Her spirits rose as she realized that, very soon, she might have the information she needed.

She'd lost her appetite, but since Peggy had gone to the trouble to fetch luncheon, she thought she'd better eat something. "Let me just have a few bites, and we'll be off. I want to ride today. It will be much faster than taking a carriage. Would you ask a groom to saddle three horses? And see if Ernest is free to accompany us again, if you will. Oh, and ask Mrs. Pawley to put some of my sugar cakes in a basket. Please then meet me upstairs—I'll need to change into a riding habit, and so will you."

Peggy shuffled her feet. "I cannot ride, my lady."

"Pardon? If you don't have a habit, I'll be pleased to give you one. I have several, including one or two I'd like to retire. I plan to order some that aren't blue," she added with a soft laugh at herself.

But Peggy showed no signs of humor. "I cannot ride. I do not know how. As a housemaid I never had reason to learn, and the last Lady Hawkridge never rode anywhere. She was very proper and always took a carriage."

"Is that so?" Perhaps riding to pay calls was not quite so ladylike—A Lady of Distinction might not approve—but Alexandra didn't want to waste time. "Make it two horses, then. Ernest and I shall do fine on our own."

"Are you certain, my lady?" Peggy did not look at all happy. "I believe his lordship would prefer you to take a carriage."

"Nonsense—he said that only because he was afraid the gas had weakened me. I am perfectly healthy today." And the sooner she finished this investigation, the happier Tris would be—no matter what the outcome.

"I would prefer to go with you," her maid said quite peevishly.

Alexandra couldn't figure why the woman would be so testy, but she decided to ignore it. "That is very thoughtful, Peggy, but there's no need. Two horses, please. I'll meet you upstairs in ten minutes."

Chapter Forty-two

Delicate notes from the harpsichord greeted Tristan when he arrived home that evening. Carrying the large, plain box he'd brought from Windsor, he made his way upstairs and paused in the north drawing room's doorway.

Alexandra sat with her back to him, focused on some sheet music, her graceful fingers moving over the antique instrument's keys. Watching her, he clutched the box tighter. He hoped she would like what was in it. He wanted to give her a nice night. Just one nice night. And, all right, it wouldn't be so bad if the niceness extended into tomorrow and the next day, too.

Their first night had been so wonderful, but since then, everything between them seemed to be going so very wrong.

As he watched, she raised a hand from the lower keyboard to the upper and hit a sour note. "Drat," she said softly and resumed. More notes tinkled through the air, sounding lovely for a few bars until she switched keyboards again and made another mistake. "Drat!"

"Good evening, sweetheart."

She startled and snatched her fingers from the keys, turning on the stool to face him. "You're home," she said, sounding surprised.

"I said I would be."

Her cheeks turned a delicate pink. "I hope you didn't hear too much of that. I shall get better with practice."

"There's no need to practice," he said cryptically, knowing she'd understand tomorrow. Already dressed for dinner, she looked beautiful in a pale green frock with a scooped neckline and his cameo on a matching green ribbon. She glanced curiously at the box in his hands, making him smile to himself. "Give me ten minutes to allow Vincent to fuss over me before dinner. Will you meet me in the dining room?"

"All right," she said, her gaze lingering on the box before she turned back to attack the keyboard with renewed vigor.

A quarter of an hour later, having instructed Vincent as to the box, he strolled into the dining room and bent to give Alexandra a long, thorough kiss. "Hmm," he murmured low, his hand wandering between her body and the back of the chair down to her bottom. "Still no drawers."

She blushed as he seated himself, her gaze going to the two footmen in the room.

"They didn't see or hear anything," he assured her in a whisper, and then louder, "How was your afternoon?"

"Peggy gave me the list of former servants," she said rather breathlessly. One of the footmen put a bowl of soup before her, and she lifted her spoon, the simple motion seeming to calm her. "Four names. I visited three of them and learned nothing."

He spooned up some soup, wondering how he would get it into his mouth between his clenched teeth. But he wanted this to be a nice night, so all he said was, "I wish you hadn't done that."

"I know." Somehow she managed to look both sorry and determined at the same time. "If it's any consolation, there is only one name left. A woman in Swangate. Unless she astounds me by being the only one to have seen suspicious dealings, I'll be finished after I talk to her."

She sounded mournful, but he couldn't help celebrating privately. And he certainly didn't want to argue and ruin this night. Instead, he made light conversation through the next two courses, his blood humming with anticipation.

Finally the table was cleared. Hastings brought in and opened a bottle of port. A footman presented a platter of fruit and biscuits. No sooner had they departed when Mrs. Oliver walked in, placed the box—now gaily wrapped and ribboned—in the center of the table, and promptly left.

Tristan poured Alexandra a very tiny glass of port— he didn't want her falling asleep tonight. He poured himself a larger one.

Alexandra glanced at the box, then lifted his empty dessert plate. "Grapes? Biscuits?"

"Surprise me," he said, thinking he couldn't wait to surprise *her*. He sipped, savoring the heady flavor of the fine, sweet wine and enjoying the quizzical look on his wife's face.

She filled his plate and took a single biscuit for herself. "How was your afternoon?" she asked, her gaze drifting again to the box.

"Extremely successful."

She took a small sip of the deep red port. "Your business in Windsor went well?"

"Exceedingly."

She hadn't touched her biscuit. "Would you mind if I asked what you did there?"

"Not at all." He popped a grape into his mouth, enjoying this exchange immensely. "I visited the shops." Seeing her startled gaze fly toward the box once more, he smiled to himself again. He seemed to be doing a lot of that tonight. "Would you like to open it?"

"Is it for me?" A tinge of excitement threaded her voice. "This was your business?"

He loved seeing her happiness. He hadn't given her enough since he'd brought her home. "Part of my business. Another parcel should arrive tomorrow." He moved the platter to make more room near her on the table, then rose, fetched the box, and placed it in the space he'd created. "Open it," he said, lifting his glass as he sat again.

The box was so large she couldn't see into it while seated. Slowly she pushed back her chair, stood, and untied the ribbon. The paper fell open, and she raised the lid, set it aside, and reached inside with both hands to part the tissue that protected the contents.

"Ooooh," she breathed.

"Take it out."

She did, lifting it by its handle. Polished silver gleamed in the gaslight. "A basket," she said reverently. "A . . . solid silver basket?"

"Sterling," he confirmed. "For your sweets. The Marchioness of Hawkridge's specialties deserve much better than wicker." He sipped, watching her stare at the basket, letting the potent liquid slide down his throat as her expression stole his heart. "It won't be too heavy to carry with you when you go visiting, will it?"

"No." She clutched it like she might never let it go. "It has a glass liner," she informed him as though he might not know.

"You wouldn't want to be trailing crumbs."

She still stood there, slowly turning it this way and that, watching the light bounce off its shiny surfaces. "It's the most beautiful thing I've ever seen."

"I'm glad you like it," he said, although *glad* seemed a very tame word. *Thrilled* would more accurately describe his feelings. He'd wanted so much to find something she'd like. He *hated* visiting shops—Vincent ordered all of his clothes—but he'd walked from shop to shop all afternoon, searching for the perfect thing. Refusing to buy anything until he found it. And it seemed he had.

She was looking a little bit shaky, so he rose just long enough to move behind her and push her chair toward the back of her knees. "Sit, before you drop it."

She lowered herself gingerly, holding the basket on her lap, her fingers tracing the chased and pierced decorations, the floral swags and raised ribbons and bows.

He moved the box from the table to the floor by her chair, where she could reach into it. "There are more gifts inside," he pointed out.

"I can see." She folded the basket's fancy handle down and pulled it back up. "Why?" She looked over at him, dewy-eyed. "When you have so much to do, why would you spend your day buying me something like this?"

Because he wanted to give her a nice night.

No, that wasn't the whole truth.

Because he couldn't say the words she needed to hear. Because he couldn't risk loving her. Because he was sure she'd leave him when she failed to clear his name, and he was hoping against hope that a silly silver basket would keep her near.

But he didn't say any of that.

"Because you deserve it," he said instead.

"I do not," she said, her voice thick. "I defy you at every turn."

"Every other turn," he disagreed agreeably. "At the alternate turns, you delight me."

She sighed and reached into the box, pulling out a book bound in fine leather dyed robin's-egg blue. The cover was embossed with gold designs, the pages edged with gold leaf. "This is lovely," she said through an obviously tight throat.

"It's blank inside. For your recipes. After you copy the ones you like, I thought you could start your own tradition. Our family could add to it every year."

"Our family," she echoed softly, not quite meeting his gaze. She set the book aside and pulled the next item from the box, her eyes widening as the fabric unfolded in all its transparent glory. "Dear God in heaven, what is this?"

"A nightgown," he said.

At that moment, two footmen returned to clear their

dishes. Her cheeks burning, she stuffed the garment back into the box and plopped the book on top. "It's lovely, too," she said quickly, sounding like she wasn't quite sure.

It took everything he had not to laugh. "Shall we take it upstairs and have a closer look at it?"

He couldn't wait to see her in it.

Chapter Forty-three

The nightgown was only the first of the scandalous garments in the box. There were *seven* nightgowns, in fact—one for each day of the week—of delicate silk gauze, gossamer georgette, and tissue-thin tiffany. As Alexandra pulled them out, she draped them on the bed. She'd never seen a nightgown that wasn't white, but these were almond and pale blush pink, powder blue and soft peach, with delicate edgings of lace and intricate, exquisite embroidery.

Under the nightgowns lay seven chemises of nearly transparent Swiss muslin, not shapeless like every other chemise she'd ever seen, but fitted to mimic a woman's curves, not plain and white, but of various pastel colors adorned with elegant trimmings and needlework.

There were stockings of the finest silk. There were satin garters with dainty rosettes.

"There are no drawers," Alexandra noticed.

Tris just grinned.

He seemed different tonight. More relaxed, less worried. She didn't know what had prompted his change of heart, but she didn't want to question it. She'd rather enjoy it instead.

After the afternoon she'd had—starting with Elizabeth's letter and ending with three fruitless interviews—

she wasn't about to risk the one thing that seemed to be going right.

By the time she finally reached the bottom of the box, the bed was strewn with garments that made her blush to look at them. She suspected there was only one sort of woman who wore these sorts of things, and she didn't even want to *think* about where Tris might have found them.

Windsor must be a very wicked town.

"Are you going to model something for me?" he asked.

She felt her face heat even more.

He chose a nightgown off the bed, of palest lavender with black lace and violet embroidery. "This one," he said, handing it to her.

It felt like nothing. Silky, slinky nothing.

"Do you require assistance with your dress?"

"Just the buttons," she said, and turned to let him unfasten them. She shifted the nightgown in her hands. Silky, slinky nothing.

"There," he said when the back of her green dress gaped open. He kissed her softly on the nape of her neck, then settled on one of the striped chairs, sipping from the glass of port he'd brought upstairs with him. "Use the dressing room. I'll be waiting."

In the dressing room, she shakily stripped out of her frock, chemise, shoes, and stockings, then dropped the nightgown over her head and smoothed it down over her hips. The fabric whispered against her legs. It felt like nothing on her body. Silky, slinky nothing.

She turned to see herself in the looking glass. Dear God in heaven, it was more shocking than nothing.

Her nightgowns all had high collars that tied at the throat. This one had a wide, low neckline. Her nightgowns all had long, full sleeves. This one had tiny puffed sleeves that started halfway off her shoulders. Her nightgowns were made of yards and yards of billowing, opaque fabric. This one was a slender column of diaphanous material that clung to her every curve.

She could see right through it.

The small bodice was split in the middle and gathered beneath her breasts. Strategically embroidered blossoms didn't conceal, but rather served to draw the eye. A narrow, black satin ribbon secured the top . . . a single tug to untie that bow was all it would take to have the bodice fall open and expose a scandalous amount of bosom.

"Are you ready yet?" Tris called.

Alexandra swallowed hard. A man didn't buy a woman a nightgown like this unless he wanted her. And heaven knew she wanted him.

She was as ready as she'd ever be.

Drawing a deep breath, she exited the dressing room, walked quickly through the sitting room, and paused in the bedroom's doorway. She dropped her gaze, then raised her lashes, giving him "the look."

Juliana had said it would make men fall at her feet, and it seemed she had been right. Judging from the expression on Tris's face, Alexandra figured it was a good thing he was sitting.

The way his eyes widened and filled with hunger made her heart begin to pound. He rose and started toward her. He'd already stripped to his trousers and turned down the gaslights, and the contours of his naked torso gleamed in the faint glow.

She met him halfway, licking suddenly dry lips. "Will you kiss me?" she asked softly, reaching up to sweep that always unruly lock off his forehead.

It worked this time. He crushed his mouth to hers.

This—the two of them together without the realities of life coming between them—was the *one* thing that seemed to work. She wrapped her arms around him and let herself sink into the kiss.

He tasted of rich port and hot desire and his own unique flavor she'd come to crave. Her fingers twined in the too-long hair that covered the back of his neck. As his hands wandered, a shimmering haze seemed to creep over her, obscuring her thoughts, dissolving her bones.

She leaned toward him, into him, pressing herself against his hard, warm body, wanting already to take him inside her.

"Hurry," she whispered.

"Not tonight," he said with a low laugh, pulling the pins from her hair and dropping them to the floor with little *ping*s.

He'd removed all the garments from the bed, and he laid her upon it, gently, spreading her long curls out over the pillows. Unable to resist him hovering above her, she reached to touch his bare chest, to smooth her palms over taut skin and muscle.

"You're beautiful," she said.

"That's supposed to be my line."

"But you are."

"*You're* beautiful," he countered, his gaze wandering the length of her in the transparent nightgown.

She knew he could see everything . . . and if his expression was any indication, he plainly liked the view. She flushed from her head to her toes. Wordlessly, his gaze locked on hers, he shucked off his trousers, climbed up beside her on the bed, and proceeded to kiss her until her head swam.

When he finally released her lips, his mouth trailed past her chin and down her throat, blazing a warm trail toward her breasts encased in the gossamer nightgown. His lips skimmed the violet flowers, his breath hot through the thin material. As she arched up to meet him, he closed his mouth over a nipple, suckling through the fabric.

A Lady of Distinction would definitely *not* approve of this nightgown. It was so flimsy and immodest, she felt his mouth on her almost as though the garment wasn't there. But it *was* there, and she wanted it gone. She wanted his mouth on her skin. This was torture. Pure torture. Her fingers dug into his shoulders, but he just switched to the other breast, lavishing it with similar torturous attention.

She really couldn't take it.

She tunneled her fingers into his hair and lifted his head, noting his look of stark surprise. "Here," she whispered, pulling one end of the black satin bow that secured the nightgown's tiny bodice. It fell open, baring her to him, and she held her breath.

After a moment, she raised her chest, offering her breasts to him like they were some irresistible sweet.

Not, however, a sweet there was a recipe for in her family's cookbook.

His lips quirked in a half smile, and he moved down, skimming his mouth across her nightgown-clad stomach instead.

More torture. He kissed across her waist and down her belly, tender kisses she could feel, but not the way she wanted. He kissed his way down one of her legs, slowly and sensually, and even more slowly and sensually up the other.

She was melting. She was dying, and she was melting. She was melting into the bed, and if he didn't touch her skin—bare skin—she'd dissolve into a puddle of need.

"Tris," she whispered.

"Hmm?" He spread her legs, pushing the nightgown down between them to kiss the insides of her thighs. Each kiss sparked a thrilling spurt of pleasure, not only where he was kissing, but also higher. Where a hot ache was building to unbearable proportions.

"I want this nightgown *off*," she told him. "I cannot stand this."

He raised his head for a moment, his smile one of masculine pride. "Ah, then I am doing my job," he said. And he returned to it, spreading her legs even wider to place a kiss in the most intimate place imaginable.

She shuddered and gasped, and he kissed her there again. This was wicked. It was more wicked than the nightgown. It was more wicked than the most wicked thing A Lady of Distinction mentioned in her entire, pedantic book.

And it was making that hot ache escalate to something all but unendurable.

Then he inched the nightgown up to her waist and kissed her in the same place without it between them.

And that was more wicked than anything she had ever imagined.

"Oh!" she breathed as she felt his mouth caress her, wet and hot, his tongue soft and slippery sweet. She wanted to say more—her mind shouted *You cannot!* and *You shouldn't!*—but all she could seem to manage was that little mewling *oh!*

He widened her legs with his hands, releasing a hum of pure enjoyment that vibrated all the way to her core as his tongue found the secret place her fierce ache was centered.

And then she quite simply couldn't say anything, couldn't form anything more than incoherent little moans. But that *oh!* must have made an impression, because he flicked that place again and again until she sobbed with pleasure, arching against his mouth as waves of exquisite passion rippled through her.

Only when the last tendrils of sensation had faded did he finally lift his head and draw the nightgown farther up and off.

Still trembling with the aftermath of his loving, she thought she might expire from utter bliss when his warm weight came over her, when he slipped inside her to join his body with hers. She wrapped her arms around him, squeezing tight, wanting more than anything for him to find the same pleasure he'd given her.

And she was shocked to find the feelings building in her once again.

He moved slowly, reverently. "Look at me," he whispered, and she raised her languid lids to see him gazing into her eyes, the familiar silver darkened with desire. He bent his head to take her mouth, and she tasted herself on his lips. The blood rushed faster through her veins.

Tristan took his time, deriving joy from her reawakening, the warm slide of her skin against his, the sweet shudders as his tongue swept her mouth. He could feel warmth turn to heat, feel her wrap herself around him, feel her quiver as the passion spread through her supple body. And when they were both ready, her beautiful low moan sent him hurtling over the edge.

It was, without a doubt, the most gorgeous span of time he had spent with any woman ever.

And now he had to end it.

Their bodies still joined and clinging, he kissed her forehead, both cheeks, her nose. "I need to leave you now," he whispered before settling full on her mouth.

"Hmm?" she murmured when he finally allowed them both to draw breath.

He *hated* this. But he had no choice.

"I'm going to sleep in the queen's bedchamber. Vincent will lock me in."

She blinked hard, and her soft mouth dropped open. "You're going to *leave* me?"

He eased out of her, wincing at her little sound of loss. "Just until morning," he promised as he levered himself to her side. "For your own protection. If I sleepwalk again, I don't want to be able to leave the room. I don't want to be able to get to you or to anything that might harm you."

"I don't want your protection, Tris." He'd never heard such hurt in her voice. And disbelief. "I want you here with me. How can you make love to me and then just . . . leave?"

"How can I not? How can I keep endangering you night after night? What kind of man would that make me?"

She offered no answer, but her eyes were pleading. They were going to destroy him, those eyes. Destroy his resolve, and destroy everything he was trying to be. Before that could happen, he climbed from the bed and went to fetch his dressing gown.

Chapter Forty-four

Alexandra lay in her marriage bed, stunned.

And alone.

She could scarcely believe Tris had left her. Not after the evening they'd just spent. Her gaze went to the filmy lavender nightgown pooled on the floor, to the silver basket and the beautiful book beside it. Gifts, she knew, from his heart.

Perhaps he couldn't bring himself to say he loved her, but men—especially enterprising men like Tris—didn't care to visit shops. Only love could drive him to spend his day choosing such perfect presents for her. Presents that demonstrated thought. Presents that showed he understood her. Presents that fit *her*, specifically, not any other woman.

Well, with the possible exception of the wicked underthings. But she didn't want to think about other women those might fit.

Of course, he'd left for Windsor before learning she'd gone off to interview three former servants. Perhaps he wouldn't have bought her beautiful things if he'd known that. Had he really left her alone in bed as a precaution to protect her? Or was he drawing away because he was angry she wouldn't call off her investigation?

She didn't really believe it was the latter, especially considering the way he'd made love to her. She blushed just *thinking* about that. Those hardly seemed like the actions of an angry man. But she wasn't sure, because perhaps he had been angry but then found himself lost in temptation when he saw her in that wicked nightgown.

She just wasn't sure. And she wanted answers. And she wasn't the type of person to sit and wait for answers to come to her. Or lie in bed and wait for answers to come to her, either. She was the type of person who went out and found answers for herself.

One would think Tris would have figured that out by now.

If he thought she would just meekly go to sleep while he locked himself in another room, he had best think again.

She rose and washed up, then retrieved the lavender nightgown, hoping he'd still find it tempting enough to entice him to talk. A few more kisses wouldn't be unwelcome, either, she decided as she wiggled back into it. Her pulse quickened at the thought.

After covering the nightgown with a very modest wrapper, she took time to brush her tangled hair and pin the front off her face. Feeling she looked as well as she could for a woman so recently ravished, she made her way from the room.

No sooner had she opened the door than Rex came trotting up and followed her down the corridor to the queen's bedchamber.

She knocked briskly on the queen's fancy gilded door. "Tris?"

Rex barked.

"I'm sleeping," Tris lied.

She knew he was lying, because if he were sleeping, he wouldn't have answered her, would he? Besides, he quite obviously wasn't in bed. She could hear him on the other side of the door almost as clearly as though there were no barrier between them.

"I want to talk to you," she said.

"We'll talk in the morning."

She wondered whether he was sitting or standing.

Whether he was upright or leaning against the door. Was he wearing his dressing gown still, or was he stark-naked?

That image made her heart skip a beat. "I want to talk now."

Rex barked again, adding his own demand.

But Tris was having none of it. His heavy sigh emanated from the room. "The door is locked, and only Vincent has the key."

"I'll get it from him, then. I want to talk. And I want you to come back to bed." She pictured him lying beneath the turquoise and gold canopy with the absurd ostrich-feather poufs at its four corners. "You hate this room."

"I'd hate hurting you even more. Vincent has gone to sleep—you're not to bother him. Go to bed, Alexandra."

"No," she said. She needed the door opened in order to tempt him again with the wicked nightgown. But she wouldn't bother Vincent. For one thing, she hadn't the slightest idea where the man slept. She'd have to schedule another appointment with Mrs. Oliver to learn where everyone was lodged.

In the meantime, she pulled a pin from her hair and stuck it into the lock, poking it around.

"What are you doing?" Tris asked after a moment.

"Picking the lock." She'd seen Griffin do this more than once, and she'd read of many a protagonist doing it in books. Surely it wasn't that difficult. But despite the fact that she was producing many clicks, nothing seemed to actually move.

Rex barked his encouragement, slapping the wall with his tail for good measure.

"Are you giving up yet?" Tris asked, sounding amused.

"No." She dropped to her knees in order to get a better angle.

"Now?"

"No." Clenching her teeth, she rooted around harder. "Now?"

"Drat," she gritted out. This wasn't going to work. She plopped to sit on the floor and leaned sideways against the door. "This is ridiculous, Tris. You belong in our bed."

"It's only one night. A few hours. I'll see you in the morning. Good night, Alexandra."

"Good night," she returned, but she didn't move.

Rex gave her a disgusted look and padded away, his huge paws thudding on the wood floor.

"The dog gave up," Tris pointed out. "It's time you did, too."

She never gave up. Perhaps that was a character flaw rather than a trait to be admired, but regardless, there it was. She didn't go back to bed. If she couldn't tempt him into more kisses, perhaps she could at least get her answers. "Are you doing this because you're angry with me?"

"I'm doing it to protect you."

"Are you certain? Because I know you're unhappy that I won't give up the investigation."

"That has nothing to do with this," he insisted—rather patiently, she had to admit. "Except in a peripheral way. If you'd stop your investigation, perhaps I'd stop sleep-walking, in which case I might not fear doing you harm in the night. But it is not anger driving me to do this. It's concern and sheer fright. Can you not understand that?"

She could, damn him.

If she hadn't been blinded by hurt, she'd never have thought any different. He had convinced himself he was a danger to her, and unless she proved otherwise, he would stay convinced. But he didn't *want* her to prove otherwise.

What an impossible mess she found herself in.

But she did understand. And she also understood that in his own, twisted way, he was acting honorable by doing this to her. Damn him.

"I love you," she said.

He didn't answer that. Not that she found *that* surprising.

She shifted to sit with her back against the door, her knees drawn up toward her chest. She wrapped her arms around them. Just because she understood didn't mean she didn't find his attitude exasperating. "You're acting like your father," she said.

That elicited a response. "What the devil do you mean by that?" A rather hostile response. "A single glass of port hardly makes me a drunk, and I rarely gamble."

"You said he was so convinced love would never happen for him again that he never bothered trying to find it."

"I also said I don't believe each one of us necessarily has a perfect person."

"You didn't mean that."

"The hell I didn't. We're not all of us destined for bliss, Alexandra. The sooner you accept that, the happier you'll be."

"Like *you're* happy?" she countered softly.

He was silent so long, she wondered if he had fallen asleep. But then he shifted against the door, and she knew he hadn't.

She'd have to give him more time. Three women he'd loved had left him. No, make that five—his mother and his sister had left him, too.

The women he'd loved had been leaving him since he was seven years old.

She laid her head on her bent knees, hugging herself. "I'm not going leave you, Tris. No matter what I do or don't learn tomorrow, I'm not going to leave you. Ever. Not next week or next month or next year. You married me, and you're stuck with me. If you open the door, I'll be right here. Always."

As it turned out, she was right there for only part of the night. As the tall-case clock in the round gallery struck four in the morning, she woke, stiff and sore, and took herself back to bed.

Chapter Forty-five

"Good morning, my lady." Peggy bustled into the bedroom and threw open the drapes. "It's nine o'clock, and I brought your breakfast." She placed a tray on the bed. "Shall I have the carriage brought round for your visit today?"

Nine o'clock? Alexandra blinked in the harsh light, wondering where the night had gone while at the same time happy those long, uncomfortable, restless hours were over. She struggled to sit up against the pillows and took a slow, bracing sip of hot tea. "I wish to ride again today. The sooner I complete this final interview, the happier my husband will be."

"I've been thinking, my lady. Perhaps, since you enjoy riding, it is time for me to learn."

"That's a fine idea." Alexandra spread jam on her toast, checking first to make certain it was cherry. "We shall arrange for a groom to give you lessons."

"I meant today. I believe I should start riding with you today."

"Oh, I don't think so." Picturing middle-aged Peggy mounting a horse for the first time, Alexandra hid a smile behind her teacup. "I shall be in quite a hurry today, and you'll need a few lessons before you go galloping off. I believe I shall just take Ernest with me and get this done."

She'd quite enjoyed riding with Ernest yesterday. Unlike Peggy, who talked her ear off, he was quiet and deferent. He never asked to come in during her interviews, nor did he ask what happened afterward. He allowed her time to think.

Peggy scowled, clearly unhappy that Alexandra was going off without her again. As she helped her into a riding habit, Alexandra did her best to ignore the maid's bad mood. Peggy had seemed so pleasant and accommodating the first few days—even going to the trouble to make the list—and it was good of her to want to learn to ride.

When she was dressed and coiffed, she handed Peggy her gorgeous new silver basket, waiting for a reaction.

There was none. "Yes, my lady?"

"Please ask Mrs. Pawley to fill this with the rest of my sugar cakes. I shall meet you in the main parlor."

"As you wish," Peggy said coldly and took herself off.

Alexandra heaved a sigh as she started downstairs. If the woman was going to sulk whenever things failed to go the way she wanted, perhaps she'd be happier with a different lady's maid, after all.

When she entered the main parlor—or rather, tried to—her mouth dropped open. "What is this?"

Inside the room, three footmen were rearranging the furniture. Outside, two muscular strangers were blocking the door as they maneuvered a large object through it.

An excessively large object.

"A pianoforte," one of them said in answer to her question.

"I can see that." She hurried around to the front and read the name above the keyboard. "Erard," she breathed in wonder, running her hand over the shining, dark mahogany. Sebastien Erard was known to build the very best pianofortes—why, it was said that Beethoven himself owned one. "And it's *six* octaves."

"Begging your pardon, ma'am, but we need you to move."

"Right. Of course." She looked toward the three footmen. "Might any of you know where Lord Hawkridge is at the moment?"

"The vineyard, I believe." One of the Johns hefted a small table onto his shoulder. "Or so I heard him tell his valet before he left this morning."

"Thank you," she said and turned away—then turned back. "Um . . . where is the vineyard?" Hopefully it wasn't as far from the house as Griffin's. "Will I need a horse?"

"Not at all." The man set down the table. "Just walk across the west courtyard, past the icehouse and through the hornbeam arch. You cannot miss it."

It was a pleasant walk. The icehouse was brick with a domed roof, and she found the long hornbeam arch to be delightfully shady. At the far end of the leafy tunnel, she exited to find sloping land covered with rows and rows of staked vines, the spaces between them wide enough only to walk single file. Spotting Tris in the middle, speaking with another man, she hurried toward him, her skirts brushing the vines on either side.

"Excuse me," she heard him say as she came up. "I'd appreciate privacy for a moment." The man tipped his cap and walked a decent distance away, bending to tend a vine.

"A pianoforte?" Alexandra said the moment he was out of earshot. "An *Erard* pianoforte?"

Tris's eyes looked silver in the sunshine. She thought perhaps she saw an apology in them, mixed with excitement at surprising her. "I did say another parcel would arrive today."

"That's quite a parcel," she said, determined to forget last night. Or the last part of last night, in any case. "Thank you. Thank you ever so much."

She threw her arms around him, feeling euphoric when he wrapped his arms around her, too.

Their kiss was sweeter than the fruit ripening in the sun all around them and as heady as the wine it would become. "I hope you'll enjoy it," he said when their lips reluctantly parted.

"Oh, I will. The men delivering it made it clear I was getting in the way, but I can hardly wait to try it." The world seemed brighter this morning, as though the queen's bedchamber last night had been no more than a bad dream. She breathed deep of the fragrant air, reaching to touch a bunch of grapes. "How fat they look!"

"In a month, they'll be ready for harvest."

She started walking along the row, touching a plant here and there. "The vines seem so sturdy. Their trunks are so wide."

"Compared to Griffin's vines, you mean?" Sounding amused, he followed behind. "A hundred years or so from now, their trunks will be wide as well."

"If he can make his vineyard pay well enough to keep it."

"He can make it pay. With the duties raised during wartime to almost twenty shillings a gallon, French wine is no longer affordable for a man of moderate income. People will be happy enough to stock their cellars with what Griffin produces."

"If it tastes as good as yours does, they will." She paused to pluck a grape and sniff it. "Is this a certain kind of grape?"

"Undoubtedly, although I confess I don't know the variety. In the old records they are noted only as English sweet-water grapes."

"Well, they make truly wonderful wine," she said, popping the fruit into her mouth.

"I'm glad you think so," he said and added teasingly, "as long as you drink only half a glass at a time." He shot a glance to the other man. "I'm afraid I am not finished here."

Swallowing the sweet flesh, she nodded. "I must leave, anyway. Ernest is no doubt waiting with our horses. We're going to visit with the final former servant. Lizzy, her name is."

"I wish you wouldn't." A hawk wheeled overhead, and a sudden breeze kicked up, making the vines rustle around them. She saw something twitch in Tris's jaw. "I sleepwalked again last night."

"I'm sorry," she said, meaning it. He looked tormented. "Have you ever before suffered these incidents so closely together?"

"Never. It's always been weeks—if not months or years—between episodes. But this morning, after locking myself in that room, I woke to find the window wide open." He sounded totally disgusted that his plan hadn't worked. "The lock kept me from sleepwalking around the house, so I sleepwalked outside instead."

"Did you wake up outside?"

"No, but that doesn't mean I didn't go out. In the past, I've often ambled around and ended up back in my bed."

"But the queen's bedchamber is upstairs. You would have killed yourself climbing out that window. I'm sure you simply opened it because you wanted fresh air." When she saw that he was going to argue, she put a hand on his arm. "Let me go see Lizzy. And then this might be over, and maybe you'll be able to sleep."

He just looked at her for a while. Just looked. And it made something tighten in her chest, because every time she thought they were making progress, stepping forward together, it seemed they took two steps back.

But she *had* to go see Lizzy. Her sisters were being ostracized already, and this was her last chance to discover information that might lead to a solution for them all. Her last chance to prove to Tris that he wasn't the dangerous man he feared.

"You may not be happy with what you learn from Lizzy," he finally said, the warning sounding bitter on his tongue. "And it's not going to change anything." Then he turned and left her, his shoulders looking tense beneath his dark blue coat as he strode toward the other man.

The hornbeam arch didn't seem nearly as delightful when she traversed it in the opposite direction. And at the other end, Vincent, Hastings, and Mrs. Oliver all stood waiting for her.

"May I help you?" she asked, puzzled.

Hastings glanced at the other two and then spoke for all three. "May we have a word with you, Lady Hawkridge?"

"Of course."

"Lady Hawkridge," Hastings repeated, then stopped.

"Yes?"

"We're concerned," Mrs. Oliver continued. Her kindly chocolate eyes *did* look concerned. "These mishaps that keep occurring . . ."

"We fear that if someone did indeed murder the last Lord Hawkridge," Vincent hurriedly finished for her, "he may be trying to kill you now to stop you from finding him."

Alexandra blinked, taken aback by the mere idea. It had not, of course, occurred to them that Tris might be causing the mishaps while sleepwalking, since other than Vincent—and she was certain he would keep Tris's secret—they probably had no knowledge of his night wanderings. But it had never occurred to *her* that it could be anyone else. For a moment, her heart raced.

Then she told herself not to be ridiculous. "I appreciate your concern," she said carefully, "but I truly believe both incidents were accidents."

"But what if they weren't?" Hastings asked.

"Everyone has assured me the marquess's death was natural," she reminded him.

"But what if it wasn't?" Mrs. Oliver blurted. "What if there is a murderer among us? Should you continue your investigation, even worse could happen."

It was obvious that recent events had them nervous and suspicious. Even of each other. Mrs. Oliver was looking at Hastings. Hastings was looking at Mrs. Oliver.

And they were both looking at Vincent.

"We brought this up for your own good," Vincent said now, his gaze steadfast. He had too much dignity to shrivel under their scrutiny. "We worry for you. If you would discontinue—"

"I cannot," she interrupted. "You are all dears to worry for my safety, but I must leave no stone unturned in my quest to clear my husband's name."

The three of them exchanged glances and subtle sighs. "Do please be careful, then," Hastings finally said.

"I will, I assure you. Thank you for coming to me with your concerns. I consider myself very lucky to be surrounded by such caring people."

She watched them walk off, praying that she was right and they were wrong. She felt a little shaky. The thought of Tris attacking her was one thing—she didn't believe it and never would. But the thought of someone else . . .

She didn't believe that, either, she decided firmly.

And besides, even if it were true . . . there was a good side to that.

The quiet ride with Ernest had done little to calm Alexandra's nerves. She was still shaking when she dismounted in front of Lizzy's small cottage. For the second day in a row, Hawkridge's villagers had stared at her as she rode through. Between that, defying Tris, and dealing with the doubts the staff had brought up, she was a wreck. Walking up the pretty flower-lined path, she half hoped this interview would lead nowhere, because that would mean this would all be over.

No, she thought with a sigh . . . she didn't really hope that. But perhaps she felt that she should.

The woman who answered the door had soft white hair, kind blue eyes, and a pronounced stoop. "Yes, dearie?"

"Might you be Lizzy?" Alexandra knew that, unlike the others, Lizzy had retired rather than leaving for a new position. Still, she hadn't expected someone quite so old. Lizzy looked ninety if she were a day. "I'm Lady Hawkridge."

"A new Lady Hawkridge!" Lizzy's weathered face crinkled with delight. "Come in, dearie, come in."

Alexandra waved to Ernest where he was patiently waiting with their horses, then stepped inside. The cottage was a single room with a living area on one side and a bed on the other. "Would you care for a sugar cake?" she asked Lizzy, pulling one from her silver basket.

"Why, thank you." The woman pulled a chair out from the simple oak table and gestured for Alexandra to sit. "I will have one, if I may."

"I've been told you were employed at Hawkridge Hall when the last marquess died."

"And for sixty-two years before that." She munched on the cake, seating herself across from Alexandra.

"My husband, the current marquess—"

"I remember your husband, my child." Lizzy licked crumbs off her fingers. "Bless you. It is long past time that dear boy's innocence was proven."

For what must have been the dozenth time, Alexandra's hopes soared. "Did you see anything that night or morning? Anyone suspicious? Have you reason to believe anyone at Hawkridge Hall may have wanted the marquess dead?"

"Alas, no." Lizzy's hand inched toward the basket. "But someone must know something. Whom have you talked to so far?"

"Everyone," Alexandra said with a sigh, handing her another sugar cake.

"Names, dearie. I want names."

Lizzy devoured two more sugar cakes while Alexandra recited the list. "How about Maude?" Lizzy asked when she was done.

"Maude?"

"The marquess's old nurse—after his wife and children passed on, she was the closest person to him. If anyone saw anything that night, it'd have been she. She left very soon after he passed . . . I wonder if she's still alive." She reached for yet another sugar cake, her face wrinkling so much in contemplation that her eyes all but disappeared. "Maude was old as dirt even then."

Alexandra felt an urge to laugh, though she wasn't quite sure whether it was from the joy of learning her search wasn't over yet or the wrinkled old woman across from her calling someone else old as dirt. "Do you know where Maude went, by any chance?"

"When she left, she was headed for Nutgrove. Maude was born there, and she said that there she'd die."

Alexandra could only hope she hadn't already.

She gave the rest of the sugar cakes to Lizzy as a thank-you and hurried back outside, unable to believe her good fortune. Not only was Maude her most promising lead yet, but she remembered passing through Nutgrove on the way here. It would be a simple matter to stop and talk to Maude on the way home. And with any luck . . .

Elated, she slanted Ernest a glance. "Are you up for a good gallop?"

"If my lady pleases," he said stoically.

She mounted, shoved the basket handle over her arm, and lifted the reins.

Tris had an excellent stable, and she had borrowed a fine mare. She flew over the countryside, the horse's hooves pounding the dirt road at a measured, rhythmic clip. Her hat tumbled back, held on only by its ribbons. She laughed, enjoying the fresh air, the light wind, the renewed hope that she just might be successful in this search, after all.

She didn't hear a snap. There was nothing to warn her. Her saddle just slid sideways and off—and she screamed as she went with it.

Chapter Forty-six

Clucking her tongue, Peggy placed a glass of water by Alexandra's bedside. "Whatever did you learn from old Lizzy that made you ride off so recklessly?"

"I don't wish to speak of it now. My head hurts."

"Hmmph." Peggy leaned to plump her pillows, which Tristan suspected only made Alexandra's pain worse. "Serves you right for going off without me there to watch out for you. If you ask me, you should go home until all these dangerous happenings cease. I vow and swear—"

"No one asked you," Tristan interrupted, rising from one of the striped chairs. *He'd* be vowing and swearing if he had to listen to her a single moment longer. "Leave us. Lady Hawkridge needs her rest."

"Well!" Peggy said and took herself out the door, closing it more forcefully than necessary.

Alexandra winced at the resulting *bang*. "You could be a bit kinder to her."

"Why in blazes do you put up with her?"

"She has her moods, but she is nice and helpful most of the time." She threw off her covers. "I'll have a talk—"

"Stay in bed!"

"I'm fine, Tris." As though to prove it, she sat up and swung her legs off the side. "A little bumped and bruised, is all—"

"You are *not* fine." He walked closer and slid his

hands into her hair, probing gently. His fingers met a hard, raised lump. "No wonder your head hurts."

He'd nearly had a heart attack when Ernest rode up with Alexandra, scraped and bleeding, the two of them sharing the same horse with her mare tied behind. Thankfully, most of her wounds were superficial and had cleaned up rather nicely, but he cringed to see the remaining bruises.

Right now, he was grateful for Juliana's concealing nightgown, even if it *was* hideous.

He stepped back. "You took several years off my life. You're going to be the death of me, Alexandra, if you don't manage to kill yourself first. Or if I don't manage to kill you instead," he added in a disgusted mutter.

"Don't start that again. You were miles away when this happened."

"Leather straps do not simply split all by themselves. Someone must have cut partway through it sometime before you left." He paced over to the fireplace and leaned an elbow on the mantel, watching her. "Like me, last night, when I climbed out that window."

"Leather can weaken over time," she argued. "And you didn't climb out a window. The room felt overwarm in the night, so you got up, opened the window, and went back to bed." A thread of exasperation—or perhaps desperation—tinged her voice. "Must you make everything more complicated than it is?"

But it couldn't be as simple as she was claiming. This incident fit the pattern perfectly. The window had been wide open in the morning, and he had no memory of opening it. And, once again, his wife had been injured by an *accident* he'd had clear opportunity to arrange.

"Come sit by me," she said after an awkward moment of silence. She patted the mattress beside her.

He crossed the room and sat, but not too close.

He didn't feel worthy of touching her.

"You would never do anything to hurt me, Tris," she said quietly. "If I believe that, why can't you?"

Because his nights were voids in his memory. Because

too many coincidences were impossible to ignore. Because someone else had died on a night when he knew he'd wandered.

He sighed. "This has to stop."

"I can't stop. That would mean dooming my sisters to dreary lives as spinsters and ourselves to an unhappy marriage."

"You *must* stop. Hastings came to me after you left, along with Mrs. Oliver and Vincent. They said they speak for the entire staff and are concerned that someone may be after you."

"They've all been accidents," she insisted stubbornly.

"What if they *weren't* accidents, Alexandra? Our own servants are worried for your safety. Have you any idea how frightened that made me while I waited for your return?" He was surprised he had any hair left, he'd run his hands through it so many times. "And then you rode up, all bruised and bloody—"

His voice broke, and he tried for a calming breath. *Tried* being the operative word.

But he had to calm down, because she was hurt. And seeing her hurt made *him* hurt in a way that Griffin's fists hadn't. He didn't want to yell at her.

He just wanted to make her understand.

He took a second breath, and then a third before he continued, as calmly as he knew how. "Someone could be after you in order to stop this investigation, or it could be me during my stressful, sleepwalking nights. Either way, you must cease."

"I won't," she said stubbornly.

It seemed she said everything stubbornly. He had never met anyone quite as stubborn as Alexandra.

That made it very hard to maintain his newly acquired calm. "They are looking at Vincent," he said, the words coming out in a staccato cadence. "He is the only one who was new at the time, and his skin is darker than theirs, and they are *looking* at him."

"I'm sorry for that." She truly did look sorry. "Is he overwrought?"

He shook his head. "*I'm* overwrought."

"I'm sorry for that, too. But can you not see, Tris? If these three incidents were accidents, there is no reason for me to discontinue my efforts. And if they weren't accidents, there is even *more* reason for me to persevere. Because if someone is after me, that would mean your uncle was, in fact, murdered—and if there's a killer, that means we can find him and clear your name."

Tristan stared at her, mute, unable to believe his own ears. He was stunned by her convoluted logic.

Was he supposed to be grateful she was putting her life on the line in order to prove his innocence?

Well, *he wasn't*.

He finally found his voice. "Am I to understand you actually think it is good news that someone might be trying to kill you?"

"Yes," she said shortly.

He hadn't been expecting a different answer, but he still recoiled. He wasn't sure which would be worse: to have Alexandra's investigation prove he'd committed the murder himself, or to have some other murderer cut short her search by cutting short her life. Either possibility was chilling. And that wasn't even taking Vincent into account. If this continued, people would be looking for a scapegoat. The man could be prosecuted and convicted regardless of his innocence—a Jamaican ex-slave was unlikely to find justice in this world.

But she was hurt, he reminded himself. And so he said very calmly, "You must stop." And then he remembered something that made him wonder why they were arguing about this. "You're finished now anyway, are you not? You interviewed Lizzy, and now you're finished."

"I'm sorry," she said, and she really did look sorry again. "But Lizzy gave me another name today. I'm not going to stop until I've talked to Maude."

"Maude." A vivid picture of a sweet old lady flooded his mind. How odd. He hadn't thought of the woman in years. Not at all. It was as though she had somehow been stripped from his memory.

"You knew her?"

"She was a kind woman. Uncle Harold's old nurse. His nanny, actually, when he was a child." For some reason, talking about her was making him feel uneasy, but he couldn't figure why. It was ridiculous, really. "She was his children's nanny after that. And when he lost heart and fell ill, she nursed him all over again."

She shifted on the bed to face him. "Why didn't you tell me about her?"

"I didn't remember her." Strangely enough, it was true. Not that he'd have assisted Alexandra's search even if he *had* remembered. All he wanted was for her to stop.

Maybe if he told her several hundred more times, she might start listening.

Probably not.

"Evidently nobody else remembered Maude, either," she said. "I find it very odd that she wasn't on Peggy's list."

"She was a little bird of a woman, quite elderly. I wonder if she's even still alive."

"Lizzy wondered that as well, but I'm hoping she is. As she was closest to your uncle, she is my best hope for information. Ernest and I were on our way to see her when I took my little tumble."

"It was not a 'little tumble,'" he snapped, forgetting to stay calm. Leave it to Alexandra to trivialize such a thing. "You could very well have broken your neck." Remembering something, he dug a small bottle out of his pocket. "I fetched this from my uncle's rooms."

"I thought you avoided going in there."

He shrugged, handing it to her. "I thought it might help you. Dull the pain and help you to sleep. It's laudanum."

"How old is this?" She popped the cork and sniffed. "There's hardly any in here."

"You'll want to take only a little, anyway. You can overdose on laudanum."

"I don't hold with taking medicine. Not unless I have

to, and I've told you, I'm fine." She replaced the cork and handed back the bottle.

"Lie down at least," he said with a sigh. "Your head will feel better if you rest."

For once, she listened, which made him suspect she felt worse than she'd admit. "It's dented," she said mournfully when she was once again settled on the pillow.

"Your head?"

"My beautiful basket." She gestured to where someone had set it on a table. "It took the tumble with me."

He rose and went to examine it in the light from the window. "It's not too bad. I don't expect anyone would ever notice, although I'm certain we can have it fixed."

"No." She gave him a shaky smile. "I believe I shall think of it as a battle scar."

"I only hope your own battle scars end up being so minimal." He set down the basket. "Maybe Peggy was right. Maybe you *should* go home until everything here is back to normal."

"This *is* my home," she said quietly.

The simple statement touched him to the core. Despite all his worry, all his dread, all the anger beneath the surface of his calm, her words warmed something deep inside him.

"I'm not sleepy," she said. "I hurt, but I'm not tired."

That was why he had brought the laudanum, but he wouldn't force it on her. He should have known she'd be too stubborn to take it.

Her family's cookbook and the blank book he'd given her were stacked together on the night table. "Here," he said, handing them to her. "You can copy the recipes you wanted." He shifted on his feet, and then, unable to help himself, added, "And think about whether continuing this investigation is really wise."

Her eyes flashed, as he'd known they would. "If Maude knows nothing, there will be nothing left to investigate. But I'd be a fool not to question her."

He'd known she would say that, too. "It is not foolish

to protect yourself, nor to abide by your husband's wishes."

She kept quiet for a moment, but something in her expression hardened. "This is beautiful," she finally said conversationally, turning the blue leather book over in her hands. After another moment, she looked up at him. "But I hope you haven't been trying to buy my cooperation with these gifts, because my convictions are not for sale."

He *hadn't* known she would think him so calculating. The warmth inside him went cold as he walked out the door.

Chapter Forty-seven

LEMON PUFFS

Beat the whites of four eggs till they rise to a high froth. Then add as much sugar as will make it thick; then rub it round for half an hour, put in a spoon of lemon peel gratings and two spoons of the juice. Take a sheet of paper and lay it on as broad as a sixpence and as high as you can. Put them into a moderately heated oven half a quarter of an hour, and they will look as white as snow.

Give these sweet-and-sour biscuits to a sour person you wish to turn sweet. My husband has never proved immune.
—Elizabeth Chase, Countess of Greystone, 1747

All that long afternoon and evening, Alexandra had a lot of time to think. After a short nap, her head felt better. The rest of her was achy, but not intolerably so. She copied some of her favorite recipes as Tris had suggested, then called for Peggy to help her dress for dinner. The maid was still in a snit, so for once she didn't babble, which suited Alexandra just fine. When she was ready, she waited for Tris to come escort her to the dining room.

A tray arrived for her instead.

She ate little, the food sticking in her throat. She knew she had hurt Tris terribly. *I hope you haven't been trying to buy my cooperation* . . . even as she'd said that, part of her had been shocked to hear the words come out of her mouth. She wondered what had happened to traditional, accommodating Alexandra. This quest for truth and justice had turned her into a woman she scarcely recognized.

And it was tearing apart her marriage.

At ten o'clock she changed from the dinner dress into one of her new nightgowns, a sheer blush-colored confection that she hoped would tempt Tris to forgive her. She belted a wrapper over it and waited. The clock struck midnight before she heard his footsteps in the corridor.

She hurried to open the door, to welcome him, to do what she could to mend things between them. But he wasn't coming toward her. At the far end of the corridor, he was opening the door to the queen's bedchamber.

Dressed only in tight trousers and a white shirt, with the collar open and the sleeves rolled up to expose his forearms, he looked worn out and wonderful all at the same time.

"Tris," she called softly.

He turned. "Good night."

"You're not going to sleep in there again, are you?" She started down the corridor, forcing a smile to her lips. "If you're going to go out a window anyway," she said lightly, "there hardly seems a point."

"I had bars put on the windows. I won't be going anywhere tonight."

"Bars?" Having reached the room, she looked past him and inside. It was dark outdoors, but she could just make out faint stripes that must be iron rods outside the glass. "That seems a little extreme, does it not?"

"Nothing is too extreme to protect you," he said unblinkingly. Unemotionally. Unfeelingly.

She swallowed hard, any pretense of normalcy gone.

"I'm sorry for what I said. Please don't pull away from me, Tris. I love you."

"Good night," he said again and turned to enter the room.

Although she certainly hadn't expected to hear those three words echoed back at her, neither had she expected them to be ignored entirely. "Wait," she said, grabbing his wrist.

She'd been fighting it all along, but she knew what she had to do. She'd thought of little else for the past few hours.

He glanced dispassionately down to her hand. "Yes?"

His skin felt warm, but his arm felt tense. She grasped him tighter. "I'm not going to do the last interview. I'm not going to talk to Maude."

He looked up and blinked. "Why?"

"It's the only way I can prove I love you. The only way I can prove I will stay with you even if you remain in disgrace. I don't care about society, Tris—I don't need their parties or their approval. I never have. I was doing this for you and for my sisters. But my sisters will cope. You're my husband, and you're more important. My loyalty to you comes first."

She couldn't think of anything else to say. So she waited. He looked down again to where her fingers gripped his arm, and she released him and waited some more.

"All right," he finally said. "Thank you. I am sure I will sleep soundly tonight." Then he stepped into the room and closed the door between them.

He was going to bed without even so much as a kiss.

While she stood there, stunned, Vincent walked up, as if on cue, and slid a key into the lock. "Are you all right, my lady?"

His low, musical voice failed to soothe her. "I'm fine," she said woodenly. "I believe I shall go make some sweets."

"Now?" Vincent asked in surprise. His gaze went to her bare feet.

"Now," she said, belting her wrapper tighter.

She refused to spend another night on the floor outside her husband's room.

"Well." He seemed at a loss. "The ovens will be cold. Let me accompany you downstairs and light them for you."

She fetched her new recipe book before following him down the gaslit staircase, flipping pages as they crossed the great hall to the back passage.

"Lemon puffs," she decided. According to some long-dead cousin or aunt, they were supposed to turn a sour person sweet. Heaven knew, given Tris's current attitude, she could use all the help she could get.

In the kitchen, she gathered eggs, sugar, and lemons while Vincent started the brick ovens. Just as she began separating the first yolk from the white, Mrs. Pawley walked in. "What is going on here?" she asked through a yawn.

The cook's round body was covered by a plain, voluminous white nightgown—not at all transparent—and her feet were as bare as Alexandra's. Still dressed like a perfect gentleman, Vincent answered with great dignity. "We are making lemon puffs."

"We?" Alexandra and Mrs. Pawley said together.

"We," he confirmed, reaching for a lemon.

Mrs. Pawley went to a cabinet and took out a bottle of sherry and three glasses. When she filled Alexandra's to the brim, Alexandra didn't protest. She took a big sip instead, feeling the rich wine warm her all the way down her throat and into her stomach.

She hadn't realized she'd been so cold.

She pushed up her sleeves and cracked another egg.

Grating sugar, Mrs. Pawley eyed a bruise on her arm. "You had a rough day, from what I've heard. Are you up to this, my lady?"

"Oh, quite. I'm halfway healed already." She took another sip, deciding the sherry must be healing her even faster. "Tomorrow I am sure to be good as new."

Two kitchen maids wandered in, also wearing plain

nightgowns. "What is going on here?" one of them asked.

"Come in," Alexandra said brightly. "We're making lemon puffs." She took another sip. "However did you know we were in here?"

"They sleep right down the corridor," Mrs. Pawley said, fetching another bottle of sherry and two more glasses.

There was much beating to do of the egg whites, in order to make them nice and stiff. And after that, they were supposed to be rubbed together with sugar for half an hour. Alexandra appreciated all the help. She was a bit sore to be doing something so strenuous, and while the others had their turns, she could relax and drink more sherry.

Before long, three housemaids and two footmen had joined them, and it was quite a while before her turn came to beat the eggs. In fact, she was so busy sipping sherry that she missed her turn twice. When they weren't occupied beating eggs, the servants took turns telling jokes. Alexandra thought they were quite the funniest jokes she'd ever heard, and when she told one or two herself, everyone laughed even when she stumbled over the words.

She rather suspected they laughed mostly because she was their mistress, but she couldn't bring herself to care.

By the time the lemon puffs came out of the oven, shiny and white as snow, five bottles had been emptied and the kitchen rang with laughter. "You must serve these to my husband first thing in the morning," Alexandra told Mrs. Pawley as she peeled the finished puffs off the brown paper on which they had baked.

"Our fine master cannot abide sweets in the morning," the cook pronounced with formal reserve. Then she dissolved into laughter that brought tears rolling down her plump cheeks. Everyone else laughed, too. One of the footmen—Alexandra couldn't remember his name—even snorted once or twice.

"For luncheon, then," Alexandra instructed. Noticing

no scullery maids had joined them, she waved a hand magnanimously—or rather, flung it somewhat flamboyantly. "You may leave this mess until morning," she trilled as Vincent grabbed her to stop the momentum from tipping her over.

She quite liked her new servants, she thought as she giggled her way up to bed, Vincent close behind in case she should fall. She'd never had so much fun in the kitchen at Cainewood Castle.

The lemon puffs had better turn Tris from sour to sweet, because she wasn't going to be leaving Hawkridge Hall anytime soon.

Chapter Forty-eight

The next day, Alexandra was *not* good as new. To the contrary, her head ached abominably, her stomach felt queasy, and her body was stiff and more sore than ever. She didn't know whether Tris was served the lemon puffs with luncheon, since she couldn't seem to force herself out of bed. Even the daylight seemed to make her hurt.

Peggy came in from time to time, clucking and leaving Alexandra cup after cup of strong, hot tea. Alexandra wasn't certain whether the clucking indicated sympathy or disapproval, and she didn't really care. As long as Peggy left the drapes closed tight and the gaslights off, she could ignore the clucking. She ignored the tea as well for the first few hours, but after a while she started sipping it, and after a few cups, she started feeling a bit better.

By late afternoon, she finally felt well enough to dress and rejoin the world. Since her battered body did not really want to move, she allowed Peggy to help her, enduring still more clucking. At long last, she made her way painfully downstairs, going straight to the main parlor and the new pianoforte.

It was magnificent. She walked around it reverently, trailing a hand along the fine, polished mahogany. Finally, she stopped in front and hit middle C. The single note sounded so rich it sent a tingle down her spine.

She sat down to play, choosing Beethoven's Piano Sonata No. 14, long one of her favorite pieces of music. *"Quasi una fantasia,"* he'd called it . . . "Like a fantasy."

Indeed, only a few notes into the first movement, she lost herself in the fantasy that was the beautiful music coming out of her beautiful new pianoforte. The minuet and trio that made up the second movement flowed more easily from her fingers than ever before. And when she reached the stormy final movement, she played it with more passion than she'd thought herself capable of producing.

As the last note faded away, she heard applause. "Brava," Tris called from the doorway.

She turned to him with a tentative smile. "You're not scandalized? Most of the older people of my acquaintance find Beethoven's style too emotional and therefore unfit for young, impressionable ladies."

"Do you think me that old?" he wondered aloud.

"I remember a time when you thought our six-year difference made me much younger than yourself."

He nodded slowly, as though he were remembering, too. "You played the piece wonderfully," he said, "scandalous or not."

"It's a wonderful pianoforte." She wouldn't pretend modesty, because she'd played better on it than she ever had before. "I thank you for it."

"I didn't buy it to bribe you," he said quietly.

"I know."

The two words hung between them for a long, silent moment. "Shall we go in to dinner?" he finally asked.

It was her turn to nod. She rose so stiffly, he came to help her, placing a hand beneath her elbow to lend her support. Funny, but when she was playing, she'd forgotten all about her assorted aches and pains.

Not to mention the awkward state of her marriage.

If Tris wasn't dismissive, he wasn't particularly friendly, either. Their dinner passed in relative silence, the rattle of dishes and clang of cutlery more prominent than conversation. It seemed forever before Hastings placed the bottle of port on the table and left them alone, closing the dining room door behind him.

"None for me," Alexandra said.

"Hmm." Tris poured some for himself, a wry smile curving his lips. "Could it be you overdid it in the kitchen last night?"

He'd heard. Well, of course he'd heard. Not only was he the lord of the manor, his own valet had been there as witness.

"I made some lemon puffs," she said, ignoring his implication.

"Yes, and they're quite delicious. I had two after luncheon. While you were sleeping off the drink."

"I was sleeping off the pain," she protested. "My body is complaining even more today than yesterday."

He nodded. "That is not unusual following an injury. You will doubtless feel better tomorrow." He paused for a long sip, then met her eyes, his own a penetrating gray. "I will take you to see Maude tomorrow."

She couldn't have heard right. "Pardon?"

"We'll take the curricle, since I'm certain you won't feel up to riding."

Tristan watched the parade of emotions cross her face: disbelief first, followed by relief, and then cautious joy. "Are you sure?" she asked.

"I'm sure."

"I told you I was giving up. I meant that, Tris. It's what you wanted."

He took her measure for a moment and decided she was sincere. "Are you trying to talk me out of it?"

She shook her head emphatically.

"I appreciate your willingness," he told her. He appreciated that more than she'd ever know. "But I cannot allow you to give up."

Although he feared learning the truth, he couldn't let her wonder all her life if she might have restored his reputation and spared her sisters grief. But he also couldn't let her ride off again with only a footman as protection. Not when a murderer might be after her.

"Thank you," she whispered, her eyes shining.

He nodded shortly. "Whoever is trying to stop you— if not myself—is obviously part of this household."

"They were *accidents*, Tris."

"Let us not go over this again, shall we?" He raised a brow to emphasize his point. "In case someone should try to follow us, I don't want anyone to know where we're going or what we are doing."

"All right," she agreed slowly.

"We shall say you require fresh air to aid your recovery, so we are going on a picnic. A honeymoon picnic."

"I suppose it won't hurt to be cautious."

"Have you told anyone about Maude?"

"No. I've been languishing in the bedroom since the accident." When he cocked his head at her, she added, "Maude's name never came up in the kitchen."

"How about Ernest?"

"Not with him, either. The man doesn't care to talk much. Besides, we'd only just got underway when the strap on the saddle snapped. I didn't have time to say anything before, and after . . . well, on the ride home I didn't feel much like making conversation."

He supposed she wouldn't have—she'd have been occupied gritting her teeth against the jarring pain of that ride. "Good. Then no one has any reason to suspect we'll be doing anything besides enjoying a honeymoon picnic." He rose, yawning. He hadn't slept much last night. Having one's wife offer up a sacrifice tended to disturb a man's equilibrium. "We should both get a good night's sleep."

A hesitant smile curved Alexandra's lips. "Shall I go up and change into another of my new nightgowns? Or do you wish to come along and help me?"

"Neither. I shall be sleeping in the queen's bedchamber again. For your safety." He leaned and pressed a kiss to the top of her head. Hearing her disappointed sigh, he raised her chin and met her eyes. "You are still entirely too bruised and hurting for any love play. When we've finished this thing you've started, perhaps we will both feel better."

For a long while after he left, Alexandra just sat in the dining room. She'd thought since Tris was being so cooperative, he'd want her back in his bed. And she'd wanted so much to be there . . . even if only to be held.

He was right: She was battered and bruised. But it was her heart that had taken the beating.

On her way from the dining room to the stairs, she nearly bumped into Mrs. Pawley.

"My lady! Will we be seeing you in the kitchen tonight?" The cook's blue eyes danced. "I expect we shall have a great crowd to assist in the sweet making. There are many who are sad to have missed our little impromptu party."

Alexandra hated to disappoint the staff, but a party was the last thing she felt like tonight.

"I'm afraid not, Mrs. Pawley," she said, watching the light fade from the older woman's eyes. "Perhaps another time."

"Very fetching," Peggy said, eyeing Alexandra's chemise-clad form in her dressing room the next day. Alexandra blushed, knowing the new garment was all but transparent, but Peggy only smiled. "I'm so pleased to see that you're feeling more the thing today."

"Oh, I truly am." Alexandra wondered at her maid's sudden good mood, but she wouldn't risk ruining it with any questions. "I am going on a picnic today!" she said brightly instead. "What do you expect I should wear to picnic with my husband?"

"With your husband?" Peggy flipped through a few dresses, then held up a pretty blue frock for Alexandra's approval. At her nod, the maid started toward the bedroom, slanting a sly glance over her shoulder. "Are not the two of you rather estranged?"

Alexandra sighed, supposing their separate sleeping arrangements had prompted much speculation belowstairs. It was so tempting to tell Peggy the truth about everything, but she'd promised Tris she would stick to their story. "I am hoping a picnic will help us reconciliate," she said carefully. "And—" A knock at the door interrupted her. "Yes?" she called, hurrying into the dress.

Tris poked his head in. "Mrs. Pawley has requested your silver basket to fill with our picnic luncheon."

A clever ruse to support their story. Still unbuttoned, she fetched the basket and brought it to him. "Please ask Mrs. Pawley to include some lemon puffs," she said, thinking she needed some sweets to bring to Maude. "I haven't found a chance to even try them yet."

"Will do." He planted a light kiss on her lips, a kiss that turned to more when their mouths clung for a long moment. "Are you about ready?" he asked when he pulled away.

He hadn't kissed her for days. Her lips tingling, she wondered whether the kiss had been for show or for real. "Almost."

He smiled, reaching around her to run a finger down her bare back, making her shiver. "I shall wait for you in the curricle," he said, then walked away.

She slowly closed the door.

"It looks like you're reconciliated already," Peggy commented as she did up her buttons.

"We're both trying." Blushing for the second time inside of ten minutes, Alexandra took a seat at her dressing table so the maid could work on her hair.

"I wish to apologize for being such a crab the past few days," Peggy said from behind her. "I admired you so for your investigation, and I was disappointed to find myself no longer part of it." She deftly twisted and pinned. "Do you expect you could ever forgive me?"

"Of course," Alexandra said. Peggy had been her strongest ally until that first time she went off without her, and she'd missed having a woman here at Hawkridge to confide in. "I collect I haven't been a very pleasant person myself the last day or two."

"But you're the mistress," Peggy pointed out. "You're allowed to be a crab." They both laughed; then Peggy sobered. "I fear for you, though. All the buzz in the servants' quarters is that someone is after you—I'm thinking you should be leaving Hawkridge to save your life, not going on picnics."

The maid's concern warmed Alexandra's heart. "I know tales of danger have been bandied about by the prattleboxes belowstairs, but I assure you there is nothing to fear. A few unfortunate accidents do not a plot make. Besides, my investigation is all but over. I have only one person left to interview."

Peggy sounded surprised. "Did you fall from your horse before visiting Lizzy, then?"

"No, I spoke with Lizzy. She told me of another departed servant called Maude." Too late Alexandra remembered Peggy's propensity to gossip and Tris's wish that no one learn about Maude. She watched Peggy's face in the mirror. "I wonder why she wasn't on your list?"

"We all thought the old woman was dead," Peggy said, looking shocked. "Are you certain she isn't?"

"Lizzy wasn't sure, but I hope not. I collect I will find out tomorrow when I try to pay Maude a visit."

"You'll take me along this time, will you not?"

"If I'm still not up to riding, most assuredly." Alexandra turned to her maid, putting a finger to her lips. "Tell no one else, I beg you. You know his lordship doesn't want me continuing this investigation. I cannot risk any word reaching him concerning my plans for tomorrow."

"Mum's the word," Peggy promised. "But I do believe the old woman is dead. Why make the journey at all when you'll most likely put your reconciliation in jeopardy for nothing?"

"Perhaps you're right." Hoping to keep her maid in such good humor permanently, Alexandra made a big show of sighing. "I shall think on it," she told her and rose to collect her bonnet.

Chapter Forty-nine

"Peggy thinks Maude is dead," Alexandra told Tristan as he helped her into the curricle. "But I want to try to visit her anyway. You won't mind, will you? Even if the journey proves to be fruitless?"

"I said I'd take you, and I don't intend to go back on my word. But whyever would Peggy say she is dead?" He climbed up beside her and pulled the hood over their heads to shield them from the bright sun. "I thought no one knew about Maude."

She winced. "I mentioned her without thinking. But it's just Peggy," she added quickly as he lifted the reins. "I made her promise not to tell, and she also believes that I plan to visit Maude tomorrow, not today. I made the timing very clear."

Annoyance tightened his jaw, but he didn't want to start this outing with a disagreement. As he drove away, he told himself firmly that what was done was done. Nothing untoward was likely to come of it, since it was plain no one was following them. By all appearances, everyone had bought their story that they were off for nothing more interesting than a honeymoon picnic.

Alexandra took up the silver basket and wrapped their luncheon in one of the large napkins, leaving only the lemon puffs in the bottom. "For Maude," she explained. "Thank you so much for doing this. It means a lot to me."

He slanted her a glance. "It means a lot to me that you were willing to forgo it."

"I'm glad," she said softly and left it at that. They rode silently for a few minutes before she turned to him again. "Would you care for something to eat?"

He shook his head. "I'm not hungry."

"Neither am I. I'm too nervous to eat. This is our last chance . . ." She trailed off, and little was said for the rest of the ride.

But he hadn't missed the "our." *Our* last chance.

Like most servants, Maude had not gone far from the place of her birth to find employment. Nutgrove was less than an hour away, an hour Alexandra spent rubbing up against Tristan. Innocent though she had come to him, she was a temptress, and he suspected she knew it. Their kiss earlier that morning had been intended for show, but the feel of her mouth on his had jarred him to the core.

He wasn't ready for this—he couldn't allow her to steal his heart. She was about to come to the end of her search. Once she believed he would never be free of scandal, it would only be a matter of time before she left him.

He couldn't bear to think of that—to think of going on without her. Alexandra's presence had changed the very substance of Hawkridge Hall, filled it with music and life and lightness that he now knew had been missing for years. Even the servants walked with more spring in their steps and smiles upon their faces. He didn't want to go back to the way it had been without her.

He could no longer imagine living there without her.

He couldn't imagine living *anywhere* without her.

But it was only a matter of time . . .

And that, of course, was assuming she was convinced he would never be free of scandal. The other possibility—that she would discover he was guilty of murder—was even worse. Then she would leave immediately. And he wouldn't be able to blame her.

Hell, she'd be a fool *not* to leave immediately.

So he sat beside her, determined not to succumb to her temptation. Meanwhile, his body reacted to every move she made. Her head on his shoulder prompted him to wrap an arm about her involuntarily. He found himself breathing in tandem with her. Her thigh pressed to his was a constant reminder that she wasn't wearing drawers.

All in all, despite his anxiety concerning what she might or might not find, he was rather relieved when they passed the signpost that read "Nutgrove."

Alexandra immediately sat straight and called excitedly to an elderly gentleman walking a tiny dog. "Good sir! If I may bother you . . . might you know the direction of a woman who goes by Maude?"

And it was the oddest thing . . . but just hearing Alexandra say "Maude" again, that vague, niggling sense of unease Tristan had felt two days ago came back.

The old man cupped a hand to his ear. "Eh?"

"Maude!" she shouted as they rolled along beside him. She turned to Tristan. "What is Maude's surname?"

He shrugged. "I never thought to ask." He'd forgotten her. How was it that he'd forgotten her?

"Maude!" Alexandra yelled again. "Might you know anyone named Maude?"

"Ah, Maude." The man smiled, revealing gaps where he had lost several teeth. "Down the corner," he said, gesturing and pulling his dog's leash in the process, nearly choking the poor little beast. "Turn left. Honeysuckle Cottage."

"She's alive," Alexandra breathed, hope flooding her brandywine eyes. "Dear God, I hope she knows something that will help us."

"It could be someone else named Maude," Tristan cautioned, that sense of unease growing stronger.

"It isn't. I just know it."

Somehow he also knew it wasn't someone else. And in any case, there was no sense arguing the matter, when in a few minutes they'd know for sure. "Honeysuckle Cottage," he muttered. "That isn't much of a direction."

"The man seemed to think it would do," she said as they turned the corner. "Look! There it is!"

Sure enough, about halfway down the lane stood an old stone cottage wreathed in pale-flowered honeysuckle vines. No sooner had the curricle rolled to a stop than Alexandra hopped down, basket in hand, and started for the door.

Tristan just sat there for a moment, feeling the unease tangle into a knot in his gut.

Finally, he climbed down and followed her. "You're supposed to wait to be handed down," he chided.

"Oh, bosh," she said and knocked on the weathered wood. "There are some things more important than propriety."

How much she had changed since he first met her.

She shifted on her feet. "What is taking her so long? Sweet heaven, I hope she's home. Lizzy said if anyone saw anything that night, it'd have been she."

And suddenly he knew why he'd forgotten Maude. He *hadn't* forgotten her. He'd simply pushed her clear out of his mind.

She'd been the person closest to his uncle. The person most likely to have seen him if he'd sleepwalked into his uncle's rooms that night.

The door swung open, and Maude stood on the other side, leaning on a cane and looking much like Tristan remembered her. A faded dress hung on her slight frame. She'd always seemed so frail she might break. "Good afternoon, Maude," he said.

Her pale green eyes widened, looking apprehensive. "Lord Hawkridge?"

She knew something. She wouldn't look like that unless she knew something. The knot tightened in Tristan's gut.

He wrapped an arm around Alexandra's shoulders and forced a smile. "This is my wife, Lady Hawkridge."

Alexandra reached into her basket. "Would you care for a lemon puff?"

"No. Thank you." Maude's blue-veined hand went up to pat her gray curls nervously. "Why are you here?"

The knot twisted. "We wish to talk to you," he said. "May we come in for a moment?"

She looked like she wanted to say no, but then turned abruptly, her cane tapping across the wood floor as she led them inside and to a small table. "These are all the chairs I have," she said, her voice wavering.

There were two. And they were rickety. "I am perfectly content to stand," Tristan said, helping the elderly woman to sit while Alexandra took the second chair. He made a mental note to send the old nurse some decent furniture next week—that was, assuming he wasn't locked up in some prison. He'd been the marquess for less than a day before she'd departed, but that was no excuse for not seeing that a long-term employee wasn't comfortable in her retirement.

Perhaps he'd have done that if he hadn't forgotten her.

Maude held on to her cane, still leaning on it even while she was seated. Alexandra reached across the little table to touch her other hand. "I've been told you were very close to the last marquess," she started gently.

"Y-yes." The old woman's eyes looked everywhere but at her.

"Do you remember anything that happened the night he died?"

"Y-yes."

Tristan stopped breathing.

"Did you see anyone go into his room?" Alexandra continued. "Anyone who might have done him harm?"

"Y-yes."

Alexandra sent Tristan a startled glance—a hopeful glance—before she looked back to Maude expectantly.

No further information seemed to be forthcoming. Tristan thought he'd expire if he didn't breathe. He wished Maude would accuse him already, so he could breathe.

Alexandra's gaze darted to his again before her smooth hand tightened over the wrinkled one. "Who was it, Maude?" she whispered, her eyes flooded with not just hope, but a measure of self-protective doubt.

The cane crashed to the floor as Maude covered her face with her hands. Beneath her cotton dress, her bony shoulders shook with racking, silent sobs.

Terrified and resigned, Tristan crouched beside her chair. "Maude? What is it?"

"I'm sorry. I'm so sorry," came a muffled wail through her fingers. "It was a mistake, I swear it."

"Of course it was a mistake, but that doesn't make me any less guilty." Ignoring Alexandra's gasp, he eased Maude's hands away from her face. "Whether intentional or not, I'm still responsible for his death."

His life was over. Or at least it was meaningless, which was the same thing.

"I'm s-sorry," Maude repeated. She stared into space, tears rolling down her parchment cheeks. "It was a mistake."

Except for the painful knot, he felt dead inside. So dead inside he wouldn't have thought he'd have it in him to feel sympathy for her. But she seemed so damned miserable. "What was a mistake, dear lady?"

Her tears flowed faster. "The l-laudanum."

Tristan dug a handkerchief from his pocket. "The laudanum?" His memory flashed on the almost-empty bottle he'd taken from his uncle's rooms and tried to give to Alexandra. *You'll want to take only a little,* he'd told her. *You can overdose on laudanum.*

He hadn't thought the knot could tighten more, but it did. He must have poisoned his uncle with that very same bottle.

"I just wanted him to stop hurting." Maude took the proffered white square and dabbed her eyes with it, then balled it in her fist, staring at her hands in her lap. More tears splashed down on them. "H-he was coughing. He couldn't sleep. I gave him too much. Too much. I used all of it." She was babbling so fast Tristan couldn't seem to keep up. "Perhaps I gave it to him twice that night. I didn't intend to. I couldn't remember. I am old."

"Could you mean . . ." Her words were confusing. A mist had obscured his brain. He'd stopped breathing again. "Do you think you may have accidentally caused my uncle's death?"

She nodded and met his gaze, her eyes reddened. "I should have died instead of him."

"No." He couldn't catch his breath. His vision clouded. His pulse felt thready and weak.

"I told you," Alexandra murmured.

He was innocent. He hadn't killed his uncle, after all.

Relief flowed through him, blessed relief after all these years. He felt a different kind of weakness now, and light-headedness, too, and giddiness, like Alexandra when she drank too much wine.

Alexandra. She'd had faith in him all along.

"Maude." He swallowed past a lump in his throat. "Will you tell this to the authorities?"

"Th-they're going to hang me."

"I won't let them." His knees hurt, but he remained crouched there, holding both her hands, when all he wanted was to collapse in relief. "You did your best, didn't you? Always? You cared for my uncle when he was a child, then his children, then him again. No one will hang you for doing the best you could. Everyone makes mistakes."

He heard a little noise from Alexandra and turned to see her. A fat tear rolled down her cheek, cracking his heart.

"They're going to hang me," Maude repeated.

"No." He looked back to the older woman. "I won't allow it. I promise your safety, Maude, if you will only explain what happened to the authorities."

She stared at her lap. "You promise?"

"I do. No one will hurt you. You can come back to live at Hawkridge, if you like. We'll take care of you."

A long moment passed when all Tristan heard was the beat of his own heart pounding in his ears. Then finally

Maude lifted her red-rimmed gaze to meet his, her eyes filled with gratitude and relief of her own.

"I will talk," she said. "I lied to the sheriff before, but this time I will tell the truth."

When Maude's door closed behind them, Alexandra and Tris paused on the garden path and turned to each other. And just stood there, looking at each other, for a very long time.

"Alexandra," Tris finally murmured. He took the basket from her hand and set it on the gravel, then cupped her face in both hands. He searched her eyes, rubbing his thumbs beneath them as though gently swiping away tears. "I've never seen you cry before," he said softly.

"I wasn't crying," she said as her eyes glazed, proving her a liar. "It was just that when you said everyone makes mistakes . . . well, I'm sorry for mine, Tris. I'm sorry I was so obstinate that I drove you away."

Slowly he shook his head. "I'm not sorry you were obstinate. Look where it led. I was too obstinate to see you were right." He shook his head faster, harder. "I even thought Maude was telling me I was guilty."

"Everyone makes mistakes," she reminded him with a watery little chuckle. She blew out a shaky breath. "Goodness, Tris, we did it."

"*You* did it," he said. "By God, you did it." Then he swept her up to twirl her in a wide circle right there in the cottage's little garden.

Her heart soared. "I told you," she crowed. "I told you that you weren't responsible for your uncle's death." He set her on her feet, where, unable to help herself, she rose to her toes and pulled his head down for a smacking kiss. "I knew you couldn't have hurt him. And you haven't done anything to hurt me, either."

"They were accidents. You were right about that, too." He yanked her close and squeezed her so hard she felt every one of her unhealed bruises.

"Oof!" she said with another laugh. "Maybe now you *have* hurt me."

"I'm sorry." He set her carefully away and bent to retrieve her basket. "But I've never been so happy to hear 'I told you so' in my entire life."

He led her back to the curricle and helped her climb up. Then he climbed up beside her and pulled her close for a kiss so long and thorough, it completely stole her breath.

"Let's go home," he said, lifting the reins.

The curricle jerked as they pulled away. She unwrapped their luncheon, spreading the napkin over her lap with all of Mrs. Pawley's offerings. She was starving. She couldn't remember ever being so hungry.

"Everything is going to be so wonderful," she said, taking a big bite out of a chicken leg. "All of society will have to apologize to you, and my sisters are both going to marry dukes."

"Marquesses aren't good enough?" he asked with a raised brow.

She slapped a chicken leg into his open hand. "I suppose marquesses will do."

They laughed and ate all the way home, talking about their future. Tris still hadn't said he loved her, but she really didn't care. She was certain he did, and if it took him ten years to admit it, she would just wait.

"I have never been so happy," she said as they headed up Hawkridge Hall's drive. "I never thought I could marry you, and now look at us!"

The whole world seemed bright in her elation. The sun sparkled on the Thames, the sky had never been a more brilliant blue, and birds trilled in the trees along the drive.

Tris was more cautiously optimistic. "I am thrilled to know I'm in the clear, but let us not celebrate until the authorities have taken Maude's statement. At the rate the law moves, she could die before they get out to Nutgrove."

"Dear God—"

"I was jesting," he said with a grin that would have been annoying if it wasn't so wickedly charming. He pulled up before the steps. "That old woman will probably outlive us both. Besides, I am going to find the sheriff right now and drag him there directly. But it won't do to celebrate prematurely. Let me take care of tying up the details, and we can celebrate tonight."

Tonight. His voice, deep with meaning, sent a tremor rippling through her. Passing the reins to a groom, he lightly jumped to the gravel and came around to hand her down.

She rose, ducking her head to avoid the hood and sticking her low bodice in his face in the process. His gaze lingered there for a moment, and she wondered whether he was staring at his cameo or her bosom. But her breasts tingled as though his eyes had touched her.

A faint smile curved his lips before he grinned up at her and held out his hand. "You waited this time."

"I would wait forever for you, Tristan Nesbitt."

"I can hardly wait for you," he murmured, forgoing her hand to grasp her under her arms and swing her down. "Don't tell anyone the news—I want to announce it together tonight, after everything is settled." He kissed her forehead, her cheek, finally settling on her mouth for a long, satisfying moment. Drawing back, he smoothed a stray curl from her face. "You must be exhausted, considering your injuries. Go inside and have a nap while I take care of getting Maude's statement. I may even bring her back with me." He pulled her close once more, running his hands down to her drawerless bottom as he claimed her mouth for another kiss. While her senses were still spinning, he reached back into the curricle for her silver basket and pushed it into her hands. "Go, will you? Before I'm tempted to go upstairs with you."

She watched him climb back up and drive away before she turned to go into the house, swinging her basket as she headed upstairs and into their bedroom. She *was* exhausted. Peggy seemed to be nowhere about, so she kicked off her shoes and burrowed, fully dressed, under the covers, where she dreamed of her wonderful new life while her husband secured their future.

Chapter Fifty

Alexandra was still snug in bed when she heard the door quietly close, followed by the *clack* of an engaging lock. She opened her eyes and yawned. Light streamed through the windows, and she hadn't expected her husband home until dark. Everything must have gone well.

"Tris?" she queried, rolling languidly to face the door. She couldn't wait to see him.

But what she saw instead was Peggy.

Holding a gun.

For a moment, that was all that registered: Peggy holding a gun. It was surreal, really. Why would Peggy be holding a gun?

Then Alexandra's sleep-fogged brain cleared a little, and she bolted upright in the bed.

"I'm sorry," Peggy said, walking closer. She hadn't aimed the gun; she just held it in her right hand. But the hand shook. She was nervous. Which made Alexandra more nervous than she already was, which was very nervous indeed. Her heart was hammering against her ribs and threatening to climb out her throat.

Her maid was walking toward her, holding a gun.

And then Peggy raised it, and Alexandra was staring down the barrel of a gun. A gun pointed at *her*.

It was, quite undoubtedly, the most frightening moment of her life.

She stared down that barrel, thinking it the longest, darkest, most menacing thing she'd ever seen.

But she couldn't just stand there staring at it. She had to get her mouth to work. She had to *say* something. "Y-you cannot shoot that," she stammered desperately, still wondering why Peggy had a gun. "It'll be heard. You'll be caught."

"But my mother won't," Peggy responded through clenched teeth. "And at this point, that's all that matters."

"Your mother?" Alexandra squeaked. She inched toward the edge of the bed. Peggy was too old to still have a mother. Or at least she'd never mentioned a mother. What in heaven's name was she talking about, and why did she have a gun, and would that hand *ever* stop shaking?

And then something clicked in her head, just as her feet hit the floor. "Maude is your *mother*?"

"Yes," Peggy gritted out, and she brought her second hand up to steady the first, and her shaking finger moved toward the trigger.

Alexandra didn't think anymore. She just sprang, one palm hitting the maid's chest while her other hand grasped her wrists and forced them up toward the ceiling. A sharp *bang* rang out, the recoil making them both fall as plaster rained down on top of them.

Peggy dropped the gun. Or rather, it skittered from her hands and went clear under the big bed.

Relief sang through Alexandra's veins. The bullet was spent. Peggy couldn't shoot her anymore, at least without reloading. And first she'd have to get the gun, which was under the bed. All Alexandra had to do was get out of the room. She'd run for help.

She scrambled up and dashed for the door, reaching for the key.

"Oh, no, you don't," she heard just before hands clenched painfully on her shoulders, wrenched her back, then bodily tossed her on the bed.

Whoever would have guessed Peggy was so strong?

Alexandra twisted on the mattress to see her, then blinked, her heart racing even faster than before. This wasn't Peggy, not the Peggy she knew. Or thought she knew. Peggy didn't have such a deranged look in her eyes.

And this deranged woman was coming after her.

There was no way to get to the door without going through Peggy. Alexandra slid off the far side of the bed and went under it.

It was dark, and she didn't fit very well, but she wiggled and wiggled some more, forcing her way under the bed, straining to reach the gun. She didn't think that Peggy had supplies to reload, but she wasn't going to take any chances. Her heart beat so loudly it seemed to be thundering in her ears, ricocheting around the cramped space. If she couldn't get the gun, maybe at least under here she'd be safe from Peggy, and Peggy's crazy eyes, and Peggy's strong, hard hands.

A fist started pounding on the door. And then another, and another, all accompanied by wild, angry barking.

"Lady Hawkridge!" Mrs. Oliver called. "Was that a *shot*?"

"Are you all right?" one of the footmen asked.

"Open up!" That was Vincent, followed by a vicious kick at the door.

Alexandra had warned Peggy people would hear. But being right brought no satisfaction. The doors at Hawkridge were thick, and the hinges were heavy, and there was nothing Vincent or anyone else could do.

"Oh, no, you don't," Alexandra heard, then felt someone tugging on her foot, dragging her backward. Peggy. She yanked her ankle from the maid's grasp and wiggled farther under the bed, trying to regain lost ground.

The pounding on the door grew louder as more servants arrived, adding voices and fists to the commotion. Alexandra stretched toward the gun, almost touching it. Almost.

Then a cackle echoed under the bed, and a hand reached out and snatched the gun from her grasp.

Peggy. She'd scooted in from the other side.

And now she was pointing the gun at Alexandra under the bed.

It isn't loaded, Alexandra told herself, reassuring herself, forcing herself to breathe. There was nothing to do but back out, wiggling in reverse as fast as she possibly could, which wasn't nearly fast enough.

"I'm going to get you," Peggy said. "I am *not* going to let you take my mother."

Alexandra kept wiggling. Her heart was pounding, and her blood was pumping, and she was gulping spastically and trembling all over. But Peggy wasn't trying to reload the gun. What the devil did she want with the blasted thing anyway, then?

Rex's barking seemed to be getting even louder. "Lady Hawkridge!" the servants shouted. "Let us in!"

If only she could. She and Peggy rose from beneath the bed at the same time, on opposite sides, and as Peggy rounded the bed, coming toward Alexandra with her arm raised, it became clear what she was planning to do with the gun.

Hit Alexandra with it. Very hard, if Alexandra could judge by the maniacal look in the woman's eyes.

Panic rising in her throat, Alexandra scrambled backward, frantically glancing around. A glint of silver caught her eye. As Peggy bore down on her, she snatched her sterling basket off the table and bashed it down on the woman's dratted, curly head.

The maid collapsed like a sack of flour.

Alexandra rushed across the room to unlock the door, her trembling fingers slipping off the key. Again and again. Finally, she managed to turn it. But as she started to twist the knob, she heard a moan behind her and whirled.

Peggy was rising up from the floor.

The maid's eyes—unreasoning green eyes—radiated pure hate. One too-strong hand flexed, as though she were preparing to clench it around Alexandra's throat.

Amazingly—petrifyingly—her other hand still held the gun.

With an animal-like growl, she gained her feet and rushed headlong.

And at that moment, behind Alexandra—who indeed seemed petrified and powerless to do anything except gape in terror—the door burst open. And Rex bounded in, straight for Peggy.

His huge paws came up and knocked the maid to the ground, and before she could as much as move, he'd draped his body full on top of her.

The gun thudded from Peggy's fingers to the floor. Pinned by two hundred pounds of dog, she couldn't budge. In fact, from the looks of it, she couldn't even draw breath. Not that Alexandra particularly cared. As the servants poured in to surround her, she quietly sank to the floor and just sat there breathing.

The staff erupted in excited babbles, Peggy regained the use of her lungs enough to howl, and Rex, staying put, was barking up a storm. But Alexandra just sat there and breathed.

Until she heard a "Holy Christ" and glanced over, through many livery-clad legs, to see Tris standing in the doorway.

He looked whiter than Juliana's nightgown.

"What has happened here?" he husked out.

"Peggy." The liveried legs parted as Alexandra crawled through them, making her way toward her husband. "Maude is Peggy's mother. She thought I wasn't going to see Maude until tomorrow, and she was trying to stop me."

"With a *gun*?" Tris stared horrified at the pistol on the floor.

"The bullet is already spent." Peggy's hands had seemed as much a weapon as the gun, anyway.

He pulled Alexandra to stand and wrapped her tight in his arms. "Maude is Peggy's mother?" he asked in a dazed tone, apparently just registering her words.

"I am," Maude said, stepping out from behind him.

The room hushed as she walked slowly toward her daughter, her cane clicking as she went. Even Rex shut his big mouth and remained quiet.

"I was but eighteen when I arrived here at Hawkridge," Maude said in a flat voice, as though she had rehearsed this many times. The rhythmic clicks accompanied her resolute words. "I considered I'd landed in heaven when I was offered a position as nanny to the marquess's son. But at twenty the head groom raped me, and I landed in hell instead."

The clicking stopped as she stood there, gazing down at her daughter pinned beneath the massive dog.

"Had the master known I was with child," she continued, "I would have been turned out without a reference. I was a mite plumper in those days, but at seven months I was forced to feign illness and return home. After delivering the child, I left her to my mam to raise. When she reached the age of fourteen, I found a position for her here, but we never told anyone we were related." She heaved a great, shuddering sigh. "My Peggy, what have you done?"

Maude's eyes rolled back in her head as she collapsed in a rather graceful heap.

"I tried to scare her into leaving," Peggy answered her mother's still form, "but she just wouldn't, the stubborn chit."

Ernest knelt down to feel Maude's blue-veined wrist for a pulse. "She's only fainted," he reported.

The room released a collective breath.

"Excellent," Tris said. "Please move her to the bed and then go fetch the sheriff. The man is earning his keep this day."

He was still holding Alexandra. While they waited for the authorities, he finally released her and took her hand instead, clutching tight as they told their rapt audience all about Maude and his uncle's accidental poisoning.

Maude woke from her faint, rolled over and went to sleep. Rex remained sitting on Peggy until the sheriff arrived and hauled her away. It seemed hours before the servants finally drifted back to their jobs, leaving Alexandra and Tris alone in their room.

Well, except for a slumbering Maude and a slobbering mastiff.

Tris was still holding Alexandra's hand. "Good dog," he told Rex, then turned to her. "See, I told you he didn't hate you."

"He saved my life," she said in wonder.

"There's no need to give him quite that much credit. There were twenty-odd servants waiting to rescue you if he hadn't. They all love you, Alexandra. And I love you, too."

"You . . . what?" Had he really said those words?

He glanced again at Rex, then at Maude still in their bed. With a sigh, he drew Alexandra from the room and down the corridor. "I love you," he repeated quite clearly. And with that, he pulled her into the queen's bedchamber, used one booted foot to slam the door shut in Rex's face, and backed her up against it, crushing his mouth to hers.

The kiss was wildly possessive, a blatant statement of ownership that weakened her knees and stole her breath. And through all of it, she heard Tris's words repeating in her head.

I love you, I love you, I love you.

She'd known it, but she hadn't known how much it would mean to hear it. Tears sprang to her eyes.

"You cannot cry now," he admonished, his hands working the buttons on the back of her dress. "I cannot ravish a sobbing woman." He kissed her chin and her throat, nibbling his way down toward her bosom. "I love you. Have I told you I love you? You may not have saved my life, but you rescued it from oblivion, you stubborn chit."

Wrestling his coat down his arms, she laughed. "I did it for myself as much as for you. I'm a selfish chit as well."

"You're an irredeemable chit," he said, tossing his

cravat to floor. He started lowering her dress, then stopped and brushed at it. "How the devil did you get so dusty?"

"I scooted under the bed to hide from Peggy."

"I love you," he said and laughed, either finding it funny she'd scooted under the bed, or perhaps from nervous relief—she wasn't sure which. And she didn't really care. She felt free and easy with him for the first time ever, and that mattered so much more.

"I shall have to have a talk with Mrs. Oliver," she said, looking down at herself in disgust. "There is no excuse for such muck to be under the beds."

He laughed even harder. "I love you," he said.

"Where did Peggy get a gun?" she suddenly wondered.

Tris only shook his head. "She almost killed you," he murmured, still looking rather pale.

"I guess she did." Alexandra took a bracing breath. "Are you going to tell me you told me so?"

He shook his head again, appearing dazed.

"How can someone named *Peggy* have done so many terrible things?" she asked. "It's such a sweet, innocuous name."

That seemed to jar him out of his stupor. "I love you," he said, and this time the laugh rumbled in his chest as he held her close for a long moment. Then he pushed her dusty dress off and down, stepping back to view her in the sheer blush-toned chemise.

It seemed like forever since she'd put it on before the "picnic." So very much had happened since then.

His voice went lower and husky. "That would tempt a monk, my lady marchioness. Wherever did you get something so wicked?"

She grinned as she unbuttoned his waistcoat. "Will it also tempt a marquess?"

"Hmm. I think it just might." He wrapped her in another hug, squeezing her so tight she groaned in protest. "Sorry," he said. "I seem to keep forgetting you're still bruised. But that's because I love you. I think I will tell you I love you every five minutes for the rest of our lives."

"That won't be necessary," she told him with an amused smile. "But I'm glad you finally figured it out."

He sobered, skimming the backs of his fingers alongside her face. A hush seemed to fall over the room.

He tilted her chin up, meeting her gaze, capturing it in the intense silver of his own. "I couldn't admit it before. Not even to myself. I was too afraid of losing you. I thought I would lose you when you chose to leave, but instead I almost lost you when Peg—"

"Shhh," she said. "I know."

And they slowed down then, removing the rest of each other's clothing with the reverence the moment demanded. There were times that called for wild passion, but this was a time that called for sweet, cherishing love. When Tris finally laid Alexandra on the bed and joined his body with her, tears came to her eyes for the third time in a single day.

"I love you," they whispered together. And they soared together to a wonderland of their own making, a place they would make together time after time in the months and years to come.

Sometime later, sprawled on his back with Alexandra lying on top of him, Tris looked up at the gaudy turquoise and gold canopy. "I think I like the queen's bedchamber after all," he said.

Epilogue

CHOCOLATE PUFFS

Beat the white part of a good-sized egg till very stiff and then add a handful of sugar. To this add finely grated chocolate and then put small spoonfuls on a flat buttered pan with an area between them. Bake in an oven not overly warm for an hour or until the puffs are very dry.

Everyone loves chocolate, so these are perfect to take on a family picnic!
—Anne Chase, Marchioness of Cainewood, 1773

Two weeks later, on the peaceful rise overlooking Griffin's vineyard, in the last sweet days of summer, Tristan and Alexandra picnicked with her family once again on the red blanket. Her siblings and cousins gasped as she told the adventurous story of her quest for truth and justice.

At least, she made it sound adventurous. Griffin suspected it had been rather more dangerous than she was letting on—and he wasn't happy about that at all.

Brooding, he watched Claire lift the silver basket and turn it in her hands. "This is gorgeous. But it is dented."

"In two places," Alexandra agreed. "Peggy's hard head left quite a mark."

"I can fix it," Claire offered, having taken up an old family pastime of making jewelry.

Alexandra smiled. "I think not. I like it just the way it is."

Apparently still mulling over the tale, Corinna reached for another of the chocolate puffs Alexandra had brought. "So Peggy offered to make that list in order to control who was on it?"

"Exactly," Alexandra said. "There were others who knew Maude was alive, even if they didn't know Peggy was her daughter."

"And Tristan hadn't done *any* of those things while sleepwalking," Elizabeth said, her green eyes wide.

"Of course he hadn't." Alexandra scooted closer to her husband and leaned dreamily back against him. "I knew he hadn't all along."

"Have you sleepwalked since then?" Juliana asked him.

"Not once," Tristan said.

"And I'm sure he won't ever again," Alexandra declared.

"I wouldn't wager on that," her husband disagreed wryly, tilting her face up and back for a quick, upside-down kiss. "Something tells me this irredeemable chit is likely to cause more tension sometime in the future."

Everyone laughed. Except for Griffin. He was glad to see his sister happy, but that didn't alleviate his misgivings.

Alexandra frowned at his clenched jaw. "What is wrong with you?"

"You should have come home," he gritted out. "When all that was happening, you should have come home."

"That's what Peggy wanted, but Hawkridge is my home now." She exchanged a glance with Tristan, apparently realizing Griffin was as disappointed with his friend for not making her come home as he was with her for not doing so on her own. Extricating herself from his embrace, she rose to her feet. "Let's walk," she said, taking Griffin's arm to pull him up before he could protest.

"I could have lost you," he said as they headed down the rise to the vineyard.

"Have you not figured out yet that you're never going to lose any of us, Griffin? Not even after we're all married and gone from Cainewood. You're stuck worrying about us forever," she said all too truthfully and cheerfully.

They walked for a few minutes, sharing a healing, companionable silence that went beyond words. When they reached the vineyard, they headed into the middle of it toward where Rachael wandered in the distance.

"What is wrong with *her*?" Alexandra asked.

"I don't know. Would you care to ask her?"

"I'll let you ask her."

"Hmmph."

She bent to touch a miniscule grape. "Your vines are bearing fruit!"

A ridiculous sense of pride washed over him. "Nothing worthy of wine yet, but it's something to celebrate."

"We'll toast your success with Hawkridge's wine in a few minutes." She wandered the row, still heading toward Rachael. "Are they English sweet-water grapes?"

"They're Rhenish." A few months ago he wouldn't have known the variety, but the vineyard truly felt like his now. "Since when do *you* know anything about grapes?"

"I have a vineyard now, too, you know. It is my responsibility to learn everything about Hawkridge."

His sister always *had* been rather responsible. But she was changing, Griffin thought. He couldn't put his finger on how, but he knew it was for the better.

"You should have come home," he repeated doggedly, "but I must thank you for persevering. Because of you, Juliana and Corinna have bright futures."

"Thank you for allowing me to marry Tris," she returned, then shot him a grin that was much more impish than the old Alexandra. "And for the excellent advice you gave me the night before my wedding."

He felt his face heat and suspected he was as red as the blanket on the hill. "I think I shall talk to Rachael now," he said and walked off.

Rachael turned as he approached, her cerulean eyes laced with unmistakable pain. "Leave me alone," she said miserably. "I came out here to be alone."

"My sister sent me to talk to you."

"Do you always listen to your sisters?"

"Only when I agree with what they say." He stepped closer and trailed a fingertip down her wan face. "Tell me, Rachael. What is wrong?"

"Oh, hell," she said, then pressed herself into his shirtfront and sobbed.

He patted her awkwardly, feeling her hot tears wet through to his skin. Even miserable, she felt entirely too good in his arms. He sent a murderous glance back toward Alexandra before patting Rachael some more. "Whatever it is," he said soothingly—at least, he hoped it sounded soothing—"it cannot be that bad."

"I'm not a Chase," she whispered through a sob.

"What?" His hands froze on her slim back. "How can that be?"

"I found a letter." She pulled away, not looking quite so beautiful as she swiped at her reddened eyes. "This morning, when I was clearing out the master suite for Noah's homecoming. It was from my mother to my father. From before I was born."

He dug a handkerchief out of his pocket, and she took it and blew her nose. Noisily and not prettily. Good, he thought. She was getting less sultry and tempting by the minute. "What did the letter say?"

"It said . . . it said she would always be grateful to him for wedding her even though she was a widow already with child. She prayed I would be a girl so he wouldn't be stuck with another man's son as his heir. She—"

"Did she say she loved him?" he interrupted pointedly.

She nodded. "But—"

"They were in love, Rachael. Anyone could see it just looking at the two of them. Don't you ever doubt it."

She shrugged, following that with a long, sorrowful sniff. "But he wasn't my father. Whoever my real father was, he wasn't a Chase."

"Did the man who raised you ever, for one minute, treat you as anything but his daughter?"

"No." The tears continued to flow as she shook her head. "But I'm not a Chase. I don't know what I am if I'm not a Chase."

"You're Rachael," he said. "Noah and Claire and Elizabeth are still your brother and sisters. You still live at Greystone. Nothing has changed. What's in a name? It will change when you marry, anyway."

But her name wouldn't change if she married *him*. And he was aware, quite suddenly and uncomfortably, that the cousin standing before him wasn't actually his cousin.

Thankfully, she hadn't seemed to make that connection. "You're right," she said, straightening her shoulders and taking a big breath. She didn't really look like she believed him, but she looked like she *wanted* to believe him. And the shaky little smile she aimed at him had nothing to do with seduction and everything to do with family comforting one another. "Thank you," she added. "I don't know when you became so reasonable, but I do appreciate your calm, considered approach."

If only she knew. He hadn't been calm and considered since inheriting the marquessate. All in all, he'd felt calmer on campaign with the enemy bearing down.

Panicked would describe his current state better.

He had two more sisters to marry off, an estate that came with entirely too much responsibility, and now a cousin who wasn't his cousin.

And since she'd stopped crying, she was looking sultry

again, damn it. Those huge, amazing eyes would bring any man to his knees.

In fact, his knees seemed to be aching right now. "I am glad I could help," he said stiffly.

His voice wasn't the only thing that was stiff.

"I think . . ." she said, licking her lips, "I think I am ready to go back to the others."

"Thank God," he said under his breath.

"Hmm?"

"I'm thankful to God that you feel much better."

She cocked her head at him, no doubt remembering he'd never been a man given to prayer, his frequent use of the Lord's name notwithstanding. But she followed him back down the row, and for that he was thankful, too. Mostly because she was behind him and he didn't have to watch her swaying derriere.

It was a good thing she'd said she'd never marry him, because the last thing he needed was a wife.

AUTHOR'S NOTE

Dear Readers,

Do you know any sleepwalkers? Two of my children occasionally sleepwalk, so I know firsthand that it is not as scary looking in real life as it has been portrayed in movies. Sleepwalkers look and act quite awake—if a little bit addled—but they never remember anything of their escapades in the morning.

Much mystery has been attached to sleepwalking, yet it is really no more mysterious than dreaming. The main difference between the two is that a sleepwalker's brain wave patterns are a combination of the type produced during deep sleep mixed with awake patterns. This second type of brain wave reflects waking behaviors like walking and talking while the person is still asleep enough so that he is not aware of what is happening and is not forming memories of his actions. In adults, sleepwalking is most likely to occur during times of emotional stress and usually stops when the source of anxiety disappears.

Can people really initiate sex in their sleep? The answer is a resounding "yes!" Researchers have named this phenomenon "sexomnia" and consider it a distinct variation of sleepwalking. As to whether sleepwalkers can be dangerous, although violence while sleepwalking is not common, sleepwalkers are not allowed in the armed services of the United States, in part because of the threat they pose to themselves and others when they have access to weapons and are unaware of what they are doing while asleep. There are at least twenty documented cases where defense against a murder charge was "I was sleepwalking and therefore, ladies and gentlemen of the jury, I was not myself at the time I killed him and so deserve acquittal." The argument has proved successful more than once.

If you're musically inclined, you may know Alexandra's favorite piece of music, Beethoven's Piano Sonata No. 14, as the "Moonlight Sonata." It wasn't given that name until after Alexandra's story, though. Beethoven wrote the sonata in 1801 and dedicated it to the seventeen-year-old Countess Giulietta Guicciardi, with whom he was said to be in love. In 1832, several years after Beethoven's death, the poet Ludwig Rellstab compared the music to moonlight shining on Lake Lucerne. Since then, it has been known as the "Moonlight Sonata."

Tristan's hydraulic ram pump was invented by a Frenchman, Joseph-Michel Montgolfier, in 1796. In 1821, *Ackermann's Repository*, a very popular magazine, published an article with instructions on how to build a ram pump, calling it "A simple Hydraulic Engine, which will raise Water to a very considerable elevation, without manual force or assistance." The article included engravings very similar to the drawings Tristan sketched in this book, which you can see on my Web site at www.Lauren Royal.com. Ram pumps are still built and used today.

Unfortunately, Tristan was too optimistic when he predicted that slavery would soon end in Jamaica. Slavery wasn't abolished until nineteen years after this story, in August 1834, and, as he feared, the transition from a slave economy to one based on wage labor proved difficult.

Although gas lighting is often thought of as a Victorian invention, it actually came into use during Regency times. It was developed by a Scot named William Murdock. The story is told that, as a child, Murdock heated coal in his mother's kettle and lit the gas that came out of the spout. In 1794, he heated coal in a closed iron vessel in his garden and piped the resulting gas into the house. That was the first practical system of gas lighting to be used anywhere in the world. In 1805, gas lighting gained public awareness when the Prince of Wales (later the Prince Regent) had it installed in Carlton House, his London home. Two years later, gas lamps were installed in Pall Mall, the first street to be lit by gas. The first gasworks in the UK were built in 1812 to light the City of Westminster, and 288 miles of pipes had been laid in London by 1819, supplying over 51,000 gaslights.

Most of the homes in my books are inspired by real places you can visit. Cainewood Castle is loosely modeled on Arundel Castle in West Sussex. It has been home to the Dukes of Norfolk and their families, the Fitzalan Howards, since 1243, save for a short period during the Civil War. Although the family still resides there, portions of their magnificent home are open to visitors Sundays through Fridays from April to October.

Hawkridge Hall was modeled on Ham House, a National Trust property located just outside of London. Known as the most well-preserved Stuart home in England, Ham House was built in 1610 and remodeled in the 1670s. The building has survived virtually unchanged since then, and it still retains most of the furniture from that period. The house and gardens are open Saturdays through Wednesdays from April to October.

Those of you who have read my previous books may have recognized Cainewood Castle or some of the people in the old portraits on the walls. Perhaps one of the nineteenth-century Chases reminded you of a Chase from the seventeenth century. And if you've read *Lily*, you know why there's always a mastiff named Rex at Hawkridge Hall, even though the characters in this book didn't! In creating this new trilogy, I'm having a fabulous time writing stories for the Regency-era descendants of my Restoration-era characters, and I hope you enjoyed reading the first book of the three.

To see pictures and learn more about the real places featured in *Lost in Temptation*, please visit my Web site at www.LaurenRoyal.com, where you can also enter a contest, sign up for my newsletter, and find modern versions of all the recipes in this book. Alexandra particularly seemed to like puffs, didn't she? She made three different flavors! If you try any of the recipes, I hope you'll e-mail me at Lauren@LaurenRoyal.com and tell me which sweet *you* enjoy most.

For a chance to revisit Alexandra and Tristan, watch for my next novel, *Tempting Juliana*, due in spring 2006 from Signet Eclipse. In the meantime, I'd love to hear from you! If you'd rather send a "real" letter than e-mail (I answer both!), write to P.O. Box 52932, Irvine, CA 92619, and please enclose a self-addressed, stamped envelope, especially if you'd like an autographed bookmark and/or bookplate.

'Til next time,

Lauren

Official Rules for the
Lost in Temptation Sweepstakes

**NO PURCHASE NECESSARY.
A PURCHASE WILL NOT ENHANCE YOUR CHANCES
OF WINNING.**

Open only to U.S. residents aged 18 and up. To enter the *Lost in Temptation* Sweepstakes ("Sweepstakes"), either visit www.laurenroyal.com and follow the entry instructions posted online or type your full name, mailing address, email address (if any), along with the answer to the question listed on the back of this book and mail it to the Sponsor at the address listed at the end of these rules. (Hint: Read the prologue of *Lost in Temptation* or the online excerpt for the answer to the entry question.) The entry must contain the correct answer to the question to be eligible. Limit one entry per person. Entries must be received by 11:59 p.m. (P.S.T.) on the entry deadline date indicated in the chart below to be eligible for that month's drawing and any or all subsequent drawings. Limit one entry per person/email address for the duration of the sweepstakes. Six winners (one per drawing) will receive a necklace consisting of a cameo in a silver setting—Approximate Retail Value ("ARV" $50 per cameo).

Monthly Drawing #	Drawing Date On or about	From among all eligible entries received by 11:59p.m. (P.S.T.) on:
1	8/10/05	7/31/05
2	9/10/05	8/31/05
3	10/10/05	9/30/05
4	11/10/05	10/31/05
5	12/10/05	11/30/05
6	1/10/06	12/31/05

Entries are void if they are in whole or in part illegible, incomplete or damaged. No responsibility is assumed for late, lost, damaged, incomplete, inaccurate, illegible, postage due or misdirected entries. Winners will be chosen randomly by the Sponsor, whose decisions concerning all matters related to this Sweepstakes are final and binding. Winners will be notified by mail or email. The odds of winning depend on the number of entries received. Employees, and their immediate family members living in the same household, of Sponsor or Penguin Group (USA) Inc., their parents, subsidiaries or affiliated companies, or the agencies of any of them, are not eligible for this Sweepstakes. Void where prohibited by law. All expenses, including taxes (if any) on receipt and use of prize are the sole responsibility of the winners. Any dispute arising from this Sweepstakes will be determined according to the laws of the State of New York, without reference to its conflict of law principles, and the entrants consent to the personal jurisdiction of the State and Federal Courts located in New York County and agree that such courts have exclusive jurisdiction over all such disputes. To receive a copy of the winner's list, please send a self-addressed, stamped envelope by July 1, 2006 to the Sponsor listed below, Attn: *Lost in Temptation* Sweepstakes Winner's List. **Sponsor:** Lauren Royal, P.O. Box 52932, Irvine, CA 92619.